"This beautifully written novel and its descriptive narrative totally encapsulate the small Alaskan town of Whetstone Cove and its residents. The characters literally jump from the pages; they are both engaging and possess many interesting layers. ... The novel highlighted the beauty of nature, the importance of caring for the environment, and the results of humanity's greed for money and power."

—Lesley Jones, *Readers' Favorite*

"The novel's core environmental message...will engage anyone interested in the continued mining debate, the Green Movement, and the consequences of irreversible land damage and climate change. Gripping and captivating, emotional and poetic, with its implicit nods to the philosophies of John Muir and the photography of Ansel Adams, this book stands tall."

— Nicole Yurcaba, *U.S. Review*

"Lost Mountain is a book from the geographic heart of the biggest Alaska mining controversy of the 21st century. Passions run deep here. ... I care about her characters; her natural history observations are both sweet and sharp."

—Larry Smith, *Homer News* and *Peninsula Clarion*

"A considerable strength of the novel is its detail of place and the seasonal rhythms of rural Alaskans. This is material that Coray knows well and brings to life with fondness and accuracy."

—Nancy Lord, *Anchorage Daily News*

T0118213

LOST
MOUNTAIN

LOST MOUNTAIN

A Novel

ANNE CORAY

ALASKA
NORTHWEST
BOOKS®

Excerpts from *Lost Mountain* first appeared, in earlier form, in the following:
Cold Flashes: Literary Snapshots of Alaska
Cirque: A Literary Journal for the North Pacific Rim

Cover image: Jolliolly/Shutterstock.com
Painting, page 2: *The Marriage of Heaven and Hell*, Beth Hill

This is a work of fiction. No characters represent actual individuals, and any real events have been altered to serve the needs of the novel. The area of Southwest Alaska that is the general setting for Lost Mountain is geographically large and complex, with numerous lakes and river systems as well as several Native villages and villages of mixed ethnicity. For the purposes of simplicity, the geography has been modified with one large lake and a reduced number of communities. The communities are not meant to be replicas of any found on a map.

Library of Congress Cataloging-in-Publication Data

Names: Coray, Anne, author. | Ngai, Olivia, editor.
Title: Lost mountain : a novel / Anne Coray ; [Editor: Olivia Ngai].
Description: [Berkeley?] : West Margin Press, [2021?] | Summary: "News of open-pit mining project disrupts the remote Alaskan town of Whetstone Cove as the whole community becomes divided over where everyone stands. Meanwhile, Alan hopes to win the beautiful widow Dehlia Melven over, despite her passive stance on the mine"-- Provided by publisher.
Identifiers: LCCN 2020053336 (print) | LCCN 2020053337 (ebook) | ISBN 9781513264455 (paperback) | ISBN 9781513264462 (hardback) | ISBN 9781513264479 (ebook)
Classification: LCC PS3603.O7315 L67 2021 (print) | LCC PS3603.O7315 (ebook) | DDC 811/.6--dc23
LC record available at https://lccn.loc.gov/2020053336
LC ebook record available at https://lccn.loc.gov/2020053337

Proudly distributed by Ingram Publisher Services

Published by Alaska Northwest Books
An imprint of Turner Publishing Company
4507 Charlotte Avenue, Suite 100
Nashville, TN 37209
(615) 255-2665
www.turnerbookstore.com

WEST MARGIN PRESS
Publishing Director: Jennifer Newens
Marketing Manager: Angela Zbornik
Project Specialist: Micaela Clark
Editor: Olivia Ngai
Design & Production: Rachel Lopez Metzger

To everyone—in Alaska and around the world—who has fought for the protection of wild places.

COMES THE MYSTERY

If you take a wedding band and hold it at arm's length to the light, you can almost imagine it as the moon.

Circles do that: they make us believe in unity, just ask the Native Americans.

Hold the same gold ring against one open eye and you'll be looking as if through a glass lens: the world appears focused and clean.

But twirl that ring with a pencil tip, and you'll get a tangle of lines.

Inside that ring is a story.

Of loyalty, love, and betrayal.

Of a company, *Ziggurat, Inc.*

Of a woman at the bottom of a deep, deep lake.

—Meredith Stone, 1999

PART ONE

A Warm Spring

1

Even after summer had collapsed, after the fireweed seeds ceased clinging to their long brown stems and floated out over the bay on a northeasterly breeze, when the robins were gone, and the swans, after the ground had hardened with a resolute frost, she still expected him.

At times she would lapse, find herself lost in a trivial task such as cleaning the windows, her focus narrowed to a smudge on the glass. Or she would be sweeping cobwebs off the ceiling, remorseful for the small life-forms whose handiwork she was destroying; or looking out on an overcast day as snow accumulated on the roof of the shed—the flakes hesitant at first, only dusting the mineral paper like white ash before building into half an inch of powder.

Then again, the expectation—that he must be coming home. He'd be returning any minute, rounding the corner of the path, a lanky figure, angular as the surrounding mountains, his gait not rapid but sure. He'd be already at the step, one hand on the railing, one foot poised to ascend. And the door—it was opening now, widening to allow his passage into their spruce-walled home.

Dehlia?

It was the wind.

Dehlia?

It was the creek.

Dehlia?

It was her own invention, the recklessness of imagination. But no—this voice that asked her whereabouts, sought her presence—surely this was his, a ghost's voice.

THEY WERE MARRIED more than twenty years.

She had her work. She rose early, though daylight in winter was scarcely six hours long. By nine o'clock her desk was littered with stencils and sketches of designs.

She liked drawing when the lingering effects of dreams still governed her pencil. The faces she created were stylized, unusual hybrids of animals and people. Raven-man. Wolf-woman. Frog-boy. Moth-girl.

The best sketches she transferred to birch logs. She used tools that Phil had fashioned from old metal files: an adze for the roughing out, crooked and straight knives for the detail work. When the carving was complete, she applied paint: washes where she wanted the grain to show, thicker layers for a look of opacity. She decorated the masks with feathers or hair.

She worked in series, which often became seasonal, each requiring several months to complete.

WHEN BARBARA NELSON stopped by it was January, seven in the evening, the temperature ten below zero. Barbara slipped inside, unzipped her heavy coat, and removed her mittens. Around her boots melting snow was already beginning to pool.

Dehlia climbed to the loft and returned with a pair of slippers.

Barbara ran an admiring hand over the fur. "What are they?"

"Ugruk skin bottoms. Ringed seal tops. They came from Shishmaref."

Barbara pried off her boots and eased into the slippers. "Mmm, nice." She glanced around the room and sank into an armchair, tilting her head back so that light from the single lamp cast a half-wreath on her full face. "Comfort—that's something I haven't been feeling much of lately."

"Do you want tea?" Dehlia asked.

"Carolyn's hiring a new handyman. You heard Rick left."

"I'm sorry."

"God—after twelve years we should have figured it out. We fought a lot, but I never thought—" Barbara's voice broke, a rasp on wood. "I need to get the hell out of here. How do you do it, Dehlia? The cold, the dark... have you thought about leaving Alaska? I might go back to Wisconsin, maybe Eau Claire. My sister lives there." Barbara planted her elbows on the arms of the recliner. "Besides," she said, "there's a rumor about this open-pit mine near Lost Mountain. It sounds bad."

Dehlia turned away. In a small town rumors were as common as lice to wild ducks. If you ignored them, they usually went away. Rumors, that is. She couldn't speak to lice.

The teakettle sang on the woodstove. Dehlia filled two mugs and handed one to Barbara. Close up, the lines around her friend's eyes seemed more prominent than she remembered.

"This is such a cheap place to live," said Barbara. "I can't believe Carolyn hasn't raised the rent, with her dad and all. But I'm sick of painting. I hate stretching canvases. I'm tired of cleaning brushes, the smell of turpentine, the damn space it takes to store all those paintings. I want to do something different."

Dehlia had heard it before. But this time Barbara might be serious. With Rick no longer in her life, she might strike out in a new direction. And there was the problem of money. Could Barbara make enough off her paintings? Dehlia herself was managing, and in just two more years she'd own her house and her small plot of land. It had been a long wait, but she was almost there.

Barbara leaned forward, a flush of excitement springing like plum stains to her face. "I could learn to carve antlers, weave baskets—"

"You might want to get out of the arts altogether." Dehlia sat down.

Barbara sipped her tea. "You know, it's just the usual fear. The jolly loneliness. How do you fight it?"

Dehlia lingered on Barbara's question. Loneliness. She couldn't explain. What would Barbara understand of Phil's mysterious presence?

DEHLIA LAY IN BED, not sleeping. A great horned owl sounded: a male, searching for companionship with five haunting notes. She imagined him, feathers fluffed, eyes narrowed, perched in the cover of a tall spruce. She'd never seen an owl with a mate, though she'd heard they mated for life.

She wandered to the window, the loft floor cool beneath her feet. A cloud passed, exposing a half-moon and a jumble of stars. She touched the line of frost on the bottom of the pane. Her fingertip burned and she held it to her lips.

In the distance, the outline of Lost Mountain traced the skyline. At three thousand feet, it stood apart from the surrounding hills. It wasn't the most spectacular mountain in the country; the eastern peaks were higher, more rugged, of a more durable stone. But Lost Mountain held a special draw, both mythic and wild. Dghhili Shtunalgguk, the Dena'ina called it, literally "Mountain Where She Lost Her Way." The story spoke of a six-year-old child who'd been separated from her parents when she fled camp in the middle of the night after a terrifying dream. It had taken three days to find her.

Back in bed, Dehlia ran one hand up and down Phil's side: the sheets were smooth but cold. She pulled up another blanket and hugged her arms to her body. And at that moment she sensed that her world, her defenses, were only illusion, and in the right circumstance all would collapse, leaving a hole so huge and raw that no flannel wrap, no images of swans or ermine or snowshoe hares could fill it.

2

The Cessna 207 descended over blue-green lake ice. From the pebbled shore rose a gradual slope of mixed forest: spruce and birch and pockets of water-hungry poplar. Alan leaned forward for a better look, taking in the rooftops—twenty? thirty?—all deep blue and postcard pretty. A network of narrow trails and some larger ones, more like roads, spidered out from an oval center populated by several large buildings and a creek winding between them. So this was Blake Parsons's creation. Whetstone Cove, an artist's town. Well, maybe "town" was the wrong word. This place was smaller, and surrounded by wilderness. "Hamlet" would be better, but it wasn't an Alaskan word. And this wasn't a village. One thing was certain: in a place this size you'd get to know your neighbors—maybe too well. He'd worked in the bush, he'd been just a little farther west, in King Salmon and Dillingham, and he knew he could make either instant friends or instant enemies. He hoped he wouldn't be squirming like an octopus with no suction cups in the company of so many intellectuals.

The plane banked sharply and lined up on the end of the gravel strip. Alan's stomach jarred as the wheels of the main gear touched down; then the nose wheel made contact, and the aircraft slowed and came to a full stop. He was here now, for better or worse. The faint smells of exhaust and engine oil filled the cabin.

The pilot climbed out and circled around the nose of the plane. Derek Johnson: Alan's link to civilization. Alan found him cocky in a charming kind of way. How did Derek pull it off? Alan's own confidence was tough enough, but it was far from impermeable.

He craned his head to see the crowd at the end of the airstrip, presumably here to greet him. That was decent. And among the brown Carhartt work jeans and jackets he saw a flash of red: a scarf, sported by a woman with long, wavy black hair. She was on the tall side, and pretty. A good distance away, but he felt suddenly short of breath. Must have been the high altitude. But Derek had only flown at two thousand feet, well below the mountain peaks, through a spectacular pass. And now they were almost at sea level.

Another woman stepped forward. A husky build: Carolyn, no doubt, the one who shouldered the burdens. The town leader, she'd described herself to Alan on the phone. She had a wide smile... would she at least be fair? That was often the best you could hope for with bosses.

Carolyn and Derek exchanged greetings with the ease of those who've worked together a long time. Derek shoved his hands in his back pockets and Carolyn touched his arm before giving herself some distance.

"Another perfect landing!" she said to him.

"A student pilot could have aced that one." Derek swept his arm expansively. "Look at this: fifteen-knot breeze, clear skies—" He grinned at the bystanders. "I suppose you'd like to meet your new handyman." That burned Alan. He was hired as a solar tech, not a handyman. There was nothing inherently wrong with the generic label; he'd spent enough time in bush Alaska to know that flexibility was key. Lodge owners, air taxi operators, boat captains—all required their employees to wear different hats. But he wouldn't mind being at least called a solar technician. Derek opened the passenger door and Alan jumped to the ground. It felt good to stretch his muscles.

Carolyn extended her hand. "Alan Lamb. I'm Carolyn Parsons. Welcome to Whetstone."

Alan gave her a firm shake, and she more than matched his grip.

Some in the crowd waved. About twenty people had come to greet him, many in baseball caps and rubber boots, perfect for April weather. It was late in the month and it had been a warm spring; the snow had already melted. A tall, Nordic-looking man approached, a Pomeranian under one arm. The dog's blonde fur matched the color of the man's mustache.

"Dan Broderman." He didn't offer his hand; his eyes were a cold sea-blue. Not the kind of blue you'd want to go swimming in.

Alan started to speak but Dan made an about-face, as if he'd simply been reporting for roll call in the army. Down his back swung a long ponytail.

Derek unloaded the plane and Alan sorted his things from the rest of the freight: personal items; a tote full of food; his box of electrical tools, solar catalogs, and installment guides. A burly man named Stew drove up with a four-wheeler and trailer. Stew drummed a palm on Alan's tote, half the lid covered with duct tape.

"Nice repair job." Stew's voice spilled out like gravel from a pail. He gave Alan an approving nod. "Made in Alaska."

Alan nodded back. *One friendship secured.*

The ground was littered with gear. Stew loaded the trailer and thumped the four-wheeler-seat. "Hop on."

Alan looked back once as they made their way down the wide trail with a sign that read Cat's Eye to see the woman and the red scarf already disappearing.

CAROLYN HAD EXPLAINED it over the phone—there were no vacancies, so Alan would have to bunk at someone else's place for the time being. Okay, he'd figured, why not give it a shot. Maybe it would be an easy way to get acquainted.

After a bend in Cat's Eye, Stew turned right onto the Inner Circle, then another right onto bumpier, brushier Zircon, and dropped him off in front of a small cabin. Alan climbed the leaning entrance steps, duffel in one hand, guitar case in the other. Inside, the cabin was spare: a rough-hewn table situated near a long low window; a corner kitchen with a propane stove; a crude sofa against the back wall topped with thinly padded cushions; two bedrooms. A thermometer outside the window read fifty-three. He unlatched the door on the woodstove: only a layer of ashes and a half-burned round of birch. Behind the stove a wide, six-tiered bookshelf rose almost to the ceiling.

He peeked in the tiny bathroom at the sink and cramped shower stall. A plastic shower bag hung from a ceiling hook. There was no toilet, but Alan was no stranger to outhouses. At least there was a water drain.

Back at the bookshelves, Alan scanned titles—all alphabetized according to author. He ran a finger over the T's, stopping at three paperbacks, the name "Trotter" in block letters in the middle of the spine. *In the Sea's Wake, The Spurious Night, The Elected.* Alan took down the first book and thumbed to a random page.

So I learned about sadness. It had been all these years my phantom twin, reticent, aimless, who sat at the fringes of conversation but preferred repose. When I killed him he didn't even whimper, and for the first time I was happy. I had discovered anger, that carnal delicacy, rich and immediate as marbled beef, and I tore at it, I swallowed the fat and greasy meat with unclouded satisfaction. Finally I could *act.*

Wow, anger as motivator—I can relate. Alan closed the book and replaced it. He was struck by the quiet: no buzz of traffic, no hum of appliances. It was the kind of quiet you could either love or hate. He'd probably find it at times pleasant, but too much of it could grate, working under his skin until he'd be forced to seek some respite: a decibel-heavy session with Burton Cummings, a good, hotheaded debate about the state of the world.

Alan headed to the empty bedroom. Not since the two years following high school had he shared quarters with another man. Now he feared he might be too set in his ways to adapt to another's routine.

He worked unhurriedly, tossing his things on and around the bed—except his guitar, which he removed carefully from its case. He leaned the instrument in one corner.

At the mirror, he combed his hair with his fingers. This morning he'd trimmed his beard, thinking, *No gray to speak of yet. But it's all downhill from here.* He'd been wearing the Van Dyke for a year now; it was mostly functional, covering the scar on his chin. It had been a jagged two-inch cut, and the doctor had done a poor job of stitching it. Once Alan had been proud of the scar, but no longer. The beard made him look older, more mature, though he rarely saw his face anymore without reminders of life's progression. You could be sad about it, nostalgic about your disappearing youth, but everyone was on the same street. Hell, then. Might as well try to be happy. Go with a smile. He needed to present his best side.

He hadn't always. Six months ago he'd walked off his job, fed up with bureaucracy. It was meant to be for a new solar installation for remote Forest Service cabins, but the paperwork and regulations had kept him from getting past the glass office doors. He'd resigned by way of a curt message on the director's voicemail. Not the best way to handle it. But Jesus, there was a time for principles. Sometimes you had to say your piece and move on. And he wouldn't stay long in Whetstone—two, three years. He knew about small towns. They made you claustrophobic after a while. Besides, he wanted his own place. He'd go back to Homer and build, but he had to save up to buy a lot. Land was expensive there.

Shortly, he heard footsteps and the clunk of the front door.

Mike Trotter was slight but well built, with cropped hair and black-framed glasses. "Greetings. Looks like we're going to be roommates for a while." He struck Alan as a little stiff, but personably so.

Alan shook his hand.

"I hope you like salmon," said Mike. "It's about all I eat."

"Of course," said Alan.

Mike pulled out a jar of canned fish. Alan watched as he emptied the contents into a bowl and mixed in some powdered potatoes and reconstituted dried eggs. Mike fried the patties in a sizzling skillet and set them on the table with a cold dish of leftover beans and rice. Lunch was ready in what seemed an instant.

"Sit, my friend," said Mike, gesturing.

Alan did. He speared two patties and spooned out the leftovers.

"This is fancy as it gets," said Mike. "Don't want to strain the budget. Writing fiction isn't the most lucrative proposition." He took up the serving spoon. "Thank God for grants."

"I saw your books. I'd like to read them."

Mike adjusted his eyeglasses. "I'll expect an honest report." He picked at his food. He wasn't dainty, just mildly disinterested. "Of course, you could sample other local fare. Meredith's the poet."

"So you help each other out?"

Mike gave a honking snort. "A poet?" Then he grew serious. "Meredith's brilliant. The problem is, she knows it. Talk about competitive. She'd be a man-of-war in a relationship."

The guy was a straight shooter. No bullshit. Alan took a mouthful of fish. This was going to work.

Mike went on, spilling out names of other residents. "There's Barbara. The guy she lived with just left. You're his replacement, the way I understand it. Barbara's nice, but she's too impulsive." Mike chewed and pushed his glasses back up on the bridge of his nose. "And Dehlia."

"What's her story?"

"Husband died, let's see… about a year and a half ago. Good artist. She makes masks."

"So say I wanted to live here and do what you do, what…?"

"Put in your application and wait 'til I move on."

Alan scooped up the last of his rice. He eyed the remaining salmon but slid his chair back. "I'm not a writer. I'd rather make a difference."

"A difference."

"Yeah. I mean, books aren't going to"—he gestured to the remaining patties—"stop these fish from dying out if water temperatures keep rising. CO_2, climate change. This stuff is real."

Mike pushed his plate away. He picked up one of four chunks of red ore—about the size of golf balls—from the windowsill and fidgeted with it. "Where are you from, Alan?"

"Here. Born in Seward, raised in Palmer. Why?"

"Most Alaskans prefer greenbacks to Greenpeace. You don't sound like an Alaskan, is all."

"I've been told that. I'll take it as a compliment." Alan said it, then wondered if it sounded too curt. "My sister fishes Bristol Bay," he added.

"Oh, family loyalty. I see." Mike rose and moved to the woodstove. He crumpled some newspaper and tossed it inside the firebox with a few sticks of kindling. He lit the match, and smells of smoke and sulfur drifted into the room.

At the sink, Mike worked the hand pump.

"A well, even," said Alan. "You live in luxury."

"Thank Blake for that. The guy was amazing. And had a better aesthetic sense than his daughter's. Carolyn has a good business mind, but there's a commercialization infiltrating the place, an increase in tourists—we call them 'Patrons of the Arts.' They're just clients. But 'patrons' sounds more magnanimous. They come to our art presentations and craft talks, to get a sense of what we do here. And buy our baubles."

Alan laughed.

"Of course, it's billed as a flightseeing tour so we get more people." Mike swiped a paper towel over a plate as he cleared the table. "I'll probably last just one more year. I'm about out of money, and the research for my next novel isn't working out. I'd hoped to meet some people in Valatga, but you can't just drop in on a village—or any place—and expect to understand it. You have to live there a while."

Alan didn't disagree.

"Here," said Mike. "Take a look." He unfurled an old, weathered map of Alaska on the table, pinning the corners with the chunks of ore. Southwest of Anchorage and Cook Inlet, Alan located Lake Hélène, with Whetstone penciled in on the north shore.

Mike pointed down lake. "Valatga Qayeh. Valatga means 'tent.' It's a Russian loan word. Qayeh is 'village' in Dena'ina. So, 'Tent Village.'"

Alan ran his finger along the shore of Lake Hélène and stopped halfway between Whetstone and Valatga on an unnamed peak. "What's this mountain?"

"Lost Mountain. There are mining claims around there, but it's too remote for any real development." Mike pointed to a small lake. "That's Moss Lake. The salmon come up the Harmon, into Hélène, up Moss River, and spawn there. They spawn in this lake too, but Moss is a major spawning ground. This area's a nursery for Bristol Bay."

"Fish are important," Alan said.

"Life blood. Must be why the Christians assigned the symbol of the fish to Jesus Christ." Mike straightened and said something unintelligible.

"What does that mean? Sounds like Greek to me."

"It is."

Alan wanted to laugh again, but there'd been something reverent in Mike's delivery.

AFTER SUPPER ALAN cleaned up and Mike sat reading. Outside the kitchen window, a bird feeder swung in the breeze. Chickadees flitted back and forth.

Alan scoured the skillet and set it on the surface of the woodstove to dry. The still-wet bottom popped and sizzled. Mike had fallen asleep, head angled to one side, his glasses resting precariously on the arm of the couch.

Mike stirred. "What time is it?"

"Just after ten."

"Oh." He yawned. "I don't usually conk out so early."

"What're you reading?" Alan asked.

"Proust. *Remembrance of Things Past.*"

Alan chuckled. "That explains the nap."

"Not too fond of tea parties and table talk?"

"No time for that stuff. There's a world to save."

"Don't be a zealot," said Mike. "Just save the fish."

3

The walk to the airstrip had disrupted Dehlia's routine, if routine was the right word. Her eating habits had become sporadic since Phil's passing—today's dinner, if it happened at all, would be close to nine o'clock. Now she fixed herself a late lunch: sliced apples and cheese, and a piece of cherry pie.

She thought about the newcomer. How would he settle in? He seemed cheerful enough from her brief glimpse, but for many Whetstone was little more than a stopover. People around her came and went, and it usually didn't pay to establish friendships except with long-term residents. Even Barbara talked often of leaving. That's how it was: transience was life, was art. But something about Alan intrigued her. He looked rugged, on the neat side of being disheveled, with his shock of dark hair and well-kept beard. Fit, and good posture. Not quite model status though—the magazines would want a thinner cut to the legs. His dress was typical, jeans and work boots, but he wore them well. Was she really thinking these things? They seemed so shallow. Yet, at the airstrip, she'd felt like a trout following a spinner, lured but not ready to strike.

When she finished eating, she rinsed the plates and silverware. She needed a task and she didn't feel like carving. Her long to-do list lay across the room. But on the windowsill was the tray of garden starts, many now tangled and competing for space. Lettuce, kale, Swiss chard. They would have to be transplanted before they went in the garden. Especially the lettuces, their delicate leaves clinging to one other so earnestly it would be hard to separate them without tearing. The kale would be easier, a vigorous, cold-weather crop that could tolerate wind and cold and hard handling.

On the island butcher block she spread out sheets of newspaper and laid down a stack of plastic pots. As she scooped out the potting soil, her hand bumped the table and dirt sprayed across the paper.

She smiled. All that coverage—government spending, conflicts in the Middle East, the faces of celebrities and world leaders—so quickly obscured. And by dirt, no less, like inverse laundering.

She disliked politics, the constant haggling, the failure of either side to admit they were ever wrong. She'd quit reading the paper years ago, weary of disputes that often seemed more like gossip than reportage. The best use for newspapers was absorbing water from wet boots. The copies she had were outdated, passed on by Barbara. Whether others' actions were right or wrong was not a judgment Dehlia chose to make. Such calls danced on a political balance beam, too narrow to maintain one's equilibrium. You fell off, to the right or left. Why mount at all? Like that mining project. Even if the rumors were true, Dehlia resolved that should anything more come of it, she wouldn't get involved.

She didn't want to jeopardize gaining title to her land. She'd put in twenty-three years; she had only two to go and she would own it. That was the contract she and Phil had signed. Dan Broderman had signed a similar lease-to-own contract, the way Blake had first written it. Later Blake had turned the agreements into lease only, with no opportunity for purchase. He had felt that a vibrant arts community would require a constant influx of new blood. No one else in Whetstone, besides Carolyn, knew about these early agreements. And what was it about Carolyn? Dehlia wasn't sure if she could be counted on to honor the contract, especially if Dehlia opposed her in some way. It was that amendment, the nondisclosure part of the agreement stating that Dehlia wasn't to discuss her pending land acquisition with any other individuals, particularly residents of Whetstone. And of course, after Phil's death, in a swirl of confusion and uncertainty about her future, she had talked it over—with Dan. She had to, she needed clarification about the legal matters, which in the past she'd always left to Phil. It was his work, after all. Surely though, Dan wouldn't mention their discussion to Carolyn—or broadcast it throughout Whetstone. Dan was a friend.

LATER, SHE SAT at the kitchen table, this time with her list in full view: *return library books, clean closets...* She stared at the paper, overcome once more with the exhaustion of widowhood. These moments were less frequent now, but they still fell, like a late-summer rain, draining her will and strength. Cleaning the closets was a task she'd been avoiding; mostly, they contained Phil's personal things. Clothes, shoes, his satchel.

His photo hung near her desk. Now she lifted it from the wall. It was her favorite picture of him, his pose relaxed but expectant, eyes fixed on some distant point.

How clearly that day on the California coast returned to her. In the background the steel-blue Pacific's jagged waves contrasted with the foreground's pale, roundly sculpted rocks. Sandstone, Phil had said, geology his second calling.

Again she saw the sea lions plunge awkwardly into the water, and comic pelicans on broad wings, their pouches stuffed with fish. The two of them had explored the rugged littoral, guessing at the names of flowers and an exotic cactus-like grass. Later they'd visited the small multi-denominational temple one of the locals had insisted was a must-stop for any tourist. Set on the edge of a grassy field, it resembled a misshapen sombrero. Inside, stained glass, sculpted woods, and a central floor mosaic lent a peaceful aura to the tiny room. And in that quiet space she'd felt that their future would be steadfast and lasting.

She traced the outline of Phil's narrow jaw and held the image to her chest. Then she wrapped the photo in a clean towel and slipped it, face down, into the top dresser drawer. She paused, removed her gold wedding band, and tucked it beneath the cloth.

4

Alan and Carolyn watched Derek Johnson's back as he picked his way down the Inner Circle, which would start him back to the airstrip. Apparently Derek had spent the night with her. The saturated ground, churned in the ruts to a dark, dense mud, formed little wells and troughs. The ruts were no surprise to Alan. That was pretty much the nature of four-wheelers: they scarred the country. But he was impressed that Whetstone had only two and that they were shared by everyone in the community. He'd be doing a lot of walking.

The day was still, with a featureless layer of altostratus clouds. Last year's leaf litter lay clustered in windblown mounds on either side of the trail, and light from the weak sun fell over the tops of the tall spruce as Alan walked beside Carolyn. From this perspective he could only glimpse the mountains he'd seen on his way in. Rugged five- to six-thousand-foot peaks that looked like a rock climber's Eden. The *country* was what drew visitors to Whetstone.

Although Carolyn walked with purpose, she was not unfriendly, chatting about the layout of the town and bits of history. Occasionally a sluggish mosquito landed on their necks or wrists, but these early pests were easily brushed aside.

"I know you've only been here one night. But do you think it will work staying at Mike's?" she asked.

"I like him," said Alan.

"Of course, I'll get you into your own place as soon as I can." Carolyn pointed left to a wooden sign marked Emerald. "That'll be the shortest route to the community center. But we'll go up Garnet. It's wider."

Soon they heard the high-pitched drone of the 207 and looked up to see a waggle of wings. Derek was saying farewell. The craft straightened and continued its northeasterly course toward

Anchorage. The city was only a hundred and fifty air miles away, but now that the plane was gone Alan felt the sense of isolation.

"You said you'd see him in a month. Is that when he brings in the first"—Alan scanned his memory for the right word—"patrons?"

"A plane load a day—six people, five days a week."

"Healthy operation."

"It's because of the flightseeing part. The intrigue of the wild gets them here. Derek spends an hour on the coast, looking for bears. So we get a lot of repeats, friends of family and friends of friends. It allows some of the artists to do quite well financially."

"And this goes on all summer?"

"Five months. Except for the two weeks we take off to put up salmon for the year. Mid to late July is the peak of the run here."

They turned left at the end of Garnet and Carolyn drew a circle in the air. "This is the town center. Most of your work will be on this side of the creek." She continued down a narrower trail that looked like it would barely accommodate the four-wheeler, and Alan made a mental note to spend a day brushing it out.

When they reached the generator shed, the first thing Alan did was survey the surrounding vegetation: not forty feet from the building's edge, mature spruce rose like turrets above snarls of leafless birch and spindly willows. The shed itself, a sixteen-by-twenty-foot post-and-beam structure, was blackened near the bottom where oily exhaust found egress through two steel pipes. Two five-hundred-gallon fuel tanks stood nearby. The *chug-a-chug-a-chug* of the generators studded the late afternoon air.

Inside, Carolyn handed him a pair of hearing protectors. He studied the two identical thirty-kilowatt behemoths. They were recently painted, supported with solid steel skids. Someone had stenciled BABY BLUE on the first; the second bore the label THE TWIN. Behind a freestanding middle partition sat a forty-eight-volt battery bank, above it a large sine wave inverter and breaker box. There was an auto-start system—good. That would save him a lot of time. Screwdrivers, wrenches, and files stippled the back wall; one window cast a dim, murky light on a workbench cluttered with bolts, loose wire, and dirty rags.

Carolyn headed for the door, indicating for Alan to follow. They stood in the only clearing.

"Loud, huh?" said Carolyn.

"You should have heard those old one-cylinder Wittes. Make these guys sound like purring kittens."

"What do you think?"

"Looks like a decent setup. Any major breakdowns?"

"Baby was rebuilt in '95, and Rick repainted them both. I'd like to extend their life as long as possible. I can hardly afford the price of fuel anymore, let alone a new generator. So, what about the solar panels?"

"It'll take some figuring, but it looks doable. You'll have to be willing to cut some trees though."

"How many?"

"Can't say for sure. I'll have to study the sun and get some compass readings. Probably two acres."

"Two *acres*?"

"Yeah. That's the downside of solar." Alan caught himself. "But," he said, "don't worry. Losing a few trees will be worth it for what you'll save in fuel, I swear."

SHE LED HIM down a footpath. Soon they were stepping over deadfalls and swiping branches from their faces.

Over Carolyn's broad shoulders, Alan could make out the creek, its ice just beginning to loosen around the banks. In a few weeks it would be flowing swiftly, but it wasn't big enough to raft on. A planked, arched bridge, large enough for two to walk side by side, spanned the water.

A bright red helicopter appeared, penetrating the quiet like a slur of the tongue. *Whump- whump-whump.* It hovered directly overhead, then swayed heavily away. A large white Z painted on the metal belly eyed them from above.

"What's that doing here?" Alan asked.

Carolyn shrugged. "I think they're taking geological surveys."

Alan didn't know who "they" were, but he didn't ask. Though it was strange that Carolyn was so breezy about "geological surveys." You'd think she'd see them as some kind of threat. The helicopter was intrusive, almost as loud as the generators had been.

They crossed the bridge, following another poorly groomed trail choked with brush. Highbush cranberry, currant? It was hard to tell when they weren't yet in leaf. The trail intersected finally with a wide swath, and ahead he saw what had to be the storehouse. The building was enormous. It resembled an airplane hangar and was finished, like Mike's cabin, with shiplap spruce siding, stained brown. With the blue metal roof, it was clear that Blake had wanted to stick to a theme.

As Carolyn swung open the heavy, planked door, Alan caught the room's earthy odor of grains and dried beans. From a central beam hung a large scale, suspended by cables and a bright, sturdy chain. Dozens of stainless-steel bins paralleled the walls. Carolyn opened the first, marked *White Flour*. "Everything's in bulk. Just bring your own container, weigh your stuff, and record it in the log." She pointed to a spiral notebook.

"Wow, organization." Alan walked from bin to bin, reading labels. There was coffee and tea. There were four other flours, and brown and white rice. There were cereals, sugar, and five kinds of pasta. He moved to the next aisle. He was between pinto beans and split peas when the door opened and a woman walked through the door, small as a sapling, with hair like ripe strawberries and a splay of freckles across her upturned nose.

Carolyn introduced her as Patricia Abbey.

"I'm a songwriter," she told Alan. "I play guitar and harmonica." She stood up on her toes enthusiastically and came back down.

"Oh, Mike mentioned you. Said you were Alaska's Bonnie Raitt. I play some myself."

Her face brightened. "Really? Fantastic. You bring your guitar?"

"Well, yeah, but—"

"Great! I've been dying for someone to jam with. Why don't you and Mike come over next Friday? I'll invite some friends."

Alan rubbed the back of his neck. "Not sure I'm ready to play in front of strangers," he said evasively.

"Oh, come *on*. No one here cares if you make mistakes."

Alan didn't argue.

"Friday, then—say, seven o'clock? Mike knows the way."

CAROLYN CONTINUED WITH the tour, but it wasn't long before she looked at her watch. When they walked past the library and the art building, she didn't offer to take Alan inside. And she hadn't shown him the post office. "One more thing. I want you to meet Dad."

Alan hesitated. Should he protest? He'd gotten a good picture of Whetstone. Surely this meeting could wait? Mostly, he didn't know how he would react to Blake. Alan had a brief vision of the old man wearing pajamas and a bib, gurgling into a bowl of cold oatmeal. He didn't know much about strokes except that the range in severity and recovery was wide. His Aunt Trudy had suffered a moderate stroke but regained her faculties by practicing multiplication in her head. Mike's account of Blake painted a bleaker picture.

CAROLYN'S HOUSE WAS more spacious than Mike's, but it had the same sense of order. They entered through the kitchen, which opened directly into the living area. Cracks in the milled spruce flooring had been caulked, and the surface painted a coffee-cream brown. The furniture faced out; beyond four picture windows the creek made its stealthy, under-ice journey to the lake. Over the back of a wheelchair slumped a grizzled head.

"Amy?" Carolyn called. There was no reply. "Amy's one of our caregivers. She must have stepped out." Carolyn beckoned and led Alan around the wheelchair where he confronted the seated figure face to face.

Alan's first impulse was to look away. But he didn't, and then it got easier. The cheeks were just cheeks, not sinkholes. The wiry, gray beard was not scrub lichen. Even the skin—pale and sickly, with forehead liver spots—could have belonged to any elderly white male. Carolyn knelt, and Alan tentatively followed suit. A stale smell of urine, not unlike the residual odor of theater popcorn, floated up through a mask of soap.

"Dad." Carolyn shook the top of his left hand.

The old man did not shift his gaze. His eyes were flat, like button eyes on a rag doll.

"Dad." Carolyn shook his hand again. She made a few passes over his mouth with a handkerchief. "Sometimes he wakes up. You can never tell when."

She leaned forward and whispered something in Blake's ear. There was a slight twitch around one eye, as if the button was beginning to lose a thread, and a wispy curl of lip that looked like an effort at speech.

Carolyn whispered again. Then she drew back. "This is Alan Lamb." She guided Alan's hand to her father's. The skin of Blake's hand was cracked and translucent.

"Hello, Mr. Parsons."

If there was a response, Alan could not be sure. Perhaps he only imagined a light reciprocal pressure. Alan stood and Carolyn folded her arms across her chest. Her look was not one of pity exactly, but it contained pity's distance. It was clear that Carolyn's compassion for her father was backed by a fierce determination.

"People tell me he should be in a home. But I won't ship him off like some cadaver in a box."

But at some point, people need to live their own lives. Is it worth it, in the long run—the emotional drain? Even if you've managed to work around the physical one.

As if reading his thoughts, Carolyn pointed to a family photograph on the wall, whose color had faded where the sun beat through. "*This*," she said, "is my father."

The lean-muscled man in the photo smiled so broadly that Alan raised the corners of own lips. On Blake's left stood a teenage Carolyn, and, presumably, her Dena'ina stepmother, long dead. It was because of her Native claim, Mike said, that Blake had ended up with so much land, doubling the size of his homestead. Surrounding it now was national park that precluded further development. How had Mike put it? Practically the whole north shore of the ninety-mile-long lake to himself. *Shame he can't enjoy it now.* Alan glanced at the wheelchair and back to the photograph.

And again Alan was amazed at the making of Whetstone, the ambition of the project. He couldn't imagine building a town—a house was work enough. He'd fantasized about building his own place, but a town, that was something else. A toothpick diorama of one would be daunting.

Alan wanted to express something, a germ of warmth that had begun to sprout as he'd studied Blake's photograph. "I wish I'd known him," he said, and Carolyn frowned.

5

The sun crept in through the east window and cast a bright swath on the kitchen counter. Now the reading glasses held a promise of perfect vision, and the flower vase, painted with flying geese, looked as if it, too, could lift and soar. Outside, the birch trees were taking on a viridescent sheen, and the ground was drying up; new spears were poking through sweeping mats of dead winter grass. Soon the undergrowth would be laden with horsetail and ferns. It was almost May.

The books waited, stacked on the coffee table, ready to go. Dehlia slipped them in her backpack. What to wear? Mornings and evenings could still be cool, but by midday it would be too warm for her wool coat. Her teal windbreaker would do.

As she backed out of the upstairs closet, a hand tapped her shoulder—a touch so palpable that she was surprised to turn around and find no one there. It reminded her of a dream she'd had weeks ago, when she'd wakened to find Phil sitting at the edge of the bed. He'd held her arm lightly and said, *Dehlia, there's something... something...* She'd struggled to sit up, pressing her elbows into the mattress, willing some point deep in her subconscious to lift her head, while the effort at speech similarly overwhelmed her. *Yes, of course, I'm listening,* she tried to say. But the words would not come out, and when she finally woke for real she could feel his hand losing its grip and see his image fading, then he disappeared at the entrance to the loft. For a long minute she waited, still believing he'd been there in bodily form, before she rested back on the pillow and fell asleep.

Now she shook her head as if to clear it, looked right and left and again behind her. "I know you're there," she said aloud. "What do you want from me?"

In the cramped library Darlene McCoy was at her desk, sorting books from a big box of donations. When Dehlia walked in, Darlene yawned and lowered her glasses, resting them by their attached chain on her buxom chest.

"Dehlia, Dehlia, how are you, love?"

Why did Darlene have to croon? She'd always been obnoxious, but in a friendly, grandmother-forcing-sausage-and-eggs-on-you sort of way.

"Fine, thanks." Dehlia swung down her backpack and worked open the zipper. "I have some books."

Darlene shuffled through them. "You should be reading romances, girl pretty as you." She made a tsking sound and tossed the books on a cart. "There's a new guy in town."

Dehlia picked at the peeling varnish covering the wooden countertop.

"I tell you, something happens to Stew, I'll be like those Eskimo women in the old days. They figured six months was enough for grief."

Dehlia bit her lip. She could tolerate the lecturing. Darlene had a good heart, and Stew was a northern-born John Chapman who didn't plant orchards but would fix a carburetor for any neighbor. He'd even sworn off the booze to save his marriage.

"My mother always claimed," said Darlene, "that patience is overrated. Before you know it, you'll be ninety."

Dehlia turned her back and perused the bookshelves. *How can you understand, Darlene. A year and a half isn't long enough.* Instead she said, "My mother never gave me advice."

Darlene didn't appear to be listening. "Ever read Alaska biographies?"

"I'd rather read about Rome."

"There's Wally Hickel. His book might not be all wisdom but dig deep enough you might find some wit. Or Jay Hammond, *Tales of a Bush Rat Governor.*"

Dehlia faced her. "No, nothing political."

"There's more to those books than politics, you know. Anyway, politics are coming to Whetstone. Better get prepared." Darlene's mouth turned down and her chin puckered like a sun-dried fruit.

"Wait." Darlene flipped through the antiquated card catalogue. "Fiddlesticks. I was going to give you a book about Sojourner Truth.

But it was checked out two years ago and never returned. Which reminds me. There's something Phil had that never made it back. It's called *Geology, Economics, and the Law*. See if you can find it sometime, would you, love?"

Darlene scribbled the title on a scrap of paper and Dehlia folded it and tucked it in her back pocket. The title was completely unfamiliar. Not that he'd carried many law books home over the years—a lot of the research for his work was done right here at the library, on the Internet. And through contacts in Anchorage. That's what she'd been told, and she had no reason to doubt it.

6

O ne bad thing about instruments," said Mike, as Alan slung his guitar to Patricia's living room floor, "is they're not very portable."

"Depends on the instrument." Patricia glanced from Mike to Alan to her six-foot-three companion, looking them each up and down with raised eyebrows.

"This is what I married. A woman of immodesty and impropriety." The tall man stepped forward and stretched out his hand. "Dale Abbey."

Alan's first impression of the couple, an odd match given the incongruity of their heights, quickly faded.

Patricia gestured to the counter. "There's homebrew, or cranberry juice for teetotalers."

Alan zeroed in on the beer, chilling to perfection in a pan of ice. He popped open a bottle, took a long draught, and wiped his mustache. "Where'd you get the ice?"

"From the lake," said Dale. "Usually lasts through mid-August under sawdust."

"No offense, Trotter, but this is colder than it would be from your root cellar."

Mike shrugged. "British heritage. I like warm beer."

Alan turned back to Dale. "Some of the new refrigerators only draw a hundred watts."

"We don't plan on living here that long. A fridge is something we can do without. Plus, I enjoy putting up ice."

A freckled little girl wearing a plaid skirt stepped into the room, holding a doll upside down by one leg. She leaned against Dale. "Daddy, we're not going to live here very long?"

He stroked her hair. "No, chicken little. We'll have to send you to a real school pretty soon."

"Mommy can teach me."

"You'll want to learn more than Mommy can teach. You'll want to make friends."

She looked at Alan. He winked at her.

"He can be my friend."

"Alan's an adult. You'll want to make friends your own age."

"Oh." She squirmed away from her father's side.

Patricia took her daughter by the hand. "C'mon, Allie, let's go fill the ice bucket."

The minute the girls slipped out the door, Dale leaned toward his guests with conspiratorial intensity. He laid one hand on Alan's shoulder, the other on Mike's. "Boys," he said, in a low voice, "I have some heavy news. But I don't want Patricia to hear it yet. She'll get all fired up, and this is her night to kick back. She never gets to play with another musician." He gave Alan a meaningful look that said, *You're filling an important role here, don't blow it.*

Mike waited with a half-scowl.

Dale said, "The mining project, near Lost Mountain? It's for real. Open pits are the worst. When they're below the water table you have to keep pumping out the hole that fills up. You deplete the groundwater. Creeks and rivers dry up. Then there's acid rock drainage that gets into the water systems. We need to look out for our fish."

Mike stepped to the side and Dale's hand fell from his shoulder. Mike said, "Who's your source?"

"Sheila Grady." Dale dropped his other hand from Alan's shoulder. "Who can you count on if it isn't the postmistress?"

"Don't rule out her soft-spoken partner," said Mike.

"Julie?" Dale chuckled. "Yeah, why do you think she works with wool? It's been around since the Cro-Magnons. Most reliable fabric ever."

"They couldn't build the infrastructure," said Mike. "Too expensive. Logistically impossible. There's not a town within a hundred miles of that site connected to the road system." He took a long pull of beer. "I'm saying those are still rumors, and in a month they'll have all the potency of a can of Coors."

Alan's mind was working overtime—even through the homebrew, which was like Coors to the tenth power. That meant the chopper he'd seen with Carolyn was doing surveys for some mega-mining project. So much for the quaint little artist community.

"They're already talking grants to communities," said Dale. "Thirty, forty, fifty thousand. For waste improvement, renewable energy, money for schools. Anything to buy support."

"But no one here would—" Alan broke off when Patricia's footsteps sounded outside the door.

Dale passed a virtual zipper over his lips and motioned his guests to the living room, where a pair of couches and several armchairs formed a circle. In the corner an old yellow Lab looked up sleepily from his bed. Alan walked over and petted him. The dog was a nice distraction.

"Chowder's seventeen," said Patricia. "Doesn't move much these days."

Alan gave the dog's head a final pat then rose, picking up his smile where he'd last dropped it.

Patricia picked up Alan's guitar. "Do you mind?" she asked after the fact.

"Of course not," said Alan.

She thumbed the strings and adjusted the tuning pegs. *Far out on the ocean, Where land's a distant sight...* Her voice was rich and sultry, and her fingers made deft transitions from chord to chord. Soon he was transported to another time and place, a rental with a wrap-around deck overlooking Kachemak Bay, where he'd often sat watching the boats leave harbor, wondering if some vessels were never destined to be moored—and worrying that this was a flaw in his own character.

Patricia struck the last note and tapped the body. "Nice guitar." She handed it back to him and picked up her own. She indicated the songbooks on the coffee table. "I see you brought some music."

Alan leafed through the sheets, looking for traditional favorites. He let Patricia take the lead, and by the time they got to "Sittin' on the Dock of the Bay," he'd grown comfortable with her rhythms. A knock at the door interrupted them.

Patricia turned to Allie. "Open the door, pea pod."

Allie sprang from the couch. "Hi, sweetie," said the first of two women, and Alan made quick note of her, an attractive brunette just north of plump. Then his gaze met her companion's. Something fluttered in his chest: wingbeats of a trapped moth. *That red scarf.*

The woman looked away self-consciously and removed her coat, revealing black hair that fell well below her shoulders. She wore a turquoise T-shirt, slim cut with a V at the front, and a silver chain around her neck. It was apparent that she chose her colors and styles carefully. A true artist.

Dale rose. "Barbara, Dehlia... this is Alan Lamb."

Alan stood and nodded to each in turn.

Barbara laid a warm hand on his arm; Dehlia dipped her head like a songbird. She didn't take his hand, and Alan was glad for it. His palm felt like it might erupt into flame.

Dehlia touched her temple, as if correcting some inner thought. "I hope you like it here."

Barbara poured two beers and handed one to Dehlia. The women sat across from Alan, Allie between them. He was relieved to have Barbara lead the conversation. She launched into a story about a weasel visiting her woodpile; she'd been feeding it bacon, and twice the animal had snatched it from her hand. Allie sat wide-eyed as Barbara made little dashing movements with her hand to show how quickly the weasel moved. The whole time Alan trained his eyes on Barbara, but there were Dehlia's wrists and forearms... They seemed possessed of a lean fluidity, and he knew that she was not without strength. Gradually the moth in his chest grew still.

Soon there was a second knock—another couple. The woman wore a necklace and bracelet and the man had three posts in one ear. All gold.

The man grinned. "We're here, the party can start." He motioned for Alan to remain seated. "Bryce Peterson. This is my wife, Jen."

"You're the jewelers, right?" Alan said. As if it wasn't obvious.

"I suppose Mike's pretty much filled you in on everyone."

"Not everyone." Alan could feel Dehlia's eyes on him.

Jen poured a glass of cranberry juice and Bryce opened a beer. He pulled a flask from his back pocket. "Chaser, anyone?"

Dehlia keyed in. "Neat, please."

Alan relaxed.

Dale turned back to Alan and Patricia. "How about 'Me and Bobby McGee'?" Dale fished two dollar bills from his wallet and dropped them at their feet. He opened wide his wallet's flaps. "I'm busted flat," he said. "Supporting the arts is tough on the bankroll."

"You musicians and jewelers have it made," said Mike. "Try writing fiction."

"Can you do 'Woodstock'?" Dehlia asked suddenly. "The way Joni Mitchell sings it." The liquor seemed to be loosening her inhibitions.

Alan grimaced and shook his head. But now he looked her full in the face. He no longer felt shy. She smiled back but immediately studied her hands.

"The slow ones are tough for us to pull off," said Patricia. "But I'll play it." Guitar in hand, she fretted an E minor. "Okay everyone, think 'G.' God, gold, gardens."

It was a long, five-and-a-half-minute song, melodic and filled with yearning. The lines drifted through the room like mist across the water, the words "land" and "celebration" rising above the rest of the lyrics as Patricia lingered on them.

"For me," she said, placing her palm on the strings when she finished, "it's about idealism. Setting the soul free. Is that Whetstone or what?"

The room grew quieter. Alan drank his beer.

Patricia hesitated. "I want to share my latest. I don't know where it came from. It's called 'Blake's Dream.'"

Alan shifted in his chair. Could an old man like that, a decrepit stroke victim, still dream? Was it possible that Blake's subconscious was still intact? But maybe Patricia meant another kind of dream. Maybe she meant an aspiration or ambition.

She started playing. Alan recognized the lonely yet full-bodied sound of A minor, but she fingered the chord differently, lower on the fretboard. From there he became mesmerized by her intricate fingerpicking style. She creatively added suspended notes, allowing tones from one chord to flow into the next, which gave the music dissonance and a dark, ominous ambiance. The refrain was the most disturbing:

> *You think I'm sleeping*
> *But I'm working on a plan...*

Patricia lifted her guitar from the cradle of her lap. No one spoke. She looked at Alan. "Your turn."

He shook his head. "I'm not a songwriter."

Bryce took a pull from his flask. "We want Alan," he chanted, his fist beating the air. The others took his cue. Even Dehlia joined in.

"Okay, okay. I'll do a couple of tunes my nieces wrote. This is Willow's. It's called 'Michael's Song.'" Alan took a sip of beer and pointed at Mike. "Don't worry, Trotter. I don't have you in mind."

Mike groaned and Alan scooted forward. He closed his eyes for a moment to enter the mood. He knew who he had in mind—that lovely woman sitting across the room.

> *I think it started with your smile*
> *I saw it and I wanted you to stay for a while.*

As the familiar vibrations ran through his body, his voice grew stronger. This was going better than he'd thought. Having an audience was flattery at its finest, and it was more important than ever that he play his best—for her. When he finished he said, "All right, one more. 'Summer Storm,' by my niece Camille." He looked at Dehlia—deliberately and a little too long—then back at his guitar.

> *Water on the front porch shining, silver in the light*
> *Thunder in the mountains rolling, lightning in my sight*
> *Wind across the water making patterns in the rain*
> *Playing tricks with light and shadows, blowing through*
> *my brain*

He was in full control now, tipsy enough to give his playing a rough edge without being sloppy.

> *And you're so far away*
> *I dare not think of where you are*
> *Listen to the wind, sing along with my guitar*

"Remarkable. Good playing, good songwriting," said Patricia.

Alan gazed again at Dehlia. *Holy mother. It's impossible. She's gorgeous.* And he was filled with dread: somehow, during his time here, they would discover one another's flaws. Now the moth was in his chest again, beating harder.

42

7

It was after midnight when Dehlia and Barbara finally strolled away from Dale and Patricia's porch, the sky still camp-robber gray. After the drinks and music and conversation Barbara was giddy, and she looped an arm through her companion's with a sisterly affection.

"Barbara, didn't that song about Blake spook you?"

"That wasn't all that spooked me. God, did you see how he looked at you? *All evening!* I think he's in love."

"Who... what are you talking about? You're crazy." Suddenly Dehlia disliked the sound of her own voice. No line existed between insincerity and lies.

"Don't deny it. You lucky dog."

Dehlia struggled to keep her balance. "Barbara, I... I'm not looking for a man right now. I'm... not ready. I feel... things... I'm not making sense." She stopped and took a deep breath. "I'm a little drunk."

"I don't believe you."

"I *am!*" Dehlia said. "Drunk, I mean." She swayed dramatically. "I mean I'm not... oh, forget it. Help me walk."

Barbara drew close. Dehlia concentrated on her footsteps and leaned into her friend. Years of use had worn ruts in the dirt trail and she walked in the center, where spruce roots jutted up from the compressed earth. Barbara, wearing XTRATUFS, sloshed heedlessly through the puddles. To a stranger they'd make an odd sight: Barbara, broad and bulky, supporting her taller companion, whose gait was unsteady as that of a young moose.

Dehlia stopped again. "I'm not proud of the whiskey."

"Come on, once, twice a year? All that time, with Phil and his, his... you know." Barbara pressed her hand to her own lips. "Shut up, Barbara. It's none of your business." She kissed Dehlia on the check. "Know what I miss most about Rick?"

But Dehlia could only think of Phil. Sometimes she wished she'd confronted him. How would their life together have been different? Forget it. Her husband was dead. And he'd been good in so many ways. She wanted to share her experiences—Phil's voice, his touch—but she was afraid her friend would scoff. Barbara knew too much.

Barbara pulled her along. "What I miss most," she said, "is I don't have anyone to blame anymore. When I lose my sunglasses or don't put the dishes away, guess who's responsible? Me. I guess I'm relearning how to live with myself."

"Mmm," Dehlia murmured. It was an admirable admission, the need to accept responsibility. But Barbara was only talking about the practical, housekeeping part. There was emotional responsibility as well, and this was much more complicated. Alone, everything was reflected back on oneself. There was no one to hide behind anymore.

"I see you quit wearing your wedding ring," said Barbara, leaning in. "Now you just need to stop thinking about yourself so much. You live in a *community*."

8

Alan stared at the drafting paper, a sheet so large it nearly covered the table. Against the blue grid, the penciled diagram was a confusion of radiating lines, the notations mostly unreadable from erasures. For the first time he understood how Blake had arranged the lots, the sixteen parcels laid out around the town center like facets on an oblong gem. Four in the middle, inside the Inner Circle, and twelve on the outside. Only two undeveloped lots. No wonder all those trails names: Garnet, Sapphire, Agate, Emerald…

He tossed his pencil on the drawing. Damn it all. Why did his laptop have to break one day before he flew in? He'd thought it would be good to work the old-fashioned way, with pencil and paper; now he wasn't so sure. He turned down the radio—tuned all morning to a Dillingham station—then leaned back in his chair and watched Mike cut circles into flattened biscuit dough with an inverted drinking glass.

"What's wrong?" said Mike. "Can't take Willie Nelson? Turn that off if it's bothering you."

Alan sighed. "It's not the music. This project's too complicated. I'm used to working with square lots. These trapezoids are driving me nuts. And the wires running to the new lots are okay, but the old ones are a mess. I'd like to throttle the guy who sold that stuff to Blake—you can't run residential wire underground. The insulation will crack, in time. So I'm looking at redoing the power supply to half the houses, trying to locate the old lines, digging them up—"

"Can't you just cut them and run new wire?" Mike thought everything had a practical solution.

"Last I checked, copper was seven grand a ton and the recycle centers were paying about a buck seventy a pound for electrical wire. Without that trade-in, Carolyn won't be too happy with the cost of the renovation."

"Aren't you on the payroll? You must be working for peanuts if it's worth her while to issue you checks for pick-and-shovel work."

"I'm not charging her for that."

"That's generous," said Mike. Then, with a touch of bitterness, "Must be nice to be able to afford working for free." He punched out another Ship's biscuit, reshaped the dough, and picked up the rolling pin.

"Looks like you're the one rolling in dough." Alan picked up his pencil but he sighed again. "Can't even read my own writing. I need a gallon of gas and a blowtorch so I can start over."

Mike peered at Alan over the top of his glasses. "Mind if I make a suggestion? First of all, redraw it. Second, get some colored pencils so you can distinguish what's what. You know, red for the new stuff, blue for the old, that kind of thing."

Alan stared at the diagrams. "Yeah, good idea. You were probably one of these kids that got five stars for penmanship. My teachers always said 'handwriting sloppy.'"

Mike cleared his throat. "It'd be painfully boring if we all excelled in every subject."

"Don't be so diplomatic, Trotter. Just tell me my drafting skills suck. I'd rather hear it from you than—"

"Shh. Listen." Mike grew still and pointed to the radio. "Turn it up."

Alan rotated the dial and the voice rose.

"…between the communities of Whetstone and Valatga Qayeh. Today Ziggurat, Incorporated announced its acquisition of a one-hundred-percent interest in the Fly Creek Mine Prospect, thought to be the largest gold and copper deposit in North America. Already environmentalists are raising objections over the mine's location near one of the richest salmon-spawning areas in the world. In other news, the city council…"

"Damn! Abbey was right!" Mike's voice drowned out the newscaster's. "Did you hear that? Largest gold and copper deposit in *North America*? Near Lost Mountain, practically in our backyard!"

Alan clicked off the radio. "There goes the country. And my sister's bread and butter." Sarah. Just what she needed, with her debts and her teenage girls to raise. Salmon was her means, fishing all she knew. With a gigantic mine operating upstream from the Bay, it was only a matter of time before chemicals leached into the groundwater and streams, and the fish and other wildlife would suffer. His old protectiveness surged up again.

"I love it," said Mike, as he placed the last biscuit on the baking sheet. "Ziggurat. A Babylonian or Assyrian temple—in the heart of Alaska. Here's a prediction: in ten years we'll all be going there to pray—for our salvation." He set his mouth then gave it a twist. "I wonder how long this has been going on. The helicopter traffic must be out of earshot."

Alan nodded. He was getting the picture. "No way to access the country except with those eggbeaters. I saw a chopper when Carolyn was showing me around. It had the Ziggurat logo."

Mike looked surprised. "We plebeians always get left in the dark. You'd think we would have been told *something*. A project like that could run this community through a juicer, and all we'd get is the pulp."

Alan knew it was true. The environmental track record for big mining companies was dreadful, the pattern always the same. The millionaires moved in, drilling and blasting began, minerals were extracted, groundwater poisoned, and the company departed, leaving locals to clean up the mess. He'd heard stories about water turned so toxic from mining waste that it could melt aluminum ladders and iron shovels. How could any freshwater creature survive that? The fish couldn't, of course, but what about the bears and birds and moose and wolves?

Mike glanced at his watch. "The mail should be sorted now. I'll run over and see if the paper came. Mind throwing the biscuits in the oven? They take about fifteen minutes, but check them in ten." Mike wiped the flour from his hands onto his pants, slipped into his tennis shoes, and hurried out.

ALONE, ALAN FELT a mixture of vexation, yearning, and self-doubt. News of the mining project added to his sense of something lurking, as if a giant shark had moved north, into a river system, and was circling in a nearby watery outpost.

What was he doing here? Why had he ever pursued solar tech work, why did he feel such a compelling need to promote things that were ecologically sound? *Don't be a zealot,* Mike had cautioned, and Alan knew that Mike had hit on something. Not just *something,* but Alan's deep and personal reasons for his commitment to the land. Environmental work made him feel like he had a purpose, like he could salvage a part of himself that had been trampled on.

God, he didn't want to revisit that. *Think about the present* was his new mantra. Oh, that was sweet. So here he was in this isolated community with a job too big for his capabilities, haunted by a woman he couldn't find the courage to court. Since that evening at Patricia's, he'd seen Dehlia only in glimpses.

Now, hunched again over his diagram, he stared gloomily at the trail from Mike's house to hers. Only three lots away, but they seemed the size of small countries. He went back to his figures, adding lengths of wire on his calculator, multiplying that amount by the going price per foot, subtracting what he could get for the old copper. He entered the information on his expense chart, knowing that if it seemed a big sum to him, it would seem like even more to Carolyn. She'd mentioned more than once her need to keep costs down.

An acrid odor wafted from the oven.

"Damn!" Alan grabbed a leather glove and removed the cookie sheet, flinging the scorched biscuits onto a dinner plate. He placed the second sheet of uncooked rounds in the oven, hauled over a chair, and sat down.

As he waited, he fidgeted with the glove, noticing signs of wear at the fingertips, the stains of dirt and oil. He thought of all the cowhide turned hand protection scattered across the country, the leather-covered palms that clutched steering wheels, turned screwdrivers and wrenches, encircled shovels and chainsaws. In Whetstone alone, how many thousands of gallons of fuel had passed through glove-gripped nozzles, all that fluid moving from tank to container to machine, to burn and disperse in the form of CO_2 and poisonous gases?

Fuel. You can't eliminate it; you can only reduce it. He needed a tally of Whetstone's energy needs for the last ten years, and a projection of the savings Carolyn could expect from his solar installation. The projections would be the most difficult. It was almost as impossible to predict the fluctuating cost of fuel as it was the weather. When prices dropped, it never helped his solar panel pitch—people always fell back on what was cheapest and most convenient. Still, Alan had an innate optimism that a great shift would someday be underway, and it gratified him to think that he was already doing his part, though his contribution might be so slight as to be scarcely noticeable. The faintest star in a distant sky.

9

Stepping back from the mask she'd hung on the wall, Dehlia examined it critically. She liked the loon image, but the human mouth was too conspicuous; it needed a subtler touch. At the same time, she'd been resisting this revision. It felt like work, an academic modification that had little to do with inspiration.

She picked up the leaflet she'd left on a corner of her desk. She scanned the passage, wondering if she'd missed something.

> The loon song has inspired cultures for centuries...
> Early Inuit cultures buried loon skulls in graves.
> Because of their mournful song, the loon was thought
> to act as a guide into the netherworld.

Skulls, graves, the netherworld. The words popped out at her. How had she not focused on them before? She read on.

> People from the Faroe Islands thought that the call
> of the red-throated loon flying overhead meant it was
> following a soul to heaven. The Ojibwa thought that
> the call was an omen of death.

An omen of death. Again she sensed that she had somehow passed over these words. Perhaps she'd been unable to acknowledge them. But perhaps she was at last ready. Now her decision to do this series was made clear. Of course, it had been spurred by the loss of Phil. Like most artists, she had not knowingly chosen her subject—it had chosen her.

SHE WAS A CHILD—maybe eight or nine. She sat, arms wrapped around her knees, on damp ground. Surrounding her were cottony tufts that looked like blooms. She plucked a stem, twirled it, and ran the white seed head across her cheek. It was softer than the brush her mother used for rouge.

From a nearby lake came an eerie cry—low at first then rising, echoing out into the vast landscape. Dehlia froze. There was a pause, then it came again. Even at this young age, without the words to express her feelings, she recognized the beauty of its song, the wrenching and powerful lament.

Her father called and ran to embrace her. "I didn't know where you were. I was worried."

She pointed in the direction of the lake. "There's something out there."

"That's an Arctic loon." He took her hand. "Come on, we're leaving."

BACK IN THE CAR, there was no more arguing. Her mother sat stone-faced, looking out the passenger window. When they reached her uncle's house, her father said, "We'll go in and pack our things. We'll stay in Fairbanks tonight."

Inside, the little woman with the brown and wrinkled skin who was her uncle's wife sat sewing a pair of mukluks. She looked at Dehlia and smiled.

Over the next two weeks, they reversed their trip north, her parents exchanging time behind the wheel but not words, her father the only one speaking, announcing the arrival of every town along the way where they stopped for gas or food or bodily relief. From Delta Junction through Canada, all the way home to Mt. Pelier, Vermont.

The endless road. Dehlia stretched out in the backseat with stacks of paperbacks, reading dog and horse and wildcat stories through the Yukon Territory's gravelly stretches before taking up her sketch pad and drawing pictures of those same animals when the tires at last hit pavement. The near absence of sound an immediate relief to her ears, her body no longer subjected to the tiresome bumps imposed by potholes and dips.

The aftermath, her mother asking, "What, Drew, were you hoping to accomplish? The dreariest place on the planet a sweet little highlight to this dreary marriage?"

AN ARCTIC LOON, the last in her series. The loon's body, in profile, made up half the mask. The other half was a man's face. Dehlia knew this man, yet she did not know him. His face was painted an ashen blue.

Before her husband's death, she had never seen a corpse. She'd always arrived too late, in time for the funeral service only, when all that was left for viewing was an urn or coffin set beside a photograph of a healthy, smiling face.

She was ignorant of death's palette, unaware that bodies don't always look alike in the first postmortem days, various diseases lending the skin a different cast: grayish-white, yellow-brown, lemon-yellow, white. But that February day when Stew discovered Phil lying prone on the trail, and hoisted him onto the snowmachine and pinned the body on each side with his knees and drove him home, when Stew wrestled him inside and onto the floor and she saw the color of his skin, his lips, his fingernails, she knew. She knew the finality, she knew the cause. She saw Phil walking, then felt his sudden shortness of breath, the pain in his chest radiating to his shoulder and arm. She saw him fall and stumble and crawl, his will sheared away by some great force that likewise coaxed and reassured him, voiceless but somehow communicating that the snow on which he lay was beautiful and soothing. Dehlia saw and felt these things even as she turned away and clutched the sleeves of Stew's grimy Carhartt jacket and nearly lost her footing. Stew held her as she choked and only repeated: *No—No—*

Later, after the radio call and the arrival of other living, breathing bodies and the hugs that did not comfort, Dehlia's gasps became less frequent, her tears controlled with fewer dabs of tissue. Arrangements were made, and Phil's body rearranged. Someone brewed coffee and tea. Stew left, then returned carrying Phil's satchel, flung erratically off the trail. Food was prepared. Someone handed Dehlia a bowl of soup. She took it and held it a moment, but the tomato, chicken, and peppery aroma made her nauseous. She pushed it away, afraid that she might be sick.

That night and the next people stayed with her. They sprawled on the couch or slept in chairs; they cooked and did dishes and swept the floor. A state trooper arrived with paperwork, and the body was flown to Anchorage for cremation. The body whose blood had pooled, whose extremities had turned a sickly blue. So that Dehlia could no longer look at photographs of Phil without seeing traces of that last color beneath his cheeks, in the hollows under his eyes. And for a long time after, she would wonder if something could have been done. If she were somehow in league with a formidable spirit who severed the once solemn vows made between woman and man.

10

In appearance, Dan Broderman's house didn't differ much from the other homes in Whetstone. What Alan noticed, as he approached, was the smell. It didn't take him long to recognize: it smelled *fishy*.

He knocked. He could hear music—loud, symphonic brass—and he rapped harder. The house front had no windows, and after a few minutes he walked to the corner of the building and peeked around the side. Instantly, an alarm sounded. *No, not an alarm, a damn siren.* Alan quickly ducked away.

Almost as soon as it was triggered, it stopped, as did the music. Both noises were replaced with a high-pitched yapping. The next instant, Dan stood in front of his door. He wore a black apron and a toothpick stuck out from between his teeth.

Dan removed the toothpick. "Motion detector. Keeps the bears out of my freezer." He studied Alan. "Are you a bear?"

Alan looked at him quizzically, and Dan laughed: *hree, hree, hree.* Mike had warned him about Dan's eccentricities, but Alan wasn't prepared for this. Dan's mirth was a good nine licks left of convention.

"What I mean is," said Dan, "are you predator or prey?"

Was this open hostility or just some twisted sense of humor? "I must be prey," said Alan. "I'm a Lamb."

This set Dan off again and Alan decided his move had been a good one.

"What do you want?" Dan folded his arms across his chest.

"I'm tallying energy needs. Mind if I come in?" The yapping continued inside the house. Dan slipped back inside. When he reopened the door the Pomeranian had stopped. Dan allowed Alan entrance. Across the room, the dog, confined to a kennel, growled at him then lay down.

The smell of fish was strong. Alan quickly located the source: on a long counter lay the carcasses of two salmon. Their bodies, void of spots, identified them clearly as sockeyes, but they lacked the characteristic hooked snouts and humped backs of late-season fish. And their bodies were still silvery, not the deep red they would take on closer to spawning. They looked like they'd make great steaks. A few rolls of rice paper lay nearby, along with a brayer and an assortment of inks and brushes, and thumbtacked to the wall were several prints in progress. The salmon had been reproduced with rubbings of black ink, but on two prints Dan had painted in more detail: eyes and scales and even lines on the dorsal and tail fins, and hints of silver and green on the body and mouth.

Alan sat down at the kitchen table. "I'm interrupting your work."

Dan remained standing but did not remove his apron. He flipped a wrist upward; he would tolerate the disruption—barely.

"I've heard about what you do," said Alan.

Dan flicked a dead fly from the windowsill. He reinserted the toothpick.

"How do you get the ink to stick with all that slime?"

"It's not rocket science," Dan said curtly.

Alan was annoyed. Was some of that slime fixed permanently to Broderman's skin? He decided to forego the niceties and get to the point. "I understand you keep your fish frozen." He pulled a pen and notebook from his pocket. "I need to know what your freezer draws."

"Eleven hundred and seventy watts." The number sounded straight from the manual.

Alan recorded it. "How many hours a day does it run?"

"Depends. In winter I only plug her in when it's twenty-five degrees or warmer. In summer I might run her five hours a day. She's well insulated, with glass batts and a down quilt." The toothpick traveled up and down.

"Other energy needs?"

Dan made another gesture. "It's all on file. Hasn't changed in twenty-seven years."

On file? Carolyn hadn't mentioned anything about that. Alan stood.

"How long are you planning on staying?" Dan asked.

What does he mean, how long am I staying? I'm leaving, obviously. Then Alan realized Dan didn't mean staying to visit him, he meant staying in Whetstone.

"That depends," Alan said, "on a lot of things. I'll see you around."

He left Dan at the kitchen table. A grunt was all that Alan received in the way of a send-off.

On the trail, the after-effects of Dan's inhospitality pulled at his chest like an undertow. As if to add injury to insult, the chopper he'd seen on the tour with Carolyn bored down, a blister-red bead, over the town center. As the wooded path closed in around him, he heard it circle twice before growing distant. *What the hell was that thing doing here?*

WHEN HE GOT BACK to Mike's house, Alan peeled off his jacket and tossed it on the couch. He sat down hard and tried to keep his knee still. He stood again. He clomped into his bedroom with his boots still on, then unlaced them and flung them off. Back in the kitchen he picked up the coffeepot, swirled it, then set it down. Again he sat on the couch.

Mike came out of his room, a pencil behind one ear.

"Shit. I didn't mean to bother you."

Mike set the coffeepot on the stove and lit the burner. "What's up?"

"Nothing."

Mike adjusted the flame. "Sure?"

Alan glared. He ran a hand through his hair. Mike poured two cups and handed one to Alan. He pulled over a chair and sat.

"Son of a bitch," said Alan.

"I hope you're not talking to me," said Mike. "Easy, we're roommates."

Alan rubbed his cheek as if he'd been hit. "Sorry."

"Come on. Tell me what happened."

"Broderman."

"Oh, got it."

Alan leaned backward and sighed.

Mike sipped. "Don't take it seriously. Broderman's hot and cold. Catch him on the right day, he might act like your best friend."

"I think he's had it in for me since day one, at the airstrip."

"Maybe he's jealous that you're the latest attention-grabber. Not to disappoint you, buddy, but novelty always wears off."

"He ever been married?" *Could Broderman have eyes on Dehlia? That would explain his animosity.*

Mike looked thoughtful. "Not that I know of. But then, bachelorhood isn't an exclusive category. You?"

"No... she decided, after ten years, we weren't compatible. I moved too much." Alan's grip on his cup loosened a little. "Okay, she told me I was too reactive. I needed to learn to rein it in. Her words."

Mike took off his glasses and rubbed his eyes. "All our sad little sagas." He grimaced and replaced his glasses. "I lived with a woman for six years. For three of those she was having an affair with the vice president of the company she worked for. Insurance."

Alan looked at him with a deadpan expression. "God, Trotter, that's a very unique and tragic story."

Mike paused for a long second. Then the two of them were laughing.

"Don't take that wrong," said Alan, catching his breath.

Mike waved his hand.

Alan tossed back the last of his coffee. "What kind of insurance?"

"Health," said Mike. "I even bought shares in the company."

AFTER MIKE WENT BACK to his writing, Alan was still restless. He slipped on his jacket, wandered to the shed, and unzipped his fly. Nearby, a scrappy blue tarp covered a pile of spruce rounds. *Nothing like a piss to get the venom out of your system.* But his conversation with Mike had already accomplished that—now he just needed to work off some nervous energy.

He found the axe inside the shed wall, right in its place, where Mike had left it. He peeled back the tarp and set a round on the splitting stump.

The first pieces cleaved easily. Straight grained and solid, they flew from the axe head like startled birds. Within minutes, Alan had shed his jacket, and the pile of wedge-shaped pieces around his feet grew steadily. He kicked them aside and went for the next round. Again and again he imposed his will on the wood, delivering each *thwack* with punishing precision.

Digging deeper in the pile, he came across a round from a different tree. Gnarly and punky, its fibers seemed to absorb the steel.

Alan struck once: *thwump*. Working the axe loose, he struck again: *thwump*. He swung a third time, a fourth. Finally, the round gave way.

For four hours, Alan worked. By the time he'd stacked the last piece of firewood under the eave of the house he was tired but satisfied. He was calmer now. And he had something substantial to show for his effort, though he knew in a day or two his shoulders and back muscles would remind him that labor always came with a price tag labeled pain.

11

A southwest breeze skimmed the darkening ice. Nearby, catkins jutted forth like prows of tiny ships on a cluster of willows, their sudden red pollen insisting on a change of season. Slender shoots of wild onions poked through sun-warmed rocks.

Dehlia had the beach to herself. She liked walking alone; this time of year and nearing the dinner hour, she expected to meet no one. Only in July would the beach see heavy traffic. Then the lake would be open water, deep and sometimes dangerous, with foaming whitecaps in a heavy storm, like a roughened mask, obscuring its serenity.

One year ago she'd paddled her canoe into the quiet heart of the bay; there she had scattered Phil's ashes. Dipping her spoon into the small brass urn, she was surprised at the coarseness of the contents, especially the bits of charred bone. It didn't fit with her conception of death or death's aftermath; if death was eternal then its leavings should be fine, like well-ground flour, imbued with the grace of easy dispersal and lift. But the spoon was mostly ineffectual, and finally she had simply inverted the urn and dumped Phil's remains over the side of the canoe, as if they were gravel from a trowel. Then it was over, and there was only a sparkle of sun. She rinsed the urn but then held it below the surface of the frigid water, where it quickly filled and sank.

One year. *It was final, done. All the best things: the talks about consciousness, the universe, the weather... and the bad: the fastidiousness, the distancing.*

She shifted back to the beach and the equally transitory present. At her feet, scattered in grassy patches between rocks were clumps of weasel snout, the plants' waxy leaves already splaying with age, the three-inch flower spikes browning from the bottom up. Only the tips, with their tiny purple flowers, remained in perilous bloom.

What a funny but charmingly descriptive name—weasel snout. Dehlia dropped to one knee and inhaled. The flowers were always surprisingly fragrant.

Might the mild spring be a precursor to a favorable summer? No use making predictions. Alaska summers could usher in a stretch of forty-day sun on the one hand, or forty-day rain on the other. What did look imminent was a storm. To the north against a cerulean sky loomed vertical cumulonimbus, cotton white on top but charcoal dark on the bottom. She'd seen their anvil shapes build to what seemed three times the height of Lost Mountain, and even that was deceptive, based on a perspective not much higher than sea level. In truth, these clouds could stretch to forty thousand feet.

Likely within two hours she would hear the first rumblings of thunder. Then would come the dry-spit crackle of lightning, and finally, the rain. Only the lightning scared her. A couple hiking in the mountains behind Anchorage one year had been struck by lightning and hospitalized. The lightning had traveled completely through the man's body, blowing out the soles of his shoes.

A half mile farther she was suddenly cold, and in the next instant she glimpsed movement in the distance. It was a person, darkly clad. Could it be Alan Lamb? She'd been trying for days to put him out of her mind, to take trails that he would not. Yet she was drawn to him, and remembered his expressiveness when he played his music.

The person climbed a steep outcropping and stood for a moment on the edge, facing the lake. Then he or she sat down and was obscured by brush. Dehlia stopped. Whoever it was deserved privacy.

Before she turned to reverse her direction she caught another movement—something brown and bulkier at the edge of the woods. It didn't take her long to recognize the animal as a bear. Likely a boar. It stopped to sniff the air, then proceeded. Something about its pace was uncanny; the bear appeared to be *stalking* something. The person—where was she? No, it couldn't be a woman, not out here alone, probably without a gun. What a silly thing to think. Plenty of women in Alaska carried and could fire a weapon.

The wind was still blowing from the southwest, in her favor. Dehlia wasn't concerned for her own safety. The bear was a quarter mile away, between her and the outcropping. No doubt the bear *did* have the other person's scent, however, and its strange behavior was alarming. What if there was a mauling and she could have prevented it? But she wasn't in a position to do much.

Instinctively she cupped her hands to her mouth and shouted a warning: "Halloo! Bear! Halloo..." But her words were promptly carried off in the wind.

The bear, at least, heard. It stopped, then lay down, watching her. Dehlia waited. She shouted again, to no effect. The person stood and began walking in the direction of the airstrip. Yes, she realized now, it *was* a woman. But who? Patricia? Meredith? Within a few minutes the figure disappeared, and still the bear did not move.

She let out a long, shallow sigh and looked at her watch. The minute hand ticked interminably, moving from seven to eight to nine, ten to eleven to twelve, before starting another round: one to two to three, to four to five to six, until twenty circuits were completed. Dehlia turned and stepped slowly at first, in keeping with the ticking still in her head. When she looked back, the bear had not moved, and before long she resumed her customary pace.

By nine o'clock, when she was nestled in near her woodstove, the rain was falling hard.

12

Alan woke in the middle of the night. He lay for a few seconds getting his bearings. The rain had stopped when he'd gone to bed, but he opened his eyes anyway and peered up at the underside of the eaves. No droplets fell.

He rolled on his side and on his back again. Dehlia. What was her house like? Who entered her dreams? All he could do was invent things, wild and spurious particulars that only augmented his fascination and intrigue. He knew he was stricken—an adolescent's infatuation—but he shoved that thinking aside.

He'd gone so far as to imagine their future together, moving from Whetstone to Haines to Halibut Cove, from yurt to sailboat to semi-subterranean home. He'd had fleeting images of children. No, she was probably too old. They could adopt then, a handsome boy from Guatemala or China, athletic and quick witted, the kind of kid who would finish his homework and take out the trash without prodding. She would have a studio, of course. It would have tall, arched windows—a Gothic look—and face the flower garden. He would always visit at noon. He'd steal up behind her and they would move to the closet—all female artists had closets in their studios!— and lose themselves in a flurry of silken clothes. He felt the stirrings of arousal, but as he shifted again the bruise on his shinbone where a chunk of firewood had walloped him quashed his desire.

It wasn't often that he was unable to sleep. Kate had been the insomniac, yearning for just three hours of uninterrupted rest. Not that they'd spent many nights together—she'd gone her own way, married he last heard. Anyway, he didn't want to think about Kate. Rehearsing the past was a lot like removing scar tissue from old wounds. Maybe the healing hadn't been pretty, but it usually sufficed.

How did Dehlia perceive him? Did he come across as too common, a jack-of-all-trades, run-of-the-mill bush rat? She seemed so damned sophisticated, as if she'd at least earned a Master's, if not a Ph.D. Like it or not, schooling was usually the thresher that separated the classes, and Whetstone was, generally speaking, a well-educated community. He had never finished college; by his third year he still hadn't decided on a major, and when job opportunities led him in different directions, he opted for financial independence. The upshot was that he knew a little about a lot. Someday, though, he'd go back to school and be able to say, *I'm qualified, okay? An environmental engineer.* A title to dress himself up in. Then he and Dehlia could walk side by side, she in her red scarf.

He almost slapped himself. *Get a life, Lamb. Get practical. What you need is an excuse to go see her.*

SHE WAS SITTING near her garden on a length of cottonwood, so still he almost believed she'd been sculpted. As Alan approached, Dehlia put her hand to her heart and gasped. But then she patted the log, beckoning him to sit. She pointed to a clearing framed by a copse of willows.

A raven atop a flat stone was trying to snatch something—or some *things*—in its beak: chunks of hot dogs, good old American fare—Oscar Mayer's or Hormel's—brownish-pink beauties made from cow guts and pig lips. The bird pecked and hopped awkwardly. Somehow it managed to load all but one piece in its beak but then dropped its entire cargo and began again the painstaking process of collection.

"I've been here twenty minutes," she said. "It could take half. But it insists on all six."

"Well, there's proof that greed isn't unique to humans. Or maybe we should compliment it for persistence." He looked at her. Her dark hair, backlit against the sun, created an aura, almost saintly. "You buy hot dogs just for the birds?"

"You probably thought I ate only free-range chickens."

"I was thinking more along the lines of escargot. Topped off with a bottle of French wine."

"I prefer Sonoma. Chardonnay."

The raven tried to regather its bounty, its black-marble eyes darting from the two of them to the trail, then to the sky.

"So, did you come to visit, or can I help you with something?" Dehlia stretched her legs the way people do in a theater after a long movie, ready to exit.

Alan swallowed. "Since you put it that way, the answer is both. Mike tells me you're on the fuel committee here and are used to working on charts and graphs. I was wondering if you'd work with me on some. I need to show past expenses, and projected ones, with and without solar panels. I thought you'd be a good person to ask." He held his breath.

It seemed to Alan an ice age before she answered. "How soon do you need me?"

"How soon do you need me?" He felt silly repeating her words. "I'll take help when I can get it, though there's no real pressure of time, I guess. How soon does your schedule open up?"

"That depends. Summer season's almost here." She gave him a sideways glance. "If Carolyn wants you to help with patrons around here, you won't have time for much else. I'll help you, but only when the season's over, in October."

"October?"

"It will be better. Trust me."

"Can we shake on it?"

But she didn't take his hand. Her eyes were trained forward. At that moment the raven took flight, all of the meat lodged in its beak.

"See?" said Alan. "He figured out a way not to settle for less."

Dehlia smiled—almost.

PART TWO

Fall Yellows

1

Dehlia was right. Summer was a blur.

Each morning, Alan would drive the four-wheeler to the airstrip to meet Derek, who always arrived promptly between nine-thirty and ten o'clock. The day's visitors would spill out of the Cessna, most of them clean-shaven men and lipsticked women, sportily dressed retirees with white teeth and good manners. Alan would lend a supporting arm to the occasional infirm passenger for the climb into the four-wheeler trailer. Soon the wobbly senior would be seated on Naugahyde pads, feet surrounded by daypacks and handbags. And Alan would give his customary warning: "Be sure to hold on to the hand grips—there'll be bumps along the way."

Then he would start out, keeping a slow putter ahead of Derek and the remaining clients, who would walk the entire mile to the town center. Alan would leave them in town to hear the artists' morning presentations, eat their lunch, and take a tour around Whetstone, after which they would return to the art building for the afternoon art presentations and a stroll through the displays on the back wall. Each artist was obligated to showcase their work, the pieces either hung or set on Plexiglas shelves, along with photos of their other available artwork and a price list. Carolyn would answer questions and fill in with anecdotes. She would open a bottle of wine, decanting it into glasses that bore the inscription "Whetstone" and make a toast to all.

She'd give her speech about supporting the arts, how they represent cultures throughout the ages but are often undervalued in America. Carolyn would urge them, in her diplomatic but persuasive way, to take an art object home or to buy one as a gift. The guests would make several purchases; those that didn't fit inside purses or handbags were laid in the back room for packaging and shipping.

At 5 p.m. Alan would return, and the trip was reversed. Back at the airstrip, with the passengers loaded, Derek would open his window and yell, "Clear," before the propeller swung into motion. Then the plane would barrel down the runway, kicking up gravel and dust, and be gone.

Alan heard Carolyn's speech the first week only. It didn't take him long to catch the drift: for all the pretense, the wine and smiles, the intent was the same: to zero in, like a good smart bomb, on the pocketbook.

He couldn't fault her for that. It was her business, her livelihood. But when he stumbled upon her application to Ziggurat for a renewable energy grant he took it as a personal affront.

He hadn't stopped in at Carolyn's looking for trouble—he was only there to drop off a list of needed supplies: copper joints, ground wire, some lengths of cable.

Amy, Blake's caregiver, came to the door, whisking him in as if she were cleaning a scrap of carpet with a hand broom. A breezy blonde with pink fingernails and youthful exuberance, she didn't look older than nineteen. Now she whispered hurriedly. Her husband was home with the flu, and she needed badly to check on him. Carolyn was at the storehouse.

"Can you watch Blake? He's completely conked out. I'll be gone thirty minutes, I swear."

Alan studied the old patriarch. The back of his wheelchair had been set at a recline, and Blake's profile appeared chiseled in stone— as if his face were a marker atop his own grave. Against Amy's urgency he seemed to be saying, *All will be well if only I'm allowed to sleep.*

What the hell. Why not. The idea of attending to Blake wasn't particularly intimidating, so content he seemed in his somnolence. "I'm happy to help," said Alan.

Once Amy was gone, Alan removed his sneakers. He tiptoed into the room, remembering that the quietest walk was from ball to toe, and very slowly. He'd read about that once—a man deep in the forests of the Sierra Madres had used the technique to escape a pair of Mexican drug runners. But there were no woods here, and no one was after him. Alan relaxed and leaned against the kitchen table, palms resting on the edge. He stood that way for several minutes, not sure what he would do if Blake woke up.

Alan quickly grew bored. He looked around the room for a magazine or book, anything to kill time. But Carolyn's shelves were remarkably bare. The only thing that caught his eye was an external frame backpack and a jacket that he knew belonged to Derek. So Derek did spend time here, and he and Carolyn probably had something going. It was as Alan had figured. He decided then to venture into the other wing of the house, where he might find something else of interest—maybe a family album that would mortar the story of Blake and his town.

He moved down a short hallway and passed the bathroom, where he stopped, feeling suddenly like a snoop. He should turn back. This was private living space and he had no business sniffing around like an overwrought hound. He retraced his steps and stood watching Blake. Something about the relaxed pose, the outstretched arms, one gnarled finger pointing ahead, read like permission, and Alan found himself again in the hallway.

Ahead were two closed doors—bedrooms, probably—but another door hung open. This must be Carolyn's office. He'd come this far, what was wrong with a peek?

Her desk was orderly—so orderly that it drew his eyes directly down, where the pencil near a typed page lay like a smoke flare. It was an application. Alan skimmed the contents, noting the Ziggurat letterhead and a deadline, December 31st. He stopped on the third paragraph:

PLEASE DESCRIBE YOUR RENEWABLE
ENERGY PLAN

And to the side, scrawled on a notepad:

Purchase solar panels to reduce reliance on diesel. Use a portion of grant funds to pay a solar energy technician for installation. Request reimbursement of funds already applied to project.

Underneath was written: $50,000? $75,000? $100,000?

Alan felt the blood surge to his face, as if he'd stepped inside the bowels of a steel mill. A renewable energy grant from Ziggurat! Bad enough that Carolyn was asking the mining company for money for the panels—but for his wages? The thought of his labor being supported from Ziggurat's coffers was like acquiring some ghastly disease.

His first impulse was to take the application and ruin it with a flurry of blue ink.

Alan. He said his own name under his breath, putting hard brakes on his overcharged brain. *What* are *you thinking?* He wasn't going to destroy Carolyn's application. For one thing, it wouldn't do any good—she'd simply acquire another. Worse than that, he would be the obvious culprit.

ALAN TRIED HARD to put his discovery behind him. Acting on it would come to no good. That was what always happened. The time he'd called his boss a soulless pen pusher interested solely in his own advancement had earned him nothing but a poor evaluation. Or when he'd coerced Kate into a ten-mile hike to punish her for not siding with him about the neighbor's wayward cat... she'd paid him back with a box of dog biscuits for his birthday. Or the worst: when he'd tried to straighten out Sarah's ex... his sister was still struggling, trying to raise her two young girls on her own. What if he challenged Carolyn about her grant application? That would end his stay in Whetstone, call a halt to any chance he'd have with Dehlia. Indignation was a dangerous thing, a mad stallion that could rear up with the slightest provocation. He was better off checking batteries and oil levels. So he told himself: *Keep clean, stick to your routines...*

Which didn't change much. Only Derek's did. Starting in late June, Derek no longer accompanied the patrons to the town center, instead taking wing as soon as he unloaded the plane. He'd secured supplementary work in Karshekovski, he told Alan, but he didn't elaborate. "Just another pocket-padding job," he said, slapping his rump.

Karshekovski was the mail hub, fifty miles south. Maybe Derek was starting to fly bigger planes. That would end his role as Whetstone's pilot. Yet he was always waiting at the airstrip by five o'clock to fly the clients back to Anchorage. It was this kind of dependability that Carolyn needed for her operation to be successful. That, and the way Carolyn could greet people—day after day with the same bright smile, somehow convincing them they were tops, like prizewinners at a county fair. But now her smile was a tarnished charm.

IN LATE JULY, Alan's unrest took a backseat to nature's rhythms. The salmon had arrived. When the fish were in, all else fell by the wayside. Everyone participated; this was the chance to stock up on a year's worth of protein, and no one took it lightly. Throughout the community, pressure cookers were pulled down from high shelves. Nets were hauled out, knives sharpened, canning jars collected and counted.

Alan was happy for the break. He looked forward to spending time near the water. Mike's place was about half a mile from the beach, but they clipped along. When he and Mike broke out of the woods they found Allie, sprawled on the rocks, busy building miniature cabins with driftwood sticks. She flashed a smile and Alan tipped his hat to her.

"Good day, gentlemen," Dale called from farther down the beach.

Alan surveyed the shoreline. The lake, opaque now with glacial silt, had risen in the last weeks. Six nets, roughly three hundred feet apart, extended into the water, their corks and buoys dabbling like ducks in a fifteen-knot breeze. People wore bright yellow rain gear or fish aprons. Two nets down, Alan recognized the tall figures of Dehlia and Dan Broderman. Why, for Christ's sake, was she fishing with him?

He waved at her, but she didn't see him.

Mike and Alan joined Dale at their fishing spot. Dale tested a rope threaded through the single pulley, which was attached in turn to an iron stake driven into the beach gravel. Alan had never seen this particular setup, and he looked at Dale curiously. "We haul the net in every time a fish hits," Dale explained. "There's another pulley underwater, anchored under the buoy. The net is attached to the line. Stew gets it all set up with the skiff."

"Got it," said Alan. He looked around. "Where's Patricia?"

"Waiting at the house for the first delivery of fish. We trade places—she refuses to be chained to the kitchen." Dale smiled from his towering height. "Some call it equal division of labor. I call it spunk." He held up a thermos. "Coffee?"

Mike and Alan nodded, and Dale filled two travel mugs and lifted his own. "Cheers."

Alan raised his cup. "To Allie. Only kid I know who doesn't have a gizmo grafted to her hand."

Dale said, "It's only because she lacks peer influence. We'll see what happens when we move to town in a couple of years. But then, Patricia's a shade stubborn."

Mike snickered. "How do you maintain domestic tranquility?"

"Easy. I give in. I'd rather be happy than right."

They sipped their coffee. The day was pleasant, with scattered clouds that only occasionally obscured the sun. In the last weeks the mosquitoes had thinned, and the breeze was enough to keep the rest at bay. Most of the snow had melted from the mountains, but crescents and half-moons hung in the deeper valleys. Two bald eagles, one immature with a marbled body, the other with full white head and tail, rested a few feet apart in the tops of spruce trees. When the fishing was done the birds would likely scour the beach for scraps.

At the sound of the four-wheeler Alan looked toward the trail head. Stew appeared and drove down the beach, his big upper body almost dwarfing the Honda.

"Any news of the mine?" Mike asked. "One radio report is all I've heard."

Alan's discovery at Carolyn's weighed on him. Should he share it with the others? He'd kept mum for weeks now; he hadn't even told Mike.

"Heard Zig's flying bigwigs around," said Dale. "And the exploration site sees more choppers every day. Henry Davis told me they're doing core samples. Could be a rumor, but that's what he said."

Mike looked out at the water.

"Who's Henry Davis?" asked Alan.

"New mail plane pilot," said Mike.

"He's inexperienced," said Dale. "That's why he got a job with Southwest Air. They're all cheap labor opportunists."

"So at Whetstone we're—what? Socialist altruistic leftists?" Mike grinned crookedly, and Alan could tell he was joking.

Dale gave him a serious look. "Come on, Mike. We have plenty of pachyderms here. The ones who left the savanna moved to bush Alaska. Just because someone's an artist doesn't necessarily make them an ass."

Alan liked the banter. But where did Dehlia fit? He and Mike had never discussed her politics. He'd just assumed... "What about Dehlia?" he blurted.

"Dehlia?" said Dale. "She's neutral as a Swiss canary."

Alan wasn't sure what that meant, but it sounded innocuous enough. He looked her direction, but she was leaning over a tote.

"What I'd like to know," said Mike, "is how we get stuck with this 'liberal' label. I usually vote Democratic, but I'm a fiscal conservative. And liberal, according to my dictionary, means advocating for individual freedoms. But that's what conservatives want too. They're all about individual rights—the right to bear arms, rights of business owners"—he gestured to the lake—"being able to fish in your own backyard. They want government out of their personal business. Unless, of course, the government is handing out crop subsidies or corporate welfare."

"Name someone who isn't a walking contradiction," said Dale. "Here we are living this idealized life, but who's supporting us? I'm Patricia's manager. I know where the money comes from, and it isn't Harlem or Appalachia—it's from the upper crust. We need these sweet capitalists. And a lot of them are liberal as hell. By which I mean, generous with the dollar."

"They're not buying many of *my* books," said Mike, with that trace of bitterness familiar to Alan.

"That's because you don't write pap, Trotter," said Dale.

"High standards are only half my problem. I need a benefactor. The cream rises to the top on a raft of bills."

Alan glanced at the sun. Either the temperature was warming or he was heating up from the inside. The wind had freshened. "At least you're doing it," he said.

"What, writing? So did Melville. What did it bring him but poverty and despair?"

"Long-lasting fame."

"Doesn't do much good if we're not around to witness it."

"I've thought about that myself," said Alan.

"Have you," said Mike.

"Time to lighten up, boys," said Dale. He pointed west, where the corks of one net bobbed and jerked like punch-drunk fighters.

"Wouldn't you know it, the women get the first fish."

It was Meredith, the poet, fishing alongside Blake's caregiver, Amy. Alan imagined Amy's pink fingernails and wondered how the polish stood up to the rough work of hauling in nets. Amy pulled the rope hand over hand, and the net moved sluggishly toward shore. Meredith yanked the salmon free, her dark curls flicking in the wind, then she struck it with a driftwood stick and tossed it into a nearby bucket.

Meredith slapped the fish on a wooden table set up on the beach and picked up a butcher knife. With the first cut behind the gills appeared a pool of dark blood. She flipped the salmon over and put more of her body into it, slicing through the tough backbone. Then she drew the severed head to the table's edge with the tip of her knife and dropped it in the bucket. One upward slice through the belly and Meredith reached inside, pulling out innards and skeins of orange eggs. She scraped away strands of glutinous slime, sliced off the fins, and hacked off the tail. The whole process took her less than two minutes.

"She means business, doesn't she?" Mike looked on with both reproach and admiration.

"Poetry in its purest form," said Dale.

"Ouch," said Alan.

"I'll stick to prose," said Mike.

"I don't trust that woman," said Dale. He didn't explain.

They turned back to their own net. Within twenty minutes two salmon hit, this time dragging the corks well under the surface. Alan loosened them from the net. He hit the fish over the head exactly as Meredith had done. Their bodies convulsed then lay still.

By one o'clock their tote was loaded, and Dale stuck a ten-foot pole with orange flagging into a sand-filled bucket. "Our pickup symbol," he said. "Stew drives the four-wheeler over and delivers the fish to Patricia."

"Nifty," said Alan. "Mind if I go along and see the other half of the operation?"

2

"Milady"—this was Dan Broderman's latest form of address—"it would please me immensely if you would apparel yourself with these new gloves. They are twelve inches in length, twenty-one mil, natural latex rubber, with a flock lining for easy removal."

Dehlia reached for them, but Dan rolled up the cuffs then held each glove open for her in turn. As she slipped her hands inside Dan pulled the cuffs over her arms. "Ah yes, the color of gold. That is fitting for a lady of your station."

"Don't be silly. I'm no different from anyone else."

Dan wagged a finger. "I beg to differ, Milady."

Dehlia didn't contradict him. She knew that others saw her as exceedingly good and pure, and she tried to maintain this image because in a way it had become her duty; she didn't want to disappoint. Partly it was widowhood. After Phil's death people treated her as if she were a glass angel on a glass shelf. She couldn't blame them, but their caution, their solicitude, was apparent. When you lost someone dear, you lost for a time a part of your identity, because others viewed you through a lens washed clean by sympathy.

Except for Barbara. What had she said, after the party? *You need to quit thinking of yourself. You live in a community.*

Along with fishing equipment, Dan had brought lawn chairs to the beach, and they sat now, facing west. At the next net Dehlia recognized Bryce and Jen, and after that, Dale and Mike and Alan. Alan... admittedly, his name had a nice sound.

Beyond the group of men she wasn't sure who was fishing. It might be Meredith with Amy, but the poet was hard to pin down. Dehlia usually saw her from a distance; Meredith seemed always to take a different path. Then it dawned on her: the person she'd seen last spring, the one the bear was stalking... now she knew for certain: it had been Meredith. How could she have missed the clues?

Meredith was taller than Patricia, with a leaner build but broader shoulders. And the way Meredith walked, with a lift to her carriage, should have been unmistakable. Why was the bear stalking her? And yet, why not? It could have been following anyone.

Dan opened a bottle of ginger beer and the yeast-carbonated liquid gave a fizzy burst of air. He filled two pewter mugs, pouring the contents as if he were a priest administering some ancient rite, or perhaps a chemist gauging the potency of a new and dangerous concoction.

Dehlia peeled off her gloves. She was startled by the first sip. She'd drunk Dan's homemade soda before, but it had been years and she'd forgotten how sweet it was.

A plane flew overhead, too high for her to identify.

"Grumman Widgeon," said Dan, looking up. "My choice of bird, if I were a pilot and flying for pleasure. The duck part of my nature would deem me amphibious."

"And if you needed employment?"

"I'd fly a Thrush. My hopper would be filled with fish, not fuel. I'd be a piscatorial St. Nick, stocking poorly populated lakes."

She shouldn't have laughed. It only encouraged Dan to drone on. Did she know that pilots working for Fish and Game had once dropped fry from too low an altitude? After some experimentation, they found that releasing the fish from two hundred feet allowed them time to enter the water head first. The survival rate increased dramatically.

Dehlia imagined the fish when they first met the air, their sideways disorientation until some subliminal instinct, or perhaps sheer gravity, turned them so they survived the fall. She wondered if a human body could similarly right itself, and she thought of incredible human feats—divers plunging off the cliffs of Acapulco, skydivers using their hands like fins to steer during a free fall. And she thought of human motivation, what a strange and beautiful and sometimes horrible thing it was. And she came at last to why people choose certain paths, and the direction her own life had taken.

She'd flirted once with becoming an archaeologist, of digging into the dark and murky *Homo sapien* past, traveling to East Africa or Java, unearthing potsherds and fragmented bones. It was the mystery that drew her. Still, like all fields of study, the novelty would wear off, moving from fun to job to drudgery. So what had she done? Majored in ancient history, and stuck, in the end, to art. She didn't regret it. But as a profession, art was not without risk. She was completely without savings.

"Dan?" She ran a finger over the pewter engraving. "How committed are you to this community? I mean..." She dropped her voice. "I'm worried that I'm selfish. About getting my land and my house. No one else here, except us, have that privilege."

"You've paid your dues, Milady. Do not doubt your entitlement." Dan pressed a long finger on her forearm.

She didn't like those words: privilege, entitlement. They made her feel queenly. But she wanted to believe him. All these years... for what? She took a long sip from her drink and leaned back in her chair, letting the sun warm her face. Gazing at the expanse of water and the steep mountains that cut down almost to the shoreline, she was overcome with awe. It must have been what Blake felt when he'd first laid eyes on this country. It was a beautiful place to live. Sometimes she even thought that she deserved it. If she was careful, if she kept her opinions to herself, kept her composure—she had only to wait, and everything would be all right.

3

Patricia was wearing shorts and a baby-blue spaghetti top when she met Alan and Stew outside her house. Alan scanned her shirt front: *Girls Say Yes to Boys Who Say No / NO FLY MINE.*

"Glad you're taking a stand," said Stew, and Patricia grinned and smacked him on his bearded cheek. He unloaded the tote then fired up the four-wheeler, leaving Alan and Patricia alone in the yard. Alan hauled the tote to the porch. He guessed the catch to weigh about twenty-five pounds.

Inside the house, the counter was covered with pint jars, washed and inverted on a dish towel. A large pressure cooker sat nearby. The wood cookstove emitted a steady, radiant heat, and despite the open windows the room was stuffy.

Patricia carried in the first fish. Alan expected her to say more about the mine, but she was all business. He understood. When the salmon came, people shifted into another gear.

Patricia laid the salmon on a butcher block and cut three steak-like pieces. She trimmed them and turned over a jar, adding salt before stuffing in the fish, her freckles a blossom of miniature roses. She wiped the rim, set the lid in place, and tightened the ring. "Voilà. Bones and all." She handed him the knife. "You cut, I'll fill."

Alan was charmed. There was nothing ambiguous about her directive. He took up the knife, gaining speed as he worked. But Patricia seemed always a step ahead of him. Her fingers were supple and strong, the result, no doubt, of all her years playing the guitar. How would a woman like Patricia suit him? No, she was too outspoken, too much a mirror of himself. He needed someone like Dehlia, someone who would soften his hard edges.

Patricia carefully loaded the jars in the silver cooker and added water before tightening the lid. She stoked the fire and passed a hand over her forehead. "Whew, hot, huh? Sometimes I feel like

I'm inside this thing. I keep hearing about Ziggurat, I'll blow my lid."

Alan glanced at the part of the gauge labeled *Caution,* and he looked again at her shirt. He suddenly felt compelled to tell her about Carolyn's grant application, but if there was any way to sabotage it, the fewer people who heard about it the better. *Sabotage?* He realized then why he hadn't told Mike.

"In case you think I'm not talking about the mine, I'm doing my homework first," said Patricia into the silence. "Advice from my friend, Dr. Sanders. She's a scientist."

Patricia slipped out to the porch and returned with two glasses that tinkled as she walked. Alan sat down with her in the living room and held the iced lemonade against his cheek, relishing the coolness. Once he had played music here; now the entire cabin was transformed into a fish haven.

Patricia dipped a finger in hers and sucked it dry. "So... been playing your guitar?"

"Not as much as I'd like."

Patricia took a long sip of her drink. She brought her knees up to her chin and rested her sandaled feet on the couch. "Seen Dehlia lately?"

Alan blushed. "No." He picked at a stray thread on the worn knee of his jeans. "Actually, she was fishing with Dan Broderman. I don't think she has time right now for a local mechanic. Or chauffeur, or gas man, or whatever the hell I am," he said, allowing himself to wallow in self-pity.

Patricia studied him. "Give it time. She's still grieving, I think."

Alan didn't want to give it time. But nothing was going to fall in place according to his schedule. "What was her husband like?"

Patricia hesitated—long enough that Alan wondered if there was something she felt she shouldn't reveal. But maybe he'd just imagined it, because she simply said, "Phil? Hard to get to know. A lot like Dehlia, really." She rose to feed the fire. "I have this theory that there are two kinds of people. Those who gossip and those who don't. Most do, of course. That makes Dehlia an anomaly. If you don't talk about others, others don't talk so much about you."

"Governing the tongue. Must take a lot of willpower." He knew he was speaking for himself.

"I just think gossip doesn't interest her."

"What does?"

"Her art, of course. And animals." Patricia sat back down. "She should get a dog." With that, Patricia pursed her lips and sucked in her breath.

The old Lab rose stiffly from his bed and sauntered over, joints stiff as pegs on a cribbage board. "Chowder, poor guy." Patricia patted him on the head. "You need to stretch once in a while."

The dog crossed the room and laid his chin on Alan's knee. Alan scratched him behind the ear and looked him in the eyes. "Chowder. That's not short for chowder head, is it? I bet you're smarter than the whole pack of humanity."

"He likes you."

"Yeah, I miss having a dog. My old Collie, Luke, he was the best guy ever. I could tell him all my troubles and he always listened."

"Speaking of listening, I want you to have something." Patricia pulled a CD case from the drawer of the coffee table in front of her. "Take it, it's my first recording."

The label was simple, a watercolor of a single fireweed in bloom and *Patricia Abbey* typed in a light, fluid script. Alan picked it up and turned it over. The back was blank except for the price: fifteen dollars.

"I want to pay you for this." Alan reached in his back pocket and pulled out his wallet.

"It's okay," said Patricia. "You don't have to."

"I want to," said Alan, and he laid a twenty-dollar bill on the coffee table.

Patricia got up again to check the cooker. Steam spewed from the small outlet on the lid. "We're exhausting!" She placed the weight over the outlet at ten pounds and set the timer. "Let's get the next batch ready."

As before, Alan cut fish and Patricia packed the pieces, until another sixteen jars, brimming coral pink, were ready to be processed. An hour and a half later, Alan lifted the heavy cooker from the stove and carried it to the porch. He would be repeating this routine with Mike many times in the next week, and now he had the experience to be a real help. Patricia set out two lawn chairs in the shade of an old birch. Within minutes, a *ping-ping-ping* erupted.

Patricia laughed. "The lids are sealing." She strummed an invisible guitar. "No botulism for you, babeee..." she sang. "What do you think, would it hit the charts?"

4

Somehow salmon fishing came and went, somehow the sweet July heat evanesced. And August? August came in like a frog and went out like a fish, Dan Broderman liked to say. Well, *usually.* There were dry Augusts, with temperatures sometimes in the high seventies, when even glacial-fed Lake Hélène was temperate enough for swimming.

This August had that all-too-common autumn feel, as if a lean gentleman stood in the corner of a theater dimming the lights and ushering people to their seats, laying a cool and manicured hand on their shoulders. Already it was the middle of the month; bats appeared, little jet fighters navigating by some precise, internal instrument. Dehlia watched them at dusk from her kitchen, knew them too as premonitions of September's flying leaves that would be taken unwillingly to air, most wind-whipped from their branches then swirling and descending in confusion.

Before long she could expect a visit from Alan Lamb. Perhaps Barbara had been right: don't shut the door too soon.

SATURDAY DAWNED CLEAR, and again she wrestled with how to spend her time. How much easier it was to clean bird houses than closets, especially when those closets contained your husband's personal effects. The clothes and the shoes, those were the hardest of all.

Outside, she leaned the aluminum ladder against the shed and began climbing. When the legs shifted against the high gable she almost lost her footing, but she kept going, one careful rung at a time. When she reached the top, she unlatched the doors of the little fourplex, revealing bunches of straw interwoven with feathers. So much about swallows baffled her. How did the fledglings learn to fly? *They simply took the plunge.*

Dehlia removed the first nest. In the center was a single, unhatched egg. She fingered the tiny shell then let it fall.

A shadow swept the ground and she fumbled to grip the ladder. "Dolly!"

"I'm sorry! I didn't mean to scare you." Even talking about fright, Dolly's pacing was deliberate. It was the only thing in her speech that betrayed her Native heritage. She had no trace of an accent.

The nest had rolled against Dehlia's chest and hung up on a ladder rung. She picked it up again and held it, palm tipped down, for Dolly to see. "You know, your baskets always make me wonder why some bird nests are so loose and fragile. The swallow nests, especially."

Dolly looked up and squinted against the sun. The hood of her sweatshirt was tied tightly under her chin, accentuating the roundness of her face. "I use wild rye grass for my baskets. Wild rye is a good strong grass."

Dehlia laughed. "Maybe you could teach the birds something."

Dolly thought about this. "I think we could learn more from the birds."

Dehlia laughed again. "You're probably right. But you're a good artist."

Dolly dropped her gaze. "Do you want to go berry picking? I'm going down the lake with my cousin tomorrow. He's coming up in his boat." She stood now with her arms crossed, looking at where the egg lay, white and whole and lovely in the trampled grass. "I know the best place for blueberries."

"Thanks for thinking of me. I need to clean my closets."

"Oh, work. There's always work." It was more of a statement than a reprimand. Dolly waved and turned away.

Dehlia stared after her. She dropped the nest, and it fluttered down and landed in the bough of a nearby spruce. *I should have said yes. A change of scene would be good for me. What do I owe him now?*

"Dolly," she called after her, but it was too late. She pulled out another nest. No eggs. The young ones had all made it. She dusted the wood with her fingers.

Dehlia, why the allegiance? Accept that he was not always present, that you've fashioned him into someone other, someone greater, than he was. Why perpetuate the myth of him? She pulled out the last nest. A fully developed chick that had lacked the courage to fly. *You're grieving not just the person that was, but the person that wasn't.*

The summer after Phil had died, she'd tried to rescue a wounded swallow. She'd fed and watered it, but something had eventually killed it, probably a hawk or weasel. She had recorded the incident, as if the process of writing it down could soothe her. And maybe it had, the notion—whether real or not—that her words had been received. Even then, after all that time, she'd wanted so much to communicate with him.

She'd left the notebook open on the kitchen table and had gone to tend her garden. Who knew whether his passing spirit could apprehend her script.

5

SOUTHWEST ALASKA GOLD DEPOSIT DRAWS ATTENTION

The newspaper headline loomed at him as Alan walked in, rain dripping from the brim of his Australian hat and the sleeves of his raincoat. He leaned over the table and read the caption on an aerial photo of a meandering stream as he peeled off his wet garments.

> Fly Creek headwaters support numerous sport fish, including rainbow trout and Dolly Varden, and serve as a spawning ground for sockeye salmon.

Ironic that the newspaper was finally covering the mine—right on the heels of salmon fishing. A map of Southwest Alaska indicated the site. Alan sat down and pulled the paper closer, zeroing in on the first paragraphs.

The gold deposit was worth about ten billion dollars, estimated at 26.5 million ounces. Copper could weigh in at 16.5 billion. To transport the ore, the article said that a new road and port would need to be built, as well as new power facilities. But the payoff was the provision of jobs for locals in an economically depressed area. For drilling and operation, Ziggurat had applied for rights to almost thirty-five billion gallons of ground and surface water. *Per year.*

Alan frowned and skipped around the rest of the article, reading subheads: "Staking claims, Megabucks." He focused on "Tons of tailings," scooting his chair closer to read about the waste rock—all the rock that didn't contain enough value to pulverize, that was just in the way. There were comparisons to Fort Knox, near Fairbanks, and Red Dog near Kivalina, with the projection of spent rock from the Fly Creek Mine topping out at three billion tons.

"Jesus," Alan murmured, "three billion." It was hard to imagine that huge pile of discarded rock—and the potential for it to turn toxic and forever ruin the water systems. What would Sarah do if the Bristol Bay fishery failed because of this project? Her boat wasn't paid off and she had her daughters to put through college. All because of her deadbeat ex-husband.

Paging back, he forced himself to read the entire piece word for word. It was a long article, and fifteen minutes into it the facts and figures blurred. He rubbed his eyes, pulled Mike's parka from the coat rack, and lay down on the couch.

It was a light, unsatisfying sleep. Even as he fell into it, he retained an awareness of his surroundings: the austere room with its bare walls and floor, and not even the tick of a clock. He turned over, the thin foam beneath him unable to offset the wooden framework, which seemed to inch upward as the cushion sank, soring his shoulders and hips.

Then he was rowing, his arms pumping, but the craft was unseaworthy. It wasn't a boat exactly—and in place of oars Alan was holding an iron rod. He was stabbing at the earth. He had to dig a firepit... he had something to burn. The grant application! What had he done with it?

Then he was back in Whetstone, Carolyn leading him through a thicket. "I need you to look at the third lot," she said. Then, in Carolyn's place was Blake, not younger but nevertheless mobile, walking ahead and motioning Alan to follow. Alan tried, but it was difficult, the ghostly father of the town disappearing behind a web of trees.

Suddenly Alan was alone. He wandered into the big storehouse. Dan Broderman was standing with his back turned, weighing something on the huge scale. Alan slipped out undetected and followed the trail to the library. Again he felt Blake's presence, as if the old man had urged him to enter the building and uncover some dark secret. Inside, the room was lit with an eerie blue-white light.

He woke. He blinked a few times and saw Mike at the counter. "You hungry?" Mike held up two paper sacks. "Jen gave me a loaf of bread and some lettuce."

Alan yawned. There was a weight on him. He threw off Mike's

heavy coat and set about building a fire. "What's up with Bryce and Jen?" He held a lighter to the newspaper, watching as stock market and budget reports transformed into a black rose.

"I take it you read the paper."

"Yeah." Alan shook his head. "Fly Creek… may fly—or may not?"

"The pun's been made, but it's no joke. Ziggurat is resolute, and the state's behind it, by all indications." Mike handed Alan the lettuce. "Why don't you cut this up." Mike plunked down a metal bowl and a paring knife on the table.

"I ran into Patricia at the post office. She found a speech the lieutenant governor made to the Anchorage Assembly," Mike said. "His boss—Queen Beehive—a commercial fisherman, no less—said, 'Just visualize it as a hole in the ground twelve hundred feet deep.' Can you dig that? That's deep enough to bury the Eiffel Tower. Whether or not you like that monument aesthetically, you have to admit it's impressive in size."

"I've never been to France." Alan crunched a mouthful of lettuce. It was juicy and deliciously sweet.

"Look at it this way. About half the height of Lost Mountain, inverted." Mike took a can of chicken from the cupboard. He flipped back the opener on his Swiss Army knife, punched the steel rim, and settled into a rhythm.

Alan shook his head. "I'm buying you a real can opener for Christmas, I swear."

"Great. Let's keep the mining companies in business."

"Point made. One for Trotter." Alan marked an invisible chalkboard.

Mike spooned the chicken on top of the lettuce and sliced the bread thickly. The two men sat down and filled their plates. Mike chewed thoughtfully. "If Bryce and Jen take a stand against this mine, they could influence a lot of people. I wanted to gauge their reaction when I brought it up."

"And?"

Mike brushed a few crumbs from his sleeve. "There was lot of 'we need to wait and see' and 'lots of hearsay—'"

"Jen must not have been too upset with you. She sent you home with some decent victuals." Alan smeared a big slab of butter on his bread.

"Figured I'd get more information if I took a diplomatic approach."

"Shrewd. You could have been a lawyer." Alan pointed at him with his fork, then set it down. "What else do you know?"

"Patricia's writing letters to the editor, collecting data. Just watch. You put that firecracker in a drum, she'll make a hell of a bang."

Mike shoved his plate to the side and picked up a piece of the red ore he kept on the windowsill, placing it in front of Alan. "This specimen belonged to an old timer, a miner by the name of Hiram. He was convinced there was a lot of capital in these hills." Mike fingered the ore, rolling it back and forth like a clunky marble. "Every summer, every day, ten years straight, Hiram hiked up Lost Mountain to his test pit. Six feet deep. Might as well have been his grave. He left a broken shovel in it, kind of a testament to his dream—and failure."

"Six feet." Alan said as he held his hand just above the surface of the table. "Or twelve hundred." And he stretched his arm upward to the full extent of his reach.

"Yeah. Two hundred times the depth," said Mike.

6

Dehlia didn't read the article in that week's paper. She overheard the talk but she didn't dwell on it. Instead, she worked on her carving, she harvested greens, she waited for the visitor season to play itself out. She felt suspended in a little bubble of time, but was always aware that summer would soon be ending. Of her promise to Alan: *I'll help you, but when the season's over, in October.* On days spent at the art building she prepared lunches, conversed with patrons, and took pleasure in watching other artists at work.

She loved watching Julie spin. Wool was all softness and resilience, unlike her own medium. Wood was durable but stubborn, requiring steel tools to shape it into submission. Now Dehlia sat with the patrons and relaxed to the hypnotic effect of the wheel as Julie's foot pumped the treadle and her sure hand drew the wool and twisted it into yarn.

The door opened and Patricia broke the trance, a yellow bandana holding back her bright-red hair. She motioned for Julie to continue but remained standing at the far wall.

At her loom, Julie separated the warp threads and ran a weft of orange through the opening. The weaving, set at an angle for all to see, showed a salmon net on a driftwood stump, high on the beach where waves couldn't tangle it. The viewer looked out to open water and rugged mountains, whose slopes were highlighted by a setting sun. It was a scene Dehlia knew well. How many times, after a long day fishing, had she taken it in?

Julie wouldn't finish the piece in time to offer it to these visitors. But someday, Dehlia thought, the weaving would hang in a room in Miami or Boston or Los Angeles, and as years passed, it would become a mere fixture, receiving nothing more than an occasional glance, so that only its removal—noticeable by a scarcely perceptible rectangle on the wall—would indicate that something was missing.

ANNE CORAY

It would be like the disappearance of an acquaintance. Alan Lamb. If he left Whetstone tomorrow, would his departure be like that?

Patricia crossed the room and took up an empty seat at the front. She shoved her hands in her jacket and sat on the edge of her chair. Something in her posture was repressively explosive.

Julie turned and addressed the small crowd.

"Weaving," she said, "has a long history. Tools and textiles have been found in tombs and ruins of Egypt and Peru. Byzantium is remembered for its beautiful silk weaving, and the Flemish weavers for their work in wool. Unfortunately, there was a loss of quality when machines replaced the handloom. The technology brought child labor and long work hours and factories sprang up overnight. With more burning of coal, the Black Country appeared in England, and Lancashire and Yorkshire were transformed into the greatest textile centers of the world. Chimney sweeps—young boys, heads shaved so they wouldn't catch fire—would climb inside chimneys to remove the soot, which would eat away their skin with cancer, so the boys usually did not live much past seven or eight years of age."

A sad, communal sigh rose from the audience. It was brave of Julie, to speak so openly about mortality.

"That's why," Julie said, "I've become an advocate for a more leisurely way of life. Faster is not always better." She looked out the window. "Now there's talk of a mining project nearby, so big it would swallow every lake in a one-hundred-mile radius. At stake is our salmon, our sustenance."

Just then Patricia sprang from her chair. "It's happening! Right now, down the lake. Dolly and I found fifty-six dead salmon, at the mouth of a stream near the exploration site! We're horrified."

Julie stared while the patrons murmured among themselves. Dehlia closed her eyes. *No good. All this will only come to no good.*

7

Patricia and Dolly's story about the dead fish circulated quickly. Alan heard it before Mike and ran to his house to share the news. Here was evidence, exactly what they needed. No one could dispute it now. The mine was already destroying the fish. What would Sarah do? And all the other Bristol Bay fishermen?

But Mike was boringly sage. "Halt right there. Proof is sorely absent. The salmon could have died for a number of reasons. And I hate to remind you, there is no mine. There's only a mining prospect. Our fight needs to be methodical. Scientific."

Screw science then, Alan felt like saying. But he knew that was exactly the opposite of what was needed. Why was Trotter so often right? Science was their one true ally. But it was slow.

A WEEK LATER, Alan parked the four-wheeler in front of the art building. The new projector screen that Carolyn had asked him to drop off was for Greg Reynolds, the photographer. Greg claimed the smaller screen didn't do his pictures justice. Couloirs, glaciers, waterfalls—for these, his audience deserved something impressive, he said, on an eight-by-ten scale.

It was a fine September day and Alan didn't intend to stay. But Dehlia was presenting this afternoon. He'd given more thought to her rebuff—was it a rebuff or had he just read it that way?—and determined to play it cool. Let her think his interest was casual, then hers would be more likely to ignite. But he couldn't stand the wait anymore. He'd never seen her at work, and surely Carolyn wouldn't mind if he sat in.

Alan muscled the large screen to his shoulder and into the lobby. He propped it in a corner and stepped inside the main space, where he spotted Carolyn among the milling guests. The artists hadn't arrived yet.

Alan took a breath. Since finding Carolyn's application, he had always been careful to be himself, the self that Carolyn was accustomed to. The affable Lamb. But she had no reason to see him any differently. He'd revealed nothing to anyone of his discovery, and he'd left her desk immaculate, just as he'd found it. He grinned and stepped forward. "Carolyn."

She waited for the proper lag in conversation, then lifted a finger. "Excuse me." She turned to him. "Yes, Alan."

He made his request, finding eye contact easier than he'd expected.

"I don't mind you taking the time off. But Dolly Monroe is presenting first. Just so you know."

Alan vacillated. Staying for Dolly's presentation would set him behind another half an hour, and he wasn't much interested in basketry. He decided to stay.

He wandered around looking at the recent displays, all labeled, with names of the artists beside them. He gave a nod of approval to Darlene's stained glass series of wildflowers. He admired Billy Barr's ivory carvings: one of a polar bear swallowing a fish, another of a man with a spear bent over a seal hole. Inside the perfect circle was a nose with two tiny nostrils, and the slightest suggestion of the seal's head.

He passed by Dan Broderman's fish prints. Gyotaku: a Japanese art form, Alan read. Three prints were displayed, and he recognized two of them from the day he had stopped in at Dan's. Okay, they were well done, even if there was a smear of ink in one corner. Maybe some cosmic hand had produced the error. It was a satisfying thought. Then Alan stood before one of Dehlia's masks. He recognized the watchband-like markings of the common loon, but the human features were ambiguous. Still, there was something simple and unadorned in the work, so very *quiet*. That was it, the quiet. That was beauty. Alan reached out and drew a calloused finger down the portrait's cheek, but there was no give to the dense wood.

He looked around the room. People were seated now, and he settled next to an elderly gentleman, a balding version of Mark Twain who Alan had shuttled to the art building that very morning.

The man took his hand off his cane and placed it on Alan's shoulder. "You'll be driving me back this evening? I want to give you something."

Alan thanked him. He didn't get much in the way of tips, but occasionally someone would press a ten- or twenty-dollar bill into his hand. Sometimes he would pass it on to Derek, who would return from town with smoked oysters, stuffed olives, or a six-pack of imported beer. He had even requested a bottle of Sonoma Chardonnay, which he'd wrapped in a pillowcase and tucked away in a corner of his bedroom.

Dolly and Dehlia walked in together, Dolly with a tote bag and Dehlia with a large chunk of wood under her arm. She was wearing a backpack. She caught Alan's eye and sat down in the front row, facing away. Her long black hair looked freshly washed, and it hung freely over the back of her chair like a glossy curtain.

Soon Dolly laid out her long grasses, some plain, some dyed, on a side table and sat, a basket in progress in her lap. She waited for the audience's attention. Her round face and dark hair indicated her Yup'ik ancestry, but Russian genes gave her a taller stature. Thirty years ago, Alan thought, she must have been a very beautiful woman. Dolly picked a blade of grass from a pan of water, split it lengthwise with her fingernail, then threaded it into a large-eyed needle. She began sewing, working counterclockwise, adding clusters of grass to form the basket's coil.

Loop over loop over loop... Alan admired her patience.

She worked without speaking for ten minutes. Then she came to a figure on her basket, one of several motifs. "A wolf," Dolly said, "and here is a raven, here is a caribou." She explained that the theme of the basket was relationships—in this case, how ravens led wolves to the grazing animals, who gave themselves up to the wolves, who in turn left scraps of meat for the ravens. "Everything is connected. If one thing is disturbed, it upsets the balance, the circle of life."

Alan glanced at Carolyn. Had she heard Dolly's words? *If one thing is disturbed, it upsets the balance, the circle of life.* But Carolyn was bent over a notebook.

Dolly collected her things and Dehlia stepped up. She placed the chunk of wood on the table and laid out a set of knives and chisels and a felt pen. She wore a short-sleeved tangerine top with gold trim along the neckline.

"Birch is heavy, especially when it's green," she said, hefting up the round of wood and letting rise and fall in her arms, as if gently bouncing a baby. "This piece weighs about fifteen pounds." She set it back on the table. "For carving, I prefer straight-grained trees with few knots."

She peeled the papery, white skin from the outside of the log, leaving the tougher cambium layer. With the felt pen, she drew a few quick lines: placement for eyes, nose, mouth, then arcs to indicate the top of the head and the chin.

"I'd like to use a full log to demonstrate how I begin." She picked up the largest of her tools. It looked to Alan like a carpenter's adze, but it was cruder, with a two-inch blade that was fastened to the handle with a hose clamp.

Chip, chip, chip. Dehlia worked, turning the wood one way and then the other. Chunks of wood fell away at her feet, some the size of large peanuts.

"The adze is for the rough work. It's very fast." She held up the adze for all to see. "The blade is wide, so I can take out big chips of wood with it to get the overall shape of my mask. It's made from an old metal file that's been ground down. This isn't for detail work, obviously." She turned the wood over and began hollowing out the back. Alan was surprised by her precision as the steel hit the surface of the wood. He'd split enough birch to appreciate the effort involved in carving. Soon he was lost in the sounds and rhythm of her strokes, in watching the long, lean muscles of her arms and the charming tilt of her head as she examined her work from one side and then the other. Before long a face began to emerge.

Dehlia set the piece down. She pulled something else from her backpack wrapped in a plastic garbage bag. "The plastic keeps the wood moist and prevents checking," she explained. "It's a way of controlling the humidity, making sure the wood dries out slowly." She grinned. "You wouldn't believe how many pieces I've thrown away because I was in a hurry to dry them. One of my best ever ended up with a big crack in the middle of the forehead." Her smile gave way and she said, "Seriously, good art takes patience."

She withdrew a half-finished mask and held it up. "I'm starting a new series. Of swans." The swan in this mask was a subtle outline of the bird's bill and upper body, placed along the temples of a boyish face. "I always merge human and animal faces," Dehlia continued. "I'm not sure why. Maybe because I think there are animal traits in humans and human traits in animals. I love reading about animals."

She made some cuts with her straight knife. "This knife works best for things like feathers," she said, before picking up another tool. "My favorite is the crooked knife. It has a bent tip and cuts both ways." She carved on one of the eyes, and slivers of wood fell away. "My tools need to be kept very sharp." She worked a little longer, then handed the knife to the woman seated nearest. "I'll pass this around."

When the crooked knife was handed to him, Alan tested its edge. Sharp enough, but it would dull quickly. He imagined sitting in Dehlia's kitchen—though he'd never set foot in her cabin—honing her knives as she mixed paint. Her presentation had deepened his interest. Who was this woman, simultaneously shy and bold, so utterly mysterious?

Mark Twain nudged him playfully in the ribs with the handle of his cane. "Is your caravan ready?" he asked.

"Not for an hour or so," said Alan. "Excuse me. I need to get back to work."

But then he was standing in front of Dehlia. He laid the crooked knife on the table. "That was fantastic," he said. "I learned a lot."

She looked down, smiling.

Carolyn opened a bottle of wine at the back table and the patrons gathered around her. There was a hush as the liquid fell into the glasses, with sounds like a softly burbling fountain, then the murmuring of guests as they toasted to Whetstone.

"I wish I could stay," said Alan.

"I wish you could too," whispered Dehlia, and when her eyes moved from his hands up the length of his arms and rested finally on his face, he was almost certain that she meant it.

8

Dehlia's trip to Anchorage was unexpected. That was her excuse for not bringing along Phil's clothes: she didn't have time to sort through them to look for stains or frays or loose buttons. And it was only a short, one-day trip, a supply run that Carolyn had asked her to make. She could hardly refuse.

She left Saturday morning, on a plane loaded with passengers that Derek had flown in from Karshekovski. The three men were executive types, and Dehlia guessed that the woman—whose eyes rarely wandered from her laptop—was their dedicated assistant. A Native youth was seated in back. Dehlia immediately stuffed in her earplugs and pulled out a paperback. She wasn't in the mood for small talk.

The weather was benign. Derek quickly gained altitude, flying well above the mountaintops. Dehlia preferred it when pilots skimmed the ground, but flying higher was safer, providing plenty of glide time to select the best landing—or crash site, in case of engine failure. But it was also dull, and before long she'd fallen asleep, not waking until they touched down at the small airport.

Once out of the plane Dehlia hung back from the others, who stood in a tight circle, preoccupied. Maybe they were involved with the mining project. Whatever the case, Dehlia saw no reason to make overtures. With luck she'd never see these people again. Unless those dead fish were somehow connected to the drilling exploration. God, she hoped not. After a brief consultation with Derek they went their own way, and Derek, in a rattletrap van, drove Dehlia to Costco.

The sudden intrusion of vehicles assaulted her senses. She winced. Compared to the quiet calm of Whetstone, this world of whizzing automobiles, horns, and screeching tires was harsh, and the reds and yellows and greens of some of the cars clashed with her artist's sense of subtlety. It was always like that when she first came to town, her incredulity fading as she became, if not inured, at least able to adapt.

At Costco she muscled a giant empty cart through the entry then averted her eyes, trying to escape the fifty or more television screens, all pulsing with the same image. She steered the heavy cart through the crowd, experiencing an odd relief in her anonymity. Children sniveled or stood in mute protest, trying to cajole their mothers into buying brightly colored cereals or treats. Beautiful or dumpy shoppers and suits with cell phones chattered and gesticulated to the air. Elderly couples methodically studied their lists and debated brand-name products.

She didn't have to pretend friendliness. Even her occasional "Excuse me" as she pushed the cart around a difficult corner could carry a hint of exasperation. No one knew her and no one cared to. What a different feeling from Whetstone, where your reputation was molded so precisely by what you said and did, where your behavior was under constant surveillance. In the city, you could easily slip away from such scrutiny.

Then she ran into Meredith.

RATHER, MEREDITH RAN into *her*. Dehlia heard the clatter of the two carts as she was bent over a sack of brown sugar. The sound struck her ears like tin on lead.

She straightened.

"Sorry!" Meredith backed away. "I didn't see—"

And in that instant, Dehlia recognized her, and saw again her figure on the outcropping, and the bear, following too intently. "W-what are doing here?"

"I flew in yesterday—on business." Meredith backed farther away, making room for a complete about-face. Then her cheeks flushed scarlet and she said hurriedly, "And personal things." She combed her hair with her fingers. "Getting my hair done."

Dehlia stared at Meredith's ringlets. Were the curls natural or permed? Did she dye her hair? How much time did she devote to her appearance? These were the kinds of assessments most women made regularly. But you had to be careful. Dehlia had seen the way some women looked others up and down, judging heights and weights and sexuality. It could all get mean and petty. But Meredith's high cheekbones and slim hips were impossible to ignore. How many men had eyed her lustfully? Even Phil? Perhaps... no, impossible. Dehlia wanted suddenly to tell her that she looked lovely, but there was a stern look in Meredith's dark eyes and shadows beneath them that spoke of ill health. So Dehlia only mumbled something about timing and coincidence, and Meredith turned and was gone.

BY THE TIME Dehlia finished shopping she was fifteen minutes late for Derek's scheduled pickup. The checkout lines were enormous, stretching and bending like dull-witted anacondas. She'd gone back for another cart, the first grown too heavy to move. Why had Derek abandoned her to do this job alone? Then she spotted him; he'd come inside looking for her, and was waiting impatiently next to the cashier as she inched her way forward.

HE DROPPED HER OFF at the mall in the heart of the city, saying he'd pick her up at six. He didn't state his business, and Dehlia, no longer peevish, looked forward to being alone.

The mall had changed since her last visit. The quality of the shops had declined: where once there were high-end stores selling men's clothing and stereo equipment, now there were kiosks selling cheap jewelry and trinkets. The bank had shrunk, but you could buy caramel corn. There was a shabbiness to the interior, probably born of competition with other malls that continued to sprout up as the city expanded.

She bought a salty hot dog from a gloomy vendor then shopped half-heartedly for a new blouse but flinched at the price tag of the one that caught her eye. After an hour of wandering, unable to decide what to buy—she didn't have to buy anything—she walked three blocks to the thrift store and rifled through racks of assorted clothes. Some were stained or worn, others looked as if they'd come directly from the department store, but all were now tinged with a musty, old-carpet odor. She did find a blouse, eventually—lust red, a great buy in great condition, that would require only light washing. Who had it belonged to? A doctor's wife, perhaps, cleaning out her closet because her husband was taking up his practice in another state. Maybe a compulsive shopper who bought ten times more than she needed, then once a year deposited a trunk load of clothes in the donations dumpster. Or a woman of modest means who had died a premature death—cancer? suicide?—and whose one surviving sibling had been forced to dispose of her belongings. Someone was always left to attend to that difficult task.

9

"Don't make any Saturday engagements," Mike said as he approached.

Alan set down the axe. He was splitting kindling behind the house after a sordid rendezvous with equipment bolts. Cleaning rusty hardware had turned a one-hour job into an afternoon.

"I'm tied up Sunday for a couple of hours, but Saturday's free. Why?" Alan tried to be casual. Was Mike taking it upon himself to hook him up with Dehlia? He'd heard she'd gone to Anchorage last weekend, but she'd be here on his next day off. He tried not to get his hopes up.

"Ziggurat's giving mine tours. They're shutting down for the season at the end of the month. It's an opportunity. I think we should go."

"Seriously?"

"Seriously, what?" Mike frowned. "Is the company giving free tours? Yes. Do I think we should go? Yes."

Alan reached down to pick up the kindling shrapneled around the splitting stump. "Sounds like sleeping with the enemy." He dropped the sticks into a nearby bucket.

"Military strategy always involves understanding operations on the other side. How can we fight them if we don't know what they're up to?"

MIKE MADE THE ARRANGEMENTS, and Saturday morning Alan found himself in the co-pilot's seat of a red Bell LongRanger helicopter. The seatbelt was an IQ test: a cam lock, round-buckled affair that took him three tries to fasten.

As the chopper lifted off from Whetstone's airstrip, Alan couldn't help marveling at the machine's performance. It was a technological masterpiece, a flying top that would have had Leonardo da Vinci immortalizing every moving part in pen and ink. Looking out the Plexiglas window, he was struck by the tremendous visibility. It had been months since he'd even been in a plane. From the air, the burbling creek he loved to walk along took on a different character. It carved a strong connecting line through the community, not dividing, but holding everything together with its constant flow, as if a master architect had carved a watery initial into the lush forest for all to see. He tried to follow its source, high into the hills, past the thick spruce, but it became lost in alder and willow. This land was immense, the helicopter minute as a dragonfly in its breadth. Sunlight fell like a floodlight on the birches and poplars, and fall yellows leapt up with a lawless vibrancy below. He felt not only physically lifted, but transported, gazing at the panorama from all sides. Even so, he harbored a faint contempt.

Was it ethical to send thirteen choppers an hour to a mountaintop so heli-skiers could plow back down through powder without extending a single muscle in an uphill climb? To hover over birds' nests at ninety decibels? Plus, fuel consumption for most helicopters was astronomical.

The pilot, a self-assured Bristow Academy graduate, had no such qualms. His expertise was like morality insurance, a policy for a select few who'd paid their dues and had risen, in their own estimation, to a bar well above self-judgment.

Mike sat in back with the tour guide, a British aristocrat named Cheryl whose manner treaded the muddy water between programmed and rehearsed. She kept her head at a perfect incline and spoke cheerfully with her exotic accent.

Although the intercom system was good, Alan didn't ask questions on the flight in. Mike had warned him to keep his confrontational urges in check, at least until the tour was over.

They flew straight for a while then crawled up the shoulder of Lost Mountain. On the mountain's peak, termination dust gleamed china white, and an eagle swept high over a deep gorge. Soon they left the timbered area; the new terrain revealed alpine tundra populated with dwarf birch and scrub willow, the deep red of bearberry plants, and pockets of white lichen. Meager groups of black spruce stood as the tallest trees around. Despite Moss Lake further south, the country looked dry, like caribou country, composed of rocky patches, ponds, and a few seepages on the valley floor.

The first stop was an overlook, a ridge that offered a perspective on the operation's reach. Alan knew that the mine site encompassed twenty thousand acres, but this seemed dimensionless. Mike whistled into the vastness.

Cheryl explained that at the height of summer's activity, ten drilling rigs ran at once, but this late in the season they were down to three. She pointed east, then west, then south.

"That's rig number one, and that is number two. Number three is a bit more distant." Her stress fell on the numbers—one, two, three—with "tew" sounding like a cross between a tulip and wood for cabinetmaking.

Alan squinted and made out the third rig.

"What do you do with them when they're not in use anymore?" asked Mike.

"We transport them by helicopter back to our base, the same way they are brought in."

"You mean Karshekovski."

"Quite."

"How many copters do you have?"

"Ten, we have ten."

"One for every rig," said Alan.

THEY TOUCHED DOWN to visit rig number two, a thousand feet below the ridge where the wide valley flattened to an undulating slope accented with green patches of brush, and grasses and sedges that had not yet been nipped by frost. In a treeless area like this, removing the surface covering would be a breeze—with no need for clearing, the bulldozers would be able to defile the landscape in no time. Alan and Mike were given orange hardhats that matched the vests they'd been required to wear. Alan was glad for his XTRATUFS; the ground, deceptively dry from the air, held substantial moisture. *What had that article said? Rights to thirty-five billion gallons of ground and surface water a year.* When toxic waste infiltrated the groundwater—and it would—gravity would move it downstream, into the Harmon. Maybe that had already happened.

Number two was a state-of-the-art sonic drill rig, manned by four workers and set on a deck of timbers. They were currently drilling "overburden," Cheryl explained—any soil, gravel, glacial fill, or vegetative matter that covered the mineral-rich ore. The drill's current depth was a hundred and thirty feet, but elsewhere core samples had been taken from over six thousand feet below ground.

Alan and Mike watched the drill power upward, spewing brown water when it exited the hole. The men slipped a plastic tube—like an elephant condom, thought Alan—over the shaft, and the slurry slid out. The ten-foot core samples were halved and placed in long skinny boxes, marked on one end with the depth, location, and date of drilling.

"Where do the workers sleep?" asked Alan. The only significant building was twenty yards away, a large Weatherport on a wooden platform, presumably for easy dismantling.

"Oh, they are flown back to base every evening," said Cheryl.

Mike nodded at the plywood outhouse. "Funny design," he said. Alan had noticed it too: fin-like projections that rose straight up, on both sides of the boxy structure.

"Yes, well, they are slung in with the helicopters. But we found that they were twisting during flight, and so we had to attach these wings—we call them wings—to keep them stable in the air."

Alan laughed inwardly. Leave it to a mining company to perceive their shitter as some kind of heavenly creature. Wings indeed.

He let Mike have the co-pilot's seat on the return. In back, the empty seats between him and Cheryl provided just enough space for him to be provocative.

"When you start pulverizing rock, how will you deal with the dust?" Alan asked.

"Dust could be a problem," Cheryl said. "It's one of the things we're working on."

"What about the tailings pond? What if there's a breach?"

"What's underneath is quite solid. It wouldn't move far."

"But what if there's leakage?"

"There will be a monitoring well at a lower level."

"And if there's leakage at the monitoring well?"

"We would add another well, and another if necessary."

Alan saw a hundred monitoring wells strung across the tundra until they reached Moss Lake.

"How would the plastic liner for the tailings pond be replaced—if it tore?"

"Of course it couldn't be replaced," Cheryl said, with a hint of disdain.

He couldn't seem to push her buttons, but he tried again. "Who writes the EIS?"

"ESIS, Environmental and Social Impact Statement. We're only in the exploratory drilling phase, after which we'll apply for permits. The ESIS is one of the last steps."

"Who will edit it?"

"It will be peer reviewed by qualified scientists."

"Why the hell did fifty-six salmon die downstream from the exploration site?" There, he'd said it.

"I have no information about this. Who is your source and when did this incident occur?"

Alan clamped his jaw. This was going nowhere. He was like a lab animal trying to escape a series of trapdoors. Only there was no outlet, and the experiment was designed to see at what point he went crazy. Or simply gave up.

10

The shirts smelled faintly of lavender, oils added to the detergent Phil had used to do the laundry. Breathing in the scent, Dehlia wondered how it could linger for so long, held in perhaps by the plastic garment bags covering his clothes. Clothes that hung like mummified, fleshless relics in a far corner of the closet. She was struck by two competing images: Phil, leaning over the outdoor washtub, dutifully scrubbing away; and her mother in Greece, head bent over lavender bushes loaded with small blue flowers.

The trip to Greece was tainted by her mother's escape from a failing marriage. And even if that weren't true, would those images—a woman and a throng of flowers, and Phil washing clothes—be enough to outweigh these hollow bodies before her? The clothes were their own worn corpses, embalmed and perfumed, awaiting—what? A decent burial? No—not that. A rebirth, an afterlife. Once more she buried her face in the shirts and inhaled. Someone else should wear them. She'd put off the task too long.

Gently, she rolled the first shirt off its hanger and laid the garment on the bed. Lightweight and forest green, it had complemented Phil's complexion and sandy hair. She turned the shirt face-down and draped the sleeves against the backside. Then she folded the shirt in thirds and straightened the collar before setting it in a cardboard box on the floor next to her. She reached for another shirt. The next was tan, the third rust. Nine shirts. The ninth month. What of nine lives?

In another box she put in Phil's jeans, and on top of them his T-shirts and socks. His underwear made her pause. There were even decisions involved with donations. Surely Goodwill wouldn't take them? She tossed them in a pile to burn.

Above, on the high shelf was the satchel. She would get to it eventually.

She reached into the closet again to make sure no clothes were left. At the far right her hand brushed his lambskin leather jacket. Of course. How could she forget?

Off the hanger it looked limp, forlorn. She stroked the pliable leather and ran it across her cheek. So soft, it was almost a match for human skin. She set it in the second box.

STEW ARRIVED PROMPTLY at 2 p.m. Dehlia watched from the doorway as he turned the four-wheeler up the path and backed toward the house, steering expertly to keep the attached trailer from jackknifing. He climbed off, grizzled as an old dog, and removed his baseball cap. He wiped his brow and replaced the cap, the fabric of his blue T-shirt straining against his tattooed biceps and midriff bulge.

Dehlia indicated the boxes, already transferred to the front porch. "There's not much. I guess you didn't need the trailer."

"No problem. This is just like hauling a little bug." He patted the aluminum side. His wedding ring hit the rim and the tinny sound contrasted sharply with his gruff voice.

They set the few boxes in the trailer. "Wait," she said. "There *is* more. What was I thinking?"

Inside, she pulled the curtain back on the downstairs closet. She tossed out several pairs of footgear: tennis shoes, dress shoes, hiking boots, slippers. She found Phil's blue canvas backpack with the leather reinforcer on the bottom, and stuffed the shoes inside.

"Sit down a minute," she said to Stew as he walked in.

He heaved into the larger recliner. Again the baseball cap came off his head. He laid it on one knee where it gave him something to fidget with. "Season's about over," he said conversationally.

"Thank goodness. Five days a week with patrons wears me out." Dehlia moved toward the kitchen. "What can I get you? I have raisin cookies."

Stew patted his belly. "No, I'm startin' to look like an October griz gittin' ready to hibernate."

"Now that's an exaggeration, Stew." But she sat down, resting her hands in her lap. "How's Darlene?"

"Bossy as always." Stew chuckled. "But she's worried about this mine. Just heard the governor changed the regs so that mining companies can dump pollutants into salmon spawning areas. They call 'em 'mixing zones.' Gotta wonder if that's what happened to those fish Patricia and Dolly found. Some scientist name of Sanders sampled the water near there for acid. It was high."

Dehlia bit her lip. Was it true? This project wasn't going away—if anything, it was escalating. People were out there in board rooms, this very instant, making plans. But what could she do? She had her property to protect. "What kind of pollutants?" she asked anyway.

"Who the hell knows. Pollutants is pollutants. Ziggurat's already using all kinds'a crap just to test drill. They claim it's nontoxic, but they ain't sayin what's in it." Stew's face reddened. "Explosives, fuel, oil, grease, antifreeze, water treatment chemicals, herbicides, pesticides, road de-icing compounds... they'll need all that to operate. Jus' wait 'til they start processing. They'll be using cyanide to separate out the gold."

"I really don't know much about it."

"Most people don't. 'Less of course you get cyanide or mercury poisoning, then you'll make a point to learn a whole lot in a hurry."

"Won't there be some safety net?"

"This is about money, not human health."

Net. Julie's weaving. That scene—the salmon net wasn't in the water, it was beached. And there was no skiff in sight. Was Julie implying that fishing had ceased? Was the weaving meant as a bad omen? Perhaps Julie had been depicting a time in the future when there were no fish left to fish. That was unsettling. Dehlia couldn't let herself think about it. Better to concentrate on the late afternoon sun, falling now with slant abandon on the yellowing birches and crimson fireweed leaves. She needed some fresh air.

Stew sensed her readiness. Again the cap went on his head, and he placed both hands on his knees. He rose and picked up Phil's backpack.

She waved from the porch as he drove away, grateful that he'd volunteered to transport the boxes, grateful that no one questioned her decision to send the clothes to Anchorage. Usually hand-me-downs stayed in the community, but Dehlia couldn't bear seeing another man in Phil's clothes. It would be too much if she ran into him: the urge to stare and compare, or worse, to stop the man mid-stride and brush a bit of dirt from a pant leg, or straighten a collar or shirt cuff. Because Phil would have wanted, always, to look his best.

11

Alan yawned. He repositioned his pillow and hooked his hands behind his head. He'd been awake for some time and already it was nine-thirty, but he had no obligations until afternoon. He'd gotten up once several hours ago to relieve himself; next to the door sat the plastic mayonnaise jar half-full of urine, cap securely tightened.

He remembered seeing a chart once on composting that compared nitrogen percentages in different materials. Some things, like blood and fish scraps, were amazingly high, but nothing topped urine. What a shame, all that liquid gold getting flushed away daily, almost hourly, then treated with chlorine before being discharged back into rivers and streams.

Alan groaned. Was this all he had to think about? Maybe he was avoiding his real problems, his role as "handyman" in the community, and Carolyn's grant application. He'd arrived in Whetstone uncertain about the job, and even now his duties were ambiguous. Or perhaps he should say "subject to change." Carolyn, if anything, had become increasingly vague.

Was the solar installation contingent upon her getting the Ziggurat grant? From her notes it sounded like she was hoping to buy the panels then get reimbursed at a later date. He saw no reason for Ziggurat to deny her the money. So what was her holdup?

No doubt she'd already sent in her application. He realized now the foolishness of trying to subvert it. No, it was more than foolish, it was preposterous. But he hadn't considered it *seriously*—he'd just let his fantasies do a few handsprings. Hadn't he?

At least she'd given him the go-ahead to clear the two acres of land set aside for the solar panels, though he sensed a lack of enthusiasm when he provided updates on his progress. Progress— hardly the right word. Working alone with an old chainsaw whose air filter clogged every minute, plus sharpening worn chains and refueling, made the job move at a snail's pace. Compounding the problem were the endless odd jobs, the shuttling of visitors and gear. But all that was about to change. Soon October would be here, and the patrons—he always laughed at the word—would be gone. That would give him two more weeks, if the weather gods were kind, to finish felling and limbing the trees before snowfall. He had to get going—there wasn't much time.

And then? Should he use the weather as an excuse and urge Carolyn to go through with the installation before the grant deadline? At least he'd know then that his wages through Christmas would be clean. But he'd promised first to deliver the fuel charts and power assessment. And for that he needed help—from Dehlia.

He gave another groan, but this one was more of anguish than exasperation. When could he—should he—see her? Today was Saturday. She would be free. Maybe he should take her for a canoe ride. No, not today—he had another woman to escort.

THE POET WAS waiting for him outside her cabin with a small pile of boxes and one suitcase beside her. From a distance Meredith looked beautiful, dark hair cascading down her back in ringlets, full lips reddened with lipstick, eyelids shaded blue. Hadn't Cleopatra, at least the Hollywood version, looked like this? She was dressed for town, wearing heels, slim-cut jeans with zippered calves, and a black, shawl-like black wrap with fringes that she kept flipping back, revealing bare arms and a lemon-yellow sleeveless top. *Killer bee.*

He turned the four-wheeler around in the circular drive and pulled up alongside her. Closer, he saw that Meredith looked haggard beneath her makeup, and he felt a surge of compassion. Why was she leaving Whetstone, and what was she seeking? There was so much about people's inner lives that others could never know—and he knew her exterior self not at all.

She greeted him coolly.

"Not much gear," he said, looking at her small pile.

"When you don't own much, you don't have much to lose." After a beat she added, "All my worth's on paper."

An odd thing to say. Alan loaded her things in the trailer. Two of the boxes, marked *Fragile!!*, were just the right size for pint jars. So she was taking her salmon with her. Good for her. She'd done the work of processing it, and anyway, these fish belonged to everyone. That was why people here cared about defeating the mine, even those who didn't plan on making Whetstone their permanent home. They understood the importance of fish from all angles. Personal, spiritual, economical.

Meredith climbed on the seat behind him and Alan drove down Sapphire and onto the main trail, Opal. Once inside the town center he pulled up in front of the library. Meredith drew her knees to her chest and covered her body with her black shawl, never looking back as he loaded a blue canvas backpack full of shoes and the boxes of clothes that Stew had taken from Dehlia's and delivered this far. They were Phil's, Stew had said. Alan was happy to shuttle them on. Maybe Dehlia's willingness to let go of Phil's things would allow him to get one step closer.

When they got to the airstrip Derek wasn't there yet. Alan killed the four-wheeler engine.

"What's in the backpack?" Meredith asked suspiciously when they climbed off.

"Phil Melven's shoes."

"And the boxes?"

He shrugged. "Clothes, I guess."

Meredith looked startled. "That's going to town?"

So it's not okay for a widow to send off her dead husband's things? What do you care? You're leaving.

Meredith swallowed herself in her shawl and her eyes shifted from the backpack to the boxes as if assessing their worth. "Oh, just clothes and shoes." She turned away.

What was her problem? Alan looked at his watch. He wished Derek would hurry up. Something about Meredith unnerved him. He remembered Dale's comment when they were fishing: *I don't trust that woman.* He was starting to feel the same way.

He wandered to the edge of the strip and breathed in the pungent smell of highbush cranberries.

Meredith sat on the gravel, her back to him. Hunched over, she resembled nothing more harmful than a small spider, caught uncomprehendingly in its own web. Then he heard the welcome drone of the Cessna and he hurried back to help Derek load the plane. What was Meredith to him anyway? He'd never see her again.

12

H all-e-lu-jah," said Barbara, clapping her hands. "The patrons are gone! No more presentations to prepare, no more lunches and small talk, no more price lists to update. Now we can just be artists!" She sashayed across the room to the kitchen table. "Ladies, let's celebrate."

Dehlia and Amy exchanged glances as their friend pulled from a cabinet an array of spirits: gin, sherry, brandy, absinthe.

"It's not even three o'clock, Barbara," said Amy.

"But it's October first. Independence Day for Whetstone. Besides, how often do I have you two at my house? We need to prove to the guys that we can tie one on." Barbara set out three cocktail glasses and a bottle of tonic water.

Dehlia didn't know which guys they would be proving anything to, but she accepted a glass of brandy. Barbara poured, filling Dehlia's glass to the brim. She vowed to sip slowly and leave a good share untouched.

Amy put her hands out, pink stop signs one shade lighter than the spots of rouge on her pale cheeks. "None for me. Ken expects me back in an hour."

"What do you have to do that's so important?"

"Nothing, just pick the last peas, make dinner..."

"You were right with the first word," said Barbara. "*Nothing.*"

Amy scowled. "It's not like I have anything to celebrate. Just because the patrons leave, my job doesn't change. For Ken and me it's the same drool, same diapers."

Barbara reached for the absinthe—an ornate bottle one-third full, with a slender neck and wide, flaring body. She pulled the cork, and the smell of licorice wafted from the foul green liquid. She poured herself three solid fingers and nudged the bottle toward Amy. "You should take a *day* off."

"Oh, all right. But not that stuff. Give me a gin and tonic."

Barbara slid Amy's drink across the table. "Sorry, dear. No ice."

Barbara held up her glass. "To friendship. To heartache. To all the single women in the blessed, cursed, world."

"I'm hitched," said Amy, "but I'll toast to you two. I admire women living on their own."

At the first mouthful, Dehlia could feel the fiery brandy spreading its warmth to her stomach. Outside, gusts of wind loosened the birches' late-clinging leaves and they settled quietly on Barbara's patio. Death was in the air, trance-like and languorous. Dehlia took a second and a third swallow of the brandy.

Barbara tossed off her absinthe and poured another, dismissing Dehlia's look of concern. "Don't worry. It's not a habit."

Dehlia and Amy sipped dutifully.

Barbara stared into her glass. "I'm going to do a painting of an absinthe drinker," she said. "After Botticelli. To counter Degas. It'll be a remake of *The Birth of Venus*. But instead of the lady covering her breast, she'll be holding a glass of absinthe. I'll give her a layered bob and pubic hair."

Amy gave a little gasp and Dehlia shook her head. What had gotten into her? Already Barbara's cheeks were flushed.

Suddenly the effects of the brandy rushed to Dehlia's head, and she laughed loudly. Barbara topped off Dehlia's drink and added a splash of gin to Amy's. Again she reached for the bottle of absinthe and poured another poisonous stream into her own glass.

Amy frowned. "Now that I think about it, you're supposed to pour ice water into that, over a sugar cube on a slotted spoon. That's how my grandmother used to do it."

Barbara signed a cross on her breast. "Confession time. It's just vodka with food coloring and anise. But I had you going, didn't I?" She pursed her lips. "Okay, ladies, now for some serious conversation. Whad I wanna know isst," she said, slurring her words dramatically, "whad ya tink about dis mine." She waved a finger, a poorly functioning metronome, from Amy to Dehlia and back to Amy, where it rested accusingly.

Amy took up the play-drunk sport, lowering her head and rolling her eyes upward. "I tink ish a good ting for da community."

Dehlia listened warily. Maybe Amy's words were just part of her act.

Then Amy said, "Derek explained it all. Did you know this project will create, like, two thousand jobs?"

Barbara snorted. "For who? For how long?" She turned to Dehlia. "What do you think?"

Dehlia swallowed more brandy. She was feeling quite intoxicated. She wanted to go home. But she was afraid if she stood her head would start spinning.

"I'm reserving judgment," she said with false conviction. *Does that make me a coward? How can I explain that I can't talk about this? I only want my independence, and to be truly independent I must put my needs first. It doesn't make me calculating or uncaring. It's self-preservation, that's all.*

Barbara straightened in her chair. "Well, I'm not. Now Ziggurat's paying people to attend meetings. Two hundred dollars a pop."

"What people?" asked Amy.

"What people? Anyone. But V.I.P.s—city and tribal government officials—get bonuses. Free travel, room and board."

"Who told you that?" Amy's eyes were cut blue gems.

"Mike Trotter."

"What does *he* know." Amy waved her hand. "Can we change the subject?" She looked hard at her drink, then took a long, defiant sip.

The women sat in silence. Dehlia wished she hadn't stopped by. Apparently Barbara hadn't yet heard about the water acidity where the dead fish were found. That was all Barbara needed: more fodder. *Change the subject. Talk about my carving; go back to Barbara's painting; talk about the light frosts we've had or when we might get the first real snow. Ask Amy how things were with Blake—no, too depressing. What about that red-tailed hawk? Animal sightings are always safe territory.* Instead she blurted, "I got rid of Phil's clothes."

Instantly Amy's expression softened. "Must be a relief. But sad too."

Barbara gazed out the window. She grew pensive. "You're letting go." She narrowed her dark eyes. "I had this dream last night about a boy I had a crush on in high school. I was holding his hand and he looked exactly like he did thirty years ago."

"I dreamed about an ex-boyfriend last week. We were in the garret of an old house. The whole thing was—ahem—very sexual." Amy was giddy again.

Dehlia couldn't remember having had such dreams, certainly not while she was married. But there'd been someone recently—who was it? *Oh yes, Alan Lamb*—and the blood rose to her face. She put one hand against her cheek to cool it.

"Sometimes"—Barbara lowered her voice—"the best ones are with someone anonymous. But I could think of at least one guy in town I wouldn't mind dreaming about." She gave Dehlia a sly smile and picked up the bottle of brandy. It swayed unsteadily in her hand. "One more?"

Dehlia shook her head firmly. She was going home. Maybe the absinthe wasn't fake after all. Whatever was in that bottle, it was dangerous stuff.

13

There was a thin drizzle with spittings of snow the morning Alan walked the Inner Circle to get to his appointment with Carolyn. His ears were cold beneath his Australian bush hat, and his thin jacket was growing damper by the minute. He shoved his hands in his pockets and walked faster.

He passed Tourmaline. Tourmaline—was that a rock or a gemstone? He'd no idea if it was used in jewelry—probably not, since it wasn't commonly known, not like jade or emerald or ruby. Who made these decisions anyway, about how precious a stone was? The rarer and more durable, the more valuable, but that didn't always translate into beauty. What was so attractive about a diamond for pure looks? A tiger-eye or star sapphire was a lot more intriguing.

He stopped, brushed wet snow from his jacket, and continued walking past an empty lot. When he got to Garnet he'd be at Carolyn's. Yesterday she'd asked him to stop by, saying she had some "business" to discuss. Why did that kind of vague language make him nervous? *Carolyn doesn't know I've seen the application.* Still, this seemed less like an appointment than a summons. It was irrational to think the worst, but if he prepared himself—

What *was* the worst? *Alan, your services are no longer needed.* But he'd signed a contract. *A contract?* What good was a contract? They were broken all the time. He had personal experience to back that up: early in his career he'd put in a solar installation for a guy who paid for the panels and batteries and wire but never made good on the labor. The contract was written clearly enough, that the amount due for Alan's work would be made in a single installment upon completion of the job. He'd never received a penny, but at less than two thousand dollars it hadn't been worth going to small claims court over. Then there was the story his parents told about when they'd first acquired their land. The contract had stated that the developer would run power to their lot, but when they asked him to follow through he refused. The developer had friends in high positions, and Alan's parents had dropped it, though it had cost them thousands to get electricity to their farmland.

If Carolyn let him go, Alan would accept her decision. It wasn't worth fighting these petty battles, especially in a small place where he would have to face his opponent on almost a daily basis. If he had to leave, he'd leave. The hardest part would be his crushed pride. And then there was Dehlia. He'd be letting her go before he'd spent time with her.

CAROLYN MET HIM at the door of her home. In the entryway, he removed his hat and boots and shed his wet jacket.

"Go warm up," said Carolyn. "Would you like coffee?"

Gratefully, he accepted the large, steaming mug and edged toward the woodstove, turning his backside to the radiating heat. He could feel the dampness seeping through the seat of his jeans, and when he shifted his feet little moist impressions appeared where his socks had leaked.

Carolyn hauled two chairs over, but he declined the offer to sit.

She poured her own cup and sat facing him. He was aware of his dominant position, looking down at her, but she didn't seem to mind. "How are you and Mike getting along?"

"Fine," said Alan. "No, great, actually. I didn't expect it."

Carolyn set her cup on her lap and circled the rim with her index finger. *She wants to ask me a favor.* "You've probably been wondering," she said, "about Meredith's place. Whether you'd be able to move into it. She isn't coming back, you know."

He shrugged. "I figured you'd let me know if it was available. Anyway, whatever works. I like staying with Mike."

"Good." Carolyn rubbed her forehead, as if relieving the week's stress. "Here's the thing. I have another couple—he's a poet—who wants to come to Whetstone. My lease is still cheap, but I could use the extra income. It'll help cover the raise I need to give my caregivers."

As if on cue, Alan heard splashing coming from a back room. Blake was getting a bath.

"I understand," Alan said, wanting to add, *how desperate you are for money.*

Carolyn circled the cup's rim again. "I'm still budgeting for the solar panels, but I want to see the charts before I make a commitment. I need a new snowmachine, salmon nets, another refrigerator for the storehouse." She paused. "Caring for dad, that's what's really costing me."

"I'm sorry," said Alan, and he was. Then, without preamble, he said, "I'm getting a dog. I hope you don't have any objection." His own words startled him. A dog? He hadn't really decided on a dog or planned the pronouncement. But he knew why he'd said it. He was feeling compelled to test Carolyn's authority. The whole grant issue was still bugging him.

Carolyn frowned. "Hmm. I'm not keen on pets. I only allow a few. I suppose"—she drew the word out and emphasized the second syllable—"if you keep it under control."

"Great. I'll keep you posted." Alan, warmed by the stove and the coffee and his own confidence, felt his spirits lift. "Anything else?"

"No, that's all."

He was headed for the door just as the wheelchair, with a scrubbed-pink Blake, in fresh sweats, appeared in the doorway. Behind him strolled Amy, her face a glisten of bright sweat. Her husband, Ken, lagged several steps behind. Alan had met him twice. He wasn't unfriendly, but he wasn't particularly friendly either. Canadian, if Alan remembered right. From Alberta or something. He wore a skullcap with a crossbones face.

Amy wheeled Blake into the living room. "We got him washed," she said. "He needs to be out of the wheelchair more, so we'll do some therapy on the mat now. The bedsores are worse."

"Yes, good," said Carolyn. "I mean, the physical therapy sounds good."

On impulse Alan crossed over to Blake and laid his hand on the old man's arm. "You stay out of trouble. I'll be hearing from Patricia what kind of ideas you're putting in her head."

He was only joking, but there seemed to be a faint smile on the withered lips. Was it possible? What exactly was going on inside that sadly diminished brain? He gave Blake's shoulder a final pat and left the house.

14

The fish were mostly humpbacked males, many hues darker than the peach blush of autumn's currant leaves. Set against olive-green noses, the colors reminded Dehlia of Christmas. At the same time, the salmon were grotesque, their bodies flattened half-moons, hooked snouts the beaks of some ungainly proto-bird, jaws equipped with wicked teeth that could cut the hand like pinking shears if a person wasn't careful. Some of the tails were partially decomposed.

Stew gaffed twelve fish from a big drum sitting outside his house and laid them in the five-gallon buckets that he'd sandwiched inside the four-wheeler trailer. More than enough for her garden, which had reduced in size since Phil's passing.

"I'll take the Honda back to the community center when I'm finished," Dehlia said. "I'll park it at the library."

Stew nodded. "I'm done with it for today."

Stew had traveled the beach that morning, collecting as many carcasses as he could before the bears or eagles spotted them. This early in October he'd returned with only twenty, giving Dehlia first pick. One November he'd counted over a hundred washed-up carcasses, and there were stories from elders who remembered windrows of them on the beaches in the fall. "Stew, you shouldn't make exceptions for me," Dehlia said.

He chuckled. "Just want to make sure you get what you need. Don't know how many will be washing up. But might be more 'n normal this year, what with those dead down lake." He lifted his cap and ran his fingers through his matted hair then waved the cap in front of his nose. "Chitlins and hominy, that's rank. I'm the Lord of Corruption."

He replaced the square of plywood on the fifty-five-gallon drum and reconnected the electric fencing surrounding it. "Had a damn bear sniffing at this thing last night. But he got his snout on that wire and took off like a mad hornet." Stew looked at Dehlia and narrowed his eyes. "Remember, when you're powering up that fence, set the energizer on low to test it out. And don't forget, it ain't measured in watts or amps, so be sure to protect the family joules."

Stew thumbed the switch and she could hear the energizer's faint but steady tick. She climbed on the four-wheeler and drove home with her bounty.

HER GARDEN CONSISTED of four raised beds. She'd already dug the trenches, and now she hauled over the buckets of fish. An insect darted into the corner of her eye and she worked it loose with her fingertip, cursing softly. The red flies, lovers of cool weather, were worse than mosquitoes: they bombarded the face, crawled around the collar and the back of the neck, and didn't suck blood but bit.

She slipped inside the house and located her gloves and bug hat, cinching the cuffs on her gloves and draping the fine-meshed netting around her head. Back at work she felt triumphant. She was invulnerable, impervious. It must have been what those ancient knights felt when they covered themselves with chainmail, except that Dehlia's armor was delicate, a tightly woven nylon. On another hat it could have been a widow's veil.

As she laid the salmon in the ground and shoveled dirt over them, she was glad they were being put to good use. Not like soldiers buried in the field of some foreign country. What good were the deaths of millions of adolescents who gave themselves up for an abstract cause—often an invented one? But this was tangible, like concrete math: fish equaled plant growth equaled food in the mouth. And there was the crux of it all: if something happened to the fish, even if she owned her own place, things here wouldn't be the same. Well, she would have to adapt then. There were other ways to fertilize a garden. There were foods to eat besides salmon. But there was no way other than through her contract for her to acquire land, a home, except with... money.

She peeled off her gloves and laid them on a post. Now to get the fence going. She switched the energizer to low, listened for the click, then, with thumb and forefinger, rapidly grasped and released the ribbon. Nothing. She moved the switch to high and repeated the quick grasp-release. What was the trouble? Oh yes, the ground rod. Sure enough, the connection was loose. She tightened the hose clamp and tried again. There was the charge—enough to jolt a bear.

Suddenly she sensed movement behind her, but when she turned around, the woods danced only with sun and shadows. Far off, she heard a grunt, and then—was it her imagination?—Phil's voice, as if from nowhere, but huskier, deeper than she remembered. The words were impossible to make out. Then the voice faded.

15

'm still budgeting for the solar panels, Carolyn had said. So now that the patrons were gone, Alan picked up the chainsaw with new resolve. Five days straight he worked, and on the last day he stopped to observe the clearing. Funny, how his perspective had changed. When he was there day after day, focused on toppling and limbing, the intensity of the work blocked his overall view. Now he saw the carnage in full light. Fallen trunks lay helter-skelter, many on top of each other. The spruce limbs jutted forth like quills of giant porcupines; the birches resembled immense forks with errant tines. The willows had almost all been crushed, but here and there a remnant poked out with a splay of yellow leaves. The ruin hurt. Alan felt for a moment the sadness that came from knowing he, like every human being on the planet, was responsible for spoiling the land. But the two acres were only a fraction of Whetstone's three hundred and twenty, and now residents wouldn't have to travel as far for firewood.

Alan reached in his shirt pocket and unfolded the list of names Carolyn had given him. Twelve people were signed up to cut wood. He noted Dehlia's absence; maybe someone had offered to cut and haul for her.

It was nearly mid-October, but he hadn't been back to see her yet. After her presentation at the art building when he had dropped in unexpectedly, she had been warm and inviting, but he wanted to give her enough time. What had Patricia said? *She's still grieving, I think.* Still, waiting wasn't easy. "Patience," he'd heard, "you're either born with it or you're not." Alan was not.

PATRICIA WAS THE FIRST to arrive. She drove the four-wheeler like a cowgirl, the trailer bouncing recklessly behind, and she made a high-speed U-turn before coming to an abrupt halt. She wore work boots and leather gloves, and Alan admired her jaunty air. She waved at him across the expanse of downed timber.

"Where can I start?" she yelled.

"Anywhere. That's fine, right where you are!" he yelled back.

She waved again in acknowledgment and carried her chainsaw to a large spruce. The engine fired on the second pull. She'd have the trailer full in no time.

Soon Stew arrived with the second four-wheeler. Billy Barr, Dan Broderman, and Jen and Bryce Peterson followed on foot. Alan returned to his own cutting. No sense being directive—people knew what they were doing.

By noon individual piles were taking shape and several loads had been hauled away. Alan lost track of who was coming and going, but he wasn't about to go snooping around to make sure no one was taking more than their share. As far as he could tell, it was all very diplomatic.

His stomach grumbled. Killing the saw, he wiped his hands on his jeans then pulled out his lunch from his fanny pack and sank his teeth into a biscuit. He opened a pint of jarred salmon, using his fingernails to pry off the lid. The top layer was always the best, where the fat accumulated. He ate five consecutive bites, pausing only to swallow. All that work now of netting and then processing the fish with Mike paled. It hadn't been that bad—Mike was particular, making sure there was just enough air space in the jars before the lids went on, and keeping a close eye on the gauge—but he had bantered with Alan and made the job pleasant. And here was the final reward: sockeye soaked in its own juice, an oil-rich source of protein that no fish farm could produce. The intense red flesh of the wild sockeyes simply *looked* healthier. *Ah, thank God for fish. No, thank the Oceans, the Lakes, the Streams.* His stomach closed a little as the food settled. Soon his craving subsided to a more casual call for fill. He ate the last biscuit and wished he'd brought extras for later.

As he sat, sipping coffee from his thermos, he felt a wash of euphoria. Life didn't get much better. The air was crisp, and the cool temperature had driven away the flies. The buzz of chainsaws spoke of good, hard, working-class labor. But it couldn't be for everyone. If everyone in America cut their own firewood, there wouldn't be a tree left on the continent.

He looked up and caught the gentle, timbered slopes and snow-topped cap of Lost Mountain. The clearing had brought the mountain into full view. It was more impressive to him now than ever, even after flying over it on the way to the mine site. Suddenly he knew that he never wanted to set foot on it.

That mountain, it was just there. People didn't need to go digging roots from it, filling pails with its berries, hacking down alders and fixing trails. They just needed to appreciate it. To see it as a reminder that beauty isn't a thing we need to pocket.

HE WORKED UNTIL nearly six o'clock. When he shut down the saw for the last time his clothes and hair were filled with oily smoke, and he had a new tear in the knee of his Carhartts. Everyone had left except Billy Barr. Alan didn't know Billy well, but he seemed friendly enough, a retired airplane mechanic who was spending time at Whetstone to advance his carving career.

"Working late, aren't you?" Alan asked, as Billy approached.

Billy grinned. He had one front tooth missing, but vanity held little esteem in his pragmatist's worldview. "Working late yourself, aren't you?"

Alan righted two spruce rounds and they sat down. He shook his empty thermos. "I'd offer you coffee, but I don't have any left."

"It don't matter," said Billy. But when he pulled a crushed Snickers from his shirt pocket, he peeled off the wrapper and broke the bar in half, handing one share to Alan.

"Thanks, man. I'm starving."

They chewed the sticky caramel and chocolate and sat looking out at the clearing, mosses and ferns trampled into the dirt. The few rounds left were stacked in pyramids, ready for pickup. Now the stumps loomed like gravestone markers above the inert ground. In the center lay a huge mound of branches that would need to be burned. Hauling them away would take eons.

"You get all your wood?" asked Alan.

"Yeah. I cut for Dolly and Carolyn too."

"You like cutting wood, Billy?"

"Yeah, I like it." Billy was reticent but seemed content to be in Alan's presence. For his part, Alan was flattered that Billy had sought him out. At the same time, he couldn't shake his Western proclivity to converse, a nervousness that mostly took the form of questions. He learned that Billy was from a small village not far from Prudhoe Bay. Billy didn't like the changes oil companies had brought to the Arctic. "Too much money. Too much equipment," Billy said.

"What do you think of Ziggurat?"

"Fish die because of them. Too much acid in the water, that's what I hear."

"Really? It got tested?"

Billy didn't elaborate. "All them companies too big," he said. "They like poison. They poison the country."

"I wonder how much we can do to fight this."

Billy fished out a roll of chewing tobacco. He bit off a chunk and worked it around until it pushed out the bottom of his cheek like a soft marble.

"Anyway," said Alan, "I'm sure as hell gonna try."

"Yeah," said Billy. "Me too." And he spat.

16

When Dehlia met Dan at the door she discovered she had not one visitor, but two. Waggy the Pomeranian perched on Dan's shoulder like a fat falcon. "Cute," said Dehlia. "Did she sit up there all the way?"

"Oh, yes. We are well trained. Since we were a puppy." Dan lifted the dog off his shoulder and held her waist high. "And our feet, therefore, are not a mite sullied."

"Of course, let her in."

Dan lowered Waggy to the floor and removed his jacket. He'd spruced up, washing and combing his long hair before tying it back. He wore clean jeans and a Western-style shirt with pearl buttons. Dehlia smelled aftershave. He was early.

"I hope you weren't expecting anything fancy." She gave him a light hug. "I'm just making a stir-fry with some moose burger Dolly gave me."

"Anything you prepare, Milady, will be a most welcome repast. And I do hope, as for invitations, this will not be the last." He gave her a lingering look before removing his boots and heading to the table.

"I appreciate you cutting all that wood for me," she said politely.

"The pleasure's mine. Your virtue deserves my service." Dan sat and moved Waggy to the chair beside him, where she sat erect as a cartoon dog.

"Would you like something to drink, Dan? Wine? Beer?"

"A compound of hydrogen and oxygen would be most agreeable. Were it presented in a tall glass receptacle I would not say no."

She wished he'd stop. This could make for a long evening. Dehlia poured Dan some water and herself a glass of Chardonnay. She lit a burner under a cast iron skillet. "Do you remember when Phil and I were building this place? You talked us out of putting in a partition.

It was good advice. It's much easier to heat when there's just one room. But you've probably forgotten. That was ages ago."

"Oh, I do well recall that conversation." Dan smoothed his mustache and stroked his ponytail. "Memory, Milady, is one attribute with which my absorbent gray material has been generously endowed. Have I neglected to mention, over the course of these many years, that I have womb memories?"

She sipped her wine and stirred the sautéing onions, whose aroma now permeated the room and overpowered Dan's aftershave. Maybe this dinner wasn't such a good idea after all. Maybe next time she should cut her own firewood. "No, Dan, you didn't mention that."

He closed his eyes, as if propelling himself back to a state of buoyant, oblivious bliss. Dehlia wasn't sure she wanted details of Dan's uterine days, whether real or imagined. It was hard enough picturing Dan as an infant, much less an embryo.

"What was your mother like?"

"My mother. Now there's a lengthy subject."

Smart move. Now she could concentrate on dinner. The question was only meant to be a distraction, but Dehlia wondered how she might have answered it if Dan had asked it of her. All that came to mind was what her mother wasn't: generous and comforting and serene. She added snow peas and sliced peppers to the skillet. Dan prattled on—his mother had been an exceptional woman on all counts—while Dehlia tossed jarred moose meat and precooked noodles into the mix.

As she set the table and transferred the stir-fry into a serving bowl, Dan was enumerating his mother's accomplishments as a small-town librarian.

He ate painstakingly slowly, chewing each mouthful to a pulp.

She tried to slow her pace.

"I hadn't heard that anyone took a moose this fall," he said. "The ungulates are on the decline, due, no doubt, to *Canis lupus.*"

"Wolves always get the blame," said Dehlia. "Anyway, I hope they rebound. I love moose."

"And I must have been a pinniped in my past life. 'Tis fish I relish above all else."

"It's very resourceful, eating them after you've turned them into art."

Dan bowed his head, as if being credited for having developed the art form. The real inventors—Japanese fishermen two hundred years dead, who used it as a way to record the size of their catch—couldn't rise up to defend themselves.

Dehlia let it pass. She was feeding Dan's ego as well as his stomach. "How many prints did you sell?"

"It was a modest season, by all counts." Dan finished eating at last. He dabbed his mustache fastidiously with his napkin. "I sold sixty."

"My goodness. I only sold fifteen masks. But that's fine. I can hardly carve that many in a year."

"Yes, a wayfarer loves a piscatorial replica. Methinks he is seeking his ocean origins, pining for that time before he broke his covenant with water and arrived beaming on shore, finless and all cerebrum."

"Would you mind translating that?"

"What I'm saying, Milady, is that our good patrons are unsettled land dwellers who yearn to reconnect with their aquatic roots. Therefore, my prints sell reasonably well."

He stayed until almost eleven o'clock. As she cleared the table Dan fished a booklet from his coat pocket. She glanced sideways at the title. The publication was from the Fly Creek Consortium. To Dehlia's dismay, he opened the booklet and began to read aloud. They were bullet points, listing long-term economic gain: jobs, capital and infrastructure investment, taxes for state and local government.

She tuned it out, resentful that Dan could say what he wished. He had nothing at stake; he'd done his full service, his land was his own. And something—a coal of anger, lying deep in her stomach's uncensored pit, began to glow.

"So you're supporting this project?" she asked evenly. *How can you, a fish printer, who "relishes fish above all else," back something that could jeopardize your very livelihood?*

"The fishing and the mining industries can work side by side. I do believe that, yes."

"But what about those dead salmon?" Why was she being accusatory? Was Barbara getting to her more than she realized?

Dan set down his pamphlet. "Sockeye are adversely affected by temperatures higher than the mid-fifties." He was working from memory now. "Less dissolved oxygen makes it more difficult for fish to breathe. And warm water is also hospitable to microscopic foes. Parasites, Milady, bring serious infection to salmon."

"So you're saying they died because the water was too warm."

"That, certainly, is one plausible and highly possible explanation."

That made sense. Dan was probably right; one shouldn't jump to conclusions. Or maybe it was just what she wanted to believe.

Then Dan said, "I would advise you, as one who has your best interest in mind, not to cross Carolyn on this issue. The ease with which she could nullify your contract would—"

"What? How do you know that? How do you know that Carolyn supports this mine?"

"I have my sources," said Dan.

"Well, maybe, but... she can't just cancel a contract." It was exactly what she had feared could happen. And of course, she'd essentially broken it, having confided in Dan after the agreement she'd signed stated she mustn't share it with anyone.

"With the right attorney, Carolyn will receive a mere slap on the wrist and a one-hundred-dollar fine," said Dan.

Could it be true? Oh, if only Phil were alive, he would tell it straight.

17

Alan rapped on Mike's door. "You asleep?"

"If I'd been asleep I wouldn't be anymore, would I?" Mike answered, in his best sardonic voice. "What's up?"

"I'm heading to the airstrip. You planning on meeting the plane?"

"Guess I'll pass. I'm in the middle of a chapter. But I wouldn't mind a break." Mike opened his door, walked past Alan, and leaned against the kitchen counter. He took off his glasses and rubbed his eyes.

"What's the book about?" Alan sprawled on the couch, wondering how Mike could stay in his room all day when the best creative material was out there, in the world.

"This middle-aged guy with lofty ideals. He comes to this town, thinking to transform it into a model of environmental perfection, then falls in love with a beautiful widow."

Alan blanched. "Don't do this to me, Trotter."

Mike snorted. "Don't flatter yourself. I jest." Then he said, "I'm writing about an old miner, based on Hiram. But it's mostly a psychological exploration of a guy who spends too much time alone. He thinks if he strikes it rich he'll make lots of friends."

"Then he won't be lonely, at least."

"Wrong. He'll still be lonely, but it'll be worse. He won't understand that the feeling has merely grown into another manifestation of itself, something more like alienation."

"That's heavy shit, Trotter. You're making me tired." Alan lunged from the couch. He had a job to do.

TURNING IN TO the airstrip, Alan surveyed the waiting crowd: no Dehlia. He was disappointed, but it wasn't the first time. He was certain she was avoiding him. Despite his resolve to hold off his advances, he kept hoping she'd at least present herself. Maybe even engage in conversation—that would be a bonus. But each time it didn't happen his expectations fell, so his dashed hopes had undergone a metamorphosis from wounds to pangs to twinges. While it hadn't negated his interest, it kept his obsession at bay.

He'd just climbed off the four-wheeler when he heard the Cessna. He always heard the plane before he saw it. Now he scanned the sky for its dark body, trying to determine Derek's altitude. Suddenly the plane was in full view, just over the treetops. Derek swooped down, revving the engine before climbing, turning, and setting up to land.

"Impressive buzz job," said Dale, as Alan squeezed in next to him in the standing crowd.

"Amazing I still have my hat." Alan grimaced. It always made him nervous when Derek buzzed so low.

"Bet he doesn't perform that stunt when he flies Zig execs around."

Alan gaped at him. "What?"

"Yep. Got word that Derek's supplemental income is working for the mega corp. Well, I guess someone has to do it. Doesn't necessarily mean he supports the bastards. Maybe he just figures on taking them for all he can."

"Sure as hell hope so," said Alan, but he wasn't impressed. If Carolyn supported Ziggurat, of course Derek did too. Couples always snuggled up compatibly on one side of an issue, didn't they? Alan wished he could fill Dale in on Carolyn's grant application, but he'd acquired the knowledge by devious means. He had to be careful about letting word out. And maybe Dale had Derek pegged, maybe both Derek and Carolyn were willing to fatten up on Ziggurat's fodder before they kicked the company out the door with a sharp hoof.

He was glad when the plane touched down. As the prop swung to a halt and Derek climbed out, Alan experienced an odd replay of his own arrival six months ago. But this time he was on the inside, looking out. The passengers stepped down—a sighted Ray Charles and a blonde Natalie Wood—and Carolyn strode forth to greet them. "Please welcome Indigo and Indi," she said to the waiting crowd. Indigo was very dark, the color of black walnut. Next to him, Indi looked as pale as a strawberry petal.

Others came up to introduce themselves, and Alan felt slighted, remembering how Dan Broderman had dampened his own reception. But there was no Broderman today, and Alan's injured feelings were momentary. He shook the new arrivals' hands and told them he'd be shuttling them to their cabin.

There was room in the trailer for all their boxes. Indigo whistled while he worked and flashed an irresistible smile. Indi, though less exuberant, helped with the loading. Alan took an immediate liking to them. They were young, athletic, and eager to please.

WHEN ALAN ENTERED Meredith's former living quarters, something was clearly amiss. The floor was dusted with white powder that led to a gutted ten-pound bag of flour. A pattern of tracks—the size of a large man's hand—made a trail across the floor and around the partition to the sleeping area. It didn't take Alan long to recognize the signature of a brown bear.

He followed the tracks to an opening in the wall where a window should have been. A mattress, where Meredith had apparently slept, lay covered with a piece of plywood. On its surface three faint white paw prints indicated that the bear had exited the same way it had entered. Alan bent to pick up the plywood. "Wow, the window frame's still attached," he muttered. The bear must have pushed on the boarded window—which landed intact on the mattress—then walked across the plywood and into the main room, where it tore open the bag of flour.

"What's up with the window?" Indigo's voice behind him made Alan jump. "You tryin' to tell us to chill out? And this flour shower— is this some kind of voodoo art?"

"Indigo, hush," said Indi. "You're talking like it's the 1970s again." Indi rolled her eyes.

"Aw, honey, we've been through this. That was some righteous lingo came out of that era, and now as I'm a bona fide poet, I aim to bring some of it back." But he dropped the retro street talk and said more seriously, "Looks like a visit from Mr. Bear."

"Yeah, but we got lucky." Alan pointed to the window and explained what he'd deduced. "Hard to believe a bear getting into a cabin without totally trashing the place."

"This bear—*our* bear—is awfully polite," said Indi. She squinted at the empty space on the wall. "Why do you think the window just fell in?"

"Weird. More voodoo," said Indigo, and he danced backward, palms out, as if warding off some evil spirit. He grinned. " 'Course Meredith was a poet, and all us poets are witch doctors in disguise. Maybe she cast some spell to allow that bear entrance."

Alan inspected the window again. "I'd call it shoddy workmanship. Someone used finishing nails instead of casements."

Indigo peered over Alan's shoulder. "Sho' enough."

"Let's unload," said Alan. "I'll run back and grab a drill and some nails. We need to get this window in so you can have some heat."

"Oh, thank you," said Indi. She shivered in her light coat.

Before leaving, Alan looked again at the floured tracks. On the tabletop, two of the bear's prints lay on either side of a book. *Polite bear, and smart too.* Scrawled on a sticky note on the book's cover were the words, *Return to library.*

He peeled back the note and read the title: *Geology, Economics, and the Law.* He slipped the book inside his jacket. He would drop it off on the way back to the airstrip. Now what would Meredith have wanted with a book like that?

18

The morning of the last day in October Dehlia woke to a world without breath. No rustle, no susurration issued from the cushioning white. As if sound, before it could even begin to be born as a wave or vibration, was suppressed.

That was what she registered first: the absolute quiet. Outside the window the lull took a side seat and her perception gradually sharpened. The sky was just beginning to lighten, and the season's first snow covered the ground. Several inches had accumulated on the stack of firewood she'd split the day before.

It was cool in the room and she dressed hurriedly before skipping downstairs. These were the times she most missed Phil. He'd always been the fire builder, the coffee brewer, the one who warmed the house before heading off to the library.

AFTER SHE'D SWEPT the porch and taken care of morning chores, she turned her attention to the holiday. Halloween. Once again she'd been invited to Julie and Sheila's annual party. She considered not going. It wasn't necessarily a costume party, said Julie, but everyone who came treated it as such. Still, Dehlia never planned ahead enough to come up with anything original to wear.

She tossed around some ideas—Raggedy Ann, Little Miss Muffet, Little Bo-Peep—and quickly threw them out. Too complicated. It was six o'clock before she pulled on an old pair of coveralls, stuck an open-end wrench in the front pocket, and smeared on her face two streaks of Crisco mixed with soot. She was a college graduate's career nightmare—a bolt-tapping, nut-turning grease monkey.

The door was open when she arrived. Stepping into Julie's cabin was a surreal, mind-altering experience, though Dehlia was sober as a Mormon. People she usually recognized at a glance were oddly clothed or masked while others had dyed or curled their hair or used makeup to create bizarre faces. From the rafters hung skeins of handspun yarn in purples, reds, yellows, and blues. A thin curtain of smoke swirled around the colors, and candles on a central table illuminated three jack-o'-lanterns. Sheila's violin was stowed away above the bookshelf, well out of reach.

Julie waved a welcome from the kitchen. She wore stockings and a half-length dress that ballooned out from her hips. Her hair was sprinkled with glitter and she carried a small wand. "Dehlia, I'm so glad you made it. Help yourself to snacks and drinks. Excuse me, I need to shut the door. We had a downdraft from the chimney."

Julie brushed past her and Dehlia poured herself a glass of punch. She picked up a carrot stick. Watching the groups of chatting, costumed adults, she wished Barbara were there. She hadn't been spending enough time with her. Barbara, she suddenly realized, was her best friend.

She studied the jack-o'-lanterns on the table. One wore a Lone Ranger mask and a stocking cap, with two cardboard pistols pointed out from either side of its bulbous head. Another's blindfold, downturned smile, and earmuffs conveyed the classic warning, "See no evil, hear no evil, have no fun." The third, with closed eyes and a water pipe in its mouth, was all contentment.

A hand grazed her elbow. It was Patricia Abbey, in tights and a short, close-fitting smock. An archer's quiver was slung over her back. "Come and join us," she said.

Then Dehlia was in the presence of friends whose assorted props did nothing to mask the person behind them—a long beard made from an old mop (Dale Abbey); a black beak in place of a nose and a punk-style, jet-black hairdo (Sheila Grady); a rotor atop another head (Darlene McCoy); and "Mr. Choice" (Stew), one half of his face painted gold, the other half red. A bag hung from each of his hips.

"I'm Robin Hood," said Patricia.

"Rip Van Winkle," said Dale.

"Caw, caw," Sheila squawked.

"I'm a helicopter." Darlene pushed something inside her shirt and the rotor swung into motion. "Battery operated. Stew fixed me up."

Dehlia marveled at the ingenuity. Patricia said, "And now we have a mechanic to work on your engine. Right, Dehlia?"

"No," she joked, "I only work on cars."

Patricia flexed her bow "Best mechanic I ever knew was a woman."

"Maybe she was the best," said Dale, "but the smartest one I knew always said, 'Don't know nothin' bout no 'chinery.'"

Dehlia studied Stew's getup, and he pointed to his T-shirt. "I'm Mr. Choice," he said, as if Dehlia couldn't read. Drawing open the bag on his left hip—the gold side of his face—he revealed the contents: dark yellowish clumps of heavily caramelized popcorn. Then Stew opened the bag on his right. It was filled with miniature fish crackers, the kind Dehlia remembered from grade school.

"You want gold or fish?" Stew pointed from the popcorn to the crackers. "You have to choose."

Dehlia swallowed. She could feel the others' eyes on her, and Stew's voice seemed gruffer than ever. But perhaps this was part of the party, turning a serious issue—the mine—into a holiday charade.

Dehlia forced a smile. "I think I'll have another carrot, thanks." She retreated to the table just as the door opened and Barbara entered. But not just Barbara—by her side was a full-sized cardboard figure. A man, Dehlia realized, and strikingly good looking, wearing a suit jacket and jeans, and a baby-blue shirt and maroon tie. Casual but smart.

"Dehlia, I'd like you to meet George Clooney," Barbara said, striding over.

Dehlia laughed and addressed the figure. "How do you do?"

"He's shy. He doesn't say much." Barbara kissed the cardboard lips as Stew, behind them, sternly questioned more guests, "Gold or fish? You have to choose."

Julie announced dinner and Barbara insisted on a place for George at the table. "I'm hanging on to this one. As far as men go, he was quite a project, but now I've got him trained. See? He doesn't even talk back."

And Dehlia knew, even as she laughed, that she herself had been on the lookout all evening for someone in the flesh—whether disguised as a pirate, monk, or gnome—but Alan wasn't there. Perhaps she, like Barbara, should have reserved an empty seat—for a ghost, if nothing else. But the whisperings and visions she'd heard over the last year and a half had ceased. Phil, not even an apparition now, had at last departed.

PART THREE

Thorns of Frost

1

It was cold for early November, the temperature hovering between zero and ten degrees. The wind too had been almost static, building if at all to no more than five knots, and rising always from the north. Clouds of steam fog obscured the mountaintops; wispy tendrils lifted from another thin line of fog on the lake's surface.

Standing on shore, observing the white and pendulous drift, Dehlia felt smothered, but she knew the skies above were clear. Years ago on a November trip to Anchorage, she'd been astounded at the reverse perspective. When Derek took off from the airstrip she thought the poor visibility would have her clinging, white knuckled, to her handbag for the entire flight. Instead, after the plane spiraled up, she'd looked down at the dome of fog and realized it covered the lake only. Open water and cold air created these conditions—the sky itself was a blue sheet, what pilots call "severe clear." She could see for miles.

At least there was plenty of beach this time of year. The water was as low as it would get, all precipitation remaining in the mountains now in the form of snow. In June, spring melting would begin and the lake would gradually creep up.

It wasn't a stroll along the Mediterranean, to be sure. She had to watch her footing. But the scene had its own appeal: waves had left an icy glaze on clusters of stones, and the ice caps glistened in the muted light like fantastic aberrant mushrooms. Her body was warm enough in her hooded coat, but her face tingled and her nose dripped. Thank goodness for handkerchiefs.

A merganser appeared, riding the lake's ripples, the long feathers at the base of its chestnut head ending abruptly, like the profile of a punk haircut. The birds were so resilient. Even this late in the year, with the water temperature not much above freezing, stragglers could be found paddling around the bay. How could they endure the cold, cold water?

When she reached the outcropping, she turned and headed home, recalling the bear incident last May. Again she pictured Meredith's distant figure, but had the bear really been stalking her? With the passage of time Dehlia's recollection was not so frightening; surely some of her alarm had just been a wild imagination. Now that most of the bears had already climbed into the mountains looking for winter dens, the thought of them was hardly threatening.

No danger then, no need for caution, except to avoid the slippery stones. And once back in the woods the familiar trail offered even greater security. The going was easy, her boots' grip sound. Then *wham!* She was down, and hurt. Her ankle... what had happened? She struggled to one knee and bumped against an old root, just large enough to have caught the toe of her boot. Damn. She righted herself and stood shakily. Accidents happened when you least expected them, wasn't that the old adage? Of course, stupid. That's what makes them accidents.

She tested her foot, applying a little weight. Not too bad—she could hobble. It was probably just a strain. A few yards ahead she broke off a long, thick branch from a stand of dead alder. It would serve as a rudimentary cane, allowing her a more balanced limp.

She made her way slowly, thinking, a little perversely, that she rather liked the pain. With a physical injury you could pinpoint the source and more easily define the discomfort. Dull, sharp. Wincing, nagging. Excruciating, tolerable. But emotional injury was different. It advanced, then retreated, it swelled and ebbed. Finding relief from it was like trying to swim to a tropical island whose shores kept eroding, whose sheltering green palms remained diminutive and always out of reach.

2

Alan flipped open his alternative energy catalog. Dog-eared and scuffed, with scores of margin notes, it had traveled hard. He turned to the FAQs. *Will solar work in my location? How much will it cost? Is solar cost effective?* Something about the questions felt like mockery. Maybe it was the emphasis on the word "cost" and the doubt inherent in all three.

From a manila envelope he withdrew a stack of papers, load evaluation forms for every household in Whetstone. As Dan Broderman had informed him—in no uncertain terms—Carolyn did have the information on file. But the files hadn't been updated for six years. Over the past five months Alan had visited almost everyone in town, assessing people's needs. With the semi-transient nature of Whetstone it was an inexact science. Still, power draw for the community was remarkably low. There were five refrigerators and eight washing machines in total. Some people, like Stew, had small generators that minimized demand on the town's battery bank. Many had their own laptops, but the only Internet access was at the library. Dan, with his freezer, had the largest load, while Julie emerged clearly as the town's Luddite. Alan gave her an imaginary thumbs-up, thinking with amusement that she would have encouraged Edison to take up candle making.

Ah, but candles were not made of air. Throughout history they'd been fashioned from tallow, beeswax, and spermaceti, and now most were paraffin, which came from petroleum. There was no way around it: something had to be wrested from the environment to serve basic human needs—lighting and heat, and—what passed today as a basic need but was really just a convenience—electricity. Every industrialized nation was hooked. You couldn't reverse technological advancements, and few people would wipe the dust from a 1947 manual typewriter when a computer with a Pentium processor was at hand. The best one could do was go for greater efficiency. Because even solar modules taxed the environment. Alan went through the steps involved in their production: fossil fuels to run the machines that mined the crystal for the silicon, which was sliced into disks before going into cells that were framed with aluminum. It began to sound a lot like "The House That Jack Built." And the U.S. imported one hundred percent of its crystal. Still, the panels, once they were installed, provided electricity for a good twenty-five years, maybe a lifetime. No emissions.

He was getting off track. Where was he? Oh yeah. Fuel. How much did Whetstone use? Dehlia would have the figures since she was on the fuel committee. He turned back to the catalog as Mike emerged from his room. Mike's hair was greasy and flat, and his typically clean-shaven face wore a gray stubble.

"How many panels you planning to order?" Mike asked.

"Two dozen. They're a hundred-and-fifty watters. Should top sixty amps on a good day. I'll need two mounts and two trackers. I could use new batteries, but Carolyn won't want to part with that much dough at once." Unless her bankroll doubles in size, Alan thought. He imagined a bowlful of greenbacks, puffing like a Swedish pastry near the stove, dwarfing Mike's biscuits. Why couldn't he let the grant thing go?

"How much without the batteries?"

"Fifteen to twenty grand."

Mike let out a low whistle.

"Yeah, I know. But maybe Dehlia will get creative with the charts. You know, fudge the numbers to my advantage."

"Speaking of Dehlia, when are you going to see her? I've been hearing about this visit for months." Mike sniffed and dug a handkerchief from his jeans. He blew his nose harshly.

"Maybe tomorrow." Alan smelled his armpit. "I need a shower."

Mike screwed up his face. "I thought I smelled something like vinegar."

"You're one to talk, Trotter. You look like a greased pig."

"Oink."

Alan picked up a nickel from the windowsill. "Let's flip to see who gets the first soak. Heads, I win. Tails, you lose."

"Very funny. I'm calling heads."

Alan set the coin spinning upward with a flick of his thumb and slapped it down on the table. He paused. *If I win, it'll be a good omen. She'll be happy to see me.* He lifted his hand, revealing the Monticello mansion. He smiled. For the first time, he appreciated that piece of architecture.

3

Dehlia lay reading with her feet propped up on the arm of her couch. Looking up, she caught a glimpse of something moving through the trees. It was dark against the snow, too tall for a wolf. A moose? Then the figure appeared again at the head of her driveway. It was a man—but who?

Alan Lamb.

She got to her feet too quickly. Ouch! Her ankle still hurt. How did she look? She smoothed her hair at the mirror. At least she'd put on her red blouse this morning—sheer, and sheer luck. If she'd known he was coming, she'd have worn an old T-shirt, not wanting him to think she was dressing up for his visit. She sat down again, gripping her book. Her hands were moist and her throat dry. Ridiculous. She commanded herself, like a stern captain, to summon some self-control.

When the knock sounded and she swung open the door, he stood back a little, as if afraid of crossing the threshold. Their eyes met, a brief look that spoke many thoughts. Intrigue and awkwardness, fascination and doubt, difficulty and risk. He seemed more youthful than she remembered.

"I brought the paperwork for the fuel charts," he said, slinging off his backpack. "For Carolyn. We talked about it in April." He cleared his throat. "I thought you might have some time now."

She looked down. "Yes... please come in."

Alan took off his boots and set them on the rug. She hung his coat on a peg near the door.

At the table Alan pulled papers from several large envelopes. He made three stacks. He wore a jade-green shirt with the two top buttons undone, exposing fine curls of chest hair.

She stood in the kitchen. "Can I get you anything?"

He cleared his throat again but did not look up. "No thanks."

She limped over lightly with a notebook and sat kitty-corner to him. His proximity caught her off guard. Something was happening to the air. Protons were unstable, electrons were trying madly to rearrange themselves. Near his elbow was the book she'd been reading, *A Study of Swans.* "I'll take that. It's in your way."

He passed it to her, their fingers not quite touching. "Are you reading that for your carving." He seemed unable to phrase it as a question.

"Yes."

"I like your work."

"Thanks."

"Shall we begin."

"Yes."

She could get through this. *Keep your questions short. If possible, answer with no more than one word.*

He pointed to the first stack of papers. "These are load sheets. The totals are on top." He indicated the second stack. "These are projected prices for a gallon of diesel for the next twenty-five years. We'll compare them to the current price. These," he said, pointing to the last stack, "are everyone's utilities charges. They're flat rates, a tier system based on appliances."

She stared at the papers. Numbers had never seemed so meaningless. "Do you have a calculator?"

He unzipped the side pocket of his backpack. A shock of hair fell over his eyes as he bent down.

She scribbled a few notes. "We'll need recent fuel receipts. I have them."

Still favoring her right foot, she walked carefully to her file cabinet. She knelt and leafed through the folders, happy to have her back turned.

"What happened to your foot?" He suddenly sounded much less formal.

"It's my ankle. It's nothing, just a strain, I think." She concentrated on the open drawer.

"Did you take aspirin?"

"Ibuprofen."

"Have you elevated it?"

"Yes."

"You should try an elastic bandage."

"I probably should."

"I could help you wrap it."

Her heart hammered like a sapsucker.

A minute passed. Somehow she found the file marked *Fuel* and spread it open with the pretense of studying the contents on the way back to the table. She sat down again and took up her notebook.

"We'll need four graphs," she said. "One: fuel prices for the last two years and projected prices for the next twenty-five. Yes?"

Alan nodded.

"Two. Maintenance and repairs for the generators."

"Yes, and the cost of replacing them or doing a complete rebuild." He was smiling now, and watching her.

"Three. The power graph for Whetstone—what do you call it? Load."

"Yes."

"Four. Carolyn's expenses."

"Yes."

"That's it, right?"

"No, we need to figure the expenses and savings of the panels. Two more graphs." He reached into his backpack again but came up empty handed. "I guess I didn't bring that information."

This struck her as funny and she laughed nervously, a schoolgirl laugh. "I almost forgot. This whole visit is about solar panels, isn't it?"

Alan smiled again. Then his look grew serious. "I don't know, is it?"

The question hung between them along with a hundred unformed others. She was aware that outside, dusk was beginning to descend. She could hear herself breathing. This time she didn't look down. "Are you English?"

"Scottish. And you? Italian?"

"My grandmother was raised in Italy, but she was born in Greece."

"So you're Greek."

This was the threshold, and she scarcely paused before she crossed it. "You have green eyes."

"Yours are brown."

What am I doing? Timidly, her hand traveled across the tabletop and slid over his knuckles until the tips of her fingers reached his wrist.

That was all. One touch.

In the next instant he'd carried her to the couch. "Your hair. It smells like perfume."

What was there to say? It was all new, this melting, this envelopment, this warm, womanly ache igniting every muscle and nerve. She arched her neck and his lips traveled her throat, down to the curve of her blouse.

She was giving something up, she was releasing an embedded stone that had forever defined her, she was emerging, like a renegade anchorite, from the cloister of her cell. She knew there might be consequences. She knew some might not be favorable. But even if she'd been able to imagine them, she would not have cared.

LATER THEY LAY on the couch, half-dressed beneath her fleece blanket. They shifted positions but spoke little, enjoying the play of hand and foot on new territories of flesh, then lapsed into the drowsy, blissful aura that only new lovers can know.

After a while Dehlia said she should get up and stoke the fire and he said, "Yes." But she didn't rise, and later she said she should fix them something to eat. But still she didn't rise, and that made him laugh. She asked if he had to get back and he said that Mike knew where he was.

"Will you spend the night then?"

"Is that an invitation?"

"Yes."

"Then yes."

And they laughed again, because *yes* had become their word, their first inside joke, and when they finally rose to stoke the fire and eat a modest meal of scrambled eggs and toast, and she stood at the counter with a mug of tea, he stroked her neck and kissed her on the mouth.

"Can I wrap your ankle now?"

"Yes," she said, brushing aside his hair. "Can I give you a haircut tomorrow?"

"Yes."

"Say it again."

"Yes. Now you."

"Yes," said Dehlia. "Yes, yes, yes, yes, yes."

4

When Alan opened the door, Mike was at the table with a newspaper, a jar of salmon, and a box of crackers.

"Good afternoon, Romeo." Mike emptied the salmon into a bowl, mixed in a spoonful of mayonnaise, and dumped some crackers on a plate. "But come what sorrow can, / It cannot countervail the exchange of joy / That one short night gives me in her sight."

Alan bent to unlace his boots.

"The Bard wrote 'minute,'" Mike said, "but I substituted 'night.' Or did you bivouac under a tree?"

Alan smoothed his mustache and beard, trying to hide his smile.

"To quote my grandfather, you look like a skunk eating bumblebees." Mike topped a cracker with his salmon spread. "So! sayeth the wounded friend, / Are you here for five minutes or an hour hence?"

"I came to get some papers. And my guitar."

"You will serenade the lass / And she will fall about thy knees in bliss."

"Mike, stop it."

"Okay. No appreciation for extemporaneous verse, attributed to none other than Michael Trotter, Stratford-Upon-Hélène."

Alan hurried to his room. He located the solar savings and expense sheets and stuffed them in his pack, along with some songbooks, socks and underwear, and a clean shirt. He added the bottle of California wine that he'd purchased months ago. He tossed his toothbrush and Patricia's CD into a side pocket. In another he tucked in his CD player and two headphones. Was it just luck that he'd brought along the extra set? Now they could listen to the music together. He fished around for batteries. "You got any double As I can borrow?" he called to Mike.

"Yeah, I think I have some extras."

ANNE CORAY

Alan stood in the doorway of his room waiting for Mike to fetch them. But Mike made no movement. "I need to read you something," Mike said instead.

Alan tried to shake off his impatience. He hurried to the table where Mike was glued to a newspaper.

"Sit down," Mike insisted. "Listen to this: 'Gold Bounces Like a Rubber Ball. Four years ago, a single ounce of gold went for $409 on the New York Mercantile Exchange. That same ounce has now reached $860, just $15 short of gold's all-time high, and precious metals analyst Jim Dunn believes it could soon hit $890.'"

Mike ran his tongue over his front teeth, as if he were cleaning them. "Eight hundred ninety an ounce. That's four years' royalties on one of my books." He picked up the newspaper again.

"I get it," said Alan.

"With that kind of incentive, Ziggurat won't back out. It doesn't bode well for Fly Creek."

"It's not good," said Alan, but he was distracted. He should be outraged, but outrage was not foremost in his mind. He'd told Dehlia he would come right back. He needed the batteries.

ON THE WALK back to her house, Alan transferred his guitar case from hand to hand, but never had it been so uncumbersome. It was a softball, a can of soda pop. He'd hardly played over the summer, picking his guitar up only twice after the party at Patricia's. The excuses were the usual: he'd been too busy, tired after long days of labor, he didn't want to distract Mike. But in truth the mood hadn't struck him. Now maybe he would write a song. *A brown-eyed lady, she made me wait...* He'd dabbled in songwriting over the years, but he'd never shared any of his attempts. Who knew, he might even write something else—short stories to start, and he'd branch out from there. He *was* living in an artist's community. The thought was a bellows to his chest. But his guitar case wouldn't allow him to swagger.

He swung the case to his right hand, feeling boyish and strong. Life was—even as he recognized the cliché—full of possibilities. Was there any other way to say it? Well, yes. If you were a writer like Mike, you could come up with something original. Something about hope and absurdity, and the way they sometimes meshed. But he shouldn't get ahead of himself. Hung up on wish fulfillment, as his uncle Terry would say.

Terry, the fence contractor, living now in Indiana. Alan had visited him once, and once was enough. Too much corn and too many cattle, with a high point of 1,251 feet. That was flatter than Kansas. Then he'd made a two-day stop in L.A. to visit an old high school friend. He hated the congestion. Returning to Alaska, the mountains had been more than a homecoming—he'd felt like he'd been given back a lung.

And now he felt like he had a *third* lung. Could a woman really do this to you? She was even letting him stay with her! Maybe the living arrangement was temporary, but the reception was more than he'd expected. He was going to get that dog he'd mentioned to Carolyn, and the pet would be the glue holding Dehlia close to him. The dog would strengthen their bond, and in caring for it they would care more for each other. Even Mike's dire predictions about Fly Creek couldn't subdue his elation. The price of gold—what of it? The mine was a long way from becoming a reality. There would be plenty of time to fight it, and Patricia was getting a head start, with her research and letters to the editor. People in Whetstone would join forces. His sister's livelihood would be saved. His only immediate worry was Carolyn's grant. He couldn't stomach being on Ziggurat's payroll, even indirectly. But if the deadline wasn't until the end of December, Carolyn wouldn't be notified for months. That was how those things usually worked. He had more time than he'd thought.

5

A week passed. Between kisses and caresses, foolery and frolic, Dehlia carried out the mundane but necessary tasks, bringing to cooking and cleaning and hauling wood a new alacrity. She knew it wouldn't last, knew the two of them were conducting themselves like adolescents, but she gleefully allowed herself the indulgence. He was charming. He was sincere. He had fabulous hair. Of course there was the scar on his chin under his beard, where he'd hit a rock when plunging too enthusiastically into a river as a teen. He said his friends had warned him but he'd dived anyway.

Alan split firewood and the woodpile grew. He sanded the kitchen window that stuck against the tight jamb, oiled the squeaky cabinet hinge, and realigned the cockeyed door. He fixed the latch on the oven and cleaned the chimney. She finished the graphs, and he praised her on their neat and colorful execution. Now Carolyn would have a real visual.

In the evenings, sipping her Chardonnay, she learned about his family. He missed his parents, but in their late sixties they were healthy and independent, still enjoying life on their thirty-acre farm. When she listened to his tales of cleaning the chicken coop or taking slop to the pigs, it was clear that he disliked the jobs not in themselves, but because he had a better place to return—a home where love was not weighed against a lack of perfect harmony.

He missed his sister, a commercial fisherman in Dillingham. He missed his nieces. And he was concerned for their welfare. Sarah had married the wrong guy—Alan refused to even say his name. He'd gotten into drugs, started running with the wrong crowd, and hadn't sent Sarah a dime since the divorce. But she was the independent type. She wouldn't accept money or favors. She was going to make it on her own.

THE SUNDAY BEFORE THANKSGIVING Alan sat at Dehlia's table chopping almonds for the cookies he was going to bake. The sound of his paring knife fell like a muted accent against the thwack of her adze. A loud rap silenced their rhythm. Who could be calling? When Dehlia opened the door, she was as surprised to see Dan Broderman as he was to see Alan behind her.

"Ah, company, is it?" Dan held forth a small package wrapped in foil. "A gift for you. A pumpkin roll, recipe compliments of my late mother."

"How sweet." She set the package on the table.

"Indeed, and is therefore fittingly presented to a sweet lady."

She blushed. Alan watched, taking in every word.

"And with this delicacy comes an entreaty: that you join me in commemoration of the great Plymouth Colony harvest of 1621. The turkey is biding time in the freezer."

"Oh, Dan," Dehlia said, "I haven't given Thanksgiving a thought—" *Wait, that wasn't the right thing to say. What would Alan think?* Dan had caught her off guard. She hadn't been expecting a visit, much less a Thanksgiving invitation. She nudged Dan back on the porch and shut the door behind her.

"And now you may. Thursday is the day." Dan crossed his arms.

"Yes, I know it's this week, but—"

"It would be a most grievous injury should you decline." Dan placed his hand on his heart. "Your dear friend Barbara has received the same invitation."

Barbara! Not once had she thought of Barbara in the past weeks, nor had she seen her since the Halloween party. She knew what Dan was thinking. *How important are your friends to you? Have you no loyalty?* And there was something else: if she declined, would Dan talk to Carolyn about her contract? Would Carolyn then pressure her to support the mine? "Okay, I'll come." Even as she said it she felt her reluctance.

Dan smiled broadly and bowed. "I look forward to the occasion. The meal will be served at two post meridiem, or two of the clock, as we once said."

WHEN SHE RE-ENTERED the room she moved quickly back to her

carving. She didn't know how to tell Alan. Perhaps there was an angle, a way to deliver the news.

Out of the corner of her eye she watched him watching her. She feared this suddenly, their first test. Then he laid down his knife beside the almonds and stood before her, hands in his front pockets.

"What's wrong?" he asked.

"Nothing." She chipped at the wood. Here was bas relief, the long curve of the swan's neck. Untextured background, no detail yet on the breast. She flipped the mask over and worked on hollowing out the back.

"The last I heard he was inviting you to Thanksgiving dinner."

"Yes."

"You're not going, are you?"

She chipped some more.

"Stop it."

"Stop what?"

"Stop working and talk to me!" His voice was a cat's wild claw. But then he gently removed the block of wood from her lap and the adze from her grasp, and set them on the floor. He knelt. "I'm sorry." His hands were on her knees. "I thought we'd spend Thanksgiving together."

"I intended to... but he told me Barbara... was coming too. I haven't seen her in a long time, and she's... alone." She felt a sudden resentment toward language, its ineffectual and harsh salve.

Alan's jaw worked. "So he'll stoop to anything. He probably hasn't even talked to Barbara. That Don Juan of a bottom fish is laying a guilt trip on you. Must have some serious designs."

"What do you mean?"

"It's pretty clear what he's interested in. One word: you."

"Alan, I've known Dan for twenty years. He's a friend."

He stood. "Yeah," he said. "No doubt that's exactly what he's thinking."

She stared at the chips on the floor as if she could will them to reconfigure themselves and become again part of the wood, forming one, indivisible mass.

Alan ran a hand through his hair and paced the room. "How can you stand that guy? 'That you join me for the great Plymouth Colony harvest of 1621.' Why doesn't he just say fucking Thanksgiving? No one talks like that."

"Dan does."

"And that 'sweet' drivel."

She pulled on her boots.

"Where are you going?"

"To get some firewood."

"So you're through talking? Just like that?"

"They're my friends," she said.

BY EVENING ALAN RELENTED, again apologizing. He suggested that he spend a few days at Mike's. He couldn't stay at her place while she was having Thanksgiving with someone else. Yes, she agreed, that would be a good idea. She blamed herself for not having made better plans. *Better?* She laughed. She meant *any* plans. Here was an idea: what if they had their own pre-Christmas celebration in a few weeks? Barbara and Mike could come, and a few others.

She'd gotten through this without telling Alan the whole story. But she hadn't been fair to him, and she knew it.

6

Thanksgiving Day a Chinook wind moved in, its warm, moist air raising the temperature to forty degrees. It felt like April. But the slow-footed sun, which finally topped the mountain peaks sometime after 9 a.m., only to be blocked by clouds, still induced somnolence.

Alan lay in bed reading. The book, a survival story about two men lost in the Canadian arctic, was a distraction from the melancholy that roamed his room like a black ghost, watching for weakness, threatening to wrap him in its arms. More than once he'd made a willful decision to refuse the embrace. When he lost the narrative, he stubbornly went back and reread the last passage.

Mike's sharp knock gave him a jolt. "Gobble, gobble."

Alan dropped his book. "Yeah."

"Pie crusts are calling."

He forced himself out of bed. He'd agreed to make the pies for this very reason: it would at least get him moving. Anything was better than lying prone. Even if the mind lacked enthusiasm, at least the body would be busy. Alan thumped his abdomen—still surprisingly solid—and reminded himself that he had to think about maintaining muscle tone.

Not that today would help firm up any flab. Thanksgiving was all about excess: greasy turkey, spuds and gravy, buttery rolls, and booze. Why were they having turkey anyway? They should be eating spruce grouse or black bear, something local, wild, and lean. Why stick to tradition when tradition made no sense? The accompanying vegetable usually did little to offset the surfeit. Yet Alan was only against it in theory. He loved the indulgence as much as the next person. Today he and Mike would be wallowing at Dale's trough. Patricia and Allie were in Anchorage, visiting family. But Indigo and Indi would be there, along with Billy Barr. Suddenly Alan was looking forward to the company.

When he left his room he saw that Mike had already laid out the canned pumpkin and the last of the fresh eggs. Alan rolled up his sleeves and got to work.

Alan and Mike were the last to arrive at Dale's. The first shock for Alan was to find Barbara there, assuming the role of hostess. He flushed with anger at Dan Broderman. This could ruin his whole day. He entered the kitchen unhappily.

Barbara took the pies and handed them each a Bloody Mary. "You have some catching up to do, boys," she said. Mike tested his drink and asked for more Tabasco.

From across the room Billy Barr heard Mike's request, and he swaggered over and slapped Mike on the back. Billy grinned. "You like it hot too."

Mike grinned back. "Yep."

Billy's drink was half gone, but he reached for the Tabasco and added a healthy splash. They clinked glasses and sipped.

Alan welcomed the liquor. Barbara had mixed in plenty of vodka and it soothed the tight spot in his chest. He had to ask. He pulled her to one side. "I thought you were having Thanksgiving with Dehlia and Dan Broderman."

"Dan? You're kidding, right? I can take about twenty minutes of that guy."

"No shit," said Alan. But he decided at that moment to say nothing to Dehlia. He'd made his point; now she would see for herself that Broderman was an all-out liar.

In the living room, Indigo and Indi sat on a couch shielding their poker hands from Dale. Dale picked up a card and then laid down a flush.

Indigo stood and shook hands with Mike. He gave Alan a thump on the chest, the striking tone of his dark arm gleaming against his yellow, short-sleeved shirt. "It's the window repairman. The bear-proofer. How're ya doin', bro?"

Alan relaxed completely. "Good." He nodded to Indi and she smiled back sweetly.

Billy and Barbara enlarged the circle. "Turkey's almost done," said Barbara.

"Wish we had some whale meat," said Billy.

"Yeah," said Alan. "But then Dale wouldn't know how to cook it."

"True," said Dale, laughing.

Barbara placed the Tabasco on an end table. "Mike and Billy have a competition going. I just hope they don't get indigestion before dinner."

Dale reached over and picked up the bottle. "Maybe this stuff would work on bears. You train the animal to avoid human food by dousing it with pepper."

Mike scoffed. "My understanding is that bears actually relish hot stuff. Isn't that the joke about pepper spray? The bears are *attracted* to it."

"Yikes," said Indi. "That's what I carry for bear protection."

"I've heard they like it on steak but not salmon," said Alan. He was feeling more jovial all the time.

"Some claim it works if you're two feet from the bear, not downwind, and you're not too terrified to pray," said Barbara.

Alan looked at Indigo. "Any sign of that bear since I was at your place?"

"Nuh-uh. Not even a toe print."

"Oh honey, bears don't have toes, they have claws," said Indi.

"Oh, oh, oh, they do have toes. And I'm sayin' this one has fingers too. You saw that window." He looked at Alan for confirmation. Alan only smiled, and Indigo added, "I say we have a *special* bear. Half-man, half-bear."

There was laughter then, and talk of centaurs, minotaurs, and satyrs, but Billy grew solemn. "I seen a polar bear once used to be human. Everybody in my village know the story. The guy done something bad. He turn himself into a bear so he can come back and make corrections."

"Why did he have to turn into a bear?" asked Indi.

" 'Cause bears is really powerful. Really strong spirit."

"What did the man do wrong?"

"Long story. Maybe I tell you after we eat."

"So get this," Dale said, carving the turkey. "Speaking of bears, Ziggurat's hiring bear guards." Dale's ears were red from the liquor. Not Bloody Mary red, but red nonetheless. He looked like a sunburned bat.

The guests were at the table. Barbara set out casserole dishes, cranberry sauce, and a basket of rolls. Mike raised his eyebrows with feigned interest. "What are the qualifications? I could use a paying job."

"Eighteen or older, physically fit, firearm experience preferred."

"Yeah. I'd prefer it if my surgeon had experience with a scalpel," said Barbara, with a wink at Mike.

"But," said Mike, "I need to know if I'm supposed to protect the workers or the bears. If it's the bears, it sounds like the job for me."

Indigo and Indi exchanged puzzled looks. "I'm still trying to catch up," said Indi. "Who is Ziggurat?"

Over the course of the meal, while the seven of them emptied their third bottle of wine, Indigo and Indi were filled in on the mining project. Mike and Barbara did most of the talking, but Alan was proud of himself. He knew as much as they did and could do his share of explaining. When he got to the dead fish and the possible link to drilling, he turned to Billy.

"Tell them about the acid water," he said.

Billy waited, making sure they were all listening. "Dr. Sanders, she test the water. She put Dolly 'n Patricia on her team. Next summer, they test again."

Alan felt gratified. *See?* he wanted to tell Mike. *There'll be proof, soon enough.*

But Mike turned the conversation on an unsettling note: even if water samples had been taken, even though he and Alan had visited the mine site, much, much more was happening behind the scenes. Alan brooded on Mike's earlier words, from when the two of them had first heard news of Ziggurat on the radio. *In the dark. We plebeians always get left in the dark.* They didn't know the half of it.

"This town's going to have to decide what it stands for," said Mike. "Some of us are using artistic expression to make our opposition known. Like my story about this pick-and-shovel miner, Hiram. It's taking a weird turn. He's going to work for a big Zig-type company, but only so he can get assay records and alter them, devaluing the ore. The creepiest thing is, he's morphing physically, starting to look like our old patriarch, Blake Parsons. I'm convinced there's this force at work, dictating to us what to do."

Alan felt the others register the superstition then pass it off, attributing it to Mike's wine-and-vodka-induced imagination. Mike was quite drunk and enjoying courting the fringes of plausibility.

"Surely though, no one here supports an open-pit mine in their backyard?" Indi asked.

"At least four people do, that I know of," said Barbara. She pushed her plate away, empty but for a drumstick.

All eyes rested on her, waiting for more. "Greg Reynolds, for one," she said.

"Reynolds. Unbelievable," said Mike. He poked at a swatch of uneaten skin. "He's a photo-grabber. A disgrace to the arts."

"I wondered about that guy," said Alan, though he'd only spoken to him once. He was part of the know-crowd now.

"Who else?" asked Indi.

Alan held his breath. *Not Dehlia.*

"Amy." Barbara swirled the wine in her glass. "Bryce and Jen."

"Damn those jewelers," Mike said. Then, quietly, "I really like those people."

There was a long silence before Indi commented that it was certainly possible to *like* people without sharing their political views. She tilted her head and grew pensive. "But love, I'm not sure. Some people manage it, I just don't see how."

There was another silence. Then Barbara said, "Are we ready for dessert? I even have whipping cream."

Soon pie precluded politics, and Alan was thankful. He wasn't in the mood to run down the list of Whetstone residents and speculate on each one's leanings. Indi's statement troubled him: *It's certainly possible to like someone without sharing their political views. But love, I'm not sure.*

When they finished eating, Alan suggested they let Billy tell his bear story, and the party moved back to the comfortable chairs around the woodstove. Indi lay on the floor with her chin propped in both hands, eyes on the storyteller. Then Billy, in a low and secretive voice, began.

7

In the days that Alan was away, Dehlia did her best to focus on her work. Wasn't that, after all, what artists desired? Time to themselves, complete isolation, because no matter how well intended the roommate, there were always distractions—a question or comment, or just the minor things: the scrape of a chair, the opening of a cupboard, the search for the perfect spoon.

But what was the making of art itself if not a distraction from life? She'd heard it said that the most alienated artists, those who found it hardest to accept what is given, had the greatest artistic strength.

She laid down her crooked knife and wrapped the mask in plastic. Thinking too much about the whys and wherefores of art usually had a negative effect. One was better off just doing it. But the biggest distraction was the thought behind the thoughts: *He'll be returning today. He promised.*

He did come, late that afternoon. She hugged him and laughed and he shared Billy's story about the bear. This bear, he said, had once been a man. He'd come back to his village to make amends for a lie he'd told his father, the chief. As a man, he'd taken his father's favorite hunting knife without asking, and he'd lost it. When his father accused him of the theft, he'd denied it, suggesting that the father himself had mislaid it. But after a while, the son could no longer live with his lie. The village had not had fresh meat for a month, and people were on the verge of starvation. They blamed their chief. The son went on a trip, alone, and returned to the village as a polar bear. The bear came within easy hunting distance, and one of the men in the village shot it. The meat was divided among all, and no one died of hunger.

Her own story paled next to Alan's. Her Thanksgiving had been unexceptional. She told him the truth: it had been just as Alan had predicted. Barbara hadn't shown up after all. But maybe Dan really had invited her, or intended to. Maybe Barbara had simply declined.

And did it matter now? They were together. Alan agreed that the time apart had not been easy. Five days had seemed so long.

ON SUNDAY THEY walked to the beach. Much of the snow had melted on the trails, leaving the surface icy where people or machines had traveled before. When she could, Dehlia took Alan's arm to keep from slipping, but sometimes they were forced to move singly as they sought sure footing at the edges. Her ankle had healed, but she was cautious. After half a mile she insisted on going back for her cleats.

When they finally reached the beach she was relieved to find it exposed, the dry rocks providing good grip. The weather was balmy— no wind, and the sky a cornflower blue. Above the mountains, wisps of cirrus clouds were visible, innocuous as the marks of a lazy finger on a dusty shelf.

"What a day," said Alan. "Too warm though." He peeled off his jacket and tied the arms around his waist. "It's been in the thirties and forties all week."

"Alaska weather is so unpredictable."

"But isn't this *unusually* warm?"

"I don't know. I remember one time the lake didn't freeze at all."

"Mike mentioned that." Alan squatted down and dipped his hand in the water. "I don't think I'd want to go swimming though." He continued walking, but soon he stopped again. "If the water's too warm, it could be bad for the fish."

"Yes, I know." She wasn't about to tell him her source: Dan Broderman. "Even on a cold year," she said, "the lake doesn't freeze until late December. Because it's so deep."

"But there's a trend. The weather's warmer." He frowned and gave her a dark look. "Climate change is serious," said Alan. His voice carried a cold anger. "It's why we need alternative energy. We might even get solar power on a day like today."

"We could stop by Carolyn's and ask about the panels."

He turned his back to her and took a few steps away. He stood looking at the water for a long time. But when he turned around again his brows had smoothed. "On one condition." He lifted her chin and kissed her. "Okay, we can go now."

Why his sudden shift in mood? Was he that volatile, that mercurial?

There was another side to him: rash, unpredictable. And maybe unreliable. It made her fearful. *He'll be like so many others: his time here will be fleeting... I don't know him. I really don't know him at all. What if I fall in love?*

When they left the beach to angle back into the woods, it was nearly five o'clock. The sun, low on the horizon, had turned the color of a ripe persimmon. Surrounded now by near-black clouds, it looked both fierce and sad, as if protesting the inevitability of its descent.

The good news, when they reached Carolyn's, was that she had approved the alternative energy plan. Carolyn had been pleased with the graphs, and Dehlia felt a swell of pride. Alan nodded with satisfaction. He seemed eager to get the job done.

But he lingered, watching Amy and Ken, who leaned over Blake at the kitchen table, trying to snake in spoonfuls of mashed peas and pork. The dishtowel tucked inside Blake's collar was covered like a canvas with a green-white glue.

"He's making modern art," said Ken. "It's all about rejection."

Dehlia didn't find it funny. The whole scene was demoralizing. *Is this what becomes of us? Then we might as well die young.*

Carolyn motioned the caregivers away. "You two take a break."

Alan drew near the old man and looked directly into Blake's eyes. "What do you want? Salt?"

Dehlia watched. Did Alan have a special talent for working with disabled people? She saw nothing from Blake that resembled comprehension.

"He wants salt," said Alan.

Carolyn shrugged. "Unlikely." But she handed him the shaker from the cupboard.

Alan gently pried open Blake's mouth. With the first spoonful, Alan pushed the old man's chin back up. He repeated the down-up action until Blake swallowed. Alan scooped up another spoonful. Again Blake swallowed, and again. Dehlia counted: ten swallows before the food dribbled back onto the towel.

"He's finished," said Alan.

"Incredible," said Carolyn. Her skeptical look had given way to wonder.

As they headed down Garnet in the fading light, Carolyn called after them.

"Derek's coming in next week if you need anything from town."

"No, we're fine," Dehlia called back. She turned to Alan. "Do *you* need anything? I should have asked."

"No, we're fine," he said, grinning.

We're fine. We. The two of us. They turned left and walked down the Inner Circle. When they got close to Zircon she slowed. "How did you know Blake wanted salt?" she asked belatedly.

"It was just a hunch. No, maybe he liked the fact that it was *me* feeding him. Like he was trying to tell me we're on the same team."

Dehlia stopped walking at the smaller trail head. What had been a light conversation lost its fluidity, like a paintbrush that she had neglected to clean and was hardening now with its loaded pigment. What was he implying by that—*we're on the same team?* Blake and Alan, not her and Alan. And if she wasn't on his "team," then what? Where did that leave her? She had to make her own decisions.

"Alan," she said, "maybe we shouldn't see each other so often…"

8

It was like she had hit him in the gut. Stunned, Alan turned and tried to meet her eyes, barren birch limbs a backdrop to her pretty face. "What do you mean?" he said. She looked away.

"I think we need to move more slowly." She paused. "Look, I lost my husband two years ago, and it's taken me a long time to get back on my feet. I need to feel truly independent before I can make a big commitment."

Alan listened with held breath. Was she going to give him the send-off? And already he'd signed for the dog...

"You need to be patient with me," she continued. "I'm not saying I want to end it all... I... I have very strong feelings for you. But I have some things I need to sort out in my own head."

He swallowed. He knew that what he said next could explode like a hand grenade on everything they'd built, so he kept silent, giving her the lead and the chance to finish her thoughts.

When she didn't elaborate he said cautiously, "So what do you propose?"

"Give me a few days to think about it," she said.

"Okay," Alan said. He didn't know whether to feel relief or despair. He kissed her lightly on the check and stood stupefied while she walked away.

So he was back at Mike's, waiting for her again, his yearning and dread all too familiar. And now he had other worries. The temperature was dropping: five degrees, zero, then ten below.

He placed his order for the solar installation. Carolyn wrote out the check and inserted it in the pre-addressed envelope, a thick, self-sealing mantle that swallowed money like a white whale. He sensed her misgivings. As for himself, he needed to complete his job as soon as the mounts and panels arrived. The weather was dictating urgency. The transport of materials was the easy part. But the colder it got, the more the ground would resemble concrete, and he had to put in four lengths of casement pipe to use as poles for the mounts. He remembered helping a friend once with a foundation in early October near Big Lake. It was brutally cold, even for Southcentral, and digging the footings meant they'd had to break through frozen soil. The first day they poured hot water over it. The second day they tried heating it with a weed burner but only succeeded in warming the top surface. Finally they'd resorted to pickaxes, iron to ice, their savage strokes chipping one walnut-size piece at a time. It was wretched work, and it taught Alan a lesson: don't try to dig frozen earth by hand. Wait until June or later, if the location was shaded. But June was too far away.

IT WAS MIKE who came up with the plan. Alan had just walked in the door with an armful of firewood when he presented it. "Use dynamite."

Alan set down his load and put his hands to his face. The frost slowly melted from his beard. "What're you talking about?"

"Your holes. For the pipes. Use dynamite."

Alan peeled off his heavy coat. "I've never touched the stuff."

"Talk to Stew McCoy. The boy's been around a long time."

Alan scratched his head. "Man, I don't know. Sounds dangerous."

Mike leaned against the counter. He crossed his legs, then his arms. All he needed was a Stetson and a pair of cowboy boots to complete the machismo image. "Dynamite's nothing more than a big firecracker," said Mike. "Stew can handle it."

"I'll let him do the handling, all right." But Alan's resistance was short lived. Why the hell not? He needed to talk to Stew about welding the pipe together anyway. What had seemed far-fetched suddenly seemed brilliant. This was his project, it was important, and he wanted it done *now*.

STEW LED THEM to one of his two sheds. The headlamp he wore cast a bright light into the darkness. They squeezed past a lawn mower, rolls of chicken wire, and buckets of sixteen-penny nails. They passed rows of shelves crowded with paints, lubricants, bolts, and replacement oil filters. At the very back Stew opened a low door that forced the three of them to duck their heads to gain entrance into a tiny addition with one window.

Stew pointed his headlamp at a trapdoor. "That's where I keep it. Wife don't want it in the house." He lifted the trap by its rope handle and climbed down a short ladder. Alan hesitated.

"C'mon down and close the door. Yer lettin' the heat out," said Stew.

Mike went first and Alan followed, sealing behind him the murky daylight that seeped through the one tiny window like weak tea.

The root cellar was crowded with the three of them, and there wasn't enough clearance to stand upright. The air felt amazingly dry. Stew's headlamp shone on a wooden case marked with military specs.

"You build this cellar just for your dynamite?" asked Mike.

"Nope. Back in my drinking days I kept my spirits here." Stew turned his light on a corner thermometer. "Thirty-six. That's what she averages, with a fluctuation of only three degrees. Good for dynamite. Helps keep it stable. That, and turning it." Stew's headlamp bored into Alan's eyes.

Alan looked down, avoiding the glare.

Stew unclasped the box. "There it is, made with gen-u-ine nitroglycerin. Can't get this stuff anymore. Military switched to TNT, Composition B, Tetryl, and such after '78. This here's from a last run. I look it over now and then and make sure nothin's leaking."

Alan peered into the box at the neatly stacked dull-red sticks, illuminated by Stew's light. Only eight inches in length, they looked harmless. But when Stew picked one out, Alan flinched.

"Compliments of Mr. Alfred Nobel."

"Nobel invented dynamite? Then what's with the Peace Prize?"

"Don't you know explosives are the way to reconciliation?" said Mike. "It's called, you know, *enforceable* peace. That's why they gave the prize to Yasser Arafat one year."

Alan punched Mike in the arm and laughed. "Enforceable peace."

"Yeah. Rather oxymoronic." In the eerie light and cramped space Mike's humor seemed suddenly macabre.

Stew held the stick by the thumbs and index fingers of both hands. He seemed to be testing it. "Can't store this much longer. Any explosives expert in his right mind would have set it off twenty-nine years ago."

Alan flinched again, but Stew set the stick back in place, satisfied. "Give me a week," said Stew. "Meantime, you can be working on your drill holes. Pile of sand's out back when you get to mixin' yer cement. And gravel for fill. Jus' take what you need."

Stew seemed to have a solution for everything. Alan left feeling optimistic. Then he stopped in to see Dehlia.

IT HAD BEEN only two days, but as soon as he entered her cabin he sensed a distance in her manner, a coolness in her greeting that put him on high alert. Even the room was cold. She didn't slide up to kiss him and stroke his hair, as she had done many times. She was at the far end of the room, sitting at her desk, and her "hello" was formal, as if she were speaking to a clerk at a shopping center. She wasn't carving, but she had a piece of paper and a pencil in front of her.

"What are you working on?" he asked off-handedly.

"Oh, nothing. Just some calculations. Financial stuff." She turned the paper over.

Alan had seen this reaction before, the way she could suddenly clam up and refuse to engage. He might as well plunge in. Whatever she was thinking would come out eventually, and better sooner than later. "Last time we talked, you said you had some things to sort out. Did you do that? Where do we stand?" His chest heaved, but now it was in the open.

She looked at the wall where a rectangle of lighter wood indicated that a photograph had once hung. "This is hard for me, but I think we should back off a little, see each other... say, three days on, three days off."

Alan frowned and closed his eyes, trying to imagine this scenario. When he opened them again he saw by her tightened mouth that she meant it. He said, "That sounds complicated."

"Not really. You spend three days at Mike's and three days with me."

He hesitated, and she picked up the pencil and drummed the tip on her desk. Then she said, "Yes or no."

No could only mean one thing. Their foundation would crumble before the walls could be built. "Okay," he said. "Sounds like an ultimatum." He started to leave, but he walked up to her and kissed the top of her head. "I'm not thrilled, but we'll try it for a while. I'll be back in three days." Then he was out the door.

9

Admittedly, she felt a touch of guilt at her pronouncement. But also that she'd gained an edge. She would be calling the shots, not Alan. He had accepted the arrangement, at least on the surface. Yet her sense of empowerment was bittersweet. When he was away she missed his physical presence, his impulsiveness, and his singing voice when he played his guitar. She should ask him to play more often. Music was a joiner, never a divider between them. And somehow the ache that came from his absence would richen their time together, she was certain of it.

Now it was almost Christmas. Last year Dehlia had skipped decorating altogether. Alone, the holiday was dispiriting. But this year she was rejuvenated. She loved the colorful balls and the handmade ornaments: snowshoes, a miniature sled, a Super Cub, mittens, and a wool cap—clever gifts from clever friends. She hung them now from strings looped through cracks in the loft boards.

"I want to make something new. Any ideas?" Her question was only half-directed at Alan. He was preoccupied, hunched over the table writing Christmas greetings and sealing the cards in envelopes.

He set down his pen and leaned back in his chair. "How about a dog? Not a Jack Russell or Pomeranian. A real dog, like a husky."

She smiled. At least his dig at Waggy had a humorous slant. She moved her stepladder and stood with one foot on the lower rung. Sometimes creating should just be *fun*. Whimsical.

Alan went back to his writing.

"I could carve a gold pan. With a broken pick and a bent shovel."

He didn't reply.

She shouldn't bother him, he was busy. Guys didn't get too excited about Christmas decorations anyway. She hung more ornaments: an outboard motor and a fat red squirrel. She'd just learned that squirrels ate, among other things, baby rabbits. So much for their cuteness.

Alan stopped writing and drummed his pen on the table. "I don't think mining is something we should be promoting."

"Promoting?" Perhaps she hadn't heard him correctly. Or maybe he was joking again. But he didn't seem to be. Apparently he'd missed *her* humorous spin.

"Okay, maybe that's over the top," he said. "Still. I don't like what gold pans represent."

"Panning is an Alaska tradition." It was all she could think of to say.

"Just because it's a tradition doesn't make it right. People start out panning, next thing you know they're digging open-pit mines." He licked an envelope and sealed it.

Why this stretch of logic? Was he baiting her? He hadn't yet broached the topic of the mine, though she knew it was coming. Should she tell him about her land and her contract with Carolyn? Could she trust him to keep a secret? But what if Carolyn supported the project, as Dan claimed? Where would that leave her then? Oh, it was all so complicated. She went upstairs to straighten one of the strings. She considered a retort: *I'm talking about Christmas ornaments.* But what did it matter? She let it go.

HE MADE HER a late breakfast: French toast and canned peaches, with slices of fried ham. She watched him prepare the meal, feeling pampered when he insisted on doing it alone.

She drenched her French toast with maple syrup. Alan leaned forward and kissed her sweetened lips. "Mmm... I'm glad you know how to cook," she said. "Maybe you can help me with the Christmas party. Who should we invite, besides Mike and Barbara? What about Dale and Patricia?"

"Yeah, maybe," he said. But that was all.

When they finished eating, he took her hand. He had something to show her. A surprise, he said. At the library.

"What kind of surprise?"

But Alan wouldn't say.

They bundled up for the walk. The cold was still fierce, and she wrapped her scarf around her face to protect it from the north wind. No snow had fallen since the warm spell, and two days of fog had adorned the trees with triangular thorns of frost. The frost fell gently now, twinkling in the wind. Beautiful as it was, the cold didn't invite lingering. She picked up her pace and Alan matched it.

Inside the library they stomped their feet in tandem. Dehlia shed her mittens and rubbed her hands together. On a cart overflowing with worn paperbacks, lying crosswise atop the spines, was a single hardback: *Geology, Economics, and the Law.* The book that Phil had borrowed. *Oh, good. Someone returned it.*

Darlene emerged from between two walls of books. In a heavy sweater and wool pants, her stocky frame looked as bulky as a bear's. "I'll be," she said. "It's so *wonderful* to see you two together."

Dehlia looked down, but Alan caught her eye. "It is wonderful, isn't it?"

"Well, you lovebirds just settle your wings over there by the woodstove while I get you some hot chocolate. I brought my big thermos today." Darlene disappeared and Dehlia shrugged. Did they say they wanted hot chocolate?

But when Darlene returned with two steaming mugs Dehlia reached out gratefully. "Thanks, Darlene. It's freezing out there."

"Nippy enough I have both stoves going." Darlene nodded to the Swedish oil stove in the corner. "Forecast's for snow though, so it should be warming up."

"Seriously? Snow?" Alan seemed worried. "I need to get those drill holes done."

"What brings you here?" Darlene asked.

"We need to use the Internet," said Alan.

"Fine. But no chocolate on the keys." Darlene scolded with an animated finger.

Dehlia followed Alan to a computer. They still wore their coats, and they wriggled against each other like hamsters in a nest.

"Close your eyes," he said.

She waited expectantly, listening to the click of the mouse and the crackling of the fire.

"Okay, open" said Alan, and she found herself staring at the face of a puppy on the screen. A cocker spaniel? A retriever?

"Hmm." Surely he didn't mean it as a gift? She liked dogs, but she didn't want one—especially a young one. Dogs had too much energy, they needed training and attention. A person became attached to them, then they died. "How old is it?" she asked.

"Five months."

"Male or female?"

"Female. They're not so territorial," said Alan.

She'd been stalling. "It looks like it would make a good companion for someone."

"You don't sound very excited." He took a sip of hot chocolate and clicked the mouse again. He read: "I'm delighted to have found a home with Mr. Alan Lamb of Whetstone Cove."

She shifted in her chair, careful not to spill her cup.

"Listen, it'll be my dog in terms of responsibility. But *our* dog in terms of companionship." He gave her a puzzled look. "I thought you'd be thrilled." He tossed off his chocolate and scooted back in his chair. "You'll see. You're gonna love this dog." He stood to go.

His hurt confused her. Maybe she should have handled it differently. Already she'd insisted on them spending less time together. He didn't need two disappointments in a row. You had to put yourself on the receiving end. "You're probably right," she said. "I just need to get used to the idea. Really. It will be fine."

He leaned into her and his breath fluttered against her cheek. Gently, he pulled her hair back from her ear. "I love you," he whispered. His lips brushed her earlobe.

Her blood raced and she felt stricken with a hot chill. But, oh it was fine. A fine exhilaration, a fine fright.

10

By the end of the first week of December Alan's drill holes were ready. The temperature had warmed into the twenties and the forecasted snow had come and gone, the two-inch accumulation posing no threat to his work. Light and granular, it was easily brushed aside. The pipe that Derek had flown in was waiting in the generator shed, ready for assembly. *So far so good.* It was two days before the scheduled blasting. Alan had made some swift calculations; no reason he couldn't complete the job by the end of the month. He'd have to hustle, but it could be done.

He was on his way to the post office when he ran into Amy. In ski pants and a Peruvian hat she looked sassy and smart—as well as hurried. Now that he thought about it, she always seemed rushed. She hailed him before he had a chance to speak. "Where're you headed?"

"Post office."

"Great. Can you take this outbound? Some's mine, some's Carolyn's." She held it out, a white-and-blue government mail bag marked STAMPED FOR SUCCESS.

He glanced at it warily. Handing mail off to other Whetstone residents was common practice, but she'd almost gotten him into trouble the last time she asked him a favor. No, that wasn't fair. Amy had just provided the opportunity. He'd snuck into Carolyn's office of his own volition. *Of his own volition with Blake's permission.*

"Sure." His leather glove brushed her knit one as he hooked the plastic handles with two fingers, feeling the heft of the contents nudge his thigh. He slipped off his fanny pack and knelt to unzip it.

Amy had already turned around. "I have a pie in the oven," she called back, and before he knew it she was gone.

Alan folded the edges of the mail bag and tried to stuff it in his fanny pack behind his bundle of Christmas cards, but its bulge was big as a polypore on an old birch. As he reached in to transfer some of the letters to the smaller pocket in front, he caught the address on one large envelope. He could feel his stomach sink. This was Alaska, the middle of winter. But he might as well have stepped into a pool of quicksand.

Damn his luck. Damn Amy. Damn Carolyn and her damn grant. He couldn't believe she'd waited this long to send it. Now he had to deliver the vile paper, act as her obsequious emissary. He glared at the envelope: Ziggurat, Inc., Community Development Project Grants. He grabbed the zipper pull and it hissed shut.

ALAN SQUEEZED INTO the tiny post office lobby and slid onto the corner bench. Surrounded by a legion of parcel post and priority mail packages, he barely had room to sit. He set his fanny pack on his lap.

Sheila was still sorting first class, her quick fingers well suited to the job. The government didn't know its luck, hiring a violinist as a postmaster. Her layered hair flew up and down like a sail catching wind. Dan Broderman stood at the counter, Patricia and Allie in line behind him. The girls waved, and Alan made a mental note to mention Dehlia's Christmas party to them. He leaned against the arm of the bench, trying not to focus on Dan's denim jacket and the blonde ponytail that reached halfway down his back. Dan didn't turn around, and Alan was thankful for the snub.

From behind the counter Sheila sang out, "Just a few more minutes. The mail plane was late today." Even hurried, she had news for Alan. "Friend of mine's flying through next week. He can bring your dog if you're still looking for a way to get her out here." She stuffed a packet in a mail slot.

"I appreciate it," said Alan, trying to sound like he meant it. The grant application leered at him from its cave of coarse fabric.

Alan adjusted his position. The lobby was so cramped that any overflow of parcels ended up on the outside deck. Worse, the door swung inward, and room had to be made for those coming or going. When Dolly Monroe opened the door, Patricia released Allie's hand. "Go play outside, sweet pea."

"Do I have to?"

Patricia turned her around and slapped her lightly on the bottom.

Alan scowled back at Allie's scowl as she headed out the door, and her attempt to suppress a smile ended in a pout.

Dolly wore a felt hat trimmed with red fox that gave her a regal appearance. "You were next," she said to Alan.

"No, you first," he said. Anything to delay handing over Carolyn's application. He saw it going through the postal chain of hands, saw his pride sliding down a tin shoot on the other end.

"I'm on standard now," Sheila said, still moving the mail like it was her last mission.

I could take the envelope home and not mail it. No one would know. Or I could mail it after the deadline, in January or February.

Abruptly, Sheila stopped. "What's *this*?" She held up a flyer from the mix she was sorting. The glossy color collage depicted a broad-leafed plant with a giant root system, five people in silhouette holding hands, and a salmon, like a slick muscle, in mid-air. "Leaping To New Heights—Ziggurat, Inc.," she read the bold white print.

Sheila brushed away a troublesome wisp of hair and began to read the back: "Our five core principles: One. The Fly Creek Mine will benefit *all* Alaskans. Two. Coexistence of healthy fish and valued natural resources is both possible and imperative. Three. Only the world's best science..."

Patricia stretched an arm past Dan. "Let me see that!" She snapped up the flyer. "Oh boy, the propaganda pumps are working overtime."

Dan turned and gave her a cold look. "I might remind you, Patricia Abbey, that you are in a public place." He turned back to Sheila. "And you, Ms. Grady, are a public servant."

Sheila darkened. "Oh? Well, guess what? *I don't care.* Let them fire me!" But she went back to sorting, her movements now those of a miller grinding stubborn grain. Alan sat in rigid and mute attention. *I could change the zip code. It would go to Whittier or White Mountain before it gets returned. By then it would be too late to resend it.*

Patricia was still studying the flyer. Then she slapped her knee and broke into laughter. "Wait, I get it! That's not a sockeye, it's a fish-farmed Atlantic salmon. And that plant's invasive kudzu, imported to reclaim the ground cover that's been blasted into a desert. And people are holding hands because they're so full of toxins they can't stand upright without help. God, I'm *so* naïve!" She thrust the flyer in front of Alan. "See?"

"Patricia, shut up." Dan spoke softly, like a hit man you could count on to deliver the corpse. This time he didn't turn to address her. Sheila took a step back.

"Don't tell me you're in favor of this project, Dan," said Patricia. "It's obscene. No one with a lick of sense thinks this is a good idea. Look, I'll take a vote right now, right here." She glared at Alan, Dolly, and Sheila, as if daring them to oppose her.

"I already made myself clear," said Sheila.

"I agree one hundred percent," said Dolly.

"I'm with you," said Alan. *Tampering with mail is a criminal offense. But I was wearing gloves when I handled the envelope. How could anything be traced to me?*

The air was so charged now that it seemed it could power a loudspeaker. But Dan's voice didn't crackle as he cut through it. "Give me my mail. Forget the standard."

Sheila thrust her hand into the open slot marked Broderman. She secured the bundle of letters with rubber bands and slapped it on the countertop. "You have a box outside."

Dan strode out, his blue eyes boring into Alan's on the way.

Patricia grabbed two fistfuls of her hair and groaned. She made an about-face. "Take my spot, Dolly. I need to talk some sense into Dan." She marched out the door.

From where he sat, Alan could hear Patricia take up her argument. "We have science on our side. Dr. Sanders sent water samples from where those fish died to a lab, and the chemicals found were the same ones Ziggurat used for test drilling! They're in some mixture that helps move the drill through the rock." Her voice rose, but already Dan was interrupting. With the two of them arguing, Alan could no longer make out their words. He felt suddenly valiant. Patricia needed support. *His* support. He stepped outside.

Dan was bent over a plastic sled, securing his parcel with bungee cords, while Patricia stood defiantly on the porch. "Do you know the hazards of open-pit mines? Would you like a list of projects gone wrong? Do you know the salaries of mining company executives?" She cited sources, authors, dates of publication. She'd obviously done her research, and she had an amazing memory. Clearly, she didn't need Alan's help.

Dan looked up. "If you want to see environmental destruction, go to Papua New Guinea. America's mining standards are the most stringent in the world."

"Well, they're not good *enough!*" shouted Patricia. "And the state of Alaska has *never* denied permits for a large mine!"

"It can be done responsibly," said Dan. He gripped the sled's rope and started out.

"No, Dan, that's the whole point! It *can't* be done responsibly!"

Dan cast one disparaging look backward. "Rave on, cat shit, somebody will cover you up."

Patricia spun around and went back in the post office, pulling the heavy door behind her.

ALAN SCANNED THE YARD. There was Allie, leaning against an old birch. She'd heard it all; the poor kid must be scared to death. When he reached her, he patted her on the head. "You're getting to be a big girl, aren't you? I bet you'll grow up to be tall like your dad."

Allie smiled at first, but then she kicked at the snow. "Why's Mommy so mad?"

He knelt on one knee and looked her in the eyes. "Your mom is a passionate woman. She's concerned about a great big project to get gold and copper out of the ground. It would make a great big hole—bigger than you can imagine. So a lot of poison could go into the rivers and lakes and kill the fish and you won't have any more salmon to eat. Your mom's trying to protect you. Like I said, she's a passionate woman."

Allie frowned. "What's bassionate?"

"It means you feel really strong about something. It means you love something enough to get mad and excited about it."

"Oh." She paused. "Why do they want to kill the fish?"

"Well, they don't *want* to kill the fish. It just happens when they do all the digging. What they really want is the gold and copper, because it's worth a lot of money. Billions and billions of dollars."

Allie stomped her foot. "Then I don't like money!"

He patted her once on the back. "Good girl. That's a very smart thing to say. Come on." He led her back to the porch.

Patricia came out, eyes still glittering, but she took her daughter in her arms and squeezed her tight.

"Mommy, you're hurting me."

"I'm sorry, sugar snap." Patricia turned to Alan. "Thanks for taking care of her."

He nodded, wanting to say more. He'd intended to mention Dehlia's Christmas party, but things hadn't gone as planned. Patricia was angry, and there was the envelope still in his pack... the party would have to wait. What excuse could he use to postpone it?

The best of all was his work—and it wasn't a total untruth.

11

In the heart of winter summer existed only in memory. So Dehlia gazed fondly at her jars of currant jelly and blueberry and strawberry jam—ruby and purple and cloudy rose.

It was the lack of color more than the cold that made the pre-solstice weeks difficult, and she cherished any bright thing that interrupted the monochromatic landscape: grosbeaks with their pink- or yellow-tinged heads and breasts, the scarlet-capped redpolls that sometimes visited her feeder; or the occasional magpie, flaunting blue-green iridescent wings.

No wonder bird nests were her favorite cookies.

She peeled back the wax paper from eight sticks of butter and laid them in a bowl. Sitting overnight at fifty degrees—"room temperature"—they were still hard. She placed the bowl near the woodstove and began chopping walnuts.

Quadrupling the recipe proved to be more work than she'd imagined, and by the time she finished with the nuts the butter was soft enough to cream. She added brown sugar and flour, stirring with a wooden spoon, switching hands when her muscles began to ache. Why had she never bought a mixer? And why hadn't she waited for Alan? She imagined his strong, sure arm working the dough. It would take him half the time. But he had a job, and she'd decided to make this hers. The party was set for the seventeenth.

WHEN HE ARRIVED THAT EVENING, she was spooning jelly into the pressed centers of the last cookies. Her apron was wanton with flour, and she had to lean forward to kiss him.

She watched him take in the array of delicately browned sweets.

"You've been busy," he said.

"Yes. And I was going to bake even more tomorrow." She wiped her brow.

He sat at the table and stared out the window. In the fading light his face looked gloomy, and grime decorated his temple. He'd put in a long day too.

"Did you see Patricia and Mike?"

Alan rubbed his eyes. "I didn't see Mike." He stood and crossed the room, filching a can of Moosehead from the corner of her studio. He sat again at the table.

She set a glass in front of him and went back to her cookies.

In one quick pour he emptied the beer then crushed the can between his palms. A few drops spilled on the table and he wiped them with his sleeve.

She topped off the last bird nest with a dollop of jelly.

"I didn't invite the Abbeys to the party," Alan said.

"Didn't invite them? What do you mean?"

"I've been thinking," he said, "that we should have the party after Christmas. I have too much to do. Tomorrow we'll be blasting. I'll need to dig out all the loose rock, help Stew weld the pipe, pour the cement. Mike said late December could get down to thirty below. I need to get this job done."

"Oh." She tried to hide her disappointment, but she knew it was evident in the way the syllable sank, like a shark-bitten buoy. She rehearsed her work: making the dough, forming the balls, pressing out the centers. Baking the cookies for eight minutes, then again pressing out the centers before the last ten minutes in the oven. Did he have any idea? She clamped her mouth and collected the crusty bowls and dirty measuring cups, road markers of her day's labor.

She felt sore—physically *and* emotionally—as she carried the steaming pot of water from the woodstove to the sink. Okay, his work was important. He was on the clock. But did a man's work take precedence? Not that baking was woman's work. It was just what she'd spent all day on. Surely he'd known for weeks how much he had to do. Why had he agreed to the party in the first place?

He emptied his glass in a few swallows. "Can I help you?"

His question seemed somehow trivial. She pulled on a pair of rubber gloves. Was he being derisive? "No, I'm fine."

"You always say that."

Her throat caught, dampening the heat from rising to her vocal chords. He'd blown a funneling breath on that dormant chunk of coal, and she had to arrest its eruption into fire. But she had this trick mastered. She softened the hard line of her mouth and dropped soiled pieces of silverware into the hot water one by one.

Alan persisted. "Why do you always say you're fine?"

"Because I am. It's not that much of a job," she said to the window. She looked down, not wanting to see her reflection.

"I'm not talking about washing the dishes."

"Whatever you're talking about, it doesn't matter. Whatever complaints I have are small in light of other things in the world."

"What other things?"

She sighed. *What other things. Isn't it obvious? Human suffering. Poverty, rape, murder, genocide. All the horrible things humanity is capable of. Where was this conversation going?*

His voice dropped. "What about this mine? Is that fine too? I need to know how you feel about it."

What did the mine have to do with their Christmas party? This talk was maddening. She plunged her hands back into the dishwater, taking a scrubber to a flour-caked bowl. "I haven't formed an opinion yet." She inverted the bowl and vigorously scoured the outside.

"What will it take before you do?"

"Alan, I'm tired!"

She heard his chair scrape across the wooden floor. Then he walked toward her holding out his empty glass. He nudged her to one side and rolled up his sleeves. "I'll wash, you rinse."

She inched to the left, furthering the space between them.

He washed his glass and handed it to her. She rinsed it briskly and set it in the drainer.

"I didn't mean to be so hard on you." He took in a long breath and his chest expanded. "It's just that a lot of things happened today."

And she learned the story of Dan and Patricia's confrontation as the stack of clean dishes slowly grew, until she had no alternative but to take out a dishtowel and begin drying them, placing each piece in its proper cupboard or drawer. Life, she thought, should be orderly like that.

12

He'd blown it. For all his resolve to ease into the discussion of the mine with her, he hadn't been able to hold back. He'd been opinionated and argumentative. It was his damn impatience again, intruding like an ogre with size fourteen feet. On the other hand, this wasn't the kind of thing that could afford deliberation and complacency, this was an issue that called for—Action! Opposition! He couldn't seem to pin Dehlia down. She seemed so... detached.

He remembered challenging his Buddhist friend about this. Miguel, whose calm demeanor drove Alan mad. Why would anyone try to "rise above" passion and desire? Wasn't passion what made people *human*? How could a person deny his very humanity? You're getting upset, Miguel had said. It's okay to get involved with causes, but you shouldn't concern yourself with outcomes. It makes you angry. Anger and hostility are what lead to war. *Well, maybe war isn't always bad,* Alan had retorted.

But he didn't want to war with Dehlia. He only wanted her to understand. He'd have to explain to her about Sarah, why he was so personally opposed to the mining prospect. How he had to look out for his kid sister. He loved Sarah, damn it. But he loved Dehlia too. He'd even told her so, though she had yet to reciprocate with those three most longed-for syllables. Sometimes he wanted to catch the I's and You's out of the air and hold them captive, saying, *Okay, now all I need is a four-letter word beginning with L and ending with E.* Wasn't that first night together enough? And in the weeks that followed, the kisses, the laughter... Instead, she seemed already on the verge of retreat, like one of those flowers that close up at night. It wouldn't take much for her complete withdrawal. He'd do better to take on the role of teacher, explaining his position one point at a time. He could do it. He'd done it with Allie. But Dehlia wasn't a child.

Above all, he was mad at himself. He'd chickened out. He'd mailed Carolyn's application after all.

THE DAY ALAN'S PUP arrived was the same day scheduled for the blasting. D-Day, as Mike had dubbed it, for detonation. Alan considered leaving the dog in the cabin but decided against it. She was new here; she shouldn't be left alone. Nor could he pass the dog off on Dehlia when he'd promised to care for her himself.

Already he was impressed with her. She was nice looking: the feathery fur around her legs and tail indicated a trace of Irish setter, but probably not enough to make her dumb. She had just the right amount of affection: when Alan petted her she licked him on the chin. She didn't slobber. On the trail, she seemed curious but didn't strain on the leash.

WHEN HE CAME TO the clear cut, Mike and Stew were pushing dirt over the drill holes. Wires leading away from them joined in a Y and ran over the cleared ground into the woods. Alan wished he could have seen the whole setup.

Alan pulled in his dog's leash. She sat down next to him, looking up and waiting dutifully.

Stew drew him aside. "This yer new pup? Good-looking pooch. You need to tie her up." Stew pointed to a spot a hundred yards away. "Jus' follow the wire. We're about ready."

At the wire's end Alan found the rack bar, a wooden box with a plunger-like handle. He wrapped the dog's leash around a stout birch. "You stay, okay? Good girl." He petted her and walked away. She whined softly but lay down.

"What did I miss?" he asked when he rejoined Mike and Stew.

"Split the paper on every stick, then wired up the detonator caps. In series," said Stew, "so they fire simultaneous. 'Bout all there is to it."

Mike finished filling the last hole. "We all set?"

Alan looked back at his dog, who was watching them intently. He nodded.

"Well, this ain't Congress. Let's quit fartin' and get the job done," said Stew.

"How long does the blast take once the stuff's detonated?" asked Mike.

"Not even seconds. Milliseconds."

"Can I set it off?"

Stew looked at Mike critically, as if he were eyeing a Wall Street executive who'd never set foot on a dirt path. "I'll do the firin'," he said. "It's gotta be done right the first time."

Mike rubbed his hands together gleefully. "One little detail," he said. "Is this *legal*?"

Stew guffawed. "Well, we skipped the BAT FARTS—Bureau of Alcohol, Tobacco, Firearms, and Explosives. Used to be, anyway, to get a federal explosives license, you had to prove three things. One, you're a good person. Two, you need it for professional reasons. Three, you have a safe place to store the explosives." Stew looked from Mike to Alan. "I figure we can answer them questions ourselves."

Mike wiped his nose with his sleeve. He put his hand to his mouth and pulled on his bottom lip, as if considering the requirements. Then he said. "Two and three are easy. But one, I don't know." He narrowed his eyes at Alan. "Are you a good person?"

Alan smirked. "If I say I am, I guess that makes it a fact."

"Then say it," said Mike.

He placed his hand on his heart. "I'm a good person."

"I'm a good person," Mike repeated. They looked at Stew.

"I'm a shit-eatin' bugger who steals pennies from eighty-year-ol' ladies."

"Sounds like we're good to go," said Mike, and he held out a clenched fist. Alan gave him a knuckle bump and Stew stood stoically, expressionless, his massive biceps pushing at the seams of his Carhartt jacket. "Okay, boys. To yer foxholes."

Alan rushed back to his puppy.

BEFORE STEW PUSHED the plunger on the rack bar, Alan wrapped an arm around his dog and leaned over her protectively. It was pure instinct, as if he were a father in some war-torn country holding his child, as overhead the whistle of falling bombs pierced the atmosphere then erupted in muffled booms. Or, if you could believe television—the dreadful silence, which meant that the planes had moved directly overhead, that the thunderous concussion of metal and concrete and surrounding earth was imminent and very probably fatal.

But when the explosion came, it was anticlimactic, a simple *thwuump thwuump* as first one then the other circle of dynamite discharged and the frozen ground heaved up at the center.

Was this what to expect if Ziggurat developed Fly Creek? Explosions so tame they might not even cause a frog to jump? Mere buckling, like a heavy man walking across a poorly supported plywood floor? A single tremor ran through the body of Alan's pup. That was all.

13

"Y ou look like Red Riding Hood." Barbara ushered Dehlia inside and quickly closed the door.

Dehlia unbuttoned her warm coat and unwrapped her red scarf from her head. Drawing back the cloth covering her basket, she handed over a plate of cookies. "Merry Christmas."

Barbara's eyes lit up. "Yum. Bird nests and Russian teacakes." Barbara kissed her on the cheek and popped a teacake in her own mouth.

"We were going to have a party," said Dehlia.

"Oh? Why the cancellation?"

"It's complicated."

"Oh well, I'm not doing anything for Christmas either."

The room was, in fact, hardly festive. There were no decorations, just a dozen cards lining the windowsills. Against the far wall leaned the usual stack of paintings, some complete, others works in progress. But the corner easel held a new canvas, the size of a large throw rug. In the upper third a mountain contrasted against a deep-blue sky, and at the bottom, matte board cutouts glued over a wash of violet-black outlined an upside-down pyramid. If Barbara meant to depict Lost Mountain she had distorted it, changing the ridge line, giving it more of a volcanic look, and moving it right down to the water for dramatic effect.

"What are you working on?"

Barbara stood tall and squared her shoulders. "I'm using mixed media and found objects." She pointed to the middle of her painting. "This is Lake Hélène." Lifting a piece of old gill net from the floor, she draped it, lead line intact, over the water. "It'll look like this when it's done. I'm calling it *The Marriage of Heaven and Hell*, after Blake."

"Blake?" *Blake, providing inspiration for Patricia, and maybe Julie, and now Barbara?*

"Not Blake Parsons. William Blake, the painter. I stole the title from him."

"An Egyptian theme?"

"You don't see it?"

Dehlia didn't.

"It's not a pyramid," said Barbara. "It's an upside-down ziggurat. Isn't that fascinating, how it looks like an open pit?"

As soon as Barbara said it, the resemblance was clear. Ziggurat. The Fly Creek Mine. There it was again. And she'd only come to share some holiday cheer. Ironically, it was the mine, with all its controversy, that had preempted her Christmas party. It was the reason she was delivering cookies in the first place. Dehlia turned. "I should get going."

Barbara laid a hand on her arm. "You're with me, right? Against the mine? Or should I say, pro-fish?"

"Has Carolyn said anything yet?"

"Not that I know of. Who cares what Carolyn thinks?"

Dehlia shrugged. She didn't dare tell Barbara. Her friend would gossip. Her best friend.

"Dehlia," said Barbara, "you need to get informed."

Dehlia moved to the door.

Barbara picked up another cookie, scrutinized it, then set it back down. Apparently willpower came with her new enterprise. Now that Dehlia thought about it, she seemed to have lost a few pounds.

"So how are things with Alan?" asked Barbara.

ON THE WAY to Dan Broderman's, Dehlia couldn't shake off Barbara's comment. It felt like a heavy stone had been sewn into the lining of her coat. *You need to get informed.* But what influence could she possibly have on the development project? These kinds of things were always decided by people more vocal and more powerful than she. And what good would her voice be in the multitude? A person could spend years protesting a thing like this and never win. Oh, what was the point of this kind of investment?

A whole life perhaps, devoted to a failed dream of reform. Or maybe you made a difference, but it could cost you your security, your home. It was easy for people here to make big, broad boasts about their opposition when they knew they'd be moving on, but if they were really committed to settling in Whetstone long term, then how outspoken would they be? Why should she join the fight when her own future was at stake? Or did she not care about the salmon, the environment, enough to fight for them? Did she love Alan enough to let him win her to his side? Did she love him at all? What, in God's forsaken name, was love?

DAN WASN'T HOME. She left his cookies on the doorstep, hoping no animals would discover them. No sense in leaving a note; he would figure out who'd dropped off the gift. Dan was many things. Stupid, however, was not one of them. Even if he didn't recognize whose hand was involved, he would study her tracks. She'd once seen him identify Phil's tracks by the tread of his boots, a level of perception that was unnerving.

Dehlia walked back down Quartz and turned left, following the Inner Circle. Crossing the bridge over the solidly frozen stream, she continued as far as Garnet. When she moved up the trail toward Julie's cabin she heard music, and she recognized the rich tones of Sheila's violin. In the forest and approaching dusk, the sounds were especially beautiful and sad, and she remembered the night she and Alan had huddled together, seeking each other's body heat beneath a thin blanket while listening to Patricia's CDs on separate headphones. Joined though they were, they had received the music independently. And she'd understood better than ever the truth of human isolation. You could be in full body contact, but your senses were still your own. It was impossible to ever see the world through another's eyes or hear it through another's ears.

14

After the blasting, Alan drove himself like a musher training for the Iditarod. The nights he spent with Dehlia he rose in the dark and dressed by feel so as not to wake her. He built the fire by headlamp and drank his coffee to the light of a waning moon, his puppy waiting eagerly at his feet. By the time he reached the work site, a muted glow was visible behind the mountains to the east; within the next hour the trees and generator shed were no longer nondescript blocks against the snow.

He spent the first day digging. The dynamite had worked well, breaking up in one explosion not only the surface soil but a layer of frozen clay that would have taken him weeks to muscle through.

When the holes were ready Stew came to lend a hand. They set the first lengths of pipe and poured concrete footings to hold them in place, putting Visqueen tents over the holes to expedite the curing process. They built forms up the sides of the pipes and poured in more concrete, encasing the pipe in a solid, immovable wall. Alan jury-rigged a tripod of spruce poles to hold the additional sections which Stew welded together, his precision remarkable as that of the finest seamstress. Two days after Christmas Alan topped off the holes with dirt, emptying the final shovelful with an exuberant "Fa-la-la!"

He whistled to his dog. She bounded over, tongue lolling, invigorated by her search for burrowing voles. He threw a stick as far as his tired arm allowed, and watched her slalom around the tree stumps to retrieve it. He petted her when she brought it back. "Good girl. Smart girl. I knew you were a good bet."

Bet. He liked the sound of that. But it was too short. *Betsy?* That had a nice ring. And so he named her at last.

ALMOST TO THE HOUR, as Alan turned from the job site and headed back to Mike's, he could feel the beginnings of an inhospitable cold seeking entry around his collar and the loose parts of his jacket. He tucked the cuffs of his gloves inside his sleeves and pressed his earmuffs closer to his head, wishing he'd brought a wool cap.

When he got to the cabin Mike was sitting near the woodstove reading by candlelight. Despite the decreased daylight, he'd been burning less propane.

Alan made a beeline for the stove and held his hands above the hot surface. "I finished up today. Good thing. It's cooling down fast out there." The heat was so welcome it made him long for a hot tub.

"Yeah," said Mike. "Barometer's climbing fast. Forecast's for strong high pressure over the next week or two." He closed his book.

Alan pocketed his earmuffs and watched the dim flame flicker, then right itself. "How can you see to read?"

"Poverty's improving my vision."

"You need a loan?" It wasn't the first time he'd made the offer.

"I'm not rationing pennies yet." Mike opened the door on the woodstove and tossed another log on the fire. Betsy leaned against Alan's leg.

"How's the writing?"

"The usual. One brilliant sentence for every nine months of suffering."

"You make it sound like pregnancy."

"Breech birth, sometimes."

Alan chuckled.

"When's the next D-Day?" asked Mike. D no longer stood for detonation. Now it was short for Dehlia, another of Mike's jokes.

"Tomorrow."

"How's that working out, going back and forth all the time?"

"All right, I guess." It wasn't really true. And it wasn't just the inconvenience of moving from one house to another. Alan would have preferred a more permanent living arrangement. "I don't know how long I can do this. I feel like I'm on a see-saw, you know?"

THE NEXT DAY at Dehlia's, Alan checked the thermometer almost hourly. The first night the temperature plummeted fifteen degrees;

the morning of the second night they woke to thirty below. He got up at 3 a.m. to stoke the fire and adjust the rug he'd shoved against the bottom of the door to arrest the cold air. Betsy stood stiffly and lay back down, curling into a tighter ball and tucking her nose under her tail. In the morning when they both got up, the kitchen window was lined with half an inch of frost. Dehlia looked past it and smiled.

Alan followed her gaze. A lone fox, fluffed fur making a sham of its true body size, sat near the garden, black-tipped ears in contrast to its red-gold body and white chest. Before long it pounced in the snow, front feet perfectly aligned, like the palms of a diver breaking water. Then it sat, working its jaws.

For hours they watched the fox perform this casual act of hunting voles. Satisfied at last, the fox yawned, curled its tail, and lay on top of its self-made pillow. Alan took Dehlia's hand. He felt like a teenager, caught up with her in this rare and intimate glimpse of the animal world, and he couldn't bear to break the spell. All was perfect if they limited their talk. The intoxication was worth it.

The next morning was three degrees colder. "I bet the lake is freezing up," whispered Dehlia. "Let's get dressed and take a look."

Over thermal underwear they tucked the bulky legs of wool pants into winter boots and struggled into thick sweaters and down coats. They slipped on facemasks under their hoods. Once their hands were covered with mittens, their padded fingertips neither received nor delivered touch, and unable to hear each other without shouting, they resigned themselves to a mute pilgrimage. It was like walking on the moon.

When they arrived at the lakeshore, rosettes of ice had already formed on the surface. Many were joined, but there remained patches of open water where a current or light wind kept the union at bay. Yet even as Alan watched, he could see the water succumbing to its altered state, no longer able to refuse the Siberian weather's steel grip. It was fascinating and surreal, this transformation, and he felt in it something of nature's disregard, a hard-hearted stare from an entity that did not care whether Alan Lamb lived or died, or whether his small human desires would ever be realized.

PART FOUR

Snowscape

1

There was no denying it: the toughest months in Alaska were November through January. That was why even longtime residents took vacations to Hawaii and Cancún during this time of low light and confinement. But in Whetstone, the dark months allowed the artists to concentrate on their work, to find reprieve from constant visitors. Dehlia was at her most productive, taking advantage of the cold and the lull to increase her output. Alan admired her dedication. Her art was bold, all confidence and affirmation. But did her art dictate her life? Was she resolved to stay here indefinitely, until age or sickness forced her to leave?

He had his own integrity to watch out for. The grant check to Carolyn was looming—she should have it in hand by April at the latest. Should he put in his resignation then? It wasn't so much that others might find out. Carolyn might never even disclose her funding. But he'd be wearing a dress of yellow feathers *if*, just *if*, he elected to stay. And how would he ever explain things to his sister? Somewhere down the road, he'd feel accountable.

So why not quit? What was keeping him? He knew the answer: Dehlia. He didn't want to leave without her. There was only one solution. He had to convince her how bad the mine would be if it was developed. Then she would follow him out.

His timing was far from perfect. They'd gone to bed after a late meal and she'd drifted to sleep. He turned on his back and stared into the darkness as he spoke. "Ziggurat's first plan was to use this lake for underwater tailings storage." This was the latest from Patricia.

"What?" Dehlia asked sleepily.

"They dropped that. Now they want to build a dam seven hundred feet high and four miles wide to retain the tailings pond.

It'll never hold. There'll be earthquakes, erosion, flooding."

She shifted but said nothing.

"You know how much power it'll take to operate this monster? More than it takes for the whole city of Anchorage." He waited. "Dehlia." He could hear her breathing. "Are you listening?" He sat up and switched on his headlamp, resting it at the foot of the bed where its light cast ghoulish shadows on the sheets. "They're holding up Red Dog as the model for Fly Creek. That mine's the biggest polluter in the U.S.!"

She was fully awake now. She edged into a sitting position, using her palms to creep backward until she leaned against the headrest.

"How does Ziggurat explain the dead fish floating down lake? It's been six months and we haven't had anything close to an answer! The chemicals they use for their drilling mix were in those water samples from that scientist, Dr. Lee Ann Sanders."

She curled a strand of hair behind one ear and drew up her knees.

Jesus, he'd been ranting. His voice dropped. "Can you take my side?" he asked weakly.

"Alan," she said, very low, "the more you push me, the more I'll resist."

"But you don't understand. My sister… she works so hard. She has a twenty-eight-foot boat but it's not paid off. She needs a bigger engine. She still owes money on her permit. When she started fishing, the price per pound was sixty-four cents. Since then it's been up and down, so she never knows what she'll make in a year. She has gas and crew and maintenance… let me put it this way. If we organized a march, flew to Karshekovski to protest, would you come?"

"I would support you if you wanted to go." She rested her hand on his arm, so gently, so tenderly, that his whole being relaxed and he melted into sleep.

BUT THE NEXT DAY he revisited her declaration. *I would support you if you wanted to go.* Was this good enough? Alan hefted the question in one hand then the other. He wished he could rid himself of it, toss it like a bowling ball into the gutter. But he saw it land with a thud at his feet and rest there, challenging him to pick it up and go for a clean strike.

Over the next weeks, as the weather warmed, the question lost its weight. It became a pebble, a small impediment, lodged in one corner of his brain. Less looming, less commanding, but more nagging, like a dull headache. *I would support you if you wanted to go... Was this good enough?*

Work didn't help. He was an onlooker, someone who saw the motions of his body but couldn't know his soul. Alan assembling aluminum frames for the solar panels, a wrench in one hand, the other ratcheting a nut... *Was this good enough?* Alan on a stepladder, clamping and bolting on the panels, then climbing down to admire his work... *Was this good enough?* Alan running copper wire from controller to battery bank... *Was this good enough?* Alan's final connection, when a ghostly February sun poked through a veil of stratus clouds and the meter read 3.5 amps... *Was this good enough?*

The argument with himself: *Yes, take what you can get. There's still time. No, compromise is defeat.*

Maybe she'll come around. Be patient with her. Be patient.

2

Maybe it was Alan's moodiness that made her gravitate toward the dog, or maybe it was simple affection. But Dehlia grew fond of Betsy. The puppy followed her everywhere. Not in that annoying, always-under-your-feet sort of way, but with a loyal, I'm-here-for-you-if-you-need-me, don't-let-life-get-you-down attentiveness. When the three of them were out walking, it was Dehlia who Betsy started off with, before her keen nose led her to explore side trails left by marten or hares. And the first time they set out on cross-country skis on the frozen lake, Betsy returned to Dehlia when called.

"I'm jealous," said Alan. "She's supposed to be my dog."

Dehlia worked her skis back and forth, assessing her glide. "She's just testing you to see how faithful you are."

He was wearing Phil's skis and boots. When she'd cleaned the closet, they'd somehow been left behind. She was glad now for her oversight. Oh, time was a strange phenomenon, that it could so alter one's perception. Seeing another man wearing Phil's things had once seemed unbearable. Now the orange-cuffed, black leather boots looked sharp on Alan's feet; the skis' green and purple chevrons were bright accents against the fresh snow. The gear had returned to life.

THEY SKIED TO the middle of the lake, where the mountains surrounded them like emblems of a past era, and the sun, in an open sky, governed with a benign and liberal shine. Lost Mountain glinted in the distance. In this snowscape nothing was urgent, and the faint swish of nylon pants and jackets was the only sound she heard.

Alan skied up behind her and pulled a camera from his fanny pack. He trained it on their faces. "Say feta." She removed their sunglasses, leaned into him, and smiled. When he put the camera away, she took his face in her hands and pulled him close. His lips were warm and full, his mustache a little wet. The kiss was long and tender, and when it ended he ran his finger down the length of her cheek. He squinted against the bright light. They replaced their sunglasses and skied on.

The quiet was interrupted with the *whump-whump-whump* of a helicopter. Alan spotted it first, and as the noise increased, the chopper's fire-red body grew more distinct. It flew overhead then made a wide sweep over Whetstone. When it headed back toward them, Alan scowled. The chopper circled twice more before disappearing to the west, the Z on its underside whiter than the glinting snow.

"Doing assessment, no doubt," said Alan. "Some Ziggurat P.R. guy looking for the wasteland he's been writing about. All this gorgeous scenery keeps getting in the way."

Their moment together faded as the helicopter droned away.

"That's a Ziggurat chopper," he said. "It's what they flew us in when we visited the site last September. You wouldn't believe how big that drilling area is. We were on this bluff, there was all this tundra— miles and miles of it—and ponds, and drill rigs. And our tour guide wouldn't answer half my questions."

Of course Dehlia had known about his tour. But it had been easy to think of the mine site as an abstraction—something far away in both time and place. Now, she visualized where Alan had stood. She saw his figure, and Mike's, minute against the vastness of the landscape.

I should tell him. I should tell him about my deal with Carolyn, how I'm positioned to get title to my land. How I need to think about my future. But he'll think it weak of me to look out for my own self-interest.

She skied ahead.

3

Alan sat at Mike's kitchen table, lost in a rare moment of reflection. The sun. It didn't get enough press. Why didn't newspapers run daily columns touting its virtues? Ninety-three million miles away, yet its rays took only eight minutes to arrive on Earth. And talk about simplicity! It was just a big ball of hydrogen, most abundant gas in the universe, fusing into energy. Fusion... something the world's best scientists hadn't really mastered. One hydrogen atom joining another to form helium, and *pow*, there was light and heat. But it was also why the sun would eventually burn out.

Of course, that was five billion years away. For now, here was this single heavenly body beaming down on a mass of water and rock, offering warmth for bodies, food for plants, and—this was the part Alan loved best—rays to activate his panels. *His* panels—of course he'd assumed ownership. But how could he not, watching the incoming amps climb to five, twelve, eighteen, then twenty-five, with the increasing daylight and clear skies? He even ordered a solar panel and battery for Dehlia's electric fence. She'd been using D-cells; a twelve-volt battery would last her years. He was as proud as a puffer defending its underwater realm.

Mike was more skeptical. "The sun can go into hiding anytime."

"Don't spoil my party, Trotter."

Mike shrugged. "Don't get too attached."

THE SUN DREW people out. Later that week, Dale and Patricia told Mike they'd be putting up ice.

"Tomorrow, 2 p.m.," Mike told Alan. "I said I'd help. You and Dehlia should come along."

Mike was the first one on the lake. He wore snowshoes, small bear paws that left oval prints in the powdery snow. Alan skied alongside

Dehlia, the two of them following Dale's four-wheeler tracks that pointed like a double-needled compass to the northeast corner of the bay. Betsy trotted nearby and Mike kept pace with a slow jog that quickly taxed his breathing. Soon Alan could make out the Abbeys, Dale appearing taller than ever in yellow rain gear and XTRATUFS.

Allie stomped down a circle in the snow. "C'mon over here," she called. "You can walk better."

"Aye-aye, cap'n." Alan saluted her and touched the bill of her wool cap. He kicked off his skis.

"Allie, don't be so bossy," said Patricia, unloading a chainsaw and a pair of ice tongs. Her lavish freckles had darkened. She turned to Dehlia. "I'm glad you could make it."

Alan watched Dehlia for signs of resentment. He hadn't known whether she'd even accept this invitation. Not since the aborted Christmas party had he mentioned Patricia. But Dehlia was her usual cordial self. That beautiful, impassive face. She simply would not allow herself to succumb to malice, viscid and poisonous as tar.

Mike took up the snow shovel and cleared a large area, and Dale roughed out a pattern of forty-eight squares. He started his chainsaw, using the loud mechanical beast to make the preliminary cuts, his tall frame bent awkwardly at the waist, while Patricia swept fine ice shards away from the work area with a broom.

Soon Dale finished and stretched his back, and Alan reached for the saw. Patricia took a turn, then Mike. The twenty-inch bar sank deeper into the ice. How thick was it? And what would keep the whole rectangle from caving in, pitching one of them headfirst into the frigid water? Alan reassessed their tools: shovel, chipper, ropes. Anything a person could cling to or that would serve to lasso a body.

Again Dale took up the saw. Within minutes spray shot up from the deepest cut, hosing his rain pants and jacket like artillery fire. He plunged the bar in to its hilt, carving out a wedge-shaped chunk on one end to serve as a ramp.

Dale cut loose the first block and bobbed it gently up and down until Patricia was able to grab it with the tongs. Now Dale used the chipper like a pry, and Mike rushed forth with the snow shovel to offer extra purchase. The three of them wrestled the chunk free and pulled it from the open hole, where it lay like a prize fish.

The next pieces came easier. Soon they were stacked like enormous dominoes on the surface and Patricia stood back, arms akimbo. "How awesome is that. Clean ice from clean water. You know how lucky we are?"

But Alan wasn't thinking of luck. Instead he found himself staring at the vacancy, stricken with a sudden premonition: a woman, lying prone in the gelid water, her long black hair spidering out in soft waves, covering a delicate ivory back. He stepped behind Dehlia and drew her away from the gaping hole, as if his crossed arms could protect her, now and forever, from harm.

4

Dehlia dipped her brush in the yellow paint and put the finishing touch on the swan's bill. Even with this bit of color the swan seemed sad, its neck hanging down like the stem of a wilted flower. Behind the neck peered a woman's face, in profile except for the two eyes. The portrait could be read several ways: side view, frontal view, two versions of the same person.

She liked the ambiguity. The best art didn't lock a viewer into one interpretation, but allowed for new entryways with each viewing. Next year she would tackle a more elaborate form—the transformation mask, or mask within a mask, conceived by tribes of the Northwest Coast. Her favorite was from the Queen Charlotte Islands, a depiction of the mythical thunderbird, whose great beak unhinged in three panels to reveal a human face within.

What would she carve for the exterior? A fish perhaps—she'd had dreams of salmon lately: the dilated pupils a cold entrance to some undiscovered world where only lidless creatures thrive. She was growing lukewarm to her subject matter. Why so many birds? Swans were of archetypal beauty, but she was weary of their stately look. She'd singled out the swan last September because of its monogamy, as if it could serve as a symbol of fidelity to her memory of Phil. Despite the effort, her life had moved on, and she with it.

Alan. Something had to give. No, *someone* had to give. What would become of them? Was it all up to her? What was she waiting for? She knew.

He came in early from work that evening. He'd hurt his hand. A slip of his drill motor was the culprit, the screw tip boring into the meaty flesh below his thumb. He unwrapped the dirty rag he'd used to stop the blood and showed her the puncture. It looked bad, but she deliberately kept calm and didn't allow her face to express concern.

"Stupid," was all he said.

"No, of course not. Accidents happen. Don't blame yourself." She rummaged through her first aid kit and pulled out a bottle of hydrogen peroxide and a sterile bandage. He held his hand over the sink while she rinsed the wound with the disinfectant, dried the skin around it, and wrapped the bandage with surgical tape. "Keep an eye on it. Make sure you keep it clean."

"You're incredible."

"It's nothing. Anyone could have done it."

"I like to pick my nurse." He moved closer and traced her collarbone. "You could have me full time if you wanted."

She closed her fingers over his wrist. "Not yet."

"Then when?"

"I don't know."

"What will it take before you do?"

"I just need to wait and see."

"See what?"

He was so persistent. "Okay, to see where Carolyn stands on this mine. Dan thinks she supports it," Dehlia said. She dropped his hand.

Alan chewed his lip. "Broderman? What does he know?"

She shrugged.

"Anyway, what if?" he asked, running a finger along his bandage.

"I have a contract. In a year and a half, I'll get title to my land. If Carolyn honors it." Damn. She hadn't meant to tell him, but now it was out. "You have to keep it a secret. Dan thinks she might break it if I oppose her."

"Oh," said Alan bitterly. "Broderman." He curled his lip.

"And I'm not supposed to tell anyone. There's a nondisclosure clause."

"Why? What was the point of that?"

She sighed. "Blake was afraid others might resent it if they didn't have the same option. Dan and I are the only ones here who signed. Then Blake changed his mind and decided for lease-only arrangements." She pressed her fingers against her eyelids and rubbed her temples. She was getting a headache. "Can we please drop this for now? You need to take care of your hand. Why don't you go lie down for a while? And we can pretend we never had this conversation."

5

Alan lay on Dehlia's bed and stared at the rough-cut ceiling boards. Every nail was hidden, but Alan knew how much time it took to pound each one in, not to mention to measure and cut the boards. To move ladders and put up trim. Trim, not just on the ceiling, but on the floors and walls and around the windows. It was the details that slowed down construction. A lot of work had been put into this place, no doubt about that. But how valuable was this house and property, or any house or property, compared to the relationship that he was hoping to keep building? At least she'd shared some of her concerns with him. Now he understood better what he was up against.

There was also Dan Broderman. The fact that Broderman would strike this kind of fear into Dehlia enraged him. But he couldn't tell her that Carolyn probably did, in fact, support the mine, because then he'd have to tell her about the grant and that his own income was tainted. It would be utterly humiliating. Plus, Broderman could well be right about this much: Carolyn might not honor Dehlia's contract. Hadn't Alan himself scoffed about contracts that day he met with Carolyn? *What good was a contract? They were broken all the time...*

He fell asleep and dreamed that he was beating up a dead man with his left fist, striking and striking a jaw that gaped at him with pearls of bloody saliva, and his hand was throbbing.

IN THE MORNING he unwrapped the bandage on his thumb and winced—the wound had begun to fester. He cursed himself for being so careless, but the damage was done. He didn't like the color of the pus, or the reddening and swelling of his flesh. If he so much as brushed his thumb on a surface, it throbbed. He could no longer wear a glove. Dehlia urged him to check with Carolyn—she might have antibiotics. She kept all different types on hand. Maybe Amy and Ken would know which ones to use. So he did.

"I can't risk not having a backup for Dad," said Carolyn. "You understand, with the bed sores and all. But you can catch a ride to Karshekovski with Derek tomorrow. There's a clinic there."

ALAN WAS THE sole passenger as the plane took off and angled south over the frozen lake. Derek fiddled with his new GPS that displayed a moving map of the view below. They flew low over several pressure cracks, one so large it had an open lead. The land along both shores, still covered in snow, was defined by nothing but blue-gray shadows. Out his window, in the distance, Alan could barely make out the village of Valatga. Derek continued on. Compared to Whetstone's vertical peaks, the mountains they passed were rolling hills, and the closer they came to their destination, the flatter the terrain. They approached an archipelago of islands and Derek told him to keep an eye out for freshwater seals. Not two minutes later, surrounding an oval pool of water, Alan spotted twelve harbor seals hauled out on the ice, their fat bodies like a wreath of elongated dark pears.

It was a half-hour flight. Even from the air, Alan could tell that Karshekovski, a mixed Native and white community, didn't have the feel of a typical village. The layout was more structured, the houses bigger, and many buildings looked like they'd been recently painted. Two paved streets defined the town square, with gravel roads weaving threads around the perimeter. A group of homes stood a few miles out of town—maybe the elite had their own hideaway.

Derek landed on a paved strip. The airport was substantial, K-Air handling enough cargo and passengers to keep six commuter planes going. A third of their business was the government mail contract, said Derek, another third local air freight and passengers. He didn't mention the rest to Alan, but that was easy—who else but Ziggurat. One of their red helicopters was parked on the tarmac.

Derek gave Alan keys to his red Toyota. "Clinic's to the north, on the main drag. They'll fix you up." He patted Alan on the back. "Meet me back here at five." Derek headed for an office whose sign read Fly Creek Consortium.

Alan wished to hell Derek wasn't working for Ziggurat. He liked the guy in spite of the fact. Partly it was their shared history, with just enough exchanges through the pickup and delivery of clients to make Alan feel a professional—and personal—affection for him. He watched him walk away and then made for the Toyota.

ALAN WAS SURPRISED at the ease with which he took to the wheel; it had been almost a year since he'd driven a car. He left the airport and turned onto Main Street, keeping the speedometer at twenty and reading storefront signs: Betty's Grocery, Bullets & Bagels, The Eatery. These were the old buildings, the four-by-eight sheets of siding dressed along the bottom with a black mold. The newer structures, brightly painted canary yellow or denim blue, included the post office, school, the state troopers', and a community hall.

The streets were nearly empty. That made sense—it was Friday, a school day, almost dead winter, and Ziggurat's drilling was shut down until spring. But didn't the company keep a skeleton crew going all year? Come to think of it, Cheryl, the tour guide, had mentioned ongoing monitoring at the mine site.

Alan passed an elder Native woman who smiled hello. He nodded and drove on, feeling self-conscious in his borrowed vehicle. He was a stranger here, and he'd left his driver's license at Mike's. Maybe the troopers would ticket him. What else did the law have to do in a town this size?

The clinic was the last building on the street. In the small waiting room lit with fluorescent lights there was no one at the desk. A message scrawled on a scrap of paper read, "Back in an hour." *An hour from when? Just my luck.* Should he walk to The Eatery for a cup of coffee? He decided to wait.

It was a boring forty minutes. He leafed through dated issues of *Time* and *Newsweek,* wondering when one-column articles had become the norm. He finally opted for *Redbook,* images of posed and pretty women being more appealing than profiles of politicians.

When the health aide showed up, she explained that she'd gone to order a pizza. The woman's name was Annie, and she looked to be part Yup'ik. She had a round, friendly face and perfect teeth, and her black hair was held back with a lime-green elastic band.

He showed her his thumb, and she pressed on it gently with a latex-gloved finger. "Does it hurt?"

He tried to be stoic. "Some." It hurt like hell.

"When did you do this?"

"About a week ago."

"You put anything on it?"

"Yeah. But now it's infected. Not sure how that happened in the middle of winter, but it did."

She pressed again on the wound. She seemed to be stalling. "I can put some ointment on it and wrap it with gauze."

"I can do that myself." He was beginning to feel exasperated. "I flew in from Whetstone. I need antibiotics."

"I'm sorry. I don't have the authority to write prescriptions."

"Well," Alan said irritably, "who does?"

"We could call Dr. Carr in Anchorage. He might write one over the phone," she said.

"Okay," said Alan, almost pleading.

THE DOCTOR WAS with a patient and would return the call. After half an hour Alan insisted that Annie try again. "It's the end of the week. If I don't get the prescription today, I'll have to fly to Anchorage."

She set aside her paperwork and picked up the phone again, but she couldn't get past the office assistant. Fifteen minutes later Alan said, "Can you call again? Say you want to talk to the nurse."

This time the assistant agreed to talk to the doctor. Alan waited. When the phone rang he jumped in his seat. But it was The Eatery, telling Annie her pizza was ready. "Let me get it," Alan said desperately. "If the doctor calls while you're gone, I won't get my prescription."

She hesitated, then handed him twenty dollars from her purse.

WHEN HE RETURNED, the doctor still hadn't called, and Annie insisted on sharing her pizza.

Alan picked off the cheese and pepperoni and left the sodden crust. The throbbing in his hand was getting to be so distracting that he tried to take his mind off it. "The town seems quiet. What's it like here during the summer?"

"Oh, much busier," she said. "Sometimes I need help at the

clinic. And everything is so much louder. The mining company has lots of helicopters and trucks and employees."

He found that an interesting order. "I bet they spend a lot of money. Business is probably booming."

"Oh yes. It's really changed here the last couple years. Everyone's rich now."

"Where does the crew stay?"

"They rent cabins on the other side of the street. The cabins used to belong to the summer fishing lodges. They got bought out."

Alan got the picture. He was reminded of Skagway, where representatives for big international jewelers had dropped from the sky in the depths of winter and offered ten-year leases on local buildings. Who could argue with million-dollar checks at a time when the little guys were scrimping nickels?

There wasn't much else to learn about the mining company. Most of what Annie had to say about Ziggurat he'd discovered months ago. He turned the conversation instead to her parents and grandparents, finding inspiration in details of the old life. A hard life, but rich in its own way. She told him how her grandmother used to run a dog team to deliver mail around the lake, all the way to Valatga. Travel by dog team was common then in the winter. At that time, people needed to put up fish not just for themselves but for their dogs. Her grandfather trapped hundreds of beaver, trading the pelts for matches and flour and salt. And he said that his own father remembered traveling in skin boats.

Alan wanted to hear more, but then the doctor called back. It was four o'clock. When Annie unlocked the cabinet that held the precious pills, Alan felt like he'd been given food after a week-long fast. Never was he so grateful to shell out twenty-five dollars. Even if it was to a company town. Already the throbbing in his thumb seemed to be lessening.

6

O f course Dehlia's battery that Alan had ordered for her was delivered while he was away. It came in a wooden crate stamped HAZMAT, with arrows on the sides pointing up. Derek had brought it on one of his supply runs, hopscotching from Karshekovski to Whetstone to Anchorage and back.

Stew hauled it from the airstrip to her house. "Where you wantin' this?" he asked.

"Oh, just inside the door." Dehlia didn't want to bother him with more transferring.

"She's heavy," said Stew, though he handled it as if it were the weight of a small turkey.

After he left she pried open the crate. She removed the packing material and set it on the floor beside her, wondering briefly at a damp circle on the brown paper. Probably water that had leaked in somehow. She cleared a spot in the closet where the battery would sit until next fall. It would be warm there and wouldn't lose much charge.

Lifting the battery by herself didn't seem like such a good idea. Stew's description of "heavy" was a sorry understatement. The seventy-pound load pitched her forward at the waist like a dinghy caught by a rogue wave.

She braced herself. Okay, she'd only been surprised at the weight. She could do this, she was strong enough. Again she heaved up on the plastic handle, this time using her thighs for a partial rest and stepping pigeon-toed across the room until she managed to plunk the battery on the closet floor. *God—what was in there?* She knew, of course—lead. What the devil did it weigh per pound? The table of elements, high school, physical science... the lower right corner...

Oh yes, lead. Pb, atomic number 82. How easily it all came back to her. Nothing like hands-on experience to jumpstart the memory bank. And nothing like wet spots on her jeans to induce a dry-mouthed panic. How did *that* get there—it couldn't be—it must be—acid.

She stripped off her pants, then ran to the kitchen and grabbed the pitcher. In the shower stall she poured water over her thighs, watching for signs of reddening. But her skin was fine, and when the pitcher was empty she dried her cold legs and dashed upstairs for a pair of sweats.

She felt foolish now, certain she'd overreacted. She washed her jeans with detergent, pulling them in and out of the water in a simulated agitation. Satisfied, she rinsed and hung them and returned to the battery with rags, baking soda, and a pair of rubber gloves.

She found the leaky cap. No telling how it had loosened. Perhaps a young clerk topping off the cells was distracted—a phone call, a disgruntled customer, a sharp "Hurry up" from his boss. So the battery went in the crate without a double-check to make sure it was ready to ship. But no harm done. She cleaned the surface and terminals, watching the soda bubble in reaction to the acid. It would be okay.

It wasn't until the next day that she discovered the holes in her jeans. Strange—she remembered Meredith once wearing jeans that looked just like these. Dehlia had thought Meredith was trying to be fashionable, succumbing to a younger generation trend. That was understandable. Middle-aged women often slipped and zipped into crazy clothing in the hopes of garnering attention. It wouldn't have been necessary; Meredith was hardly inadequate in the looks department.

Dehlia folded her jeans and tucked them in a bottom drawer, vowing not to mention anything to Alan. It was her lesson, one she wouldn't repeat. What would Barbara do in a situation like this? Not cower, not run to her man like a lost kitten. What man? Barbara was on her own. And Dehlia was half. On her own.

7

A three-day storm with thirty-knot east winds passed through in early March. It was a typical low for the area, one that nudged the mercury above freezing and blew much of the snow off the lake. The spruce lost their dazzling white caps, became Plain Janes in olive dress. That was fine with Alan. The sacrifice in beauty had a practical advantage: it was easier for woodcutting. No snow to chunk off the limbs with a gloved fist before edging in with his chainsaw, no flakes falling in around the collar then melting down the neck. And when the storm ended and the skies cleared, the temperature returned to twenty degrees. The lake's crusty surface made travel easy.

He was ready for some sweet bodily abuse. The antibiotics had worked their magic, and the planet's tilt was performing its own sorcery, ramping up his energy level to a new high. He fitted Betsy with an old harness borrowed from Stew. She waited eagerly while he and Dehlia loaded the plastic toboggan with gas, oil, chainsaw, axe, and a thermos of hot tea. Alan secured the load with bungee cords and clipped Betsy's harness to the sled's front line. Dehlia, ready to act as anchor if Betsy gained too much speed, wore a padded belt clipped to another line at the rear.

Alan led, calling out simple commands: hike, gee, haw. Betsy proved to be a fast learner. She'd gained almost twenty-five pounds in the last three months, almost doubling her weight. She was more muscular but only a foot or so taller, with traces still of a puppy's awkwardness. Once Betsy turned too quickly and Dehlia lost her balance and fell, laughing, onto the trail.

STEW WAS IN his yard fiddling with his portable generator. He pointed to Betsy. "You got a good machine right there. What you needing with a gas-mobile?"

Alan patted Betsy's head and unclipped her. "We'd need about five of her to haul wood."

"Yep. I gave up dog teams in the sixties. Soon as snowmachines came on the market. Good thing about gas-mobiles is you only have to feed 'em when you want 'em to work. I don't need all that heated handlegrip and adjustable backrest crap though."

They loaded their gear into the four-wheeler trailer while Stew gassed up the machine. Dehlia fired up the engine and Alan climbed on the seat behind her.

Stew scoffed. "Oh, did you hear? Derek's flying choppers for Ziggurat. One thing about traitors, they're always loyal to their wallets. No better'n dogs sniffing out garbage bins to see who left the best scraps." He looked at Betsy. "No offense."

Derek? Flying choppers for Ziggurat? The news left Alan's ears pounding. So that's what Derek had been up to these last months: moving from fixed-wing to helicopters. What would this mean for Whetstone? Who would replace Derek as the main pilot? He wanted to ask Stew more questions, but Dehlia put the four-wheeler in gear, Betsy running behind.

Out on the lake she drove across the bay, skirting the ice hole that Dale had marked with spruce boughs. The open water had long since refrozen, but Alan yelled to Betsy to stay back.

Dehlia stopped the four-wheeler and Alan jumped off. "Did you hear what Stew said about Derek?" he asked her.

"Yes."

"Yes? That's all?"

"People need to make a living. We don't know the circumstances. Maybe Carolyn doesn't pay him enough."

"He gets his hydraulics worked on free of charge."

"What do you mean?"

"Forget it. Just a dumb joke. Let's go cut wood."

They walked up an incline into a stand of birch with trunks the size of telephone poles. Older birches were in the area, some gnarled or leaning, tortuous trees that would be torture on the body to split. Ahead were several dead spruce. They would require more limbing, but standing dead trees were usually bone-dry and ready to burn.

He thumped one with his fist. "What do you think?"

"They look good," she said. "I'll get the saw."

He watched her walk to the beach and unload the toboggan. He admired her work ethic, her steady, unhurried pace. She was the kind of woman a guy could live with long term in a remote setting: not one to get frazzled when weather kept you indoors for days or you ran out of butter and eggs. In many ways, she was the perfect ballast for him.

THEY STARTED WITH two spruce, Alan felling them toward the lake. Dehlia limbed with the axe while he followed, sawing the trunks into twenty-inch lengths. He helped her drag the large, unwieldy boughs away from the work area, their brittle tips sweeping the snow like coarse brooms.

They worked nonstop. When they finished, Dehlia sat down on a round and poured a cup of tea. She took a few sips and handed it to him.

He sat across from her. Like him, she was dressed in work clothes: insulated jeans, a ratty shirt, and winter boots. Her hair, braided behind her back, gave her the appearance of a bob. With this and her cold-pink cheeks she could have passed for thirty.

"You look ravishing," said Alan.

"I'm sure," she said. But he could tell she was pleased.

He thumped his seat. "A little punky, but we'll get plenty of BTUs from it." He peeled off a swatch of bark. The inside was grooved, as if etched with rivulets of acid. Fat white grubs clung to the hollows. Alan squished one with his thumb. Bark beetles: more common now with temperatures rising. They'd killed the tree.

Alan swallowed his tea and studied her. "Let's get out of this town," he said suddenly. "Come with me. We won't have to worry about your land or Carolyn, or this wretched mine."

"I want my property," she said. She closed her eyes and sat with a meditative air, as if all worldly woes had fallen away and become absorbed into some uncharted ethersphere.

But what about me? Do you want me? he almost asked, but he was afraid of her answer.

8

Printed on pumpkin-orange paper, the notice on the post office bulletin board was impossible to miss:

Special Meeting—Friday, March 27, Art Building, 7 p.m.
Following a presentation, Fly Creek Consortium will answer questions on the proposed mine.

Dehlia read it, her heartbeat quickening. Then the door opened and a breath descended on the back of her neck. "Long time, Milady. The lapse hath made me lonely."

She stepped to the side and faced the intruder. "Dan."

He tipped his head. "Honored I am to be recognized."

She laughed, though it wasn't funny. "I've been busy."

Dan closed his eyes briefly and reopened them, their blue intensity suddenly unnerving. There was something chilling in his demeanor, and he was blocking her way.

Dehlia stared at the outbound mail clutched in her hand. *Say it's great to see you. Stand straight. Smile and say goodbye.* Still, Dan didn't move. She looked at her watch. "I have to meet Carolyn in a few minutes."

From behind the counter Sheila looked on with a frown, a NO FLY MINE button in bold red letters pinned to her collar.

"And when might I see you again? At the presentation, perhaps?" Dan tapped the notice on the bulletin board. "We need longtime residents to balance these mendacious proclamations floating around town."

Dehlia bit the inside of her lip. Too hard. She tucked her scarf inside her collar and buttoned the top button of her coat. Dan stepped aside, and she moved to the counter. She handed her letters to Sheila, whose frown had given way to a smirk.

"I hope," said Sheila, eyeing Dan, "to see you on the twenty-seventh, Dehlia. We need *rational* input from the community."

Dehlia could hear Dan and Sheila begin to argue the minute she closed the door. Her lip hurt. She washed down the metallic-tasting blood in her mouth with her own saliva.

SHE MADE A beeline for the storehouse, her empty backpack swinging from side to side. She tried not to think, or to think only about the items on her list, but she couldn't shake her lie. She had no appointment with Carolyn. It was just the first thing that had popped into her head. Dan had cornered her. She shouldn't feel guilty. Her lie was nothing—just a fib, really, and no one would be hurt by it.

She swung open the door to the big building, taking in the scent of dried grains. The dim surroundings offered a welcome refuge, her wool coat a perfect camouflage. But there was no one in the building.

Then she caught movement at the far end of the room. A large, bulky shape, bending, then straightening. "Hello, Dehlia." In the vast space, Carolyn's voice sounded with an eerie echo. "I'm filling bins. If you can't find something, I probably have it here."

Oh, did you hear? Derek's flying choppers for Ziggurat. Stew's words, folded and tucked away like clean linen, came back to her.

"Okay." Dehlia pulled out her list and went from bin to bin, scooping grains and beans, then recorded her weights in the log. She'd done this many times; it was all routine. When the items were in her backpack, she paused. Carolyn was still there.

Carolyn, do you support this mine? What if I don't?

Oh, yes I do, and I'm planning on selling some of my property to Ziggurat, including yours...

Carolyn hefted a burlap sack onto a flat cart. It looked to weigh fifty pounds.

"You look like you could use some help," said Dehlia.

Carolyn lugged another sack to the cart. She drew back, stalwart as a straight-backed ox, and waved Dehlia on. "No," she said. "I'm fine. Just fine."

"So long then." As Dehlia slipped out, she remembered Alan admonishing her for those very words: *I'm fine.* Next time she would look him in the eye. *See? I'm not the only one who says that.*

9

Alan rushed into Mike's house and kicked off his boots. "Did you hear about the presentation?" He'd spent the last three nights with Dehlia and he was anxious to talk about what to expect on the twenty-seventh.

"It's going to be a bloodbath." Mike made the pronouncement almost gleefully.

"Is that why you're looking for a .22? I saw your ad at the post office."

"As a matter of fact, I intend to use it as a grouse gun," Mike shot back. "But I won't have any grievances with the birds I'll be targeting." He seemed especially jovial.

"A little late in the season to start hunting."

"I'm planning ahead. For next fall."

"I thought you were leaving town."

"Plans change." Mike strolled—too casually, thought Alan—into his room. He came out with an envelope, holding it by one corner between his thumb and fourth finger. He dropped it on the tabletop from a careless height and Alan took a seat when it landed. *Ta-dum.*

Alan fished out the contents.

> Dear Mike Trotter,
> On behalf of the National Endowment for the Arts, I extend my sincere congratulations. I am pleased to inform you that you are one of forty-two recipients for this year's fiction fellowships. This is a highly competitive grant, and the panel was very impressed with the quality of your work sample. A check in the amount of $25,000...

"Fuckin' A!" Alan stood and slapped Mike a high-five. Then, "Aw, hell," he said. And he crushed Mike's chest in a bear hug. Mike returned it with one awkward arm around Alan's shoulder.

"It's not exactly a Guggenheim," said Mike, as Alan drew back. But Mike was grinning widely, glasses askew.

"This calls for a drink." Alan opened the cabinet that housed the hard liquor and pulled down a bottle of Jack Daniel's. He poured generous shots into two mugs and the men sat across from each other at the table.

He raised his cup. "To Trotter. Who just broke into a gallop."

They swallowed simultaneously.

"Man that's rotten at ten in the morning." Alan sucked in the sour aftertaste.

"Right now bilge water would taste good." Mike leaned toward the windowsill and grabbed one of Hiram's pieces of ore. He hefted it then set it on the table, where it assumed a symbolic presence, taking on the import of Mike's defining moment.

"Twenty-five K's a serious chunk of change," said Alan.

Mike grinned again. "Every little bit helps, said the old maid as she peed in the ocean."

"How will you spend it?"

"It'll be enough for me to live here another two years. I won't find rent this cheap anywhere else."

"Most people would squander it in six months."

"Yeah," Mike said. "Last time I checked, Alaska's poverty level was thirteen grand a year. Amazing how much you can stretch the cash out with all this salmon though."

Alan kept his mouth shut. This wasn't the time to talk about fish deaths.

They sat for a while, savoring Mike's good fortune. The sun filtered through a gauze of thin clouds, highlighting the dust particles floating in the still and dreamy air. Alan could feel the whiskey raising the possibilities to new heights, like a tower atop a five-story house. It was one of those moments that would replay itself for him in years to come: a feeling of brotherhood and a heady renewal of belief.

Mike talked about his book and outlined ideas for his next. He charted his lifetime expectations, the hurdles he had yet to overcome.

Alan simply listened. He didn't understand the convoluted world of agents and publishing, and it didn't seem fair that a writer of Mike's ability would have to work so hard.

Almost as quickly as the whiskey plied them with its dizzy optimism, the effects began to settle, the stimulant slowly losing ground to its depressive counterpart. It was a gradual annexing of spirit, at first almost imperceptible. Alan reached for the bottle to offer Mike another shot. But even as he did he knew that Mike would decline. Entering the kingdom of heaven was a onetime deal.

Suddenly Alan was ravenous. He leapt to his feet and rummaged through the cupboards.

"Look in the drawer," said Mike. "Jen baked me some bread."

Alan found the loaf and set it on the table with a jar of Dehlia's blueberry jam.

Mike sliced while Alan whipped up a pot of coffee and stirred the coals of a dying fire. He sat down with Mike to eat.

The food and caffeine had a sobering effect. Alan swallowed mouthful after mouthful of bread slathered with jam. He tapped the loaf. "Jen looks out for you, doesn't she?"

"Yeah," Mike said between chews. "I guess she does."

"Think she'll be there on the twenty-seventh?" Alan had forgotten how imperative the presentation had seemed when he'd first stepped inside.

"I'm sure she will. What about Dehlia?"

"I don't know. Sure as hell hope so." The thought of trying to convince her to attend made him weary. At least he and Mike were on the same plane.

Mike's eyes were looking brighter behind his black-rimmed lenses. "I'm interested in whether Derek will make an appearance. He's been passing out handouts from the Fly Creek Consortium."

"Jesus," said Alan. Why was Derek becoming a shill for Ziggurat? As if flying choppers for them wasn't enough—he had to spread their propaganda around as well.

"So he and Carolyn are both converts," Alan said without thinking.

Mike set his mouth, in that way he had, like he'd just chewed a bitter leaf. "Carolyn will come to her own conclusions, independent of Derek."

Not until later, when Alan was at the woodpile driving the axe head through a stubborn knot, did he question Mike's statement. How the hell did Mike know? *How do any of us know anything? We're all full of predictions and convictions, but when it comes down to it, we don't know shit from apple butter. We just feel peacocky when we occasionally get it right.*

10

Dehlia woke feeling a little off. How would she describe it? Not sick, but... cloudy. A suggestion of pressure at her temples, a hint of ill humor at the back of her sinuses. Slight though, very slight. It was probably nothing.

She lay on her back and looked at Alan. She often woke before he did; there'd been just a few weeks in December when he was putting in long hours, trying to beat the weather, that he'd been on an early morning schedule. Usually, if she slipped out of bed at six-thirty or seven, she could spend an hour or more sketching.

This morning she pulled the comforter up past her shoulders. Alan was sleeping on his stomach, a not uncommon position for him, and not the most flattering. In profile he looked almost aristocratic, with his straight nose and neatly bearded chin—the kind of man who would take a woman's elbow and steer her gently and confidently down the street. Except for the shock of hair that fell over his eyebrow—his hair the giveaway that this gentleman had a wild streak, was not predictable enough to be a full confidante. And straight on, there were his eyes: too penetrating, eyes that demanded answers rather than made an appeal for them. Then that hidden scar... what else was beneath the surface? They'd been together five months. Would they last another year and a half? He didn't like their arrangement, three days on, three off. Still, she wanted no firm commitment until her agreement with Carolyn was resolved.

He stirred and reached for her. She let him wrap his strong arm around her waist and draw her close. That feeling of safety would surely be fleeting.

She dozed and didn't wake again until nine. The bed was empty now. She dressed quickly and pulled on a turtleneck to keep off the chill.

Alan was downstairs in an easy chair with a notebook across his knees. He closed it as she walked past, but she noticed the heavily scribbled page as she hurried out the door, her bladder full after the long morning in bed.

When she returned, he greeted her with a cup of coffee. She sat listlessly on the couch, not drinking it. Would the cloudiness in her head grow heavier throughout the day? Could she be coming down with something?

His pencil moved dramatically across the page.

"You must be inspired," she said.

"It's not creative. I'm writing an opinion piece about the mine."

"I see."

Alan closed his notebook again. "You slept late."

"I hope I'm not getting sick." She picked at tiny balls of lint on the cushion cradled in her lap.

He shot her a look of alarm. "Maybe you should eat something." He lowered his voice. "You *look* fine."

An hour later she was certain that the faint cloud under which she'd awakened would promptly send down a steady drizzle. No wonder the expression "under the weather." There was no stopping it now. Breakfast hadn't helped. "Maybe you should go back to Mike's tonight," Dehlia said. "I don't want to pass it on to you."

Alan didn't reply at first. He moved to the nearby window. "You don't want to go to the presentation."

"What?"

"The mining company reps are coming tonight. It's March twenty-seventh, remember?"

"Yes, I know."

"So you're claiming you're sick."

"Alan, I *am* sick."

"Pretty convenient, isn't it?"

It was as if a flurry of barbs had just targeted her heart. She felt woozy. "That's a cold and mean thing to say. I didn't exactly plan it this way."

So this explained his earlier look of alarm. He wasn't concerned for her well-being—he just wanted to make sure she didn't miss the presentation. She blinked hard, keeping her tears in check.

Then his hand was on her shoulder. "I didn't mean that."

"You did."

He held her against him. "Listen, I'd really like you to come. But I'm not going to force you."

She drew away and grabbed a tissue. "I'll see how I feel." She wiped her eyes and blew her nose.

"Fair enough," he said. "I'm going to work now. I'll either see you there or I won't."

She nodded. Then, as if to prove a point, she sneezed twice.

"Can't you take Sudafed?" He reached for the door.

"It doesn't work for me. Anyway, I probably shouldn't expose everyone else."

"People get over colds. If this mine gets built, there'll be a health risk here for perpetuity. You know what that means. *Forever.*" His hand was on the knob.

Why did she suddenly think of marriage vows? *Forever. Until death do us part.*

He turned just before exiting. "I love you," he said. "In perpetuity."

She didn't meet his eyes. Only after the latch had clicked did she mouth the words "I love you too"—words that faded like a lost fragrance, adding another touch of injury to her overall malaise.

11

The art building was packed, but what Alan saw first were the sandwiches. He stared at the quarter-cut white bread and mayo-slathered tokens of friendship on the table. He hadn't eaten. Hungry as he was, they made him suspicious. They looked like deviled Spam.

Against the north wall three strangers were setting up a computer and display table, and behind them loomed Greg Reynolds's giant screen. Folding chairs had been set out, but there weren't enough seats; Dan Broderman and some others were standing. In front was Dehlia—Dehlia!—with an empty seat beside her. She must have reserved it for him. His skin tingled at her thoughtfulness. As he wove toward her he noticed Derek and Carolyn, and on her left lurked a gray-haired figure with a forward slump—who was that? Holy Christ, they'd brought Blake. The stricken patriarch seemed the size of a small child, sinking like a slack water tide in his wheelchair, his shriveled legs wrapped in a navy-blue quilt. There was no one to watch him, of course. There'd been no choice but to bring him along.

Alan stood before Dehlia. "Is this seat taken?"

She removed her coat from the seat back. In her hand lay a crumpled handkerchief.

One row back, between Dale and Allie, Patricia was scowling at a newspaper. Maybe she didn't like the way one of her letters had been edited. Looking up, she caught Alan's eye. He sat down, Indigo and Indi on his left.

He suddenly grew self-conscious. He'd worked late, and he could smell the diesel on his clothes. "Sorry I stink. Generator problems," he said to Indigo, who was seated next to him.

"I thought that was a new soap," said Indigo. "It's cool. Makes you smell like a *man*." He made a fist and the veins popped out on his inner wrist.

Alan leaned into Dehlia. "How're you feeling?"

220

"Terrible." She sniffed again and lifted her handkerchief to her nose. Her eyelids were red.

Damn. She was here for him, not because she wanted to be. He'd been too hard on her. "Why don't you go home?"

"I'm here now."

"Thanks for coming."

He scrutinized the presenters. A young woman in a tan blouse. A man with a crew cut, and a handsome Native youth. All were casually dressed, with slacks and pressed shirts for the men, ties conspicuously missing. No bright colors, no suits or sweats—professional but comfortable, noncommittal attire. It was probably calculated. As in, *We don't want to alienate you. Trust us.*

At the back, Sheila marched to the storage room and dragged out five more chairs, passing the last to Dan Broderman. Alan expected Dan to wave her off, make a public display of refusing a seat from his rival. Alan was glad he hadn't offered to help. He'd as soon stay out of Broderman's spitting distance.

The presenters set out two stacks of booklets: *Introduction to Mining* and *Mining Careers.* Alan grabbed a copy of each. The cover photo on the first was the Fort Knox Gold Mine near Fairbanks, an immense, barren cavity terraced with access roads—small ones, probably, for equipment like front-end loaders; larger ones, conceivably, for the big trucks piled with ore that made forays in and out of the pit. Alan flipped open the second booklet and gave it a speedy back-to-front perusal, landing on the introduction: *Mining creates long-term, high-paying, rewarding careers.*

The crew cut squared his shoulders and cleared his throat. He flashed an upper-tooth reveal of a smile and pressed his palms together. "My name is Rob." He gestured to the two beside him. "And Wayne and Cora. We're here on behalf of Ziggurat, Incorporated to share information about the proposed Fly Creek Mine. I've brought along a PowerPoint, so let me run through it and give you an overview."

He smiled again. "I need to clarify that this mine, if it's developed, would be primarily a copper mine. Gold and molybdenum are also in abundance at the site, but copper is the most valuable. With the surge in alternative energy, the demand for copper is extremely high."

"Try recycling," Alan muttered. "We'd be set for decades."

Rob turned on his computer and displayed a map of Southwest Alaska. A laser pointer circled the area of exploration.

"How many acres is that?" The question came from Stew, and it was not delivered kindly.

"The main site covers several square miles. We've also been doing some drilling to the east—"

"So how many acres, total?" barked Stew.

"We don't have those exact figures. According to our estimates—"

"It's twenty square miles," Patricia said, "plus a ten-square mile tailings pond that would hold billions of tons of waste. If this mine is developed it would be *fifteen times bigger than all the other mines in the state combined.*" She rose from her seat and turned to address the audience. "Not only that, now there's a London-based company backing Ziggurat. British Global Resources. Big, big money." She made a loud *thwump* as she sat back down.

Rob pulled up a timeline. "Stakeholder consultation is part of our process. We seek input from all who have invested in our company. We've committed eighteen million dollars toward environmental studies this year, doubling the amount we spent last year."

Sheila's hand shot up, but she didn't wait to be called on. "Who are your scientists? Are they handpicked by Ziggurat?"

"We have responsible teams of consultants looking at water quality, marine habitats, wildlife, fish, and aquatic resources." The rep fidgeted with the laser pointer.

"Anyone from National Resources Defense Council?"

"I'm not aware of any consultant hired from that particular organization."

"Figures." Alan could hear the sneer in her voice. "Tell us about the chemicals you use for drilling. Tell us about the dead fish."

"Maybe now would be a good time for us to say something about socioeconomic impacts." Rob stepped back, allowing the young man beside him center stage.

Wayne straightened his shoulders. "I grew up in the villages. I've seen many of our people succumb to the devastating effects of drugs and alcohol. The thing we need most is economic diversification. People need to feel pride, they need jobs that will keep them living and working in the places they grew up. Our best young men and women are moving to the city. This mine will create renewed hope for communities." Despite his village inflection, Alan could tell he'd been well coached.

"Where are you from?" asked Stew.

"I was born and raised in Unalakleet. Now I live in Karshekovski."

"How long you been in Karshekovski?"

"Two years."

Two years. In other words, since you've been employed by Ziggurat.

Cora slid next to Wayne and raised her chin. "Everything Wayne says is true. Alaska suffers from a lack of economic growth. We need incentives; we need to keep people employed. As a lifelong resident of this state, I support this mine."

"A lifelong Alaskan? Shame on you!" Stew's outburst made Alan jump. There was a moment of shocked silence, then several people in the audience chuckled.

Patricia stood, holding the *Introduction to Mining* booklet high above her head. "How can you people consider putting this"—she tapped the cover photo of the open pit and flung the booklet aside, then gestured to the window—"in place of this?" Everyone turned to look at the landscape, surrendering to the view of Lost Mountain rising just above the trees. Patricia had picked a perfect moment: the setting sun had infused the white peak with a rare tangerine glow.

Rob shut down his computer and the image on the screen disappeared. There would be no presentation after all. Alan's spirits soared. Earlier, he'd thought half-seriously of sabotaging the generators and disconnecting the solar panels, but this was better. The people had done it.

Dan Broderman cleared his throat. "I'd like to propose that we refrain from emotional reactions as we examine the benefits of this project. Let's explore facts and gather data in a clear-headed manner." Dan leaned over and picked up a large sign: *What's Yours is Mined.*

Alan raised his hand. "Exactly how long will this mine employ people if it's developed?"

"Twenty to forty years," said Rob.

"Twenty to forty years? That's less than a person's lifetime!"

A low, eerie moan, like a wounded wolf, erupted suddenly at the end of the row. It rose to a high pitch, then broke abruptly as Carolyn clapped a hand over Blake's mouth. Blake! Was he trying to speak?

Carolyn scuttled behind him and pushed his wheelchair to the back of the room.

"I have something to say." Dolly Monroe stood. Her black hair, coiled on her head, made her taller and more commanding than ever. "In 1964, on March twenty-seventh, a devastating earthquake hit Alaska. In 1989 another Good Friday disaster occurred. It was called the *Exxon Valdez* oil spill. Today is March twenty-seventh. I don't think it's a coincidence that you presenters came on this day. If this mine is built, it will cause another huge disaster. Like the oil spill, it is preventable." She headed for the door.

Julie rose. "I second that," she said. And she, too, walked out.

Others followed: Sheila, Darlene and Stew, Dale and Patricia, Barbara and Mike, Billy Barr. Alan wavered. Part of him wanted to linger. Who would stay? Broderman, no doubt. And Derek. But what about Carolyn?

Alan stood and looked Dehlia full in the face. "I'm leaving."

She raised her handkerchief and nodded. Would she follow? As Alan moved past the sandwiches and reached the door, he heard another animal-like eruption. *Baa... baaaa.* No mistaking it. Someone was imitating a sheep. Dan Broderman, and the bleat was directed at him. He remembered the exchange he'd had with Dan, not long after he'd moved to Whetstone:

"Are you predator or prey?"

"I must be prey," Alan had said, trying to make light of it. "I'm a Lamb."

12

After the exodus Dehlia sat feeling miserable, her clogged head subject to another pressure: decision making, whether to stay or go. Either way it would seem that she was taking sides. She didn't like being in this position, especially when she'd had a legitimate excuse to stay home. Why had she let Alan coerce her into it? She hadn't wanted to come in the first place. And not just because she was sick.

Twenty-three years in a town was a long time. Dan was right, she'd paid her dues. She'd done her service. She really did *deserve* to own her own house and land. She had an investment in this place that Alan could never understand. And walking out of the room would be a slap in the face to Carolyn. Though it still wasn't clear where Carolyn stood. She'd said nothing, had not in any way revealed her position.

Dehlia, why are you still here? Is this all about not wanting to offend Carolyn?

Third grade. A new school year. Her mother had taken her shopping, made her try on a starched blue dress. The fabric was so stiff that it cut into Dehlia's waist and neck. "It hurts," she'd said. "No, it's a lovely dress, it fits you fine," said her mother. "I didn't say it didn't fit! I said it hurts," said Dehlia. Then she'd received the pinch, under the tender part of her arm, right in front of the salesgirl. A pinch so hard it wedded cruelty, and cut through her mother's rasp-sharp words, "Don't argue with me. The dress is perfect." It was a defining moment. The garment was purchased, the starch wore off, but the pain and the lesson did not.

Dehlia blinked hard. Blake had calmed down, and Carolyn wheeled her father back up to the front of the room. Greg and Dan came forward to take up the vacated seats. Dan made a move to sit next to her, but Dehlia warded him off. "I have a cold," she said.

He nodded once and gave her a berth of three empty chairs. "I'm pleased to see you have retained your dignity, Milady. We need to listen to what these gentlemen have to say." Dan crossed his legs and waited expectantly.

The gentlemen—and gentlewoman—seemed to have taken everything in stride. Perhaps it wasn't the first time they'd met with a hostile crowd. Now each took a chair, and the man with the crew cut said, "This is much more intimate." He laughed at his joke. "Seriously, I'm happy to answer any questions."

"Sir," said Dan, "given the episode you've regrettably witnessed this evening, it appears we need to talk in terms of dollars and sense, and I'm spelling that S-E-N-S-E. The only way to convince people of this project's benefits is to give them concrete figures. How much does an individual stand to earn if employed by Ziggurat?"

"An excellent question. Of course, there isn't one simple answer. As you'll see"—the man tapped the mining career booklet—"there are a number of job opportunities requiring various skills and education. So it depends on your particular career path. Also, we can't rule out financial benefits to communities. Development projects like this means better services—new construction of schools, roads, medical facilities."

A medical facility... that was something Whetstone didn't have, although the town had managed all these years without one. *What I need right now isn't medical services. I just need a cup of tea and my bed.*

Dehlia rose and approached Carolyn. Derek had shifted his chair next to Blake, who stared blankly into some distant universe. Was it her imagination, or was Carolyn eyeing her skeptically?

"Carolyn, I have a cold. I'm sorry I have to leave."

Carolyn's response was swift, perhaps curt. "I can see you don't feel well. Good night."

And Dehlia escaped into the cool night air.

WHEN SHE GOT HOME, Alan wasn't there. Was he upset or was he simply being considerate, giving her space because she was undeniably sick? Perhaps he was following the suggestion she'd made that morning, that he should stay at Mike's tonight so she wouldn't make him sick. Now she wasn't even sure if she'd meant it. She suffered a pang of self-pity. At the same time she felt oddly disencumbered, knowing that she could withdraw under the covers with a book set in another time and place. Life's dramas were fascinating when played out on a page.

She stoked the fire and fixed herself a cup of chamomile, breathing in the warm steam as she carried the balm to the loft. Then she saw a note on her pillow:

> *Dehlia,*
> *Figured I should stay w/ Mike for a couple of days.*
> *Didn't know when you'd be home or I would've waited.*
> *Hope you're feeling better soon. Betsy misses you already.*
> *Alan*

She lingered on the paw print he'd drawn at the bottom, then folded the note and laid it on her night table. The room was darkening now, softening the furniture's hard edges. She slipped out of her clothes and into her pajamas. Once in bed she held the cup of warm tea against her cheek, indulging in the utter quiet.

Resting, she allowed herself to succumb to a drowsy indifference that obliterated the smoke of human folly and left a deep, unspoken faith in the restorative power of the natural world. Somehow it would outlast us—our jealousies, our unkindness, our myriad altercations.

13

Alan had jotted the note quickly, wondering as he did what the difference was between a courtesy and an obligation. No matter, it was the right thing to do, let her know he'd decided to keep a low profile for a few days. If his note was short, at least the paw print served as a gesture of affection.

He wasn't exactly in a warm and cuddly mood at the moment. Dan Broderman's dig was one thing. But more than that, the obscene nature of the mining venture had him electrified. He was humming like a high-voltage wire, anxious to get to Mike's and let the sparks fly. He needed people he could exchange ideas with, who saw eye to eye with him on this fundamental issue. Even Mike was almost too stoic; tonight he craved the company of Patricia or Sheila. But it was late, too late to go knocking on doors and inviting himself in for a diatribe and a drink. Mike would have to do.

He sprinted down the trail in his heavy winter boots, glad he'd worn a light jacket to keep from sweating. Betsy followed, welcoming the exercise after her long wait outside the art building. She was probably starving. Alan himself was long past hunger, the pangs he'd felt earlier displaced by a keen and singular focus. Dark was approaching, and he wanted to get to his destination. He was aware of his quick pace and excellent physical condition; so much walking since coming here had firmed his thighs and butt and seemed even to have sharpened his mind.

Outside Mike's he heard voices. He stopped and listened. Alongside Mike's was a female voice, and it took him a minute to recognize it as Barbara's. Alan stood uncertainly in the cavernous night, lit by a pale and gibbous moon. Should he retrace his steps and land like a shipwrecked cabin boy back on Dehlia's doorstep?

Then Barbara caught sight of him through a front window, and she flung open the door, inviting him in with a sweep of the hand. "Alan, this is your place too!"

The table had been moved to the center of the room. Mike was busy opening bottles of Merlot, two of which Alan recognized as his own purchases.

"You planning on drinking all this yourselves?" Alan asked.

"Company's on the way." Mike filled his wineglass and motioned to Alan. "Help yourself." He grinned.

Alan reined in a good-natured jab: *Generous of you, Trotter, to offer me my wine.* He filled a glass and leaned against the counter, taking a minute to absorb the fact of Barbara's presence, the late hour, and the atmosphere, weighty with portent.

Betsy sensed the excitement, understood that things were off-kilter. When Alan fed her, she ate in nervous increments, finally retreating to her rug.

Mike pressed his hands together in mock theatrics. "Thank you for coming this evening. We're going to begin with a PowerPoint to give you an overview." His impersonation of the crew cut was good. Alan had never witnessed Mike's dramatic flair.

Barbara sat down sexily and crossed her legs, her figure like Liz Taylor's in *Who's Afraid of Virginia Woolf.* She touched the rim of her wineglass. "Excuse me, but is this wine made with local water?"

"Why, of course, ma'am," said Mike. "Not to worry. All our toxic waste flows uphill."

The impromptu skit was interrupted by a pounding at the door. Patricia and Sheila waltzed in, followed by Julie, Dale, and Allie. The women looked like conspirators, and Alan imagined them arm in arm on the walk over, leading the troupe while plotting how they would murder King Ziggurat.

Alan tousled Allie's hair and she squirmed away. Barbara poured wine for all and juice for Allie, who sat on the rug with one arm around Betsy. Barbara insisted on rehearsing the skit. When Mike said, "All our toxic waste flows uphill," Patricia burst into laughter.

"Yes, wait, no," she said, assuming the role of a Ziggurat executive. "The waste will all be contained within the tailings pond." She wore a paisley blouse with five buttons.

"Therefore," said Dale, stepping forward, "we'll just pipe water from downstream back into the mining camp. Your employees can drink it."

Patricia eyed him sternly. "Who are you and what gives you the authority to question our operation?" She put a hand on her hip.

Dale took a long pull of wine and set down his glass. He crossed his arms and looked down at his wife. "I represent the people of Whetstone, Alaska."

"You little plebeian," Patricia scoffed. "Better leave things to the experts."

Dale was on solid footing. "Explain why eighty percent of mines developed acid drainage when mining companies predicted they wouldn't. Why should I trust DNR when they start issuing permits? DNR: *Does not regulate.*"

"Oh, off with his head." Patricia waved a dismissive hand, and Dale toppled like a Greek ruin.

Patricia drew close to Mike, and Barbara scooted her chair next to Dale. Julie squared off with Mike and Patricia, trying to fortify what was left of Dale. Julie said, "The U.S. operates under an old mining law that can't kill mining developments."

"Precisely *because* it's an old law makes it a good one," said Patricia. "Why else would it have been around such a long time?"

"Longevity doesn't make it *right*," said Julie. "It's just some crazy legislation that was never changed. Like that law in Florida: 'If you're a single, divorced, or widowed woman, you can't parachute on Sundays.'"

Mike removed his glasses and stepped close to her. He cleaned his lenses carefully on the sleeve of her blouse, then took up his position alongside Patricia. "Trust us, miss. There will be adequate time for public review and comment."

"Review?" said Sheila. "I know how *that* works! There'll be three thousand pages of permits and plans, and six days for public input."

"Madam." Mike feigned respect. "With a development plan the size of Fly Creek, we promise to extend the comment period."

"To what, thirty days?" Sheila tossed her head.

Alan grabbed the broom, turned it upside down like a staff, and thumped the handle on the floor. "I'm King of the Lambs. We challenge you to a duel."

"It's not time yet for the slaughter," said Patricia.

"Coward," said Alan. "It's five to two. You're afraid we'll win."

From Betsy's rug Allie shrieked, "Get 'em, Alan!"

"See?" said Alan. "Your own daughter has turned against you."

Patricia held up her hand. "Okay, we've gone too far. I need a refill."

They all sat down, hooting and giggling.

"Could you believe those guys tonight?"

"Guess we let 'em know how we feel."

"Those people would sell their own mother into slavery."

"The Native kid was good-looking though. No wonder they hired him."

"You notice how they avoided giving us real answers?"

"We were pretty rude."

"How do you define barging into a place you've never lived and announcing that you've begun the biggest mining development in the entire U.S.?"

"It's worse than rude. It's belligerent."

"Revolting."

"Criminal."

"Yeah, criminal. Or it should be."

The wine had gone to Alan's head. This was it—exactly the conversation he'd yearned for. Now that he'd been rewarded, he felt suddenly drained. What happened after this? People took on a collective voice, sometimes they formed groups, sometimes they fought hard for their principles, sometimes they won. There was Project Chariot up north, and coal-bed methane in Southcentral, both of which had folded because of public outcry. But it was always a long and taxing battle. Tonight the role playing, the sarcasm, offered comic relief. The real work, though, hadn't even begun.

He slipped outside. The moon had risen and grown brighter. At the corner of the woodshed he laid one hand against the rough siding for support. He unzipped and aimed drunkenly at his familiar patch of snow. When he finished, he turned to go back inside, but then he was crying. He blinked hard and pressed his fists against his eyes. He couldn't help it. The cold seeped up through his jeans as he slumped down.

He had to get out of this place. He couldn't keep up this pretense any longer. *You're getting paid through Ziggurat?* Sarah's disdain wasn't hard to imagine. If only his little sister wasn't so hard up for money. If only the low-life father of her children would give her a few hundred measly dollars a month. The bastard was probably putting every dime he owned up his nose. Well, Alan hadn't exactly fixed things, had he? That drive to Anchorage in January, all the way from Homer in under four hours, with patches of black ice and a near wreck, until he was finally able to correct the wheel. Meeting the bastard at the bar in Spenard, the stink and gloom of the place, his failure... he could still feel the blood on his face. But no, it was only tears now. He wiped them away and got to his feet.

BY THE TIME he rejoined the others, he'd composed himself. Inside, he pumped up a pitcher of cold water, drank two full glasses, and offered the pitcher to the others.

"You trying to sober us up, Lamb?" said Mike, with plucky jocularity.

"Hey, anyone hungry? Let's go over to our place and have some sourdoughs." Patricia was wide awake and brimming with enthusiasm.

"It's one o'clock in the morning," Dale mumbled. "I'm beat."

"Let's do it!" Patricia was just charming enough to get her way.

Allie had fallen asleep with Betsy, so her father woke her gently and lifted her on his tall shoulders as the group set out for the other side of town. The moon lit their path as Alan walked in front, his energy rekindled at the prospect of food. He was hungry again. Betsy followed behind him.

He helped Patricia cook the hotcakes, pouring the batter into creative animal shapes for Allie—rabbit, fox, raven, frog. He ate half a dozen himself, soaked in a thin, oversweetened syrup.

Sometime that morning Mike and Barbara mysteriously disappeared, and Alan made the long trek back to Mike's alone with Betsy at his side. He woke at dawn to an empty cabin, thinking of Dehlia and missing her with a raw and unrelenting hurt. He knew now he'd be staying at least through the summer.

14

The first week of April was beautiful. Cold, though. Northerly winds and clear skies kept temperatures in the single digits, but that didn't stop Dehlia from planting her seeds for her garden. She germinated them near the woodstove, moving the tiny seedlings closer to the window when they pushed through the soil. It was the time of year when flats and pots usurped the available surfaces, and she and Alan no longer sat at the table to eat.

Since the Ziggurat meeting and Mike's party (of which Dehlia heard scant details), Alan seemed to have shed some psychic weight. Partly it was the nice weather, but he seemed to be feeling good about his work, his panels producing more power than he'd anticipated.

"Let's expand solar around the state. You can be my rep," he said to Dehlia.

"And live out of a duffel bag? That sounds... not so fun."

Did he mean it, that part about traveling, or was this just talk? He would leave Whetstone, she felt certain of it. He would be just another transient. And she would be left, a lonely widow, with no property, no investments. Only a small life insurance policy that would allow her to eke out a living as an elderly woman. The fact that she hadn't worked a regular job all her adult life was the sacrifice she'd made for her art.

DEHLIA WENT THROUGH her masks. She had carved eleven new ones, fewer than her usual annual output, but she would advertise thirty-five. She always had back inventory. Typically she gave a mask six years before relegating it to permanent storage, or worse, the woodstove. Over the years only three had failed to land a buyer, and she sometimes wondered if she shouldn't give them another push. They were good pieces, she felt, as good or better than many that had been instantly coveted. Artists couldn't gauge the success of their work by its salability. Deep down, the creator had an intuitive sense about a piece, sometimes just knew that a particular sentiment had found expression.

She needed an updated price list. One of her hardest tasks was deciding what to charge, and she sometimes spent an hour agonizing over a difference of thirty dollars. But ultimately she had to come up with a figure. The clients would arrive in a few weeks; it was almost summer. Beneath *Swan-Lady* she inked in the price on the label: seven hundred dollars.

Alan peered over her shoulder. "You should charge more. Look at CEOs. They don't work half as hard as you do."

She sighed. "I don't like this one anymore. It's too... elegant."

"I like it. It's worth at least a grand."

"It wouldn't make any difference. I'll never have real retirement money." She shifted her chair. "At least I have Phil's life insurance policy. It's small, but it's enough. Enough, if I can have my own home."

He looked at her quizzically. "I didn't know Phil left you anything."

She returned to her task. Why had she mentioned the insurance policy? She wished she'd kept it to herself. Money was a private matter. She didn't want to be judged according to her assets. A clean demarcation between a person's monetary worth and their worth as an individual was imperative.

THE LAST PART of the month the weather took a sour turn, a series of lows clogging the skies with ragged scud. Multiple showers deteriorated into sleet or hail, and the saturated but still frozen ground was as uninviting as the sky. In the restless gloom of a delayed spring, Carolyn called a community meeting. This was typical before the clients arrived, but this time she insisted that everyone be present.

Dehlia sat at the back with Alan. Dan Broderman, off to their right, cast them a critical eye. Carolyn was her usual business self, ringing her silver bell and expecting silence before she spoke. Beneath her friendliness, she maintained an air of command, her squared shoulders and wrist-crossed stance communicating that she was ultimately in charge.

Carolyn handed out charts detailing the summer schedule, and Dehlia flipped through the pages. Monday through Friday, the daily lunch with artists and patrons. Craft talks, morning and afternoon. May through September, twenty weeks, one small slice of time off for salmon fishing. It seemed like so much work, presented in this concentrated way.

When Carolyn asked for committee reports Dehlia shared the fuel consumption findings, watching Carolyn with anticipation, wishing she would credit Alan for good work. But Carolyn made the notation without comment. Dehlia was certain she saw Dan sneer.

Then Carolyn said, "One last item. As you know, Derek is no longer flying for us. I've hired a new pilot. His name is Pete, but he couldn't be here tonight. Whether or not you agree with Derek's decision to fly for Ziggurat, this has nothing to do with Pete. When you meet him, please be welcoming." Her tone softened. "Let's try to maintain our reputation as a congenial community."

PART FIVE

The Bright, Bright Sun

1

The bustle outside the art building settled down after lunch was announced, and everyone jockeyed for a place to sit. They were eating under a tarp because of the drizzle. A red-haired, freckled man with a quick smile sat at another table. The visitors were a family of five from Nebraska, along with a retired schoolteacher from Tempe, Arizona. Dehlia slid into the empty seat beside the teacher. Something about the woman seemed familiar. It was the way she wore her headband, almost buried in her full auburn hair, cut close to her neck. Or her smile, subtle as the upward curve of a dogwood leaf.

Dehlia unfolded her napkin and leaned in. Dolly, seated on her right, was entertaining the family with a story of butchering her first caribou—alone. Their questions were endless. It was always like this: so much surrounding chatter made it hard to have a conversation. "Is this your first time in Whetstone?" Dehlia asked the teacher.

The woman shook her head. "No, I was here four years ago. I remember you. You're Dehlia, the mask carver."

"Yes." Dehlia took a bowl of green beans from Dolly. "I thought I might have seen you before."

"Well, how could you be sure, you get so many visitors. My name's Helen."

"Oh, of course. You bought one of my masks." Dehlia handed Helen the beans then scooped a few French fries onto her plate and passed them on. She ladled out some borscht for the two of them.

"Yes. But it wasn't for me. It was for a friend with terminal cancer. I hoped it might give her a bit of comfort at the end, something to show that this world has many faces, and the face of death is just one of them." Helen gazed outward. There was something stately in her sadness, a glow of warmth in her face. "I don't know if it helped, but she did like the mask very much."

239

Dehlia had a brief image of her work in homes around the country, perhaps the world—pieces that had been passed on to relatives of the deceased, some displayed prominently on a living room wall, others boxed up and left in storage to be discovered a generation later. Would her art be treasured or ignored? Mounted behind an impervious glass case, or discarded with a slew of other unwanted things? Artists could never know whose hands a piece would fall into or what its fate would be. Like those Yup'ik Eskimo masks that had been destroyed by missionaries who considered them works of the devil. The irony was that the Native people themselves had laid the pieces—once they'd served their ceremonial purpose—on the tundra, to be displaced over time by rot and weather.

All was perishable. The natural world was indifferent to human creations. But how hard curators tried to overcome nature's nonchalance. How determined they were to preserve, reclaim, restore! For what? To pass on to others for study and appreciation, but also to detain the inevitable, if only for a few hundred years; to cage the wicked reaper behind bars, to dull his blade on pumice or rock. To paint a lighter face on him, who was always trying to conceal himself behind his infernal hood.

"This is excellent borsht," said Helen. She spooned extra sour cream into her bowl, a jarringly beautiful contrast to the purple-red soup. Helen winked at her. "Now I allow myself these indulgences. I turned seventy-five last month."

"My mother's seventy-five," Dehlia said, then wished she hadn't. She set down her spoon and held her napkin tightly. "I don't know where she lives. She doesn't keep in touch."

"Oh. That must be hard."

"No, it's… fine. We were never close."

Helen studied her. "It's hard either way. If you're close, the hurt is greater when you lose that person." She became very quiet. "I lost my daughter thirty years ago. I still grieve for her. Every day."

"Why? I mean, how?" Dehlia smoothed her hair self-consciously. "I'm sorry. I didn't mean to pry."

"It's okay." Helen picked up a French fry and examined it, as if the potato's harvest and immersion in hot oil were some kind of perverse parallel to human life. "It was a boating accident. Preventable, of course. Most accidents are." She bit off a piece of the French fry, chewing abstractedly.

Helen laid a hand on Dehlia's wrist. "Tell you what." Dehlia could barely make out her words amid the talk and laughter from the other guests. "I'll consider you my adopted daughter."

AFTER THE PEACH COBBLER, Carolyn announced that it was time for the tour. Helen and the other guests followed, and Dehlia and Jen cleared tables. The short, freckled man with red hair that Dehlia had noticed earlier came up to introduce himself.

"I'm Pete, the new pilot." He extended a hand and Dehlia shook it awkwardly as she balanced a stack of empty plates. "Here, let me help," he said.

"Why don't you join the others?" Dehlia glanced after them, all equipped now with raincoats and umbrellas. "But it's not that inviting out there, is it?"

"Nope. Plus, I've taken the tour already. I'd as soon be busy." He rolled up his sleeves and began collecting dishes and transferring them to the kitchen. Soon he was standing at the big double sink.

"We can do those, Pete," sang Jen, waltzing in with a handful of glasses.

"No problem. I grew up in an orphanage. I got real good at washing dishes."

"An orphanage," Dehlia repeated. *That must have been hard, never knowing your parents at all...* She took a place beside him and started rinsing.

"So," said Pete, after Jen disappeared again. "I hear you're a mask carver." He worked quickly, sloshing plates and cups with such fervor that Dehlia was afraid he'd break them. "Why masks?"

"I don't know... I never really thought about it." She was trying hard to keep up with him. She fed the drying rack. "I don't think anyone's ever asked me that particular question."

"What are you working on now?"

"I'm starting a transformation mask. One mask opens up to reveal another, interior face."

"Cool," said Pete. "But we'll never see the real face. It'll still be a mask." He laughed lightheartedly and moved to her left to begin drying.

"How long have you been flying?"

"Five years. Before that I was a baker. It was time for a change—a transformation." He laughed again. "It's still the same face when I look in the mirror though."

"Yes," she said. But was it true? Maybe in Pete's case, but not always. Sometimes a career change could completely transform a person. As could a birth. A divorce. Or a death. And she thought again of Helen.

2

Pete, in those first weeks, was as prompt as Derek had been, arriving daily at 9:45 a.m. Early May remained overcast, with occasional light rain. Not flight-obstructing weather, but poor solar energy weather, in which a few attenuated rays landed haphazardly on Alan's panels. He hoped the trend wasn't indicative of the whole summer.

He pulled up near the airstrip one morning, thinking how lucky Carolyn had been to find another pilot with a 207. For Pete the situation was ideal: not many flying hours but a guaranteed schedule for four full months.

Pete taxied the Cessna to the offloading area and cut the engine. His flying style was more conservative than Derek's; he used more of the strip when landing, spent more time going through his checklist before takeoff, and never made low passes over people or buildings. But Pete's caution might keep him grounded on bad weather days. Chances were slim that he'd be able to maintain Derek's near-perfect record.

Through the windows of the plane Alan made out one teen and two adults, presumably the mother and father. Pete opened the door, and the boy, lanky and quick limbed, scrambled out first. His parents followed. Then an elderly couple, whose feeble hands clung uncertainly to Pete's arm as they descended. Alan introduced himself, and the visitors chatted excitedly about the plane ride and the country, how remote it seemed, how quiet and beautiful. For a moment Alan thought there was no sixth passenger, which was unusual but not unprecedented for flights to Whetstone.

Then he caught movement. There *was* someone else—a woman, but her bent head hid her features. As she moved toward the door Alan glimpsed her long black hair, like Dehlia's hair, and his heart gave a flip. *No, Dehlia's hair isn't in ringlets, it's wavy. And Dehlia has been here, in Whetstone. Long hair in ringlets...* The woman straightened and looked Alan full in the face. Meredith! What on earth was she doing here? He remembered taking her to meet Derek the day she left Whetstone. She had been almost hostile to him and he'd been relieved that she was departing for good.

"Hello, Alan." She clutched a small handbag and refused Pete's arm. She was thinner than ever. And nervous, a displaced feline. He tried not to stare. The rust-colored flannel shirt she wore was too large for her. It looked like a man's.

She moved away from the milling guests as Alan backed the four-wheeler trailer close to the cargo door, where Pete was unloading. "What's Meredith doing here?" Alan whispered.

"The woman with the long hair?" Pete followed Alan's lead and kept his voice low. "There was a cancellation. She took the spot."

Alan loaded a couple of hard camera cases into the trailer. "But she's not a client. She's a poet. Used to live here."

Pete shrugged. Apparently this was news to him.

Alan wondered, not for the first time, why visitors brought so much along. They were only here for the day. He'd transferred laptops, books, and travel bags that didn't once get opened. Pete handed him a backpack. There was a name on the tag: Meredith Stone. Then Pete reached for the last item, a green nylon sack. It, too, had a tag. It, too, bore her name.

ALAN COVERED THE TRAILER with a tarp, a habit he'd gotten into this season. It was proving to be a good practice. He drove faster than usual, relieved that none of the guests required motorized transport. He parked the four-wheeler near the art building. Through the open door of the kitchen he saw Julie, Barbara, Patricia, and Mike preparing the day's lunch. Mike, wearing a chef's apron, looked up from the celery he was chopping. Alan motioned to him with a backward jerk of his head.

Mike followed Alan around the corner of the building. He frowned. "What's up?"

"Looks like you're not hurting for female companionship anymore. Lucky guy, getting to cook with all those women."

"What's going on?"

Alan paused, reveling in his secret before letting it spill. "Meredith's here." He was whispering again.

"What?"

"Meredith. She came in on this morning's plane."

"Weird. Are you sure?" Mike wiped his hands on his apron.

"Yeah, weird. And yeah, I'm sure. She has a tent. Like she plans on camping out."

Mike's frown deepened. "I can't make sense of that."

Alan loved it when Mike was stumped.

Mike said, "Did you know she sent me a postcard congratulating me on my grant? Said she hadn't been supportive of other writers all these years."

"That's not the Meredith I remember."

"Maybe deep down there's a more magnanimous spirit." Mike took a step in the direction of the kitchen. Then he seemed to remember something. He stretched, assuming a reciprocal smugness. "I have news too."

Alan waited, but when Mike didn't deliver he said, "What, you and Barbara getting hitched?"

"Hell no."

"Yeah. You wouldn't want to hook up with someone so impulsive."

"Fuck you, Lamb," Mike said. But he smiled. "No, this is more Ziggurat offal. And it isn't good. They've applied for permits to expand into the Nahoyak. That's Bristol Bay's second largest drainage. Nothing stops them. They're like a medieval empire."

"Shit." Alan scowled, feeling the pith of Mike's comment and a renewed sense of violation about the mining project. He wanted to sink his teeth into the Rat's neck and never let go. It was time Dehlia stood up against this project. To hell with her land.

Mike took another step back. "The ladies are calling."

Alan returned to the four-wheeler to wait for the guests. He sat backwards on the machine's rear rack, legs hanging loosely over the edge. Then he rested his head on the cushioned seat. His thoughts raced: Dehlia, his job, his sister, Carolyn's grant, Meredith.

It was the end of the week, and tonight he'd be seeing Dehlia. D-Day. Mike didn't say that anymore. The joke had worn itself out.

3

B oy, that ice sure look rotten. Hope somebody don't fall through."
Dehlia had overheard Billy's warning that morning in the post
office. It didn't worry her; no one traveled on the ice once it turned
green. Perhaps that was because Carolyn emphasized so forcefully
the danger. Since Dehlia had lived in Whetstone, treacherous ice had
resulted in only one near casualty: a couple from down lake had fallen
through a pressure crack with their four-wheeler. They'd survived,
but it had taken three days in a warm sleeping bag lined with hot
water bottles to elevate the woman's core temperature.

It was one nonfatal incident, making Whetstone an anomaly.
Every year, in villages across the state, reports of cold water drownings
cast palls on conversations, sobering as tallies of plane wrecks and
climbing deaths. Dehlia had heard them all, grisly tales that renewed
her resolve to exercise caution and travel only in the best weather.

But this was spring, and the rotting ice held a charm and fascination.
It was the last vestige of winter's stubborn tether: the fraying rope, the
worn chain, the final relinquishment. She had to see it.

SHE FOUND ALAN at the community generator shed, wearing goggles
and rubber gloves, and pouring distilled water into the big batteries.
It was one of many things she'd learned from him: the water must be
distilled, because water with minerals can build up on the lead plates
and shorten a battery's life. But no water at all is just as bad. If the
plates are exposed to oxygen then the acid will crystalize on their
surface and reduce the charge. She kept her distance, picturing again
her acid-riddled jeans. "It's Friday. Can you join me for a walk?"

Alan screwed the caps back on and turned to Betsy. He pulled
off his protective gear. "What do you think, girl? You won't tell if we
head out early?"

At the beach Dehlia lingered over fresh blooms of saxifrage, intoxicated by the fierce magenta hues. Finally, some color, after the long, drab winter!

Alan plucked a stem. "Five petals. This should be the lover's flower, instead of the daisy. I'd always get the right answer." He twirled the stem and removed the petals one by one. "She loves me, she loves me not, she loves me… "

His candor left her giddy. She took his hand and walked to the lake's edge. Already the ice had pulled away from shore. Betsy tested the water with one paw, then busied herself sniffing out spiders between rocks.

Dehlia guided a wedge of ice back to their feet with a driftwood stick. She tapped once, and it broke into dozens of translucent tapers.

"What causes that?" asked Alan.

"Impurities, I think—glacial silt and dust that absorb heat. Then the ice melts down in columns." She felt suddenly foolish. "I didn't mean to sound pedantic. That's Phil talking." She tossed the stick out in the bay, but it didn't sink. "One thing I know, you don't want to walk on this!"

"Yeah, I wouldn't trust a foot of this stuff."

"You never struck me as the cautious type."

"I've heard enough stories." He looked out at the shifting floes and pointed past the first small island. "I think I see whitecaps."

She squinted. It was hard to tell.

"Next time I'm bringing binoculars."

"Next time you're here this will all be open water. It's already the ninth of May."

THEY WANDERED BACK down the beach and turned onto the main trail. After crossing the bridge, they followed the trail past Quartz. This was Dan's lot, and Dehlia wasn't surprised when Alan clipped Betsy to her line. Dan seemed so suspicious lately, so unfriendly. She didn't want to run into him, and Alan must have been thinking the same thing.

Then *wham!* Just as they reached the next intersection, there he was. Betsy froze and whined softly. Waggy, snarling, leapt at Betsy's throat, and Alan grabbed the Pomeranian by the collar and threw her back.

Dehlia heard herself gasp.

Dan cradled his dog and smiled ruefully. "Nice meeting you," he said, and continued down the trail.

Alan knelt and felt Betsy's throat and ears. "You okay, girl?" But when he pulled his hand away his fingers were stained with blood.

Dehlia inspected Betsy's ear. "It's superficial," she said, relieved.

Alan ground the heel of his boot into the ground. "Don't make excuses for Broderman or his sawed-off-rat," he said.

"Why were you so brutal?" Her anger surprised her. "You could have broken that little dog's bones!"

"Hey, forget it." Alan touched her on the arm. "Let's not ruin our day."

They walked on, but she was quiet. Alan respected her silence, and she was glad for it. They relaxed, and Alan let Betsy off her leash.

Not until they reached Indigo and Indi's lot did he speak. "Meredith's old place. Did you know she's back?"

"No!" Dehlia recalled the last time she'd seen Meredith, the shadowy eyes, the groomed hair. Something about the news was disconcerting.

"She's tent camping on a knoll up there." Alan pointed northeast, but all Dehlia could see was a thicket of willows. That was odd. Why would Meredith have returned to Whetstone?

They crossed the main artery and were approaching Jasper when Betsy stopped again. Once more Alan clipped her to her line. Betsy stood rigid, ears perked except for the tips. The hair around her neck rose and she lifted her tail and growled softly. Alan pulled Betsy close and Dehlia clapped her hands.

When the animal came into view, it stood about sixty feet away and eyed them curiously. Dehlia could feel the thud of her heart. The bear rose on its hind legs and sniffed the air, and Dehlia's heart thudded louder, although she knew that, contrary to popular opinion, this was not a threatening posture.

The bear grunted and dropped back to all fours, then ambled away, giving them a wide berth. It stopped twice to look back. There was something wistful about it, but something disturbing as well; the bear looked familiar. As it wandered out of sight to the north, she recognized the dark legs, the blonde back—the same markings of the bear she'd seen last spring. What was it doing here? Where was it headed?

When they arrived in the front yard, they found another surprise: the bear had visited, leaving muddy paw prints on the porch. A hollow in the melting earth indicated that it had lain there for some time.

Alan gave Dehlia a questioning look, but she had no explanation, and despite the encounter she felt oddly unthreatened. But when Alan asked if she'd like to keep Betsy for the weekend "just in case the bear returned," she considered it. She looked forward to the companionship, and when she reached down to pet her and Betsy laid her wet black muzzle against Dehlia's face, the deal was sealed.

4

Two days later Alan knocked on Mike's bedroom door and opened it without asking. He seldom interrupted Mike's work, but today was different. "Trotter." He waited while Mike finished a sentence. "Let's head to the lake and see if the ice is out."

Mike gave him an annoyed, one-sided smile and studied his page full of scrawlings and scratchings. He pressed the butt end of his pen to his forehead, as if trying to channel his thoughts directly to the ink. As if whatever was muddled in his brain would come clear through some kind of telepathy.

"C'mon," Alan said. "It's not raining for a change."

"You're a pain in the ass, Lamb," said Mike. But Alan knew that his lack of serious protest meant he was relieved at the excuse to head outdoors.

They slipped into sneakers and lightweight jackets, Alan pocketing a pair of binoculars before leaving. The trail was still wet for mid-May, and they had to skip over puddles. By the time they reached the beach, their feet were damp. But Alan didn't care. They were like adolescent boys anticipating some adrenaline-charged adventure, oblivious to discomfort.

"Sure as shit," Alan said, pointing east. "Bona-fide water."

Across the bay the hulk of a partially submerged tree rode just above the slate-blue surface. It would likely sit there all summer unless Stew towed it out to the main lake.

Mike squinted. "Who's that?"

"What do you mean... oh." What Alan had mistaken for a tree was in fact a canoe. In the flat light the vessel looked unusually dark, and it took a minute for his eyes to adjust. He made out a seated figure. Whoever it was had taken the first opportunity of the season to launch.

Mike gave him a nudge. "Give me your super cheaters."

"What?"

Mike patted Alan's pocket. "Your binoculars. I need an extension for my corrective lenses."

Mike took them and cleaned the lenses with a ragged handkerchief. He raised the optics and adjusted the focus. "Zeiss would be better. I used to have a pair. I pawned them for eighty bucks."

"Man did you get screwed," Alan mumbled, but Mike wasn't listening. He zeroed in on his target.

Seconds ticked by. Then Mike gave a low whistle. "I'll be damned."

"What? Let me see." Alan played again with the focus. Something about the figure in the canoe was familiar, but it was too far away to make out any details other than the color of the person's shirt. Rust. Somewhere he'd seen that color before.

"You know who that is," said Mike.

"Nope. I guess it takes a guy who wears glasses to best me in the vision category."

"Meredith."

Meredith? Alan narrowed his eyes, as if that would make discernible her long hair, her beautiful pale skin, her finely sculpted nose. It couldn't be her... no, Mike was right. The shirt, of course! Now he had it. It was the shirt Meredith was wearing when she stepped off the plane a week ago. Too big. A man's.

"That shirt belonged to Phil Melven. I remember him wearing it."

Mike's words jolted Alan's concentration. He lowered the binoculars and stared at his friend. It was as if some link in a long chain had been missing and had fallen at his feet, where it was waiting for him to pick it up and weld it in place. All he needed were the right tools. He flashed on images from last fall: Meredith at the airstrip ready to leave Whetstone, the trailer with the boxes of clothes and a backpack full of shoes. Meredith's suspiciousness, the look on her face. Her questions.

What's in the backpack?

Phil Melven's shoes.

And the boxes?

Clothes, I guess.

Then the question she hadn't asked: *Whose clothes?*

Why hadn't she asked? Because she knew. She knew they'd belonged to Phil and she knew that she was going to get her hands on them. Once in town, she must have negotiated something with Derek. But why? Why were Phil's clothes important to her?

Mike elbowed him. "Close your mouth. You might catch a fly."

Alan swallowed. "So her and Phil...?"

Mike nodded. "She and Phil. Get the grammar right." Mike reached again for the binoculars.

Alan started to say more but Mike grew abruptly serious. "Jesus," he breathed. "What's she doing?"

Alan got no answer. He could see movement, nothing more. He had to rely on Mike to detail her actions. So when Mike said, "She's taking off the shirt," Alan's immediate image was erotic: a beautiful woman, bare chested, surrounded by water and snow-capped peaks. His pulse quickened.

But then Mike's voice dropped in concern: "She's standing up, she's completely naked, she must be freezing." And Alan's pulse rose again, this time in alarm.

"She's picking something up. Looks like some kind of webbing... she's struggling with it... must be heavy... like it's loaded with rocks... she's trying to put it on... she could lose her balance..."

As Mike spoke, Alan felt sweat building under his armpits, and he quickly estimated the distance between them and Meredith. He saw the only skiff in Whetstone high on the beach, turned over for winter storage, and the outboard somewhere in Stew's messy shed. He saw himself waving excitedly, his voice spiked with panic. And he knew before Mike spoke his last words—"Good Christ, she's going to jump"—that it was true, so that even as he sped away, and long before he heard the splash, he accepted that his effort was futile, that time was laughing at him like an old man with a very sick lung and an even sicker grin. Still he kept running, back up the trail through the mixed forest that swam past in a blur of dense limbs and offered no shortcut, then down Tourmaline and the Inner Circle and all the way to Stew's, where he collapsed at the doorstep, yelling "Meredith, Meredith's drowning..." where he panted and wheezed, so sharp was the pain in his chest. Then his sobbing relief when Stew stepped up with a plan of action. A plan that would take an hour to carry out, that did nothing except leave behind a defeated rescue team and those two unshakeable words:

"We tried. We *tried*."

5

The rescue team searched for hours and the state troopers were called in. Derek flew a Ziggurat helicopter up and down the bay, sweeping low, looking for signs of the body. The mining company had generously volunteered fuel and time.

That was all Dehlia knew by Wednesday evening when the community gathered for the memorial service. Somehow the town kept running; somehow Carolyn kept people on task; somehow daily visitors were whisked in and out.

Of course there was gossip. It was hard to ignore the troopers' presence, their somber, waxen faces, their holsters and flat-brimmed hats, their dark-blue slacks with gold double stripes down the outside of each leg—slacks that, even if never soiled, looked to be dry cleaned weekly. And the uniforms in turn made *them* the subject of scrutiny. They did not mingle with the crowd but strolled through like moving statues, pausing only to make their shrewd and practiced assessments.

Dehlia did not gossip. Who was she to engage in some lurid hearsay surrounding Meredith's death, when in time all would be laid clean?

On Wednesday she joined the others on the beach where a bonfire had been built out of mammoth pieces of driftwood. She quickly spotted Alan, who acknowledged her solemnly from the corner of one eye as he finished his conversation with Dale. He was drawn and unusually quiet. It was six o'clock and the light was good but gray, and it settled like a blight on his unshaven cheeks.

"I haven't seen you since Friday," she said. "Why not?"

"These have been some disturbing days. I needed some time alone."

"I understand." She leaned against him. "Betsy's fine."

"Thanks for taking care of her."

They moved closer to the fire, retreating when the heat grew too intense. Conversation came in snippets from those milling nearby.

"Tough times."

"Are you going to talk?"

"Haven't decided yet."

"I hardly knew her."

"Wonder if it made headlines."

"It was in Monday's paper."

There was a shuffling of feet, a kicking of stones. Arms randomly reached out to add more fuel to the fire. Soon Mike and Barbara arrived, and behind them, in a white fleece jacket, Carolyn, who broke the lull with a brisk directive. "Let's form a circle."

Dehlia shifted back to allow others to join in. Allie, holding her mother's hand, stared at her. As with the Ziggurat presentation, everyone in the community was present, excepting, this time, Blake and his caregivers. And where was Dan?

Carolyn cleared her throat. She locked her hands together and focused on no one as she spoke. "You've probably heard stories. Some may be true, others not. I'll do my best to set the record straight."

Dehlia breathed freely. Carolyn would make it right, dispense with any misinformation.

"Meredith Stone jumped from a canoe Sunday afternoon. Mike and Alan witnessed it, and Alan reported it. Dale and Stew and Billy searched the water where Mike last saw her. They dragged an anchor over half a mile. They explored the shoreline, thinking maybe she'd managed to swim in. Her clothes were discovered in the canoe, which miraculously didn't overturn. You've seen the troopers around town. They've completed their investigation and won't be returning. It's believed that she drowned in about two hundred feet of water."

Carolyn paused, allowing the subdued whisperings while people absorbed these facts. She cleared her throat again. "A suicide note was found in her tent. The troopers notified next of kin, an uncle living in London. There's nothing left but to pay our respects. Anyone who'd like to say something may do so now."

For a moment the only sound was waves licking the shore, reminders of the vast depths just inside the bay. Sparks from the fire shifted and crackled upward in the cooling air.

Dale put one arm around Patricia and the other around Allie. "What's happened makes me appreciate more than ever what I have. It shouldn't take tragedy to do that." He drew his girls tighter.

"Never did meet Meredith," said Indigo, "but I like her pad. Indi and I feel privileged to be here."

Stew raised a finger. "Woman that beautiful shoulda been a model. Always wondered what she was doing in Whetstone. I guess now she's here to stay."

It was an odd and not very complimentary thing to say. Why had Stew spoken at all? Didn't the dead deserve better? This was supposed to be a tribute to a fellow member of the community. Death should redeem people, not indict them. Dehlia tried to picture Meredith, in town at the post office, fishing on the beach, conversing with other women. But she had no enduring images of her, and she realized she'd never even heard her read her poetry. How was it that the two of them had never given a presentation on the same day?

She should speak, but she was tongue-tied. Had Meredith been lonely? Untrusting? What were her passions, her accomplishments? Why did she leave, and why did she return to die here? *There'd been that thought, that suspicion, the time at Costco... no, don't think that. Let it rest.* Much about Meredith would never be uncovered. Just as her body was shrouded now, sequestered in its liquid cloth. Heavier than six feet of soil.

"Whatever Meredith wasn't, she was dedicated to her art," said Mike. "And not long ago she wrote to congratulate me on my grant. There was another side to her."

Sheila raised her violin to her chin. Music flooded the night air. Gradually the strings displaced the remnants of speech as they brooded and wept, then ended with a simple, haunting melody. A fine mist began to fall, a signal for all to turn home. It hadn't been much of a memorial, but Carolyn had done her part, and Sheila had given everyone a sense of closure. The crowd broke up. Dale and Patricia began to snuff out the fire.

Alan walked Dehlia home, his brisk stride giving way to an uncharacteristic trudge. Even Betsy, tail wagging at the door, couldn't lift his mood. He told Dehlia he'd be staying at Mike's.

Dehlia watched Betsy hesitate, then trot away by Alan's side. She wished the dog would turn around and sprint back to her, showing her master that this was where they belonged. But Betsy did not, and Dehlia knew that the wish, after all, was unfair. You shouldn't wish for a thing that wasn't rightfully yours. Betsy belonged to Alan, and the dog was obliged to show her fidelity to him alone.

6

It was a gnaw, as if a microscopic rodent had taken up residence and was worrying a corner of his brain. Some days it was almost imperceptible, and Alan resumed his visits to Dehlia without betraying any outward distress—if distress was the right word. The gnaw would go away, or wear itself out.

In other circumstances he would have launched into predatorial pursuit, pinning Mike down until he got to the bottom of it. But Alan was still in shock, reliving the image of Meredith in the canoe, her preparations for her suicide. And anyway, maybe there was no bottom to get to, maybe Mike had nothing more to reveal.

So there'd been an indiscretion. Phil and Meredith had had a fling. What was the big deal? Happened all the time. And to top it off, the transgressors were two dead people. Better let that affair sink into oblivion. Dehlia apparently didn't know; it would be stupid and inconsiderate to bring it to her attention now. Or maybe she'd blocked it out. If ignorance wasn't bliss, it was one hell of a coping mechanism. And Alan understood then how people like Dehlia had an edge in life. The unprobing mind had a certain functionality; it equipped you, and the bigger your blindfold the larger your store of armor and shields.

Besides, Alan wanted to move on. The town certainly had—within a week people were back to their routines, as if the tragedy had happened on another continent, in another century. He'd seen it before, the way people took up so easily where they'd left off after someone's passing. *You'd think with a suicide it would be different.* But Meredith's death seemed to have no more effect than the aftermath of a heavy storm: you cleaned up the mess, did your repairs, and tended again to your home. A two-day job. Except that being a witness made it more difficult. And there was the gnaw, the fear that there was something more behind Phil Melven's dead secret.

Still, he couldn't shake the feeling that no one in Whetstone had really *liked* Meredith, and while he doubted that anyone applauded her death, no one seemed especially unhappy about it either. The indifference manifested at the memorial had blossomed into a breezy air that circulated throughout the community and kept spirits high as leavened bread.

Maybe it was just his perception, what struck him as a contrast to his own frame of mind. If weather was mood's great manipulator, there was no call for anyone to be cheery. June was dismal, with pervasive lows and perpetual drizzle. And the mosquitoes were intolerable. Was he alone being tested for endurance? Others had the luxury of working indoors or in a covered area with mosquito netting. Alan himself had helped erect tarps over the picnic tables outside the art building. He, meantime, was always ferrying gear or fuel, or clearing brush around the generator shed and cussing at bugs. He usually started out with a head net, but the mesh clouded his vision and inevitably the hat grew too hot. In frustration he would throw the whole affair aside and muscle forward with nippers and bow saw, severing branches with a blind ferocity, then sawing down the thicker trunks in a few short strokes. He'd work himself into a sweat in minutes, which attracted more insects and worsened his mood. He finally resorted to Muskol, spraying the toxic repellent onto his hands and running them through his sticky hair.

Even the poplars were fueled with bad intent. When their leaves broke, scores of the sticky buds fell to the ground, then clung to his clothes and gloves until he attacked them with a gas-soaked rag, coating himself with another unpleasant stench. Had they been this bad last summer? He couldn't remember.

There was no recourse. He should quit the damn job and give Ziggurat the final send-off. Every paycheck seemed stamped with the company's lurid seal. He'd already installed the panels, but he suspected that Carolyn was paying him now from Ziggurat's coffers. Up to one hundred thousand dollars, she had considered asking for.

To compensate, he tried digging up the old wire that wasn't up to code—a job that one year ago he'd idealistically hoped to complete. Copper was still worth a fortune; one raid in town on an FAA maintenance facility could have netted the thieves a scrap value of fifteen thousand dollars. But what good was recycling in the face of Ziggurat's gilded pot?

He tried anyway. He knew better—it was June, for Christ's sake—but before he'd sunk the pickaxe six inches it felt as if he were striking concrete. Funny, he'd just helped Dehlia put in her garden, but here, the shaded and clay-layered earth held like a vise. Maybe he could try later in the summer, but no—he'd already kissed the project goodbye. It was too much work, his schedule was too tight. Most important now was generator maintenance. With the weather so abysmal, the generators were working overtime and the panels were putting out few amps. He'd have to let the wire go by the wayside. It had held up for twenty years, it would probably last another ten. And Alan would be gone by then. His reasons to leave were mounting. More than ever he wanted his own land, his own home.

That was another problem with Whetstone. After a while you start feeling like a serf, always looking to someone else for permission. There was something debasing about it. He didn't want to be a tenant. And what would happen when Ziggurat moved in? He feared the worst. This place would turn into a Bible belt, but the temple would be a mound of toxic earth. All the sinners would be thrown into the open pit.

If only Dehlia would relocate. He'd have to keep working on her, try another tack. There were other communities in the state, lots of places to make friends. She'd have a studio with good light. He'd go back to school, get paid what he was really worth. It would only take him a few years. They could manage. They were creative. They could adapt.

7

On the second of July, guests at Whetstone were weathered in. The morning was benign, but conditions worsened hourly. By afternoon the question of returning to Anchorage was definitive—if there was a ceiling it wasn't measurable in feet. This was no soup fog, it was more like stew. Pete was having no part of it, refusing to put lives in danger.

When Carolyn asked Dehlia to put up a client—a reporter named Lillian from the *L.A. Times*—Dehlia hesitated. It was the day before Alan's birthday, and she'd meant to surprise him with a small celebration. Lately, they'd had little time alone. But Carolyn's request was part of living here. You helped out. With luck, the weather would improve and her guest would be gone by morning.

It ended up being a double overnighter. Dehlia gave Lillian her bed and moved to the couch, forcing Alan back to Mike's to sleep.

She made the cake anyway.

Lillian offered to help. She melted the chocolate and beat the egg whites. Though comfortable in the kitchen, a trip to the garden for lettuce made her fret about dirtying her slacks. Before stoking the woodstove, she had to be shown how to split kindling if the fire had burned down to coals. Dehlia quickly decided it was more efficient to do these jobs herself. How soon a person's bush-living adaptability revealed itself—as did personality.

Gangly, blonde, and functionally attractive, Lillian, by her own admission, had sored up both elbows working herself into her position. Reporting wasn't a job, it was a life. The trip to Whetstone was a rare diversion, but she was always on the lookout for a good story. She offered to put in a good word with the arts editor on Dehlia's behalf. "I'm sure she'd run a piece on you. It would certainly boost your sales," Lillian said.

"That's kind, but I can only carve so many masks a year." Dehlia was happy for this excuse. She didn't like the idea of having her face duplicated on one hundred thousand newspapers—or whatever number the *L.A. Times* ran.

"Think about it. Our Sunday circulation is over a million," said Lillian.

One person, one million, thought Dehlia. *What does it matter how many people appreciate my art? It's the level of appreciation that counts.*

ALAN AND BETSY arrived at six, Betsy wet and smelling like a plucked chicken. Alan's odor, reeking of diesel and sweat, wasn't much better, and when Dehlia introduced him to Lillian the forward reporter took two steps back.

While Alan heated water for a shower, Dehlia fed Betsy and tied her outside. By the time Alan emerged from the bathroom, it was almost seven-thirty.

Lillian set the table and Dehlia brought the casserole from the oven. She set out a green salad with parsley and dill and a basket of homemade rolls. The wine she chose—Sonoma Chardonnay— was straight from Lillian's childhood county. After a toast to health and hospitality, Lillian told Alan about her work. The conversation was less than riveting; Dehlia had already heard about the reporter's thirty-year career.

Lillian interrupted herself. "Dehlia, dear, this casserole is *divine*."

Divine? "It's just canned salmon."

Lillian put down her fork and gave her a sharp look. "How can you say that, 'just' salmon?"

"I only meant we eat salmon all the time."

"People I know would give a rib for this meal, and probably two if the fish were fresh."

Alan said, "Have you heard about the mine?"

Dehlia slumped in her chair. *Not again. Not another interrupted party.*

As soon as he began talking, Lillian's eyes narrowed. "Give me two minutes." She dashed upstairs and returned with a pocket-sized recorder and a notebook. Alan bolted the rest of his meal and Lillian fixed up the mike and flipped on the machine. "Please, from the top."

Dehlia picked up the plates. At the counter, she wiped the crumbs into a bowl and added a big spoonful from the casserole dish for Betsy. She pulled four boxes of candles from a drawer where she'd secreted them away, uncovered the cake, and inserted the spiral stubs into the chocolate icing. Even as she counted—*fourteen, fifteen, sixteen*—she couldn't ignore the conversation.

"I'm going to cover this," Lillian said to Alan.

"Good. The more press, the better. But... journalism. It's too... neutral."

"It's never completely objective. I'll work in a slant."

"Will it really make a difference? Sometimes it seems impossible..." Dehlia felt Alan's eyes on her. "...to convince people how bad this will be," he said.

She concentrated on her candles. *Twenty-five, twenty-six, twenty-seven.*

He continued. "There's a new bill in the works, HB 149. It would protect wild salmon stocks in the Harmon drainage. Destruction of water systems could result in a fine of up to a million bucks a day. That would send Ziggurat to its knees. Sheila said there might be a local hearing. With Alaska lawmakers."

"Really!" Lillian adjusted the mike. "Politicians coming to hear what the people have to say!"

It was news to Dehlia. *Thirty-seven, thirty-eight, thirty-nine.*

Lillian scribbled furiously. Dehlia set the last candle in place. She lit them all and walked the cake to the table, taking care that each small flame wasn't extinguished in transfer. She set the cake before him. "Make a wish."

Alan stood and kissed her, then sat back down, inhaling deeply. He blew, a big gusty breath that left every candle smoking. Lillian nodded approvingly. But she didn't stop writing.

Dehlia sliced and served. A devil's food cake, his favorite. He downed his slice in five bites.

Lillian took two hasty nibbles then went back to her notebook. "Tell me again about the plans for the earthen dam."

Dehlia picked up the bowl for Betsy. Outside, the dog ate greedily, licking her palm when the food was gone. "Good girl," Dehlia said. "Good, sweet girl."

She listened for rain but there was none. Still, the air was humid. She squashed four bloody mosquitoes on her arm, brushed others from behind her ears. Insects. She could take being bitten. It was the high-pitched buzz, the females' flight noise that rose in frequency when they were engorged, that was hardest to endure.

She patted the fine fur of Betsy's head. "Tell me, sweet girl. What should I do? Love him or keep my land?"

8

Before fishing season arrived, two more groups of guests had to overnight at Whetstone. For Alan, it was a reprieve of duty. He was tired of playing the daily charmer and, as Mike put it, serving as "transportation factory." But he was glad he'd met Lillian. That was dialogue with a purpose, not some faux friendship built on the hopes of snagging a handful of dimes. He looked forward to spending time on the beach, hauling nets instead of cameras and computers. At least it would break up the routine. If only it would quit raining. July so far was making June look like dry spit. It didn't rain, it poured. Streams and sheets, torrents and tattoos; one deluge on top of another.

The weather was finally wearing on everyone's nerves. Grumbles and curses were more frequent, impatience and brusqueness now the norm. Carolyn in particular was unhappy, and she let it be known: patrons weren't meant to lodge here and detained flights were spoiling her purse. She wasn't that poetic, but everyone got the drift. Alan knew what she was thinking. *How about those panels? Will they save me money in the long run?* Others would probably agree. Solar— go to Vegas if you want to play roulette.

WHEN THE FISH HIT, the heavens were kind for five days. The rain stopped and the sun meted out a few sly winks. In the early mornings a pale fog hung over the ridges and swales and lingered through midday, and Alan, fishing this year with Dehlia, Mike, and Barbara, watched the mountainous landscape reveal itself in slivered increments. A stir was in the air.

Dehlia was a good picker, better than most at untangling fish. Alan watched in admiration as she tackled an impossible snarl. She flipped and spun and shook, sliding expert fingers under the mesh and over the gills. Times like these he wanted to arrest her focus and direct it to him. Take her in his arms and dance with her, right on the beach. But there were salmon to clean, totes to fill, nets to pull. Then Dehlia left with Barbara to begin canning.

Patricia strode over, her red hair accented by a navy-blue bandana. "Hey boys, what's shakin'?"

"Just fish from the net," said Alan.

She smiled, her freckles seeming more prominent than ever. She turned to Alan. "How's the guitar?"

"He works for a living," said Mike. "No time for leisure, no government subsidies."

Alan scowled. *No, just mining company subsidies.*

Patricia faked indignation. "I've always supported myself."

"But you write music, not li-tra-ture," said Mike.

She snorted before returning to business. "I hope you're preparing for the hearing," said Patricia. "There's a date now, August thirty. It'll be our chance to speak out. And there's more good news. We have boycotts."

Boycotts? Alan stared at her dumbly. *Of what? From whom?*

"Big-name jewelers. Zales, Tiffany, Ben Bridge. Along with about forty-five others."

Alan still didn't get it, but Mike was nodding. "They won't buy," Mike said.

"You got it," said Patricia. "No Fly Creek gold. They're taking a stand. They pledged not to use dirty gold. They don't want their jewelry to come from a mine where there'd be such huge environmental impact. Tiffany's even running an ad in *National Geographic*."

Mike kept nodding and Alan's spirits soared. He had a sudden, renewed awareness of his whole circulatory system, down to those minute capillaries. *Three strikes, Ziggurat, and you're out.* There was the upcoming hearing. The *L.A. Times* article. And now this boycott. It was the best news he'd had all summer.

9

The letter arrived on a Friday, but Dehlia didn't open it. She didn't know why. She was tired. She'd spent the afternoon with patrons, come home, and weeded her garden. Alan played his guitar for the first time in weeks, and they'd talked about ways to hinge her transformation mask. They'd made love. He was tender with her.

The letter sat that night. On a corner of the table where she'd left it.

Later she would wonder what would have happened if he'd never learned of it, if she'd opened it when he was away. Maybe she would have accepted the gift as good fortune best left secret. Maybe she would have made her phone call and been satisfied with the response. Or maybe she would have had stirrings of concern. Knew somehow that it would change things.

She did open it. In the morning, after a lazy breakfast of scrambled eggs, she put on her reading glasses and slit the envelope—one clean swipe with the fillet knife that had been a wedding gift for her and Phil—then, with a mostly incurious second thought, she went back and read the return address: Birkenhausen & Associates, Chicago, IL. She didn't recognize the name.

The letter was written in block type, with the company's address at the top, her name and address underneath, then the date, August 4. Very formal, very clean. Dear Mrs. Melven, signed Sincerely Yours, an inked signature by Ian Birkenhausen himself. The privilege. The professionalism. One could hardly care about the contents.

But she read the contents, then read them again, trying but not quite managing to absorb the information. The little ohs and wows that escaped her lips drew Alan's attention, and he peppered her with questions.

"What's that?"

"A note from some law office."

"And?"

"It's about some trust."

"Trust?"

"Yes, a trust fund has been established in my name." She tried to suppress a smile. What was it about money—no matter how much you thought it didn't count, no matter how much you contended it was best to shun, no matter how much you swore it couldn't control your life, when it landed in your lap, well, there it was. A happiness you couldn't dispute.

"Who's the benefactor?"

"Phil. It says Phil."

"How much?"

"Two million."

"Two *million*." Alan chuckled. "It's gotta be a mistake."

She shrugged helplessly, feeling a relinquishment of power.

Alan frowned. "Can't be right. Phil's—"

Dehlia saw him struggle for the word: *dead*. "Maybe Phil set it up a long time ago and I'm just now learning about it," she said. That seemed perfectly plausible.

"Did he ever mention anything about all this loot?"

"Never."

"Jesus. When does it say you can withdraw it?"

She read the notice a third time. "The money can be transferred automatically to an account or investment package of my choice." She liked the convenience of that. Minimal paperwork. Minimal effort. But it wasn't that simple. "I have to decide on installments. I'll have to call."

Alan picked up a pen, but he had nothing to write on. She watched him do the calculations in his head.

"You're forty-three. If you live forty more years and you divide it evenly, you could have a million by the time you're sixty-three. Half a mil when you're fifty-three. Two hundred and fifty thou' in five years, that's fifty K a year." He set down the pen. "Roughly."

She wasn't sure about his backward math, but it was an estimate. *God. Everything I've hoped for, worried and waited for over the years, could be answered in this one letter. Like a snap of the fingers, a magic wand, everything I need is mine, now and forever.* And suddenly it all seemed wrong, too facile. What on earth would she do with all that money? What did others do? Invest it, so they could make more money, so the big numbers could become bigger numbers. She remembered the story of the Little Prince, who, on the fourth planet he visits, encounters the businessman. The man owned over five hundred million stars.

"And what good," the Little Prince asks, "does it do you to own the stars?"

"It does me the good of making me rich," the man says.

"And what good does it do you to be rich?"

"It makes it possible for me to buy more stars, if any are discovered."

Dehlia folded the letter and tucked it back in the envelope. She felt unexplainably sad. She wanted to go to her garden, thin carrots, pull weeds. Do the good dirty work of handling earth. But again the rain had started.

Alan was shaking his head. "Something's not right. It's a mistake."

He was probably right. It didn't add up. Plus, never in her life had she lucked into serious money. No matter. There were chores to do. Haul wood. Burn trash. She'd have to wait until Monday to call and find out.

10

The girl was young, far younger than most Whetstone visitors. A college sophomore, maybe. While Alan was loading the guests' bags into the four-wheeler trailer, the girl said she didn't want to wait at the airstrip. She asked him to point the way to the art building. She struck him then as someone with a mission.

He gassed up the four-wheeler while the others hemmed and hawed and finally declined an offer for a ride. These guests, older and slower, would take their time. They weren't daunted by the rain— several had even brought umbrellas.

Alan drove to the art building and parked under the covered area. He entered the building. The girl, already inside, had removed her boots and donned shiny black pumps. She wore a bulky, thick-collared sweater and tight jeans. One hand held a small backpack. Her cropped hair had an uneven cut that was meant to be stylish, and Alan decided that it was. Her poncho sat like a child's teepee in the middle of the floor surrounded by a pool of water. Alan picked it up and hung it properly on a hook.

The girl threw him a quick thanks. It gave her an easy opening. "I'm Ajax. Do you know Meredith Stone?"

Meredith Stone. The name sounded like a drumbeat in his head. How should he answer? He couldn't think that fast, still preparing to introduce himself.

"I've been looking at these displays," Ajax went on, with a sweep of the hand, "but I don't see anything about her. I was *so* hoping to meet her."

He took in the artwork on the wall. What loomed at him was Barbara's latest creation, just hung, a mixed-media piece she'd titled *The Marriage of Heaven and Hell.*

"Is she a friend of yours?" he asked. That was a stupid question. How could Meredith have been a friend if the girl wanted to meet her for the first time?

"No! Here—I'll show you." Ajax unzipped her backpack and pulled out a large Ziploc that held several books. She handed one to Alan—a slim volume—and he saw that the others were identical. The cover was solid white with a line drawing of a goat. *Capricorn*, it said.

"I'm a poet, see? And I got these contributor's copies of this magazine—they sent me three—because I have a poem in it, and Meredith has this poem too that I just *love,* and I read her bio and found out that she lives here, so I wanted to come and meet her..."

Was youth really that breathless? "I'm sorry," said Alan. "Meredith doesn't live here anymore." He felt calm, paternal.

He watched the thousand tiny stars in her eyes withdraw, down to a hundred, then ten, and finally, none. Just jade-green eyes. Bright though. Lucid. She could take it. At her age adjustments were easy.

"Oh." She stood for a moment, unsure what to do. Then she perked up. "But you knew her?"

"Yes."

"Would you like to read it? Her poem? And mine?" She flipped through the volume. "Here!"

What could he say? He saw the name—*Meredith Stone*—and his heart pounded again as he recalled her web of rocks, her nakedness, her plunge. Vanished. Only to appear again in a new form. He read.

BARE
For P.

Those days you came to me were not just days,
Nor even mere clichés—heaven on Earth
Or any unbearable, too familiar thing.
Oh, we were bare, all right, stripped down
To hair and teeth and nails and ring—
The last contentious, a nub of gold
That cut above my rib and bruised my neck,
That you persisted yet to wear,
For fear of losing it—or worse, her

Finding out. Oh, how deliciously it hurt,
When once you cursed

"I love you!" (reckless voice, almost hoarse)
To which I panted, *Now. Take me. Take me*
Like a bear. And so you cuffed and grunted,
And I purred and gnawed and hissed,
For no single animal was I, although I wasn't wed.
Then you rolled me over, and I played
—For one long minute—dead. Before I came

Alive again, and seizured to a spin. So now you're
Gone? What bitter trick, how trite. With you went
Your bluff, your innocence, your stealth, while I,
Mere weight—a tossed auxiliary—am left, sole witness
To your treachery. What shall I do? The knowledge
Preys. It stalks, inhales. This much I'll tell:
The dead are dead. I am refusing grief.
What were you, anyway, to me,
Other than my fuse, my blaze, my life?

He was unaccustomed to reading poetry. It took him a minute to
get the rhythm, to move from line to line to complete each sentence.
At first he didn't catch the metaphors, but then he felt like he'd been
broadsided with a shovel. And the dedication: *For P.* The "you" in
the poem—who else? The person addressed was Phil. Phil Melven.
Likened to a bear. What had Billy said? *The guy done something bad.*
He turn himself into a bear so he can come back and make corrections.
That mattress on the floor of Meredith's place, where the window
had fallen... Oh, lover boy, was this how you spent your time? When
you were supposed to be doing legal work? Or maybe you were doing
both... Alan knew then that the money, the two million, was for real.
And it had something to do with Ziggurat.

Acid seeped into the back of his throat. He could feel himself
trembling.

Ajax gave him a troubled look. "Are you okay?"

He managed a nod but the voice in his head said *No. Not even*
close. "I have a... stomachache." He fumbled, using his fingers like
he was hitching a train to couple together a string of words. "I can't
read your poem, but I'm sure it's great." He pushed the magazine at
her, but she pushed it back.

"Read it when you can."

Alan nodded again and tucked the magazine inside his shirt, where it rested searingly close to his flesh.

"Would you," he found himself asking, "make sure the visitors get their stuff? It's all in the trailer. Just undo the lashings on the tarp."

Ajax assured him that she would.

HE TRIED TO SPRINT, but his boots wouldn't allow it. His walk felt more like a hobble, the ruts and puddles mean impediments to his progress.

Mike wasn't home, but Betsy met him at the door. He'd taken to leaving her at Mike's during the day, away from the generator noise, out of the rain. He let her out briefly to pee, shut her in again, and headed for Barbara's.

Mike was there, but he and Barbara were about to leave. Lunch duty, said Barbara. Alan stood in the door, blocking their passage. He peeled off his raincoat and reached inside his shirt. "Read it," he ordered, "page sixty-three."

Mike and Barbara exchanged glances. Mike held out a listless hand and read the poem without comment. He passed the book to Barbara. Alan watched her intently and saw her wince.

"That's awful. Don't show it to Dehlia, whatever you do!"

Alan's throat hurt. It was the acid again.

Mike nodded coldly. "We knew it was going on, we just didn't know how obsessed she was."

"You *knew*? Why didn't you *tell* me?" But Mike *had* told him, in a way. "I mean, from the beginning?"

Mike shrugged. "I didn't think it was that important. I didn't know it was a heavy affair."

"We don't want to hurt Dehlia," said Barbara.

"But anyone could read this! It's been published!"

"Alan, Alan, calm down." Mike took a breath. "It's a literary journal. No one reads them."

"I read it. And you, and Barbara, and Ajax. That's four right there!"

"Okay, but percentage-wise. Forget it. It's not a big deal."

Barbara gripped Alan's arm but he shook off her hand.

"What else do you know about Meredith?"

Mike shrugged again. "Nothing. She had a lot of money."

A lot of money. "What's the source?"

Mike looked at Barbara. For once his face wore a cloud of uncertainty.

She hesitated. "A rich uncle, I heard. In London."

A rich uncle in London. Alan's mind danced backward. Patricia at the presentation, saying, "Not only that, now there's a London-based company backing Ziggurat... Big, big money." And another: the book left at Meredith's place when Indigo and Indi first moved in. *Geology, Economics, and the Law.* And Dehlia's letter, the notice of the two-million-dollar trust. This was coming together, and it was not good. He was hot, then cold. He could feel himself shaking again.

"Alan, put your coat on. Come to lunch with us." Barbara's persuasiveness was almost too much. Alan glared at her.

"C'mon, let's go," Mike urged.

He refused. He was sullen. He was proud. He said he was headed back to work.

11

The day broke clear, as if a shroud had finally lifted. Beneath sou'westers and hoods, people had scarcely noticed the transformation. Fireweed, though late, were in full bloom; monkshood were beginning to tease open their purple shades; red currants hung in plump clusters on the trails near her house, waiting to be picked. Another week and most would be past their prime. Dehlia took advantage of the sun's appearance. She plopped handful after handful of the soft ripe berries into her bucket, and in two hours she had all she needed.

She simmered the currants in a large pot, mashed them gently with a big spoon, then transferred the hot pulp into a mesh bag and hung it from a ceiling nail. The juice came quickly at first, streaming into the catch bowl before slowing to a steady drip.

Picking, juicing, straining—pleasant tasks to follow another hectic day. She'd given her presentation that morning, helped with dishwashing after lunch. Now it was almost seven, and Alan would arrive soon.

It was cause for apprehension. She hadn't seen him in three days, and he would want to know about the money, probably still thinking it was a hoax. She would have to tell him, *No, I talked to the law office and everything in the letter is authentic. The money is mine. The only thing they want is documentation on some personal account of Phil's.* But where would she find a record of that? Not in the file cabinet. She would've seen it there. Perhaps in the upstairs closet? It was worth a look.

Alan arrived and entered without knocking. He'd showered and put on a fresh shirt, but his eyes were haggard. "So what's the story," he said.

"The story?"

"About the money."

He might as well have tied a rock to her heart. She felt herself sinking. Why couldn't he go easy for a change? "Yes, it's for real. Shall I make something to eat?"

He sat down but didn't take off his jacket. "When does it all kick in?"

"I have to call back. They need information on one of Phil's accounts. I'm not sure where it is—maybe in the satchel upstairs." She frowned. "I've never been through it." Immediately she regretted sharing this.

"You've never been through it? Why not?"

"I don't know. I just haven't."

Why not indeed? It had taken her so long just to deal with Phil's clothes. She'd set the satchel aside and simply hadn't come back to it. His legal papers, she supposed. Business affairs, probably nothing worth keeping.

"Get it." Alan's voice was very low.

"What?" She swayed a little, stunned.

"Get the satchel. There's something we need to find out." His voice still lacked inflection.

"Alan... why don't we have something to eat?"

On the counter behind her the currant juice dripped steadily into the bowl, a muffled *plunk, plunk, plunk,* like the tick of dead minutes.

She looked at him. Never had she seen him so stern. For an instant she wanted to cradle him, smooth his hair, quiet him with a kiss. It was a passing impulse. She could see that he wouldn't budge. "All right," she said. *If I must.*

She climbed to the loft and found the satchel on the shelf behind an old afghan. The leather was black and covered with a fine layer of dust. She slung the strap over her shoulder and lugged the bag downstairs, remembering when Stew had gone back on the trail to retrieve it. How it had lain for hours in the corner behind Phil's corpse. When they had taken away the body, she could no longer look at it. So she had relegated it, like a hush, to the closet.

Downstairs, she hefted it onto the table and Alan fastened his eyes on it. For the first time she saw that the clasp included a little keyhole, and she realized it was probably locked. "I don't have a key," she said.

"It's just brass."

And before she could protest he pulled out his multi-tool and worked the plate loose with a screwdriver, using it as a small pry. The bent latch lay like a twisted scar before their eyes.

She unzipped the main compartment. Inside were three divisions, and she pulled the papers from each one, keeping the stacks separate. Immediately, Alan began sifting through them, his eyes steely with intensity.

"Alan…" There was no point. Nothing she could say would stop him.

He zeroed in on one of the documents. He grunted. "British Global Resources, plc, 50 Chesterfield Terrace, London SW2Y6AN, United Kingdom." He scanned the pages, devouring them, while she looked on in dismay. Then he shook them, like a wolf reprimanding its cub. "You know what this is?"

"How could I possibly know?"

"It's a statement of Phil's involvement with Ziggurat. He was bridging the gap between them and the Brits. He was helping support the Fly Creek Mine!"

It wasn't possible. He was making it up. "Alan, don't do this."

"But it's true! Read it yourself!"

He thrust the papers at her as she backed away. Undaunted, he read them aloud as she gripped the edge of the counter with both hands. She was numb. She could hear his words, but she couldn't. He leafed through the second stack, pulling out documents and reading more snippets. Each was a sharp arrow, and they were hitting the straw target of her chest while her eyes gazed blankly at nothing. Her mind felt drugged.

He moved to the last stack. He dug with purpose, a starved animal that had picked up a food scent.

She gripped the bag of currants and squeezed. The juice streamed out.

He tore out the contents of a large envelope, and his voice went soft. "I knew it. I fucking knew it. Do you know who wrote this letter? Meredith. Meredith Stone."

She squeezed harder.

"Do you know who it's to?"

She shook her head.

"British Global Resources. Attention: Paul Stone."

He didn't scan it this time. He simply read: "Dear Uncle Paul, On behalf of the legal work done by Phil Melven regarding the Fly Creek Mine and Alaska law, we request payment in the amount of five million, a sum which should both cover his services and give us enough to live on once we relocate outside of Whetstone. I'm so anxious to start my new life with him!" Alan's voice dropped. "God. I learn more by the minute."

She clung to the currant bag. Surely the red liquid was not her blood.

"So Meredith's the one who set up your trust! Your *trust*! And look where she got her money!"

Dehlia stopped squeezing. Some giant machine had just rumbled along and scooped out her insides. Was this what she had felt coming so long ago? This hurt, so huge and raw.

Alan kept leafing, sifting, reading. No, consuming. With an appetite that was no longer a beast's. It was a man's now, utterly irrational.

"Oh no. It's too much!" He was laughing. He was hysterical. "Broderman! He was in on it! He was assisting! A consultant, no less. The slimy son-of-a-bitch!"

Dehlia crumpled. She was on the floor with her hands over her ears. She remembered the story of Joseph Pulitzer, who could no longer endure noise in the last decades of his life. He had retreated to the hushed, womblike stateroom of his private yacht, or had sequestered himself in a soundproofed room that he named The Vault. Its windows were triple glazed, its double walls stuffed with insulation. She wanted to live like that. To die like that.

"Alan," she said. "Stop. Just stop."

And he came and stood above her, looking down, as she held her hands over her ears.

"It's true," he said. "Everything I said is true."

12

Alan slept not a wink. He didn't toss and turn. He simply lay, flat on his back, eyes closed, revisiting the pain. Their pain. His and hers. Like bath towels—one for each body. Nothing hurt like seeing her hurt, and he was responsible. He'd thought once that Dehlia would repair him; instead she seemed to have brought out his worst. The side that overreacted, the side he'd been trying to suppress since his time in Whetstone. Once again he'd let his impulses take over.

But how could he have known what was in Meredith's letter? It was addressed to British Global Resources. He hadn't meant to expose the affair. Neither had Phil, of course. Phil had locked his satchel. Not that Dehlia would ever have pried. And Phil hadn't planned on dying—he was in the prime of life. Like that Russian figure skater—what was his name?—who collapsed of a heart attack at twenty-eight. Phil probably never intended to leave Dehlia either. What Meredith had written about her and Phil leaving together was just some utopian dream. The reference wasn't in the poem. In the poem, Phil wouldn't remove his wedding ring. Meredith's letter, anyway, had been written earlier; Alan had noted the date. The letter was Phil's only oversight. There were no love notes, no other shreds of evidence. Phil had been careful—just one little flub.

And Meredith? Apparently she, too, had thought she was covering her tracks. There was the problem of the poem, but maybe Mike was right: who would read it? Still, she could have used a pseudonym. She could have omitted the part in her bio about where she lived. But she must have been suffering incredible guilt. So she tried to make it up to Dehlia by leaving her all that money. A trust. Ha. What had happened to the rest, the other three million? Likely it never was paid. Those multi-billion-dollar companies could only squeeze two million from their tight wallets. Alan gritted his teeth.

As if everything that had happened was the fault of some foreign executive. But money was probably what drew Meredith and Phil together in the first place. Alan could imagine how it all came to be: Meredith moves to town, learns about the mine (long before the public does, of course), the uncle finds out where she's living, asks her to do a little research, it's a bit over her head, she asks (innocently) Phil's advice, there's a mutual attraction, followed by an offer for legal services rendered, and before you know it, things are out of control. It's torrid. They've dug themselves in so far they can't get out.

It was one theory. The other was more insidious, that Meredith's presence in Whetstone was pre-planned. Like a first-degree murder, and she was her own best weapon. What man in his most upstanding right mind wouldn't have found her hard to resist? She'd lured Phil in, knowing that an attorney with local connections could be of use. The ultimate manipulator. So she could collect—a few coins at first. A bit of seed gold. Then the promise of more riches.

Hell, Alan didn't know, and neither did Mike. Last night the two of them had sat up until two in the morning, looking at it all from twenty different angles. Alan told Mike everything: about Carolyn's grant, his struggle and decision to stay on the job in spite of it, how it had left him feeling like a coward. Mike just listened. As for Alan's part in uncovering Phil and Meredith's scheme, Mike was judicious. The closest he came to a reprimand was to ask if Alan's approach had been prudent. "You'll have to decide where your loyalty is," he had said, "to your principles or your love. You can't always have both."

Without Alan, Mike admitted, everything may not have been found out now, though Dehlia would have opened the satchel eventually. And maybe it would have been easier on her if she'd discovered it herself. Ultimately, did it matter?

YES, IT MATTERS a fuck of a lot, thought Alan, achingly awake in his own bed and wishing he'd never set foot in this town. All these hidden things, so much deception. They're a wall. A barrier. A mask. *I need to tell Dehlia that.* No wonder she's a mask carver. But why was he putting the blame on her? He was guilty of holding back too. If only the two of them had been more open...

Well, too late for that, you schmuck. Look what you've done. It's over. Now you're a wreck. What would Broderman say? A bleating Lamb.

Half the night, he rebuked himself. Toward morning he'd had enough with self-pity. *Just go tell her what's on your mind.* Clean and simple. Might as well have it all out. Anyway, he needed to get his stuff.

HE LEFT AT SIX, wanting to get there early before he was faced with the day's duties, and hoping to catch her before she left the house. He strapped on his empty backpack and laced up his boots. For once it wasn't raining. He glanced at Betsy, curled on her rug. Should he bring her along? No, the dog would only deepen her hurt.

He reached her door in twenty minutes. He knocked, three good raps, and waited. Nothing. He rapped again.

She came to the window. She was dressed; that was a good sign. She opened the door but wouldn't look at him.

"Dehlia." He stood stupidly, wishing she'd meet his eyes. "I came to get my things."

She backed away, allowing him entrance.

He saw that she'd already made a pile; a few shirts, a pair of jeans, some songbooks. His guitar. He watched helplessly as she picked them up in three separate bundles and set them near the door. Then she sat with her back to him on the couch.

He filled his backpack, taking his time. He swallowed, trying to work something down in his throat. Again he said her name, again she didn't respond. He stood in the doorway. "Dehlia, can I talk?"

She gave a brief nod, and he folded his arms and leaned against the door. This would be a monologue, but it was better than nothing. He made several jumpstarts in his head before he got his beginning right. He didn't want to implore or snivel or sob. He just wanted to be honest.

"My actions are beyond apology, but... God, I'm sorry. I overreacted, like I always do. I... I've been frustrated with the rain. I think my job's at stake. I don't know if I even want this job. The only reason I'm still in Whetstone is because of you... But waiting is hard for me... I want everything to happen too fast. I didn't sleep last night. All I did was think about you, about us. And this crazy situation."

He gathered his thoughts.

"It's hard to explain how I feel about this mine. It's... personal. If Phil was cheating on you, then Ziggurat's cheating on the whole country. There was Meredith and the money, and... I had to find out... like it was my stupid destiny. Here's the thing: a few months after I got here I was at Carolyn's, and I found an application she was filling out for a renewable energy grant. To Ziggurat. For solar panels and labor to pay someone to install them."

He took a breath. "I'm the installer. Some of that money's going to me. It's been bugging the hell out of me. Maybe that's why I ended up in Whetstone—to see if I really stood by my talk. I would have left. But you... I know, I already said that."

The thing in his throat was back. He swallowed. "You think I'm exaggerating."

A third swallow. "Okay, there's more. After Sarah's divorce, I tried to help her. I went to The Buckaroo Club in Anchorage, where her ex hung out, and I jumped him in the parking lot. He beat the shit out of me. He's shorter than me, but he's a muley son-of-a-bitch. And he cut me with a broken beer bottle that he picked off the pavement. That's how I got the scar on my chin. I only wanted him to own up to his responsibilities and start sending Sarah some money. I failed her. I failed my sister. Now I'm failing her again, with this grant, this mine. Fishing is all she knows. If the fish are gone, then..."

Dehlia hadn't moved, and he saw that he might as well conclude. His voice quavered. "When I first met you, that night at Patricia's, I thought, *Is she ever fine*. That hasn't changed. I still feel that way. I've told you I love you. But I need to hear it back. I want more than three days a week. I want eight days a week, thirteen months a year." He cleared his throat. "I just wanted you to understand."

"You lied to me," she said bitterly.

"Yes," he said. "I lied. I don't deserve you."

He hoisted his backpack and picked up his guitar. He straightened his shoulders. She had nothing more to say. Something had been done that an apology couldn't undo. His first tear fell before he closed the door.

13

The weeks passed. Alan didn't come. Barbara didn't come. Dehlia didn't care; she craved no conversation. Strangely, her days at the art building were the easiest: she could explain her process, pick up her adze, and chip away at the wood without having to engage. It was all rote.

"I start with a piece of white birch. It needs to be green, so it can dry slowly without checking. These are my tools: crooked knife, straight knife, adze." She held them up, each in turn. "I do preliminary drawings. But the mask always takes on its own form."

Chip, chip, remove, incise.

If there were questions, her responses were well rehearsed. If she made a mistake, no one knew the difference.

ON THE DAY OF THE HEARING, she wore black. It wasn't meant to convey a funereal look, but to make herself less conspicuous. All summer she'd worn reds and yellows, as if to offset the dreary weather; after the rift with Alan she reached only for drab clothing, hoping to be swallowed inside the unrelenting clouds that pressed down again like layers of gray felt.

She wouldn't have gone at all, but Carolyn had ordered it: all community members were expected to be present. The hearing was scheduled for twelve o'clock.

DEHLIA WAS THE last to arrive, and the room was crammed. At the back hung a group of people she didn't recognize that had traveled from surrounding villages. Some looked to be Dena'ina, from Valatga Qayeh. A table stood next to them—they'd brought food. One man with a tie and sport coat fiddled with a huge camera; there would be

TV coverage.

Already in her seat, Carolyn was surrounded by a small entourage: Dan, Greg Reynolds, and caretakers Amy and Ken. And Blake, the poor old man—they'd dragged him here again. Who else? Derek. It had been months since Dehlia had seen him, and he'd aged.

The remaining Whetstone crowd made up a bulwark on the right. Alan sat in one of the seats with his head bent, writing. Three empty chairs loomed in the middle, and Dehlia took one of them, dead center. She felt like a leper, space on either side.

The five politicians sat in front with a stenographer, busy at her machine. Facing them was an empty chair and a long table equipped with a microphone; those who testified would address the lawmakers. She slumped. This wouldn't be so bad. Nothing would be required of her. All she had to do was listen.

Finally, the borough mayor came forward, oddly cheerful for the seriousness of the moment. "I'd like to welcome the senators and House members for coming today. We have a much bigger turnout than expected, so we'll have to limit the length of the testimonies." He turned to the panel.

There was a muffled discussion, and the chairman spoke. "Testimonies cannot exceed two minutes."

"Two minutes!" Patricia jumped from her chair. "First you tell us ten, then five, now two! We're all scrambling to rewrite our notes!"

"I'm sorry, that's the best we can do."

Patricia sat down unhappily.

People moved to the back for food, some for second helpings. Dehlia stayed put. This was going to be long. Forever. *You know what forever means? In perpetuity.* Or maybe it was the other way around: *You know what in perpetuity means? Forever.* When he'd said it, she'd thought of marriage. Marriage! How far away that seemed now.

Barbara walked by and laid a hand on her shoulder—a little touch of comfort. It said, *I haven't forgotten you, my friend.*

Eventually, the chairman announced that it was time to begin. "Names will be drawn. When you come up, be seated and state your name. Keep your testimony short. It should only address House Bill 149, a bill designed for the protection of wild salmon. It is not an opportunity to speak about the Fly Creek Mine."

There was a murmur of protest, and a female voice—Sheila's—fumed, "Oh, bullshit."

The first person was called, a man from Valatga. He walked to the front, tall and broad shouldered. He didn't flinch. "My name is Jimmy Andrew and I support HB 149."

Dehlia closed her eyes. This was a one-hundred-act play. People came up and delivered their lines. And again she thought: *all I have to do is listen.*

"Dr. Lee Ann Sanders."

There was a lull while the woman took the testimony seat.

"I'm Dr. Sanders." (An intelligent, self-assured voice.) "I'm a fish biologist, and I've been studying salmon around here for ten years. Dead salmon were found last summer near the drilling site. When the water was analyzed, it was highly acidic. Many of the chemicals we found were the same used by Ziggurat in test drilling. This is more than mere coincidence. We'll continue monitoring..."

"Dr. Sanders," the chairman interrupted.

"Salmon have incredible intolerance to the smallest amount of copper in water—just two parts per billion can affect their olfactory sense when they're trying to locate their spawning grounds. If the Fly Creek Mine—"

"Dr. Sanders, we ask that you not reference this mine in your testimony."

"Okay... *if,* say, industrial development *such as* an open-pit mine... oh, forget it. I feel like I have a muzzle on. I support this bill."

Clapping. Dehlia pulled her sweater sleeves over her hands. With her sight shut down all sound was amplified. She felt like she was inside a drum. Very large, like one of those used in orchestras.

"Please hold your applause," said the chairman.

Murmurs, voices dying down.

"Ed Durham."

A swishing, confident stride, pant legs rubbing together. Back of the room to the front.

"My name's Ed Durham and I'm a businessman. I've made good money through my investment company and stocks. Some of those are in the seafood industry. I'm a dyed-in-the-wool Republican and

I support economic development. But not this mine, this fifteen-thousand-pound elephant in the room we're not allowed to talk about. Not here, not in this place."

"Mr. Durham—"

"Every year, forty million fish return to Bristol Bay. Fourteen thousand jobs are connected to the fishery, and Ziggurat is promising only two thousand construction jobs. British Global Resources earned ten *billion* last year, after taxes. I support HB 149."

"Thank you, Mr. Durham. Brad Ford."

An overturned chair, then, "Shit!" A nasal voice. The chair re-righted.

"I'm a driller, name of Brad Ford. I worked at Fly Creek. When we were doing drill tests we sucked up all these fry out of the creek, and they were just lying there on the tundra. Hundreds of 'em. Doornail dead. I support the bill."

Coughs, a sneeze. Dehlia dropped her chin inside the collar of her sweater. Would she catch another cold? Who knew what you could be exposed to at these kinds of gatherings?

"Mary Clark."

A quiet one. She was wearing slippers, maybe.

"I'm Mary Clark from Karshekovski. I'm from a mining family. We need oil and gas to run our snowmachines and four-wheelers so we can practice subsistence. This bill will cut off all our allowable access to the country. We need jobs to get to places where we hunt and fish. If we don't have an economy, we'll create our own form of cultural genocide."

"*Cultural genocide?*" It was Mike Trotter. "Spare me the hyperbole!"

"Darlene McCoy."

Heavy footsteps, unmistakable. Dehlia could visualize her ample bosom.

"I'm Darlene McCoy. My husband Stew and I have lived in Whetstone for nineteen years. You politicians don't understand the importance of salmon here. I mean, not just in Whetstone, but in every village in the whole region. Salmon to us are like beef and corn to people who live in Iowa. I am in favor of this bill, and I support using part of the EPA's Clean Water Act to—"

"Listen—"

"No, *you* listen. It's my two minutes. I support using part of the EPA's Clean Water Act to deny use of an area as a disposal site if the discharge will harm spawning areas."

A long sigh from the chairman. The chair scraped the floor as Darlene moved away and the next person was called. "Ralph Gage."

The name was familiar, but Dehlia couldn't place him.

"I'm Ralph Gage. I'm a teacher now, but before that I worked as an environmental chemist. Fly Creek isn't like other mines. The minerals there aren't in veins. The rock has to be crushed. The copper is chalcopyrite—copper, iron, and sulfide all bonded together. Pyrites turn into sulfuric acid, and it's really nasty, basically battery acid. Some leftover rock will go acid right away, some of it will take forty to sixty years. But acid drainage can last thousands of years. Some of the leftover rock will be put underwater, to keep the acid from forming immediately. But removing all the bad rock will be impossible, because there'll be billions of tons of waste. Enough said. I support HB 149."

Battery acid? Dehlia saw her jeans pocked full of holes, her first-hand experience with the acid's caustic effects.

"Rick Evanoff."

A quick walker. Someone very fit.

"I'm from Valatga. Our people depend on salmon..." Dehlia tightened her eyes, but she was finding it hard to concentrate. *He'll testify soon, I know it. Will he mention me?* "...mine permitting in this state is done by only three people..." *Will he speak of love and responsibility and accuse me publicly for not taking sides?* "...in Nevada where a thousand fish died along one creek." *I could stand up and say I'll go away with him.* "...in Colorado metals and cyanide killed a seventeen-mile stretch of river." *This is my opportunity to speak... I can explain it all... my fears.* "...near Questa, New Mexico, acid from an open-pit mine turned the Red River blue."

"Thank you, Mr. Evanoff. Alan Lamb."

Dehlia caught her breath. She knew the fall of every footstep. He was wearing his work boots. She opened her eyes and watched him take his seat.

"My name is Alan Lamb. I've lived in Alaska all my life, and I have a sister who fishes Bristol Bay. I wish you could hear her stories. She says that standing on the deck of a gillnetter on the flood tide in late June, you can look out on the water and see five or six salmon jumping all at once, and when you turn and look in another direction you see salmon rolling everywhere, all around the boat, and you know the whole bay is alive and you're sitting on maybe half a million fish that are making a push for the river. This project is crazy, insane. This protest isn't about economic shutdown. It's about not mining in a place that's the greatest red salmon fishery on the planet."

The room quieted and people seemed to hang on every word. He had spoken eloquently, poetically. He hadn't betrayed her. Love rushed through her like a sickle.

"Three more testimonies, then we'll break," the chairman said. "Martha Brown."

Dehlia remembered her. She'd met her once, in Anchorage of all places. Gentle and wrinkled and walnut skinned. Dehlia gazed fondly at the deeply etched face, a face that seemed to rise out of shadowed centuries.

"My name is Martha Brown. I was born in Valatga Qayeh. I'm old now, so I'm an elder. To our people, the Dena'ina, that mountain, you call it Lost Mountain, is sacred. In our language the name is a little different. It is named after a girl, very young, who got lost, and so we call it 'Mountain Where She Lost Her Way.' I think about this mine so close and I think about that dynamite and how it's gonna blow up part of that mountain. And I think these people who do this are madmen, or maybe they are the ones are lost. So I hope they can be found. Just like the girl—they find her, you know. And restore her to her family. That is how I see it. That is all."

Dehlia's eyes welled. Her vision blurred, and despite her resolve to watch the rest of the testimonies she was having a hard time seeing.

"Bryce Peterson."

Bryce walked forward just ahead of Jen, and Dehlia watched their two lean figures wave like candle flames in a drafty room.

"I'm Bryce Peterson and this is my wife, Jen. We're testifying as one. We've been jewelers for fifteen years. We've made earrings, necklaces, bracelets, the works. Mostly gold. When we first heard about this mine, we thought, 'Great.' Of course. We're in the business. But we know more now. For a porphyry mine it takes *thousands of tons of crushed ore to get one little ring.* And eighty percent of all mined gold goes to jewelry. Eighty percent!"

Jen picked up the thread. "Humans love to adorn themselves. We wear shiny things, things that glitter. From now on Bryce and I will make jewelry from natural objects: beach stones, driftwood, and best of all: salmon. Yes, dried vertebrae and gill plates. They're beautiful! Today, we're starting a pool. We're going to make a gift. Do you see these rings?"

They held up their left hands.

"Our wedding rings. Solid gold. We're giving them up." Jen lifted an old gold pan from the table, and she and Bryce dropped their rings into it, where they landed with two resonant pings. "We welcome donations. We'll be giving the proceeds to fight this mine."

Dehlia's vision cleared. *My wedding ring. What value does it have now? Lying under a towel in a closed drawer.*

Patricia and Sheila rose from their seats, whistling and shouting. "Yeah! Right on!" Greg and Dan booed. One of the senators banged his fist on the table. "Quiet! Enough!"

The chairman said, "One more before the break. Carolyn Parsons."

Carolyn came forward, head held high and her face calm and determined. She rested one hand on her heart before sitting at the microphone. It was strange, looking at the back of her head. Carolyn, the town leader, appealing to a panel. But finally she was going to say her piece.

"I'm Carolyn Parsons. My father, Blake Parsons, founded this town."

Dehlia looked at the old man seated near her. Paler than ever, he didn't stir.

"Whetstone was my father's pride, and after his stroke, I carried on. I kept his dream alive. I've worked *so* hard, but he"—she choked— "he started it. We made it possible for all you artists to work."

She turned to the audience, her shoulders shaking. "I've waited until now to state my position because I wanted to know where everyone stood without my influence. And it seems that most of you have turned against—Blake. Maybe no one here has ever really loved a parent. If you did, you would understand. I don't care what it costs, I will take care of him! I will not put him in a home! We need medical services, a clinic, right here in Whetstone. And Ziggurat will make it happen. Is that such a sin?"

She turned back to the panel. "I have bills to pay. I have my father to take care of. We lost four planeloads of guests to weather this season, and today is another day without income. I've been floating this community from my own pocket. What I get in rent isn't enough. We need more revenue. Ziggurat offers community grants, and I'd be crazy not to consider them. I do not support HB 149."

She stood, and the chairman called for a short break.

Dehlia sat limply, her emotions drained. Carolyn's words had not, in the end, come as much of a surprise. It was what she'd suspected all along: Carolyn supported the mining project. Across the room she saw Alan lean in for a private conversation with Mike, then Patricia, his lips almost touching her hair. Fiery red. Dehlia would never live up to someone like her.

She walked to the back and took in the spread of food. Salmon, mostly. Baked fish, smoked fish, some in strips, some in fillets: bright orange and deep, glossy red. There was akutaq, berries mixed with whipped lard. Sourdough bread and moose stew. But the salmon was the most striking.

What an incredible thing, their life cycle. Starting in fresh water, the smolts' innate urge to travel to sea, their long swim; the adults fattening themselves on the ocean's bounty; then their taxing return—in two to four years—if they were lucky enough to avoid the perils of sea lions and seals, orcas and other fishermen's nets. To arrive here, finally, at their beginnings, to nourish the people once more. For all her years in Whetstone, she'd never fully appreciated them. She would never look at them again in quite the same way.

14

September was fading and the guests would soon be gone. The sun had finally conquered the clouds. It had been a long battle, but the victor emerged unscathed, displaying from nine to six its resilience, its mettle, its shine.

Alan watched the controller climb back to twenty amps and felt vindicated. The renewed input would never make up for losses over the summer, but these last four days had restored his faith. If the blue-sky trend continued, the boost of power should last another month. Not until November would it start to drop, when, between steam fog and lost daylight, it would be almost nonexistent.

Still, at the end of September, this here and now was a fine moment. All his labor, his calluses, his sore back, hadn't been for naught. The panels, mounted to their steel poles, were his proud flags. Never mind where the money had come from to buy them. Years from now, people in Whetstone, when asked, "Who put those up?" would say, "Alan Lamb." No one could take that away. On impulse he scratched his initials on one of the poles with the awl from his Leatherman. *Take that, Broderman.* He'd left his mark.

THE DAY PETE FLEW the last group of clients back to town, Carolyn left a note for Alan at Mike's. She wanted to talk. *Sunday, ten o'clock. Please be prompt.*

What was it this time? Did she find out that Alan had snuck into her office and found her grant application? So much for his secret; he'd told two people now. Dehlia was no longer his ally, and maybe she never had been. So what if Carolyn had found out? He'd committed no crime, and in her testimony at the hearing she'd made no bones about it: she wanted to take advantage of Ziggurat's development grants.

Outside Carolyn's door he waited. Then he paced. At his second knock, she called from inside, saying she'd be with him in a minute.

But it was more than a minute. It ended up being fifteen. *Okay, I was a little early; now you're a lot late.* He wandered off the porch and to the window.

There was Blake, on a floor mat, naked but for oversize boxers. Not much to show. Gray skin, devoid of nutrient. Mere wisps of hair. Even his bones looked starved, elbow and knee joints, collarbone and ribs. If the object was to teach anatomy, it was a grim lesson. This was a theater, harshly lit. An audition for death.

Amy and Ken attended to him, checking a bedsore, looking for bruising. Then they dressed him, Ken the lifter, Amy the fitter. In his clean blue flannels Blake looked better, but not by much.

A figure passed from the kitchen into a back room: Derek Johnson.

Shortly Alan heard footsteps, and he quickly resumed his place near the door. Carolyn slipped outside wearing a red fall coat. She'd done her hair, and she looked pretty.

"Let's sit over there." She pointed to what must have once been a patio, the cobblestones so overgrown with moss they were scarcely visible. Carolyn took a seat on a wooden bench and motioned Alan to another. In a flash of understanding, he knew what this summons was about.

He sat stiffly, arms folded, his long-sleeved Pendleton just adequate for the crisp weather. How would she play her part? He waited with curious detachment as she fiddled with a handkerchief, sniffed, and pulled out a pair of white knit gloves. "My hands get cold easily. They're more susceptible with age," she said.

Did this deserve a response? Alan decided to make it easy on her. She wasn't a bad woman. Misguided, perhaps. But her intentions were admirable enough. "I know what you mean," he said.

A leaf fell on her bench and she brushed it off, focusing on the spot where it hit the ground. How undistinguished it looked, lying now amidst the others. Some broad, some narrow, some spotted, some plain. But all were yellow against yellow, and all from the same species: white birch. Dehlia's tree. He would never look at one again without thinking of her. Her carving. Her loons and swans.

He glanced up at the branches. Leaves were still clinging. Ah, well, they'd get their turn. He braced himself for the inevitable.

"Alan, I want to say, first, this isn't what I had in mind. I'd hoped things would be different."

She was having a hard time. Should he help her? No, this was *her* job. Let her do it.

"Whetstone has changed. Whether or not this mine gets built, it has already had an impact."

All right, he could give her that much. "Yeah. I haven't been here that long, but it's already a different place."

"So what I'm going to tell you has nothing to do with your performance."

Okay, Carolyn, let it launch. If I weren't hearing it from you, you'd be hearing it from me.

"Derek and I are getting married." She looked up as if to make sure he'd heard. There was something coquettish in her speech.

Was she going to use Derek as an excuse? It didn't seem fitting for Carolyn, typically straightforward. "Congratulations. You deserve it." He meant it.

Then he watched her business side regain its edge, and almost in apology for mentioning the marriage she said, "My expenses are too great. I have to take care of my dad. But I already explained that at the hearing. There's much, much more that I'm responsible for, financially, and unfortunately the solar array has been a losing ticket. It isn't paying for itself."

For the first time Alan felt defensive. *Tell me I'm incompetent, tell me I'm bad luck, tell me you hate me, but don't blame it on the panels. Anyway, you didn't pay a red cent for them. How can they be a losing ticket?*

He kept his mouth clamped on that. Truthfully, he didn't have any proof that she'd even gotten the grant. Maybe all his agonizing had been for nothing.

"You need to give them time," he said. "It was about the crappiest summer on record. The last few days have been brilliant. Look at this sun! You'll see. In the next few years, those panels will make a huge difference in your fuel bill."

She studied her gloves. "Perhaps. I can only go by what's in front of me. At this moment." She took a breath. "Alan, I'm letting you go."

He'd prepared himself; he knew it was coming, but hearing it still hurt. *What's the real reason, Carolyn? Is it because of my opposition to the mine? What rumor… is it because of something you heard from Dehlia, from Dan Broderman?*

Now that Carolyn had let it out, the rest was easier. "It's not personal, Alan. It's entirely a business move. I can get by this winter without replacing your services. Plenty of residents can fill in with the odd jobs. If a generator breaks Stew can help, or if I have to I can call in a mechanic. Next spring, I'll look for someone who can work for a lower wage. Maybe a college student."

You didn't ask me if I'd take a cut in pay. But he knew it wasn't a consideration. Not for her, not for him. Not the way things were with Dehlia. It was all too awkward and strange.

"When can I catch a plane out?" He was ready to have it over with.

"Pete will be coming in a week. Next Sunday, figure on three o'clock. I'll have your last paycheck ready."

He almost said, "Forget it." But he stopped himself. *Don't be an idiot, Lamb. You earned it.*

"Goodbye, Carolyn. I respect your work ethic. Whetstone's an interesting place. Good luck with your dad." He stood, and two leaves fell from his lap.

As he turned to go, Carolyn said, "Thank you. Thank you, Alan."

He set out, following the trails whose names he knew by heart: Garnet, the Inner Circle, Tourmaline, Zircon. Why had Mike taken that house, or was it the only one available when he'd moved here? How had he, Alan, ended up in it? Turn left. When you hit the last letter of the alphabet.

15

It was a quiet morning, the sun gilding the trees with a light any photographer would envy. Dehlia wiped down her kitchen and sipped from a cup of lukewarm tea. On a plate nearby lay her half-eaten toast. The woodstove, as if a bodily presence, crackled faintly in the center of the room—a reminder that, since the hearing, Dehlia was ever more sensitive to sound. She picked up a vase, devoid of flowers, and held it.

She saw herself then as a woman in a painting. Like the subject of a Dutch interior, cloistered in the warmth and shelter of self. All she needed was to reshape herself, carve out a new image. Alan... she'd accused him of lying, when she herself—

Her thoughts were jolted by a knock at the door. It was longer than his, and not as sharp, but insistent in its own way. She set down the empty vase.

Barbara wore a brown leather coat and matching beret, giving her a jaunty look. She carried a cloth handbag over one shoulder.

Dehlia touched Barbara's sleeve. "Nice outfit."

Barbara brushed past. She sat squarely on one arm of the couch. "Dehlia, Alan's leaving. He lost his job."

A knot worked up in her stomach. She had thought this might happen. Not that he would be let go, but that he would depart. She sat at the other end of the couch, the big, cushioned arm a welcome support. "When?"

"Sunday. Mike told me yesterday."

Five days. She sat, absorbing the news.

"Dehlia, it's none of my business, but if you have anything to say to him, you don't have much time."

The knot tightened. It wasn't that she had nothing to say. The question was whether words could matter. Whether they would help them part on better terms or whether they would simply make things worse. She'd seen many times how words produced only more bitterness.

"You know, Dehlia, with Rick and me"—Barbara crossed her legs, then uncrossed them—"I think it was just bad communication. We could have worked things out."

"I don't know, Barbara. Some people are just incompatible."

"You and Alan made a great couple."

Dehlia hugged her stomach.

"Dehlia, why do you always avoid conflict? Conflict is"—Barbara shrugged—"a part of life."

Another accusation. Somehow she knew everything would be perceived as her fault. All that had come down. But how little Barbara knew.

"A minute ago you were talking about working things out. Now you're saying life is all conflict. So which is it?" Dehlia rocked, trying to soften the slap.

"It's both. It's communicating, and it's holding your own. And I didn't say life is all conflict. I just said it's a part."

"You know everything, the whole story, don't you? About Phil and the affair and the London company."

"Yes." Barbara extracted from her handbag a copy of a little journal and handed it over solemnly. "Meredith wrote this poem, dedicated to Phil. I thought you should see it. Page sixty-three."

Dehlia flipped through the pages. She read dispassionately, absorbing the words but no longer caring. What difference did it make anymore? Probably the whole town knew. She only felt cheated because she'd missed the clues. How could she have been so incredibly dense? The answer, she knew, was that she hadn't *wanted* to know. Or hadn't wanted to admit the possibility. She had known all along.

"Do you think," said Barbara, "there's ever been justification for a revolution? I mean, in the history of the world?"

Why was she asking? What did this have to do with Whetstone? Clearly, Barbara had been talking to Mike. His influence was apparent.

"To what end? All that bloodshed, suffering... as if justice is ever the result."

"If you're neutral in situations of injustice, you have chosen the side of the oppressor." Barbara paused. "Desmond Tutu."

It wasn't like Barbara to quote people. Dehlia figured it was Mike talking again.

"So," said Barbara, "you don't think we should fight this mine?"

"Barbara, it's more complicated than that..." She wanted to come clean now, to tell Barbara why she'd been holding out. But she should keep her secret until things were settled, legally and financially. Only Alan knew. The trust money still wasn't in her hands. "The mine has divided the town," she said instead. "It's making people crazy. Dan—"

"You mean crazier," said Barbara. "That was so sleazy, the way he was working for Ziggura—"

"Barbara, Phil did the same thing."

"But Phil was seduced by Meredith."

"Don't make excuses for him," Dehlia said. But the mention of Meredith's name had a strange effect. Dehlia pictured her, lying crippled and splayed at the bottom of the lake, in those first weeks after her suicide. A bloated, alabaster body in a web of rock, eyes locked in a vacant stare.

What had Phil meant to her? She must have been terribly in love with him. Anyone that disturbed had known great suffering, greater than anything Dehlia had experienced. For all her childhood unrest, all the hurt in hearing, from Alan, about Phil's affair, she'd never considered taking her own life. She knew she would never completely understand Meredith's pain.

Barbara stood and Dehlia followed suit. She let Barbara take her hand and Dehlia closed her eyes. They stayed like that for a long time. How warm Barbara's touch was, how tender and sure, how it spoke of commitment to seeing her through this turmoil.

SHE WALKED TO the post office in her scarf and wool coat. Winter was coming on. High up, a flock of sandhill cranes, borne on some fortuitous wind, announced their flight with squeaky, trumpet-like calls. A gust blew in that shook the birches, and Dehlia was surrounded for a moment in a yellow swirl—a figure in leaf-fall.

What might be in the mail? Surely something from Chicago, and she would need to decide about the trust. Should she use the money to buy herself a nice house, maybe in Anchorage or along the

Oregon coast? Her future at Whetstone was uncertain. Whetstone could become—she had to face it—a mining town.

She retrieved her mail quickly and left the post office, flipping through the contents on her walk back home. There wasn't much: a solicitation; a gardening magazine; a bank statement, nothing from Chicago. But wait—more news about the mine, on a four-by-six postcard.

CPR—COALITION for PROTECTING our RESOURCES now formed, thanks to a generous donation. Do your part. Help save our fish. Fight the Fly Creek Mine. The text was printed over an image of spawning salmon.

She looked up to see Dan coming down the trail. Of all the people to run into!

Ten feet away he called out, "And what are you reading, Milady?"

She opened the magazine and stuffed her mail inside. "Nothing of interest."

"I take it you've seen the latest propaganda. A coalition, they call it. Made possible by an anonymous donation of three million dollars."

She froze. That number. Three million.

"I happen to know who the perpetrator was," Dan said. "May she rest in anything but peace."

Meredith, of course. So she'd had a change of heart. What next? Why was there always another revelation, another punch? Suddenly Dehlia felt like she was spinning, as if the wind had caught her up in a great twister. She had to find her footing.

She took a step and squared off. "Dan, where did you get this information?"

He grinned foolishly. "I have my scouts."

And then she was aflame. It was the gusty wind, or Dan's smug assuredness, or a combination, but her every nerve had exploded into a river of fire; she was carried and consumed with it, and she had never felt so free. Oh the joy, the sheer and extravagant monopoly of anger, the gallantry with which it could unearth the soul.

"Dan, I know about your involvement with Meredith and Phil and British Global Resources. I don't want to hear any more about your support of the mine."

He shied like a struck horse. "Okay, I shall not offend the lady."

She walked abruptly away, then turned. "Another thing. My name is Dehlia. Don't call me 'Milady' anymore."

Dan pursed his lips. He lifted his chin and high-stepped to the right, an actor exiting a stage.

IN THE GARDEN, pulling the last of her carrots, she wondered if she'd been too harsh. Dan's role as accomplice for the London company was all about money. Or was it? Maybe Dan had encouraged Phil and Meredith's affair, hoping one day he'd have her, Dehlia, to himself. Maybe he'd tried to sway Carolyn against Alan, to get him out of town. Anything was possible. You never knew about human motivation.

She sat back on her heels, brushed off a carrot, and bit. She could taste the dirt, but underneath was an untarnished flavor and crunch. Then the forest echoed a softer crunch: the sound of a broken stick. She peered up through a stipple of yellow and green.

The bear stopped, partially hidden behind a copse of willow. She knew this bear—her third sighting. It hung back, watching, Dehlia watching back in turn. It was average sized, handsome but not exceptional. No doubt it was moving down to the river, where, at the mouth, other bears might have already congregated to fish. Later, it would climb the mountain, burrowing in for a long sleep. The time of white silence. The bear gave her a long look, then vanished, leaving not even a shadow. She knew she would not see it again.

16

Alan went over his checklist. The practical things were done: he'd packed his tools and clothes and left them at the airstrip, talked to Sheila about forwarding his mail, turned over maintenance of the generators to Stew. He couldn't help mentioning that the solar array was self-sufficient, though that wasn't news to the seasoned hand. By way of farewell, the big man punched him on the arm and gave a gruff goodbye. "Take care o' yerself. This town keeps actin' like a clogged toilet, I might be following you out."

Alan didn't feel up to the other goodbyes. There were so many people he'd grown to like: Billy Barr, one of the friendliest; Julie, weaver and spinner; postmistress Sheila; and Jen and Bryce. Indigo and Indi, still the new kids on the block, whose optimism you couldn't shake. He wished every one of them well. The Abbeys—aw hell, he had to make an exception. He couldn't leave without seeing them.

In the yard, Patricia was raking leaves while Dale and Allie hauled firewood. Patricia's bandana had loosened and fallen to one side, her red hair wild and free; in her smart jeans and work shirt she was sprightly as a colt. She set down her rake, her husband his wheelbarrow. Allie skipped behind Dale as he shook Alan's hand.

"Sorry to hear the news, buddy."

Alan met his eyes. "Just the way it is, I guess." He looked at Patricia and Allie, thinking, *What a nice family.* "You're good people," he said. "I'm glad I got to know you."

Allie stepped up and took her dad's hand. "Is Alan leaving?" she asked him, looking up. She wasn't hiding her disappointment.

Alan leaned down to her. "Yep, I need to go find more work."

"Will you come back?" She queried him directly now.

"I don't think so." Then, to soften the blow, he said, "Maybe just to visit."

"We'll probably be in Anchorage in two years," said Patricia. "You should look us up."

"What part of town?"

"Not sure yet," said Dale. "Might be easier for us to contact you. Where're you headed?"

"Timbuktu?" Alan smiled wryly. "Tell you what. You can reach me through my folks. They'll have a current number." He reached in his wallet and found an old bank receipt. He tore it in half.

"Need a pen?" Dale pulled one from his front pocket.

Alan jotted the number and address and tried to hand the pen back to Dale.

"Keep it. A souvenir."

"Appreciate it." Alan shifted his feet. "I better get going."

Dale put an arm on Alan's shoulder. "I hope we beat this son-of-a-bitch." He stepped back.

Patricia looked at her husband and smiled. "We will." She opened her arms and gave Alan a full embrace. He swore he could feel her heart.

When she drew back, she winked at him. "Nothing like a mine to get the blood running." It was a private joke.

He tried not to blush. It was hopeless. "Bye, Allie." He knelt and Allie gave him a quick hug. Then he was on his way, with waves and promises to keep in touch.

He took the Inner Circle counterclockwise back to Mike's. He could have walked through town, but this long route allowed him to pass by Dehlia's. There was always a chance... no, there wasn't. Not Dehlia, not even her house, were in sight.

Mike and Betsy met him at the door.

"You won't believe this," said Mike, so low that Alan could hardly hear him. He sounded like a mortician. "Blake's dead."

Alan's jaw went slack. "No! When did you hear that?"

"Derek came by an hour ago and dropped off your check." Mike pointed to an envelope lying on a nearby shelf. "It happened this morning, about eight o'clock."

"Jesus. After all that." Alan moved to the table to steady himself and sat down, grabbing the envelope along the way. Setting it in front of him, he let his hands drop to his lap, overcome by his last glimpse of Blake through the window, being dressed on a mat. "When I saw him last week he looked bad. Really bad. I guess his body finally gave out."

"That's one way of looking at it." Mike pulled down two cups from the kitchen shelf. "Coffee?"

"Nah." Alan was slowly recovering. "Oh, all right, half a cup."

Mike poured and set Alan's coffee in front of him. He topped off a cup for himself and took the opposing chair. "The other way," Mike continued after a long sip, "is more poetic. It was his last protest."

"What do you mean?"

"Maybe there was more upstairs than we gave him credit for." Mike touched his temple with his index finger. "Maybe he was saying fuck Ziggurat. Maybe he was standing up to big money, to the corporate takeover of his town."

"Wow. That's heavy." Alan liked it, but another part of him doubted. "C'mon, Trotter, you don't really believe all that superstition about Blake."

"Normally I'd say no, but... "

But... Alan considered finishing Mike's thought. *It makes a better story.*

"But then there was Meredith," Mike continued. "Maybe in the end Meredith was acting as Blake's seer."

Come on, no way. Meredith, Blake's seer? How far was Mike going to take this? Better to think of it all as mere coincidence. Alan shook his head. "Whatever was happening, it won't change anything. Carolyn's marrying Derek. She's casting her dice with the Rat. Her mind's made up."

"Don't be so sure. Blake's death could change a lot. I bet she's been putting in over a hundred grand a year into the old man."

Alan drank his coffee. Betsy flopped down on the floor beside him, bored with men and conversation. "Won't affect me. Betsy and I are heading out." Her head raised as Alan picked up his envelope, folded it, and stuck it in his back pocket.

Mike flicked his wrist up in a questioning gesture. "Aren't you going to open it? Make sure you didn't get cheated?"

Alan shrugged. "I guess sometimes you just gotta trust."

"Trust? Like—Ziggurat, for example?" Mike grimaced.

Alan smiled at the sarcasm. He was going to miss it. "Yeah, all those claims of good science. Water so clean you can drink it. But then, those guys aren't human. When I said trust, I was talking about the human part."

THEY WALKED TO the airstrip. Mike put his hand up to shade his eyes and looked out over the runway. "Wonder who'll be leaving town next," he said.

"Won't be Dehlia. She wants to stay until she gets her land from Carolyn. She has a contract that says she'll get ownership soon, once her twenty-five years are up. But she was afraid if she opposed the mine, Carolyn wouldn't honor her word."

Mike's eyebrows did a quizzical dance. "Seriously?"

"Yeah, I'm not supposed to tell anyone, so keep it to yourself." Alan's stomach twisted. *Fuck. So much for nondisclosure. But Mike won't tell. He's my friend.*

Mike offered to stay until the plane came but Alan waved him on. "Go write the great Alaska novel. You're up to it."

They shook hands, both reluctant to let go.

"Where do you think you'll end up?"

"I don't know, maybe Homer."

"Nice town."

"Write me a letter."

"I will."

"Good luck with Barbara."

"And with your life."

WITH MIKE GONE, Alan had nothing to do but wait. He squinted against the bright light, but with his sunglasses at the bottom of his pack he only kicked at a few stones and stared at his pile of gear. What would happen when Pete came with the load from town with no one here to pick up the incoming freight? Maybe Carolyn had forgotten to ask anyone to meet the plane. Well, it wasn't his problem.

He sat on his duffel and called Betsy. He held her face in his palms, and she gazed back, faithful to a fault. "What do you think, girl? We're on our own."

He patted her head and looked down the airstrip, trying to determine which direction Pete would land. Then he saw movement, slight at first, but unmistakable: the slender build, the easy walk. The wool coat and the scarf. And something he'd never noticed before, a squaring of the shoulders. He stood and ran a nervous hand through his hair.

She took her time, and he looked at his watch: fifteen minutes. She'd cut it awfully close.

When she approached, the first thing she did was pet Betsy. Was this what it was all about? To say goodbye to the dog?

But then she raised her eyes. "I thought I should see you off."

His heart sank, and in the blinding sun all he could do was blink.

"It's bright, isn't it?" she asked.

"You didn't bring your shades?"

She shook her head. She looked toward the lake. "I don't know if you heard."

"About Blake? Yeah, Mike told me."

"What?"

"He's dead. This morning. Early, I think."

"Oh... God." He saw her shudder, and he realized the news was completely unexpected.

"So," he said, "what were you going to tell me?"

She chuckled softly. "I thought you should know. It's about Meredith. She gave three million dollars before her suicide to fight the mine. There's a new coalition, just formed."

Alan slapped his forehead. "Jesus, where does it end?"

"That's what I've been thinking."

"How did you find out?"

"Dan told me."

"And he..." Alan fitted the pieces. "Of course. He has inside information." He set his mouth. "When you see him, tell him I said adios. And give him my best."

"Are you ser—" But before she could finish she caught his humor. Then she was laughing, and he was laughing too, and soon her eyes were wet.

When they recovered, Alan said, "Well, good for Meredith. I guess that's cause for some redemption. But maybe not in your book."

Her voice went soft. "I've forgiven her, Alan, and Phil too. I can't go through life with all that resentment."

He looked at her full on, the sun backlighting her hair, and remembered a similar image from long ago, the first day he'd gone to see her. Saintly, he'd thought. Studying her, he felt that her radiance had dimmed a little, or perhaps it was just the bright, bright sun, which a human face could never begin to match for glow. He loved her then even more deeply. Because he saw that perfection was impossible. Or rather, that perfection was imperfect. Those who turned the other cheek, who never stood by a belief with a stone of conviction in one hand, ready to upset their balance with a gutsy throw, were marred. Uninvolvement, that was it. That was the imperfection. Still, that didn't mean one should never forgive. And now he wondered, *If forgiveness is that easy, do you forgive me too?* But he couldn't bring himself to ask. Instead he said, "I suppose you've been carving."

"Not lately. But I do want to finish the transformation mask."

"A transformation mask is still a mask."

"Maybe I'll use three outside layers, and when you open the last, you'll see my real face."

He saw his chance. "You as in anyone, or you as in me?"

She smiled, and he noticed for the first time a look that hinted at possibility.

"I wouldn't know how to reach you," she said ambiguously.

Alan groaned inwardly. *Good lord, woman, if a thing like that were our greatest obstacle we'd have married seven moons ago.*

Hurriedly he pulled out his wallet and fished out the other half of the bank receipt. He patted his pocket for his pen. *Thank you, Dale, you lifesaver.*

He was writing when he heard the plane. He forced himself to concentrate. There wasn't time for a single mistake. He handed her the paper.

She looked it over before she tucked it away. "Your parents?"

He nodded just as the tell-tale thump sounded. Pete had landed.

"I'll write," she said.

He tried to stand tall. "How do I know?"

"Because," she said, "I promise."

She patted Betsy. Again her eyes were moist. "I'll miss you," she whispered. She reached for his hand and squeezed it. Then she let go, and before he knew it she was walking away.

Pete was unloading the plane. Alan moved to help him, but his eyes were still on her.

She turned once. "Alan," she said, "you were right about the mine. From the beginning." Then she continued on and didn't look back.

Alan caught his breath. Perhaps she hadn't anticipated her last words. But he knew then that he was wrong. There was something in her voice, a tone of certainty he'd never heard before. And he wanted to run after her and catch her in his arms and gaze deeper into her deep brown eyes. But he knew it was his turn to hold back.

"You all set?" Pete asked.

"Yeah. I'm set."

"It'll be smooth sailing. It doesn't get any better than this." Pete made a sweeping gesture.

No, Alan thought. It does. It does get better. You just have to give it time.

BY WAY OF THANKS

Numerous metaphors come to my mind in the way a novel develops, but the one I like best is house construction. If you are highly skilled, both as a framer and finish carpenter, you can perhaps build a house from beginning to end without a single miscalculation or oversight. More often, even professionals have to make corrections: lumber is cut half an inch too short, a window header requires extra support, one corner of a floor isn't level. The more practiced the carpenter the easier it becomes to adjust, to find alternative approaches to problems that arise. Still, many people elect to build their own homes, just as authors, sometimes with expertise in other genres, take on the writing of a novel. The result is that sometimes the design is flawed. The layout didn't accommodate all the furniture or kitchen cabinets and has to be redrawn. Sometimes a foundation needs reinforcing. But big changes can sometimes be avoided. Rooms can be added on, doors and windows can be installed in different places. Walls can be cut out, either fully or partially. This is where friends—or readers—come in. Advice from others helps make the building more solid, weatherproof, and livable. My immense gratitude to: Steve Kahn, Glenn Wright, Craig Coray, Richard Chiappone, Erin Hollowell, Dawn Morano, Ann Pancake, Sarah Birdsall. A special thank you to my nieces, Willow Coray Mason and Camille Coray, for the use of their song lyrics.

To the whole team at West Margin Press, and to my editor, Oliva Ngai, who is nothing short of phenomenal.

Anne Coray
March 2021

Anne Coray is the author of three full-length poetry collections and coeditor of *Crosscurrents North: Alaskans on the Environment.* Her work has appeared in the *Southern Review, Northwest Review, Poetry, North American Review,* and *AQR.* The recipient of fellowships from the Alaska State Council on the Arts and the Rasmuson Foundation, she divides her time between Homer and her birthplace on remote Lake Clark in southwest Alaska.